NORTHWEST PASSAGES

A Literary Anthology of the Pacific Northwest from Coyote Tales to Roadside Attractions

Edited by Bruce Barcott

SASQUATCH BOOKS
SEATTLE

Printed in the United States of America.

Cover and interior design: Kate L. Thompson
Cover art: Emily Carr, *Young Pines and Sky* (detail); oil on paper; 89.6 x 58.7 cm.
Collection: Vancouver Art Gallery, Emily Carr Trust. Photo credit: Trevor Mills.
Composition: Fay L. Bartels

Library of Congress Cataloging in Publication Data

Northwest passages : a literary anthology of the Pacific Northwest from Coyote tales to
roadside attractions / edited by Bruce Barcott.

p. cm.

Includes bibliographical references.

ISBN 1-57061-005-3

1. American literature—Northwest, Pacific. 2. Northwest, Pacific—Literary collections.
I. Barcott, Bruce, 1966-

PS570.N67 1994
810.8'09795—dc20   94-2939
                                                                     CIP

SASQUATCH BOOKS
1008 Western Avenue
Seattle, Washington 98104
(206)467-4300

CONTENTS

Foreword by Charles Johnson   ix
Introduction by Bruce Barcott   xi

FIRST STORIES   1

RED-ARM (NESPELEM)
  "Origin of the Columbia River"   3

KWAKWA̱KA̱ 'WAKW SONGS
  "Love Songs"   5
  "A Boy's Song"   6
  "A Girl's Song"   6
  "War Song"   6

WÁYI ́LÁTPU (NEZ PERCÉ)
  "Coyote and Monster"   7

LOUIS LABONTE (CLACKAMAS CHINOOK)
  "Coyote and the Cedar Tree"   11
  "Coyote Builds Willamette Falls and the Magic Fish Trap"   12

EUROPEAN ENCOUNTERS   13
1579–1792

FRANCIS FLETCHER
  from The World Encompassed by Sir Francis Drake   16

MICHAEL LOK
  from Purchas His Pilgrimes   18

JONATHAN SWIFT
  from Gulliver's Travels   20

BRUNO DE HEZETA
from For Honor and Country: The Diary of Bruno de Hezeta   20

JAMES COOK
from A Voyage to the Pacific Ocean   23

GEORGE VANCOUVER
*from A Voyage of Discovery to the North Pacific Ocean and
round the World, 1791–1795*   25

PETER PUGET
from Peter Puget's Journal   28

TRAPPING AND TRADING   31
1805–1836

MERIWETHER LEWIS AND WILLIAM CLARK
from The Original Journals of the Lewis and Clark Expedition   34

ROSS COX
from Adventures on the Columbia River   40

DAVID DOUGLAS
from David Douglas's Journal   45

WASHINGTON IRVING
from Astoria   48

POPULATING THE PROMISED LAND   53
1832–1853

NARCISSA WHITMAN
from The Letters of Narcissa Whitman   56

SIDNEY WALTER MOSS
from The Prairie Flower   60

AMELIA STEWART KNIGHT
from Amelia Knight's Journal   61

TREATY TALK   67
1854–1879

CHIEF SEATTLE
from Chief Seattle's 1854 Speech   70

CHIEF JO HUTCHINS
from Chief Jo Hutchins's 1869 Speech   73

CHIEF JOSEPH
from "An Indian's View of Indian Affairs"   75

CLOSING THE FRONTIER   81
1853–1916

THEODORE WINTHROP
from The Canoe and the Saddle   84

JAMES G. SWAN
from The Northwest Coast   88

FITZ HUGH LUDLOW
from "On the Columbia River"   92

HAZARD STEVENS
from "The Ascent of Takhoma"   95

JOHN MUIR
from Picturesque California   99

RUDYARD KIPLING
from American Notes   102

FRANCES FULLER VICTOR
from Atlantis Arisen   105

MARY HALLOCK FOOTE
from Coeur d'Alene   107

OWEN WISTER
from "The Second Missouri Compromise"   108

ELLA HIGGINSON
"The Blow-Out at Jenkins's Grocery"   114

ANNE SHANNON MONROE
from Happy Valley   118

WAGE WORKERS, WOBBLIES, AND BINDLE STIFFS   121
1917–1919

WALTER V. WOEHLKE
from "The I.W.W. and the Golden Rule"   124

WALKER C. SMITH
  from The Everett Massacre   125

ZANE GREY
  from The Desert of Wheat   129

ANNA LOUISE STRONG
  "Britt Smith"   135

A HOMEGROWN LITERATURE   137
1920–1945

JAMES STEVENS
  from Paul Bunyan   140

HATHAWAY JONES
  "The Year of the Big Freeze"   144

VARDIS FISHER
  from Toilers of the Hills   146

ROBERT CANTWELL
  from The Land of Plenty   149

H. L. DAVIS
  from Honey in the Horn   154

STEWART HOLBROOK
  from Holy Old Mackinaw   159

RICHARD NEUBERGER
  from "The Biggest Thing on Earth"   163

WALLACE STEGNER
  from The Big Rock Candy Mountain   166

BETTY MACDONALD
  from The Egg and I   170

WAR STORIES   173
1948–1957

MONICA SONE
  from Nisei Daughter   175

NARD JONES
from The Island   182

JOHN OKADA
from No-No Boy   186

THE POSTWAR NORTHWEST   191
1950–1976

WILLIAM O. DOUGLAS
from Of Men and Mountains   194

MURRAY MORGAN
from The Last Wilderness   199

OLIVE BARBER
from The Lady and the Lumberjack   202

JACK KEROUAC
from The Dharma Bums   205

GARY SNYDER
from "Night Highway Ninety-Nine"   207

BERNARD MALAMUD
from A New Life   213

JOHN STEINBECK
from Travels with Charley   220

HORACE CAYTON
from Long Old Road   222

KEN KESEY
from Sometimes a Great Notion   229

THEODORE ROETHKE
"The Rose"   236

RICHARD HUGO
from The Real West Marginal Way: A Poet's Autobiography   241

DAVID WAGONER
"Elegy for a Forest Clear-Cut by the Weyerhaeuser Company"   245

CONTEMPORARY EXTREMES 247
1971–1993

TOM ROBBINS
from Another Roadside Attraction   250

MARILYNNE ROBINSON
from Housekeeping   255

RAYMOND CARVER
from "Boxes"   259

TESS GALLAGHER
"Amplitude"   264

DAVID JAMES DUNCAN
from The River Why   269

CRAIG LESLEY
from Winterkill   274

KATHERINE DUNN
from Geek Love   279

ANNIE DILLARD
from The Writing Life   283

JONATHAN RABAN
from Hunting Mister Heartbreak   288

TIMOTHY EGAN
from The Good Rain   296

BRENDA PETERSON
from Living by Water   310

SALLIE TISDALE
from Stepping Westward   315

SHERMAN ALEXIE
"The Business of Fancydancing"   318

ROBERT HEILMAN
from "Overstory: Zero"   319

DENISE LEVERTOV
"Settling"   322

Acknowledgments   325

FOREWORD

WHENEVER WE, AS WRITERS, are asked to explain the reason why we choose to create in the Pacific Northwest, we instinctively reach for something close, the palpable, what we cannot help but touch and feel each and every blessed day: an extravagant, enveloping landscape as bountiful and generous on its enormous canvas as I suppose we as artists would like to be on our smaller ones.

Some of our best-known authors, from poets Theodore Roethke and David Wagoner to essayist Barry Lopez, from novelist Tom Robbins to emerging talents like David Guterson and Nicholas O'Connell, find a pre-given poetry almost Zen-like or reminiscent of native American mysticism in this luxurious physical presence right outside our windows, one that dwarfs, predates, and no doubt will outlive by millennia the reams of poetry and prose we write about it—mountains that rise twelve thousand feet above the sea, magnificent, rain-drenched forests, treeless desert lands, three thousand kinds of flowers, glacial lakes, and hundreds of islands in Puget Sound. (It should surprise no one that Sea-Tac was the first airport in America to set aside for its travelers a room specifically for meditation.)

This region's diversity and difference, its heart-stopping scale, and our diminutive place beneath such titans as Beacon Rock on the Columbia River or the looming epiphany of timelessness that is Mount Rainier, humble in the healthiest ways a writer's ego with the ubiquity and antiquity of the pre-human. It puts a novelist firmly in his place, you might say, as but one among countless residents in a vast democracy of creatures ranging from western bobcats to the Canadian lynx. It deflates his hubris. It nudges him naturally toward wonder and awe at this mysteriously rich world in which we find ourselves thrown, and toward taking the long view on life's problems. That sensibility—being forced to take a step back from citified busyness and cares—is, of course, the beginning of art and philosophy, both of which are enriched, or so I've come to believe, by the misty, meditative mood invoked by the Northwest's most famous element, rain. Rain and the moist, ambiguous, evening air that now sets fragments of the landscape to gleaming, now hazes other parts in weather you simply have to see as a perfect externalization of the brooding inner climate of the creative imagination.

Yet weather and woods are but half the reason why after eighteen years I've come to call this place home.

Would that I could boast I was born here, or that the region's history inspirits the props, furniture, lighting, and costumes in my fiction. Perhaps someday that will be so, but most often my stories are set in the Midwest near Chicago, or in the little farm towns and hot cornfields of southern Illinois where I went to school (or in an imagined South delivered to me in family chronicles told by my parents when I was a child). In other words, my emotional and literal "home" is the so-called American heartland, where working-class people had no tolerance for phoniness or pretense. These were not people to judge one another by their possessions, dress, family pedigree, or how often they got their names in the newspapers. Family and friends came first. What mattered to them was what you knew and could do—and belonging to a neighborhood, where they did not hesitate to share what little they had, whether that be food, labor, their home, or the skills each had developed in order to survive. That was the Midwest of my childhood.

Happily, that is the Pacific Northwest of my adult life. In Seattle, which some call a "city of neighborhoods," my friends, acquaintances, and students cover the spectrum of humanity. They are black, Chinese and Japanese, African and Hindu, from Scandinavian and German stock, Jewish, native American, gay and lesbian; and presiding over this salad bowl of human possibilities is Norm Rice, one of the nation's few black mayors. Furthermore, these are people who know things, but with no cackle or boast about their abilities. Just a few blocks from my home lives Eugene Clyde, whose intricate miniatures of sailing ships have been commissioned by the U.S. Navy (I proudly own an eighteenth-century slaving vessel he built for me). In the martial arts studio I attend, you'll find award-winning short story writer Stacey Levine sweating beside architects, general contractors, and a University of Washington sociologist. Close by in the Central District is sculptor James Washington, Jr. (check out his *Oracle of Truth* at Mount Zion Baptist Church, or *Obelisk with Phoenix* at the Sheraton Hotel); and not all that far from him live the internationally celebrated painters Jacob and Gwen Lawrence, who are just a short drive from playwright August Wilson, the two-time Pulitzer Prize winner who takes notes on humanity's foibles from the Broadway Cafe.

So, yes, when asked why I choose to create in the Northwest, I reach for the region's beauty and resources. But no small part of its treasure, I know after nearly two decades, are the people whose presence is as memorable and enriching as the great mountains beneath which they reside.

—CHARLES JOHNSON
July 1994

INTRODUCTION

There are those to whom place is unimportant,
But this place, where sea and fresh water meet,
Is important . . .
—THEODORE ROETHKE, "THE ROSE"

THE IMPORTANCE OF THIS PLACE did not strike me until I went away. I was in my early twenties, living in New York City, and miserable. A century earlier, my great-grandfather had come to the Pacific Northwest looking for a new life. I had tried my luck heading east, reversing six generations of westward progress with a six-hour flight from Sea-Tac to La Guardia.

When you've grown up in the Northwest, the cities of the East seem like vast Industrial Age ruins, places unnaturally disconnected from the earth. Looking up at the penthouses along Central Park West, I realized that I was living in a city where trees were a luxury of the rich, where access to the open sky went for a price in the millions. Escaping into Central Park from the brown stain of Manhattan, I realized how much I missed the color green.

A year later I came home, not so much seeking a new life as finding the one I had foolishly left behind. As a friend drove me from the airport, I fought back the urge to shout in exultation out the window. Trees! Row upon row of Douglas firs lined Interstate 5. Gossamer strands of fog drifted about their waists like brushstrokes in a bad motel painting. I rolled the window down and let the cool drizzle of Puget Sound dampen my face. Home. Where the world is chilly, green, and wet.

Since then, I have often wondered about the source of the Northwest's claim on me, what it is that binds my soul to a region so isolated, how it is that a climate so dark and gloomy can inspire my psyche.

I turned to books for an answer. I thumbed through Northwest classics like *The Canoe and the Saddle* by Theodore Winthrop and Ken Kesey's *Sometimes a Great Notion.* I prowled the stacks of the University of Washington's Suzzallo and Allen libraries, my neck bent in the right-angle pose of the title troller. Flecks of two-hundred-year-old leather clung to my palms as I gingerly opened the journals of the first Northwest explorers. I jotted down promising leads in notebooks—one, two, then three tablets full. I haunted Magus Books and Bowie & Company in Seattle, and Powell's in Portland, taking guilty pleasure in the arrival of new batches of Northwestiana from the collections of recently deceased bibliophiles. I read many bad books and a few very good ones. I read in coffee shops and airports and buses and cars. I read everything I could get my hands on.

This anthology is the result. The seventy-odd excerpts gathered here vary widely in subject and setting, from Lewis and Clark's travails in Idaho to Betty MacDonald's battle with an irascible stove on the Olympic Peninsula. On the surface, each answers the first question of every armchair traveler and would-be immigrant: What's it like there?

On a deeper level, the passages trace the evolving *idea* of the Northwest. In choosing these excerpts, I sought to capture the changing character of the Pacific Northwest of the mind, the different ways in which the region has been imagined and perceived—by the earliest native American inhabitants, by European fable-makers and explorers, by religious missionaries and hopeful immigrants and rowdy loggers and union radicals and novelists, journalists, and poets. Through the written word, we've given human definition to a land that has long resisted the imprint of civilization's boot. The mountains, rivers, and trees stood for millennia before humans broke the silence—brash interlopers telling stories with puny human voices. We came and created the Northwest with words. We continue to create it, and change it, with every sentence we write.

Like most locals, I use the words Northwest and Pacific Northwest interchangeably, though that may rankle some historians. "Northwest" once signified the Great Lakes region. That definition passed out of fashion around the turn of the century, but left a few misnomers for us to remember it by; I always find it curious that an Oregonian must travel two thousand miles east to attend Northwestern University.

The modern Northwest constitutes the greater portion of land drained by the Columbia River. The region's main artery actually extends halfway up British Columbia and into Wyoming, but the Pacific Northwest's cultural identity is contained mostly within the borders of Washington, Oregon, and Idaho. I say "mostly" to save me from the wrath of western Montanans, who often consider their homeland the easternmost flank of the region. But watch the cultural symbols change as you drive toward Big Sky

Country. Cowboys and steers are the icons there, not loggers and trees. Once you leave Idaho, the regional center of gravity shifts to the Rocky Mountains, and the lush forests of Puget Sound exert a weaker pull—which is why Montana does not appear in this book. A few selections from British Columbia appear early on, before the dividing line between America and Canada was established at the 49th parallel.

This is an anthology of writings *about* the Northwest, not a collection of Northwestern writers. Most writers cringe at the "regionalist" label. The tag carries the smell of failure, as if the writer got his or her specifics right but failed to translate them into universals. Many of the best descriptions of this place were recorded by writers who happened to be passing through. Which is appropriate—passing through is a way of life out here. We're a restless population, forever moving a few miles down the road, where we hear the jobs are better and the living easier. Most of our ancestors arrived only a generation ago. Our roots are shallow. The place is still settling in our bones.

Most of this book's passages were written in the era they describe. I kept historical fiction and nonfiction to a minimum so that writing styles and cultural attitudes can be seen to evolve with the times. Literary forms are dictated by the dominant genres of the day; journals and travelogues make up the early sections, giving way to fiction, essays, and poetry.

I had every intention of dispelling the Pacific Northwest's reputation for rain. As I read through my nightly stack of books, the Woodstock tribal chant—No rain! No rain!—resounded in my head. The region's famed wetness tends to be overblown, I felt, and that ignores the dry eastern halves of Oregon and Washington.

But I cannot deny the evidence. It rained everywhere I read. Lewis and Clark: "Rain falling in torrents—we are all wet as usial [*sic*]." Betty MacDonald: "All about November I began to forget when it hadn't been raining and became as one with all the characters in all of the novels about rainy seasons, who rush around banging their heads against the walls, drinking water glasses of whiskey and moaning, 'The rain! The rain! My God, the rain!'" Tom Robbins, who can turn a single cloudburst into chapters of electric prose: "Water spilled off the roofs and the rain hats. It took on the colors of neon and head lamps. It glistened on the claws of nighttime animals. And it rained a screaming. And it rained a rawness. And it rained a plasma. And it rained a disorder."

Rains a lot here. What's strange isn't the amount but the form. Clouds let themselves go in fine mists and fluttery sprays, spreading their supply so thin that one day melts into the next and the next and it's still sort of raining. The pluvial skyfall insinuates itself into our lives. Longtime Northwesterners don't own umbrellas. We just wear that old floppy raincoat nine months of the year. Annie Dillard put it best in her novel *The Living*: "It was not quite raining, but everything was wet."

As I write, at a spot on the Washington Coast not far from Lewis and Clark's soggy winter camp, I can see nothing but grayness broken now and again by the white foam of Pacific rollers arriving from Asia. This is interior weather, the contemplative oyster light that Denise Levertov describes in her poem "Settling" as "a grey both heavy and chill . . . the price / of neighboring with eagles, of knowing / a mountain's vast presence, seen or unseen." It drives us inside to tell stories.

The gloomy damp is perfect writing weather. Is it possible to imagine Robbins claiming that it "sunned a disorder"? Misery claims a thousand metaphors; happiness runs dry after six. Even in the grimmest moments of his 1853 journey across Washington, Theodore Winthrop saw the literary value of a good bone-soaking drizzle: "Poetic visions do not visit beds of roses, and no good thing or thought came out of Sybaris." Northwesterners believe life was not meant to be all sunshine and smiles. There is virtue in the miserable struggle.

I walk outside and find I cannot cast a shadow at noon. We live under this roof of dirty wash most of the year, and when the sun peeks through we dance like the circus has come to town. "What eats us here?" asked Theodore Roethke, shortly after arriving in the Pacific Northwest.

> Is this infinity too close,
> These mountains and these clouds? On clearing days
> We act like something else; a race arrived
> From caves . . .
> Bearlike, come stumbling into the sun, avoid that shade
> Still lingering in patches, spotting the green ground.

The editor of *The New Republic* recently wrote, "A recurring fantasy of mine is one day to quit everything, disappear to Seattle, buy a Starbucks franchise, and generally aim for an idea-less existence." His vision of the Northwest as a land of blissful ignorance is as common in the East as apples in Wenatchee. Over lunch in a trendy SoHo grill a few years ago, an editor friend of mine expressed surprise that any writer could make a living out here. "Where do you find your ideas?" she asked.

The Northwest has never shaken this reputation as a literary and intellectual laggard. In an 1889 issue of *Washington* magazine, University of Washington professor Edmond Meany excused the lack of regional writing by pointing to the Northwest's unfinished chores:

> No, Puget Sound has no literature. But this region has plenty of real estate, timber, coal, iron, and fish, and at present the inhabitants are scrambling over each other in their efforts to become rich out of these natural wealths of the land. There is no time to devote to the production or the appreciation of a distinctive literature.

Half a century later, Portland writer Stewart Holbrook explained the Northwest's lack of literary production by observing that "the arts do not commonly follow on the heels of the pioneer, no matter how literate the people."

Comparison with the development of other regions, however, suggests that the image of the Northwest as the slow learner in the American Lit class is not altogether accurate. Consider that the earliest European settlers arrived in the Northeast in the early 1630s, a few years after Cervantes wrote *Don Quixote*, but that the first homegrown Northeastern works— James Fenimore Cooper's *The Deerslayer* and other novels—appeared nearly two centuries later.

The Pacific Northwest, settled in the 1840s, began turning out its first serious literature fewer than ninety years later, in the late 1920s. Novels like Vardis Fisher's *Toilers of the Hills*, Robert Cantwell's *The Land of Plenty*, and H. L. Davis's Pulitzer Prize–winning *Honey in the Horn* used the local vernacular and the gritty experiences of the region's settlers to begin shaping the Northwest's identity from within.

The best Pacific Northwest poetry aspired to a level of high mediocrity until the arrival of Theodore Roethke in the late 1940s. In the decade and a half of his Seattle tenure, Roethke established himself as the leading American poet of his generation and inspired a poetry renaissance in the Northwest. Many of his students became nationally recognized writers, and some currently teach a third and fourth generation of poets and novelists.

Northwest literature succeeded in spite of the region's anti-intellectual climate. Since the early nineteenth century this has been a land for men and women of action, not reflection. College education, fine novels, poetry—these were touchstones of the genteel, class-calcified societies that most Pacific Northwesterners had fled. The most common buffoon in Northwest letters is the book-smart Easterner whose wits abandon him on Western soil. A pallid young Bostonian plays the fool in Anne Shannon Monroe's homesteading novel *Happy Valley*. In Mary Hallock Foote's *The Chosen Valley*, a young man is given a choice between going west to join his father, a rugged engineer, or staying in the East with his mother and completing his education. Foote's symbolism has the subtlety of a hammer to the head: The West is rough and manly, the East refined and emasculating. The kid heads west.

The Easterner out of his element turns up again in *Sometimes a Great Notion* and in Bernard Malamud's novel *A New Life*. Had they met during their time in Oregon, Kesey's Lee Stamper and Malamud's Sy Levin might have passed an evening swapping horror stories about the backward habits of their Western acquaintances. Timothy Egan's book *The Good Rain* contains a more sinister, nonfiction episode of anti-Easternism. Egan tells the story of John Goldmark, a rancher and pillar of the Okanogan, Washington, community, whose good name was libeled during the red scare of the 1950s. In their lowest moments the red-baiters used Goldmark's Harvard degree to plant suspicion in the minds of his neighbors. The Ivy League pedigree marked him as a man not to be trusted: If Goldmark's so smart, what's he doing out here?

My ancestors failed their way west. They went broke farming in Missouri, so they moved to Montana. They raised lousy wheat and worthless potatoes. They claimed the last and worst of the homesteading land and staved off starvation by eating dandelion greens. Floods washed their gyppo logging operation into oblivion. A plague of locusts devoured their summer crop in an afternoon. A jealous husband killed Uncle Max, though in polite conversation it was said that he drowned in the Flathead River. With each bust, they packed their wagon and moved farther into the setting sun.

The scent of shipyard jobs eventually lured them to Washington. They aimed for Bellingham, but settled in Everett when their eldest son, my grandfather, got typhoid fever from cooling his thirst in a contaminated stream.

Northwesterners take pride in the heroic aspects of their history, in the Lewises and Clarks and Whitmans. The recent year-long Oregon Trail sesquicentennial celebration proved that the cult of the head-bonneted pioneer still flourishes. But the Northwest's true written record includes many more stories like my own: darker, unsanitized histories that tell the truth about the contaminated river and the murder of Uncle Max.

Too often those stories have been drowned out by grand visions and double-talk. The Northwest was promoted as a land of milk and honey even before its promoters laid eyes on it. One of the first reports on the region came from Michael Lok, a London merchant obsessed with finding the Northwest Passage, a mythical waterway that would cut through North America and give European traders direct access to Asian markets. Lok's description, published in 1625, came secondhand from a Greek sailor (or so Lok claimed) named Apostolos Valerianos, or Juan de Fuca, who had seen the passage himself. If that wasn't enticement enough, Lok threw in a bonus. Not only was the passage there for the charting, de Fuca told him, but "the Land is very fruitfull, and rich of gold, Silver, Pearle, and other things."

For the next 350 years, the Northwest was touted as a promised land, a fertile new Eden waiting to nurture new and better civilizations. Consider just a few titles from the Northwest shelf: *Happy Valley; The Land of Plenty; Promised Land; The Land Is Bright; The Green Land; Honey in the Horn; The Big Rock Candy Mountain.* The virgin landscape offered itself to utopian settlers as a slate clean of industrial blight, political corruption, and class division. Theodore Winthrop believed the purity of the Northwest wilderness would inspire the birth of a society that would surpass the previous achievements of Western civilization. "Civilized mankind," he wrote, "has never yet had a fresh chance of developing itself under grand and stirring influences so large as in the Northwest."

The reputation persists to this day. A few years ago the English writer Jonathan Raban (now resident in Seattle) came to America and found the Pacific Northwest still hailed as the land of opportunity. "By the end of the 1980s," he wrote, "Seattle had taken on the dangerous luster of a promised city. The rumor had gone out that if you had failed in Detroit you might yet succeed in Seattle—and that if you'd succeeded in Seoul, you could succeed even better in Seattle. In New York and Guntersville [Alabama], I'd heard the rumor. Seattle was the coming place."

My ancestors bought the promise. But like many others, they found something less than heaven when they arrived. The dark side of the Northwest is well documented in its literature, although it rarely gets mentioned in the bright booster-speak with which we tend to discuss the glories of our settling ground. We've been putting up a happy front for so long that it has become instinctual. The folks back home all thought us fools for moving out West, and we'll be damned if we'll give them more ammunition to shoot us down.

But it has always been here. Look to the journals of explorer John Meares, who searched in vain for the Northwest Passage in 1788: "Disappointment," he wrote, "continues to accompany us." Consider the later Oregon Trail diaries, which read like itineraries for a Western cemetery tour: "[June 29] Passed 10 graves. [June 30] Passed 10 graves . . . made 22 miles. [July 1] Passed 8 graves . . . made 21 miles." There is a spirit in the land that continues to fight the advancing sin of civilization. "Ah, it had sounded *right* good on paper," wrote Kesey of a newly arrived Oregon immigrant in *Sometimes a Great Notion*, "but, as soon as he saw it, there was something . . . about the river and the forest, about the clouds grinding against the mountains and the trees sticking out of the ground . . . something. Not that it was a hard country, but something you must go through a winter of to understand." This side of the Northwest also has its titles—Fisher's *Toilers of the Hills* comes to mind.

You must go through a winter to understand.

If the Northwest is searching for its great literary theme, it may find it in the region's role as a catchbasin for washed-up westering dreams. Since the time of Homer, to go west has been to travel into the romantic unknown. Horace and Plutarch believed the paradisiacal Elysium described in *The Odyssey* could be reached by sailing west from the Mediterranean. The sixteenth-century Spanish explorer Álvar Nuñez Cabeza de Vaca believed that "going towards the sunset we must find what we desire." Horace Greeley's "Go West, young man, and grow up with the country" imported the sentiment to Western America. The Pacific Northwest is the final chance to find the golden land; this is where the westward dream runs out of room. To travel west from here is to strike east.

Oddballs and loners are welcome. We came out here to get away from failed farms, deranged spouses, nightmarish families, and sometimes the long arm of the law. Many of the quiet misfits in Northwest fiction—Gus Orviston in *The River Why*, Aunt Sylvie in *Housekeeping*—just want to be left alone. Seattle was flattered by its moment in the national spotlight (grunge music and all that) in the early 1990s. But we grow irritated and nervous in the spotlight, and worry that the tangles of camera cable looping across our sidewalks will end the Northwest's splendid isolation. We know that when the bloom of hipness fades, we'll gladly return to our former solitude.

Mount Rainier, Mount Hood, and their jagged Cascadian sisters are to the Northwest what skyscrapers are to New York. Nature's glorious rawness has forced generations of writers to reach deep into their bags of adjectives. Excerpts from the 1792 journal of English captain George Vancouver sound more like the praises of a judge at a garden show than the dispassionate record of a British officer: "luxuriant . . . delightful . . . a landscape almost enchantingly as beautiful as the most elegantly furnished pleasure ground in Europe . . . the country before us exhibited every thing that bounteous nature could be expected to draw into one point of view." American journalist Fitz Hugh Ludlow experienced an epiphany during his Northwestern travels for *The Atlantic Monthly* in 1864:

> We had enjoyed, from the summit of a hill twenty miles south of Salem, one of the most magnificent views in all earthly scenery. Within a single sweep of vision were seven snow-peaks, the Three Sisters, Mount Jefferson, Mount Hood, Mount Adams, and Mount St. Helen's, with the dim suggestion of an eighth colossal mass, which might be Rainier . . . I cannot express their vague, yet vast and intense splendor, by any other word than incandescence. It was as if the sky had suddenly grown white-hot in patches . . . No man of enthusiasm, who reflects what this whole sight must have been, will wonder that my friend and I clasped each other's hands before it, and thanked God we had lived to this day.

These awestruck paeans are what we've come to expect from the Northwest's chroniclers. What's surprising, though, is how often the landscape is described in terms of the grotesque or horrifying. Francis Fletcher, sailing the Northwest coast with Sir Francis Drake in 1579, reacted to a sleet storm as if the wrath of God had been visited upon his ship. Meriwether Lewis's partner, William Clark, fretted over the "monstrous trees" rolling in the Columbia, which threatened to crush his party's canoes. Theodore Winthrop cowered under "goliath" evergreens. When James Swan and his frontier cronies set a "monster tree" alight, the resulting forest fire burned for months, doused only by the first big rainstorm of autumn. An illustration in the original 1857 edition of Swan's memoir, *The Northwest Coast*, depicts a man measuring the length of his arm against the girth of an Oregon pine. The proportion of trunk to man is approximately that of elephant to mouse.

Jonathan Swift's decision to locate Brobdingnag in the then-unknown territory of the Pacific Northwest was so metaphorically accurate that it nearly has the glow of prophecy. This is truly a land of giants. Even our folk heroes—Sasquatch, the hairy half-man of the mountains, and Paul Bunyan, the Hercules of the woods—are outsized just to fit in. Literary travelers from the American East are especially susceptible to the region's grandiosity. "You've never seen anything like it for scale and magnificence," Thomas Wolfe wrote home during a visit here in 1938. "The East seems small and starved and meagre by comparison."

Living in the Northwest means coming to terms with the territory, terms not necessarily our own. It is often suggested that Northwest writers feel a special connection to nature, a certain closeness to the earth. But the connection comes by no Thoreauvian choice; ours is a forced closeness to the natural world. On clear days Mount Rainier looms above downtown Seattle, reminding us that even the most urbanized blocks cannot block out the wild. The forests and mountains impose themselves as presences around us.

In the Northeast, wrote Denise Levertov, "the word 'Nature' calls up a landscape of farms, of old cellar-holes, forgotten family burying-grounds, overgrown stone walls, apple trees lost in the woods." In the Northwest, she pointed out, "Nature" still evokes wilderness.

Lately that wilderness seems to be vanishing. On the drive to the coast, I passed hills shorn like patients for surgery, with highway billboards—PLANTED 1933, HARVESTED 1993—posted to soothe outraged environmentalists. In the coastal towns, fishing boats are up for sale. Salmon season 1994 has been canceled; the fish did not show up. The job of depleting our natural resources has been done quickly and well. Fewer than forty years separate Stewart Holbrook's 1938 prediction that loggers "will never be able to let daylight into all of the Western timber" and David Wagoner's poem "Elegy for a Forest Clear-Cut by the Weyerhaeuser Company."

This cannot come as shocking news. John Muir called for the conservation of the Oregon pine forests as early as 1889. Nobody felled a tree with more relish than Paul Bunyan, but even James Stevens's hero was aware that his band of woodchoppers would eventually turn the Northwest into a stump-filled plain. He had only to recall the tall timber of Maine and the Great Lakes region, mown low by his own axmen.

And yet, despite our progress in turning the Northwest's forests into fields of stubble, there remains an opposing sense that civilization's grip on the land is tenuous, that given half a mind the Cascades might one day shrug us, shacks and all, into the sea. Compared with other cities their size, Seattle and Portland are mere infants, alive fewer than 150 years. If we all up and left tomorrow, the trees, birds, bugs, and slugs would erase our tracks in a dozen seasons.

This is a cold country. Not cold *freezing*, but cold *indifferent*. It will go on with or without us. In a clash of the Northwest titans—Bunyan vs. The Force of Nature—the smart money rides on the pines. Hank Stamper, Kesey's Bunyanesque hero, faces down river and forest every day of his life. In the end, nature defends her own: A felled tree pins Stamper's brother to the river's edge, and the slow-rising water exacts its revenge. Hank should have listened to his father, who knew the land could not be tamed:

> Back home in Kansas a man had a *hand* in things, the way the Lord *aimed* for His servants to have: if you didn't water, the crops died. If you didn't feed the stock, the stock died. . . . But there, in that land, it looked like our labors were for naught. The flora and fauna grew or died, flourished or failed, in *complete* disregard for man and his aims. A Man Can Make His Mark, did they tell me? Lies, lies. Before God I tell you: a man might struggle and labor his live-long life and make *no* mark! None! No permanent mark at all! I say it is true.

I take great comfort in the idea that we haven't yet wounded the land beyond repair.

The place I come from—Everett, Washington—is scarred with deep furrows of family tales. Forest Park housed my grandfather's family while he rode out the fever and they scrounged for jobs and a home. A patch of wilderness near Beverly Park hid a man who had murdered my aunt's next-door neighbor. Sixty years earlier and a few blocks west, a gang of deputized vigilantes used fists, straps, and clubs to beat a group of Wobblies within an inch of their lives. The stories aren't all big. I bloodied a neighbor kid's nose on that kitchen door; I stole nickel candy from that fellow's gas-and-shop; I imagined jumping off the second-story balcony of that downtown J. C. Penney onto bags of shredded foam in the notions department below.

Just stories. But specific stories, from here and about here. We live in an age in which that part of our lives shaped by local forces is rapidly shrinking. Regional identity fades every time a news anchor mispronounces "Puyallup" and signs off a live remote "from the banks of the Willam-ETTE." Our cultural references come more often from film and television, not actual local events.

But all deep history is local. Our stories of calamitous events and unexpected triumph connect people to a place, breathe the life of meaning into a mute patch of earth. Land that has meaning is much more difficult to destroy. Keep telling stories and the land stays alive. And so do we.

FIRST STORIES

PACIFIC NORTHWESTERNERS HAVE BEEN telling stories about this land for at least ten thousand years. Up to the late eighteenth century, the Northwest was home to 125 native American tribes, speaking fifty different languages. Many tribes consisted of dozens of smaller groups; the Nez Percé alone counted 130 bands and villages among their tribal kin.

Songs and stories flourished, passed orally from generation to generation. Many of the tales were set in the "myth age," a time when the boundaries between the natural, animal, and human worlds were not yet fixed and a race of animal people inhabited the Northwest. Coyote, Fox, Bear, Badger, and others were not exactly animals and not quite gods. They were more like the Titans of Greek mythology—humans imbued with animal spirit-powers who might do battle with anthropomorphized mountains or, as in the Nespelem story that follows, with the very waters of the Columbia River.

The most important of the animal-people was Coyote, the great hero and fool of native American oral literature. (Raven often takes Coyote's place in the tales of coastal tribes.) Coyote could assume any form and was by turns wise, courageous, selfish, boastful, greedy, and cruel. "Coyote was sent by Chief to set the world in order," Nespelem elder Red-Arm once said. "He endowed [Coyote] with great magical power, so that he could surmount all obstacles." While he was readying the world for the people's arrival, Coyote amused himself by pulling cunning pranks on other animals, many as bawdy and inventive as the blushing japes of Chaucer's pilgrims.

Estimates of the original catalog of Northwest native American stories run to ten thousand tales. Of these, less than five percent survive in written

2

form. Whole libraries of oral literature had been lost by the time anthropologists began recording native stories in the late nineteenth century, their bearers wiped out by imported diseases and the misguided policies of white religious and political leaders intent on eradicating traditional Indian culture.

Even those stories rescued by print are deprived of their full effect. True native American storytelling is public theater. Narrators are actors whose delivery is full of nuance, passion, and humor, who draw upon their audience's energy and response. Limited to words on paper, we are left not so much with stories as with scripts. In his collection *Coyote Was Going There: Indian Literature of the Oregon Country,* Jarold Ramsey quotes from a letter that Nez Percé anthropologist Archie Phinney wrote after transcribing his tribe's mythology: "A sad thing in recording these animal stories is the loss of spirit—the fascination furnished by the peculiar Indian vocal tradition for humor. Indians are better storytellers than whites. When I read my story mechanically, I find only the cold corpse." Yet in reading these stories, one cannot help but find plenty of life in the body left behind.

RED-ARM (NESPELEM)

The following story was told by Red-Arm (KwElkwElta´xEn), an elder of the Nespelem tribe, to James A. Teit, a Canadian anthropologist who studied and wrote extensively on the culture of the Interior Salish peoples of Washington and British Columbia. Red-Arm told Teit that the tale here titled "Origin of the Columbia River" was common to the Nespelem, Sanpoil, and Okanogan tribes in north-central Washington. It was first published in Folk-Tales of Salishan and Sahaptin Tribes *(1917), edited by Teit's mentor, the renowned anthropologist Franz Boas.*

ORIGIN OF THE COLUMBIA RIVER

COYOTE WAS TRAVELING, and heard water dropping. He said, "I will go and beat it." He sat down near it, and cried, "Hox-hox-hox-hox!" in imitation of water dripping. He tried four times, but the noise never ceased. He thought he had beaten it, and laughed, saying, "I beat you. No more shall water drip thus and make a noise."

Shortly after he had gone, the water began to drip as before. He became angry, and said, "Did I not say water shall not run and make a noise?" The water was coming after him, and increased in volume as it flowed. He kept on running; but still he heard the noise of the water, and was much annoyed.

Now he traveled along the edge of a plateau. There was no water there, nor trees. He looked down into the coulee, but everywhere it was dry. It was warm, and he became very thirsty. He heard the noise of water, but saw none. Then he looked again down into the coulee, and saw a small creek flowing along the bottom. It seemed a long distance away. He went down and drank his fill. He ascended again, but had barely reached the top when he became thirsty. He heard more noise of water, and, looking over the edge, saw a large creek running. He went down, drank his fill, and ascended again, but had not reached the top when he was thirsty, as before. He thought, "Where can I drink?" The water was following him. He went to the edge of a bench and looked down. A small river was now running below. He descended and drank. He wondered that much water was running where there had been none before. The more he drank, the sooner he became thirsty again.

The fourth time he became thirsty, he was only a little way from the water. He was angry, and turned back to drink. The water had now risen to a good-sized river, so that he had not far to go. He said, "What may be the matter? I am always thirsty now. There is no use of my going away. I will walk along the edge of the water." He did so; but as he was still thirsty, he said, "I will walk in the water." The water reached up to his knees. This did not satisfy him; and every time after drinking, he walked deeper, first up to the waist, then up to the arms. Then he said, "I will swim, so that my mouth will be close to the water, and I can drink all the time." Finally he had drunk so much that he lost consciousness.

Thus the water got even with Coyote for kicking it; and thus from a few drops of water originated the Columbia River.

KWAKW̱AḴA'WAKW SONGS

Songs are regarded as personal property among the Kwakwa̱ka̱'wakw, who live in the land around Queen Charlotte Strait, British Columbia. (The Kwak-wa̱ka̱'wakws' former name, Kwakiutl, is a misnomer; the current name trans-lates as "those who speak Kwak'wala," the language of the village groups around Queen Charlotte Strait.) The songs of these people take many forms: lullabies, prayer songs, funeral songs, love songs, and war songs, among others. Following are songs recorded in the 1890s by Franz Boas, whose studies of Northwestern tribes run to some ten thousand pages, more than half of which are devoted to the Kwakwa̱ka̱'wakw.

LOVE SONGS

Yï'yawa, wish I could go and make my true love happy,
haig·ia. hayia.
Yï'yawa, wish I could arise from under ground right next to
my true love, *haig·ia hayia.*
Yï'yawa, wish I could alight from the heights of the air right
next to my true love, *haig·ia hayia.*
Yï'yawa, wish I could sit among the clouds and fly with them
to my true love.
Yï'yawa, I am downcast on account of my true love.
Yï'yawa, I cry for pain on account of my true love, my dear.

―――――――

Anānana! Indeed my heart is strong, for I am ready to leave
my true love.
Anānana! Indeed my heart is very strong, for I am ready to
leave my true love.
Anānana! Indeed I am true to my true love.
I pretend not to know that you are my master, my true love.
I pretend not to know for whom I am gathering property,
my true love.
I pretend not to know for whom I am gathering blankets,
my true love.

Like pain of fire runs down my body my love to you,
my dear!
Like pain runs down my body my love to you, my dear!
Just as sickness is my love to you, my dear.
Just as a boil pains me my love to you, my dear.
Just as fire burns me my love to you, my dear.
I am thinking of what you said to me.
I am thinking of the love you bear me.
I am afraid of your love, my dear.

A BOY'S SONG

Baby, baby all the children call me baby when I am playing
mischief among them.
Baby, baby all the children teaze me and call me baby.
Who is teazing the girls?
Who puts his finger into their vaginas?
Who throws stones at the children?
It is baby.

A GIRL'S SONG

When I am grown up I shall go and stoop digging clams.
When I am grown up I shall go and splash in the water
digging clams.
When I am grown up I shall stoop down digging clams.
When I am grown up I shall go picking berries.

WAR SONG

I am the thunder of my tribe.
I am the seamonster of my tribe.
I am the earthquake of my tribe.
When I start to fly the thunder resounds through the world.
When I am maddened, the voice of the seabear resounds
through the world.

WÅYI′LÅTPU (NEZ PERCÉ)

Archie Phinney was a Nez Percé Indian who studied at George Washington University, at Leningrad University, and at Columbia University under Franz Boas. After receiving his doctorate in anthropology, Phinney returned home to the reservation in Lapwai, Idaho, and eventually became superintendent of the federal Northern Idaho Indian Agency. During the fall and winter of 1929–1930, he recorded a volume of ancient Nez Percé myths as told to him by his sixty-year-old mother, Wàyi′làtpu. Those stories, including the following Nez Percé origin myth, were originally published in Phinney's 1934 book, Nez Percé Texts.

COYOTE AND MONSTER

COYOTE WAS BUILDING a fish-ladder, by tearing down the waterfall at Celilo, so that salmon could go upstream for the people to catch. He was busily engaged at this when someone shouted to him, "Why are you bothering with that? All the people are gone; the monster has done for them." — "Well," said Coyote to himself, "then I'll stop doing this, because I was doing it for the people, and now I'll go along too."

From there he went along upstream, by the way of the Salmon River country. Going along he stepped on the leg of a meadow-lark and broke it. The meadow-lark in a temper shouted, "*Limá, limá, limá,* what a chance of finding the people you have, going along!" Coyote then asked, "My aunt! Please inform me, afterwards I will make for you a leg of brush-wood." So the meadow-lark told him, "Already all the people have been swallowed by the monster." Coyote then replied, "Yes, that is where I, too, am going."

From there he traveled on. Along the way he took a good bath saying to himself, "Lest I make myself repulsive to his taste," and then he dressed himself all up, "Lest he will vomit me up or spit me out." There he tied himself with rope to three mountains. From there he came along up and over ridges. Suddenly, behold, he saw a great head. He quickly hid himself in the grass and gazed at it. Never before in his life had he seen anything like it; never such a large thing—away off somewhere melting into the horizon was its gigantic body.

Now then Coyote shouted to him, "Oh Monster, we are going to inhale each other!"

The big eyes of the monster roved around looking all over for Coyote but did not find him, because Coyote's body was painted with clay to achieve a perfect protective coloring in the grass. Coyote had on his back a pack consisting of five stone knives, some pure pitch, and a flint fire-making set.

Presently Coyote shook the grass to and fro and shouted again, "Monster! We are going to inhale each other."

Suddenly the monster saw the swaying grass and replied, "Oh you Coyote, you swallow me first then; you inhale first."

Now Coyote tried. Powerfully and noisily he drew in his breath and the great monster just swayed and quivered. Then Coyote said, "Now you inhale me, for already you have swallowed all the people, so swallow me too lest I become lonely."

Now the Monster inhaled like a mighty wind. He carried Coyote along just like that, but as Coyote went he left along the way great camas roots and great service berries, saying, "Here the people will find them and will be glad, for only a short time away is the coming of the human race." There he almost got caught on one of the ropes but he quickly cut it with his knife. Thus he dashed right into the monster's mouth.

From there he walked along down the throat of the monster. Along the way he saw bones scattered about and he thought to himself, "It is to be seen that many people have been dying." As he went along he saw some boys and he said to them, "Where is his heart? Come along and show me!" Then, as they were all going along, the bear rushed out furiously at him. "So!" Coyote said to him, "You make yourself ferocious only to me," and he kicked the bear on the nose. As they were going along the rattlesnake bristled at him in fury, "So! Only towards me you are vicious— we are nothing but dung." Then he kicked the rattlesnake on the head and flattened it out for him. Going on he met the brown bear who greeted him, "I see he [the monster] selected you for the last." — "So! I'd like to see you save your people."

Thus all along the people hailed him and stopped him. He told the boys, "Pick up some wood." Here his erstwhile friend Fox hailed him from the side, "Such a dangerous fellow [the monster], what are you going to do to him?" — "So!" replied Coyote. "You too hurry along and look for wood." Presently Coyote arrived at the heart and he cut off slabs of fat and threw them to the people. "Imagine you being hungry under such conditions—grease your mouths with this."

And now Coyote started a fire with his flint and shortly smoke drifted up through the monster's nose, ears, eyes, and anus. Now the monster said, "Oh you Coyote, that's why I was afraid of you. Oh you Coyote, let me cast you out." And Coyote replied, "Yes, and later let it be said, 'He who was cast out is officiating in the distribution of salmon.'" — "Well then, go out through the nose." Coyote replied, "And will not they say the same?" And the monster said, "Well then, go out through the ears," to which Coyote replied, "And let it be said, 'Here is ear-wax officiating in the distribution of food.'" — "*Hn, hn, hn,* oh you Coyote! This is why I feared you; then go out through the anus," and Coyote replied, "And let people say, 'Faeces are officiating in the distribution of food.'"

There was his fire still burning near the heart and now the monster began to writhe in pain and Coyote began cutting away on the heart, whereupon very shortly he broke the stone knife. Immediately he took another and in a short time this one also broke and Coyote said to all the people, "Gather up all the bones and carry them to the eyes, ears, mouth and anus; pile them up and when he falls dead kick all the bones outside." Then again with another knife he began cutting away at the heart. The third knife he broke and the fourth, leaving only one more. He told the people, "All right, get yourselves ready because as soon as he falls dead each one will go out of the opening most convenient. Take the old women and old men close to the openings so that they may get out easily."

Now the heart hung by only a very small piece of muscle and Coyote was cutting away on it with his last stone knife. The monster's heart was still barely hanging when his last knife broke, whereupon Coyote threw himself on the heart and hung on just barely tearing it loose with his hands. In his death convulsions the monster opened all the openings of his body and now the people kicked the bones outside and went on out. Coyote, too, went on out.

Here now the monster fell dead and now the anus began to close. But there was the muskrat still inside. Just as the anus closed he squeezed out, barely getting his body through but alas! his tail was caught; but he pulled and it was bare when he pulled it out; all the tail-hair peeled right off. Coyote scolded him, "Now what were you doing; you had to think up something to do at the last moment. You're always behind in everything." Then he told the people, "Gather up all the bones and arrange them well." They did this, whereupon Coyote added, "Now we are going to carve the monster."

Coyote then smeared blood on his hands, sprinkled this blood on the bones, and suddenly there came to life again all those who had died while inside the monster. They carved the great monster and now Coyote began dealing out portions of the body to various parts of the country all over the land; toward the sunrise, toward the sunset, toward the warmth, toward the cold, and by that act destining and forenaming the various peoples: Coeur d'Alene, Cayuse, Pend Oreilles, Flathead, Blackfeet, Crow, Sioux, et al. He consumed the entire body of the monster in this distribution to various lands far and wide. Nothing more remained of the great monster.

And now Fox came up and said to Coyote, "What is the meaning of this, Coyote? You have distributed all of the body to faraway lands but have given yourself nothing for this immediate locality." — "Well," snorted Coyote, "and did you tell me that before? Why didn't you tell me that awhile ago before it was too late? I was engrossed to the exclusion of thinking. You should have told me that in the first place." And he turned to the people and said, "Bring me some water with which to wash my hands." They brought him water and he washed his hands and now with the bloody washwater he sprinkled the local regions saying, "You may be little people but you will be powerful. Even though you will be little people because I have deprived you, nevertheless you will be very, very manly. Only a short time away is the coming of the human race."

LOUIS LABONTE (CLACKAMAS CHINOOK)

Louis Labonte was an early product of Indian–white relations in the Northwest. His mother was the daughter of Chief Kobayway of the Clatsop tribe. His Canadian father came west in 1811 to work at Astoria; Labonte was born there in 1818. He grew up in Astoria, Spokane Falls, and Fort Colville, learning the languages of the local tribes, sitting in on their ceremonies, and listening to their myths. Later in life he recalled some of those stories for Oregon writer H. S. Lyman, who published them in the second edition of The Oregon Historical Quarterly *(1901).*

COYOTE AND THE CEDAR TREE

[COYOTE] SAW A TREE with a crotched root, leading to a hollow within, and thinking this a fine resting place, went inside. He then asked the tree to close, and it did so obediently. This was some time along in the fall. After it was closed, he asked it to open, and it did this also. Then he asked it to close and it was closed. It opened or shut whenever he asked it to, but by and by when he asked it to open, it would not. Then he was very sorry and sat down inside the tree and cried. But he was compelled to remain there all winter.

Some time along in the early spring the birds came at his request to peck him out; but the first, the second, and many others that tried only broke their bills and were unable to make even a small hole, until this was done by a woodpecker; and through the opening [Coyote] was able to gaze abroad and see the blooming flowers and the green grass.

But still he could not go through the opening, and finally concluded that the only way was to take himself to pieces and put himself out, piece by piece. His eyes were the first parts that he thus placed on the outside, but they were seized upon by a raven who carried them away. Finally the various sections of his body were all out and collected and put together properly, except that his eyes were gone and he was blind. But he smelled the scent of flowers and felt around until he found some of the flowers, which he placed in each eye. Then, feeling his way along laboriously, and staring about as if seeing everything, was at length directed by smelling smoke. Following this odor, he was led to a lodge where there were some women. By these his misfortune was ridiculed, and they engaged in laughter as he felt for the door; but he answered, "I am only measuring your house." He was moving around in the meantime and trying to find a place to sit down, which only increased their merriment; but he answered, "I see; I see; but I am only measuring the ground."

Then one of the women said, "Can you indeed see?"

Then he, staring off, replied, "Do you see that fire?"

"Where?" they asked.

"Far off," he answered, and described the distance as far away, beyond the limit of their vision.

"No," they confessed, "that is too far for us."

Then he answered, "I can see what you do not." By which one of the women was so impressed with the strength of his sight that she immediately wished to swap eyes, and he promptly accepted the proposition; as a result of which he could see even better than before, while she became blind. He then transformed her, for her folly, into a snail, which even to this day feels its way along the ground.

COYOTE BUILDS WILLAMETTE FALLS AND THE MAGIC FISH TRAP

ARRIVING BY THE WILLAMETTE RIVER, [Coyote] found the tribes of that region in very unhappy circumstances; chiefly from the absence of any good place for catching fish, and also, owing to the depredations of certain gigantic skookums [spirits]. In order to remedy the first evil, he determined to make a fall in the Willamette River where the salmon would collect and be easily captured. He found a place at the mouth of Pudding River, the Indian name of which is Hanteuc, and here he began erecting the barrier, but finding it not suitable, went further down, leaving only a small riffle. At Rock Island, he began in earnest, but upon further investigation found this also unsuitable, and leaving here a strong rapid, went down to the present site of the Willamette Falls, where he completed his task and made the magnificent cataract which is not only a scene of beauty, but a model fishing place.

After having provided the fishery, he decided to invent a remarkable trap which would obviate the labor of fishing. He succeeded and produced a marvelous machine which not only caught the fish, but also had the power to talk, and would cry out, "Noseepsk, noseepsk," when it was full.

Determining to try his invention for himself, [Coyote] set the trap and went immediately to his camping place to build a fire in order to cook the fish. But scarcely had be begun when the trap cried out, "Noseepsk! Noseepsk!" and going down he found it full of fish sure enough. Then, returning, he began once more to prepare his fire; but the trap called out again, "Noseepsk! Noseepsk!" He obeyed its summons and found it full, and went back once more to start his fire; but the trap called for him again, and now, out of patience with its promptness, he said to it crossly, "Wait until I build a fire, and do not keep calling for me forever." But by this sternness the trap was so much offended that it instantly ceased to work, and the wonderful invention was never used by men, who were obliged as before to catch the salmon with spears or nets.

EUROPEAN ENCOUNTERS

1579–1792

TAKING A BREAK FROM HIS PLUNDER of Spanish ships and settlements along the coast of South America in 1579, Francis Drake sailed north to the coast of present-day Oregon and possibly as far as Washington. Drake wasn't looking *for* the Northwest so much as a way *around* it. At the time, North America sat like a boulder in the middle of the commercial highway between Europe and Asia. The explorer who found the elusive nautical expressway through the continent—the Northwest Passage—would reap rewards far greater than the pilfered loot weighing down Drake's hold.

What Drake found, though, was a fortnight of freakish weather that turned his ropes to ice-twine and froze his supper as quickly as he could pull it from the fire. Thus was the Northwest's reputation for nasty weather born.

The Northwest coast remained unexplored by European navigators for nearly two hundred years after Drake. Where information was lacking, imagination rushed in. In the early seventeenth century Michael Lok, a promoter of expeditions to the Northwest coast, published an account of his meeting with a Greek mariner named Apostolos Valerianos, also known as Juan de Fuca, who claimed to have found something like the Northwest Passage during a voyage in 1592. (Though his directions put his "discovery" in the vicinity of the contemporary Strait of Juan de Fuca, navigators of his day were skeptical of de Fuca's claim, as are modern historians.)

In the eighteenth century the Northwest became less a *terra incognita* than a *terra apocrypha*. Maps of the region were exercises in creative cartography, based largely on information gleaned from legends like that of de Fuca and "Bartholomew de Fonte," a de Fuca–like figure whose dubious claims of Northwestern exploration appeared in a London magazine in 1708. In this climate of wild sailing stories appeared Jonathan Swift's yarn "A Voyage to Brobdingnag," in his 1726 satire *Gulliver's Travels*. In it, a raging storm sweeps Swift's surgeon Lemuel Gulliver to the Northwest coast, where he encounters a land of forty-foot corn, cat-sized rats, and people big as oaks. In light of the de Fuca and de Fonte stories in circulation, Swift's vision seems only a few satirical steps away from what was then passing for truth.

Spanish and British explorers such as Bruno de Hezeta and James Cook recorded the first credible written impressions of the Northwest, but for these navigators literature was of secondary importance. Quite a few accounts of these voyages still survive, though they vary widely in literary style. De Hezeta's diary was a true navigator's journal; upon landing on the Washington coast, he jotted a few sentences about the Indians and the beach, then ran on for four paragraphs about the sea, the tides, the currents, and his depth soundings. Cook took inventory; his account of the Northwest coast is filled with dispassionate descriptions of sea animals, vegetation, birds, shellfish, fish, insects, snakes, lizards, and stones. His report on the native Americans is anthropologic in tone; Cook was after knowledge, not adventure. George Vancouver had a more literary mind. In his account of a voyage to the Northwest coast, he presents himself as the main character in an adventure story and weaves the dry recordings of date, time, and location into a tale of exciting discovery. Where Cook coolly observed the natives, Vancouver invited them on board ship for a gala fireworks display.

Like his rivals, Cook was concerned primarily with the Northwest Passage. Instead he found the sea otter. During a brief stay in Nootka Sound on present-day Vancouver Island, he and his crew swapped metal trinkets for a few otter pelts the Indians had to offer. Upon reaching China, Cook's sailors were astonished to find Chinese merchants willing to give them the equivalent of several years' pay for a single pelt. Word spread by mouth and through the published journals of Cook and his crew. By 1792, Nootka was booming, with Spanish, English, French, Portuguese, and American traders competing for the best deals on pelts.

The picture of the Northwest presented to European and American readers in these accounts was cautionary, to say the least. To many explorers and traders, the native Americans were filthy, treacherous devils, honest traders one minute and murderous savages the next. Journals abound with tales of sailors massacred on board or on the beach. Cook and his crew were convinced that Northwest tribes practiced cannibalism, a libel that Cook's young officer George Vancouver took pains to disprove during his later voyage to the region. Some encounters were more humorous than deadly; Peter Puget's failed attempt at trading comes to mind. The scene of the young British officer frantically waving bough and hankie at an approaching canoe (the sight of which caused the paddlers' hasty retreat) reads like a BBC comedy. Although there were a few, such as Vancouver, who recognized the delights of the Northwest landscape, the region remained a primitive, savage land in the eyes of the outside world's readers.

FRANCIS FLETCHER

In the course of his three-year circumnavigation of the globe (1577–1580), the English explorer and pirate Francis Drake summered off the Pacific coast of North America, a portion of which he christened New Albion. Drake was on his way north after a season of pillage in South America, where he had "attacked Spanish ships," wrote one historian, "till his men were satiated with plunder." He sailed up the Northwest coast for two weeks in June 1579—some believe as far as 48 degrees north—but turned back after finding nothing but sleet storms and "stinking fogges." Although Drake's log aboard the Golden Hind *was never published and no longer exists, an account of the expedition was compiled from the notes of Francis Fletcher, the ship's chaplain, and published in 1628.*

from THE WORLD ENCOMPASSED
BY SIR FRANCIS DRAKE

[JUNE 3, 1579] We came into 42. deg. of North latitude, where in the night following, we found such alteration of heate, into extreame and nipping cold, that our men in generall did grievously complaine thereof; some of them feeling their healths much impaired thereby, neither was it, that this chanced in the night alone, but the day following carried with it not onely the markes, but the stings and force of the night going before;

to the great admiration of us all, for besides that the pinching and biting aire, was nothing altered; the very roapes of our ship were stiffe, and the raine which fell, was an unnatural congealed and frozen substance, so that we seemed rather to be in the frozen Zone, then any way so neere unto the sun, or these hotter climates.

Neither did this happen for the time onely, or by some sudden accident, but rather seemes indeed, to proceed from some ordinary cause, against the which the heate of the sun preuailes not; for it came to that extremity, in sayling but 2 deg. farther to the Northward in our course: that though sea-men lack not good stomaches, yet it seemed a question to many amongst us, whether their hands should feed their mouthes, or rather keepe themselves withint their coverts, from the pinching cold that did benumme them . . . [O]ur meate as soon as it was remooved from the fire, would presently in a manner be frozen up; and our ropes and tackling, in few dayes were growne to that stiffenesse, that what 3. men afore were able with them to performe, now 6. men with their best strength, and uttermost endeavour, were hardly able to accomplish: whereby a sudden and great discouragement seased upon the mindes of our men, and they were possessed with a great mislike, and doubting of any good to be done that way, yet would not our general be discouraged, but as wel by comfortable speeches, or the divine providence, and of Gods loving care over his children, out of the Scriptures; as also by other good and profitable perswasions, adding thereto his own cheerfull example, he so stirred them up, to put on a good courage, and to quite themselves like men, to indure some short extremity, to have the speedier comfort, and a little trouble, to obtaine the greater glory; that every man was throughly armed with willingnesse, and resolved to see the uttermost, if it were possible, of what good was to be done that way.

The land in that part of America, bearing farther out into the West, then we before imagined, we were neerer on it then wee were aware; and yet the neerer still see came unto it, the more extremitie of cold did sease upon us. The 5. day of June, wee were forced by contrary windes, to runne in with the shoare . . . where wee were not without some danger, by reason of the many extreme gusts, and flawes that beate upon us; which if they ceased and were still at any time, immediatly upon their intermission, there followed most vile, thicke, and stinking fogges, against which the sea prevailed nothing, till the gusts of wind againe removed them, which brought with them such extremity and violence when they came, that there was no dealing or resisting against them.

In this place was no abiding for us; and to go further North, the extremity of the cold (which had now utterly discouraged our men) would not permit us: and the winds directly bent against us, having once gotten us under sayle againe, commanded us to the Southward whether we would or no.

MICHAEL LOK

How much of Michael Lok's tale originated with the Greek pilot Juan de Fuca (Apostolos Valerianos) and how much in Lok's own imagination has been a point of contention since 1596, when Lok's story began circulating in London. Lok was a wealthy sixteenth-century London merchant who grew steadily poorer backing expeditions in search of a Northwest Passage. With his story of Juan de Fuca, he thought he had proof of the passage's existence. Henry Wagner speculates in Apocryphal Voyages to the Northwest Coast of America *(1931) that Lok had been thoroughly discredited in 1596, and "too much money had been lost searching for such a passage by the merchants and adventurers and some fresh stimulus had to be supplied to whip them into further contributions; perhaps this was it." The story was printed in 1625 in Samuel Purchas's four-volume, 4,262-page folio,* Hakluytus Posthumus, or Purchas His Pilgrimes, Contayning a History of the World in Sea Voyages and Lande Travells by Englishmen and others.

from PURCHAS HIS PILGRIMES

A NOTE MADE BY ME MICHAEL LOK *the elder, touching the Strait of Sea, commonly called* Fretum Anian, *in the South Sea, through the Northwest passage of* Meta incognita.

When I was at *Venice*, in April 1596. Happily arrived there an old man, about threescore yeares of age, called commonly *Juan de Fuca* but named properly *Apostolos Valerianos*, of Nation a *Greeke*, borne in the Iland *Cefalonia*, of profession a Mariner, and an ancient Pilot of Shippes . . .

[He] said, that he was Pilot of three small Ships which the Vizeroy of *Mexico* sent from *Mexico*, armed with one hundred men . . . to discover the

Straits of *Anian* . . . and to fortifie in that Strait, to resist the passage and proceedings of the *English* Nation, which were feared to passe through those Straits into the South Sea. And that by reason of a mutinie which happened among the Souldiers, for the Sodomie of their Captaine, that Voyage was overthrowne, and the Ships returned backe from *California* coast to *Nova Spania,* without any effect of thing done in that Voyage . . .

Also he said, that shortly after the said Voyage was so ill ended, the said Viceroy of *Mexico,* sent him out again *Anno* 1592. with a small Caravela, and a Pinnace, armed with Mariners onely, to follow the said Voyage, for discovery of the same Straits of *Anian,* and the passage thereof, into the Sea which they call the North Sea, which is our North-west Sea. And that he followed his course in that Voyage West and North-west in the South Sea, all alongst the coast of *Nova Spania,* and *California,* and the *Indies,* now called North *America* (all which Voyage hee signified to me in a greap Map, and a Sea-card of mine owne, which I laied before him) untill hee came to the Latitude of fortie seven degrees, and that there finding that the Land trended North and North-east, with a broad Inlet of Sea, between 47. and 48. degrees of Latitude: hee entred thereinto, sayling therein more then twentie dayes, and found that Land trending still sometime North-west and North-east, and North, and also East and South-eastward and very much broader Sea then was at the said entrance, and that he passed by divers Ilands in that sayling. And that at the entrance of this said Strait, there is on the North-west coast thereof, a great Hedland or Iland, with an exceeding high Pinacle, or spired Rocke, like a piller thereupon.

Also he said, that he went on Land in divers places, and that he saw some people on Land, clad in Beasts skins: and that the Land is very fruit-full, and rich of gold, Silver, Pearle, and other things, like *Nova Spania* . . .

And also he said, that he being entred thus farre into the said Strait, and being come into the North Sea already, and finding the Sea wide enough every where, and to be about thirtie or fortie leagues wide in the mouth of the Straits, where hee entred; hee thought he had now well dis-charged his office, and done the thing which he was sent to doe: and that hee not being armed to resist the force of the Salvage people that might happen, hee therefore set sayle and returned homewards againe towards *Nova Spania* . . .

JONATHAN SWIFT

Jonathan Swift cast the American Northwest as the land of Brobdingnag in his 1726 satire, Travels into Several Remote Nations of the World, *which became known as* Gulliver's Travels. *(Swift published the work anonymously, but word got out soon enough.) Brobdingnag was a land of giants whose inhabitants, Gulliver noted, "appeared as tall as an ordinary spire-steeple, and took about ten yards at every stride . . . " On the opening page of "A Voyage to Brobdingnag," Swift sketched a map of this imaginary Northwest, reproduced here on page 21. The imagined region resembles a Spain-shaped polyp attached to a suggestive cheek of land split by the Straits of Anian, Francis Drake's name for the Northwest Passage.*

BRUNO DE HEZETA

Three years before James Cook arrived in Nootka Sound in 1778, the Spanish navigator Bruno de Hezeta landed there, claimed the territory for Spain, sighted the mouth of the Columbia River, and established trade with the locals. Although both he and countryman Juan Francisco Bodega y Quadra kept extensive diaries of their travels in the Northwest, the Spanish government considered the books state secrets and the journals remained unpublished for more than eighty years. The tactic backfired, as Cook's widely published account of his landing at Nootka later bolstered England's claim to the territory. The first English-language edition of de Hezeta's diary was not published until 1985. In the following excerpt, de Hezeta lands near what is now Point Grenville, Washington.

from FOR HONOR AND COUNTRY:
THE DIARY OF BRUNO DE HEZETA

THE MORNING OF [JULY 14, 1775] dawned with misty horizons that did not permit us to make out the schooner. At four-thirty in the morning, I landed accompanied by the Reverend Father Fray Benito de la Sierra, Don Cristóbal Revilla, the surgeon Don Juan Gonzales, and some armed men. I took possession at six in the morning (following the Instructions

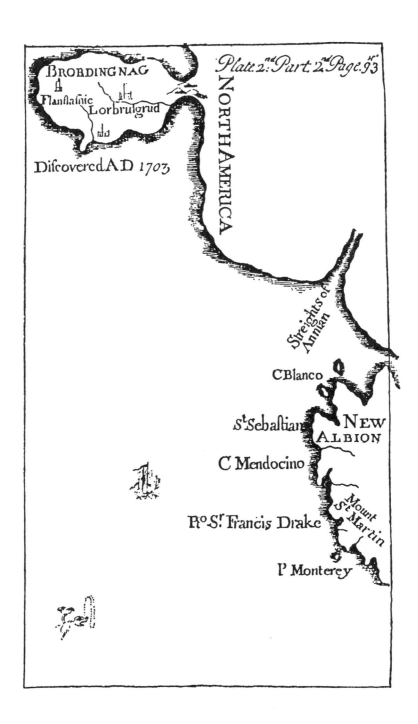

strictly in every detail), giving it the name Rada de Bucareli [Bucareli's roadstead], and returned at seven-thirty in the morning.

Only six Indians presented themselves to me ashore, young fellows, unarmed, who traded salmon, red gurnard and other kinds of fish for glass beads. One of them was dressed in a red chamois skin.

These Indians, like another nine that I left at the frigate when I departed on this mission, have beautiful faces. Some are fair in color, others dark and all of them plump and well built. Their clothing consists of sea otter skins with which they cover themselves from the waist up. I figure that this was more a matter of prevention—to defend themselves—than the need to keep themselves warm . . .

At eleven in the morning I sighted the schooner which was still anchored but diligently making an effort to set sail. At twelve-thirty their swivel guns were fired, and I, figuring that it was in danger from the nearby shoals, sent the launch with a stream anchor and cable. At two, seeing that it was joining us, I unfurled the topsails, placing myself in a risky situation, and alone I awaited impatiently to find out what event had made them call for help in order to set sail. Its commander informed me by word of mouth and in writing of the following:

> In the morning of that day, at low tide, exactly at seven in the morning, what happened was that [the schooner] found itself surrounded entirely by shoals, and consequently could not join us until high tide. In this interval, it was decided to replenish the water supply and to cut some poles for the main topsail masts. To do this, it had sent the boatswain with six other well-armed men. When they arrived on land, some three hundred Indians, falling upon them treacherously, had surrounded the boat and knifed those who were in it (so far as we know), with the exception of two men who threw themselves in the water, defending themselves. But they turned back towards land exhausted, and [the crewmen aboard the schooner] did not know whether it was reached or whether afterward they suffered the same martyrdom as their mates.

That the Indians had shown great gentleness in their manner, like that of the Indians at Trinidad, had brought their women on board this morning, and having exchanged meat and fish of different kinds for the presents of glass beads that had been given them, all [seemingly were] signs of true and sincere friendship between them [Bodega's crew and the Indians].

Despite this account of what happened, I set sail in order to get more depth. Meanwhile, in the confusion, we were trying to decide whether or not those treacherous people should be punished; and also whether the schooner should continue on, considering that on the eleventh . . . it was not able to endure the seas without lying to with extreme difficulty.

As to the first proposal, the commander and pilot were of the opinion that the Indians should be punished. Don Juan Pérez and Don Cristóbal Revilla were opposed. I went along with the latter two. This was because, in the first place, I am guided by Article 23 of the Instructions: not to give offense except in case of the need for self-defense.

Secondly, from what I knew of the terrain I realized we were in no position to inflict injury but rather to receive it.

JAMES COOK

On his first two expeditions, English captain James Cook charted the New Zealand and Australia coasts, explored the South Pacific, and circumnavigated the globe. For his third voyage (1776–1780), the Lords of the Admiralty sent him to the Pacific coast of America in search of the Northwest Passage. Cook found no passage, but discovered a commercial bonanza: Northwest fur. His account of that voyage, co-authored by James King and published in 1784, was an instant best-seller. The first edition sold out in three days, with some readers offering more than twice the retail price for the leatherbound three-volume set. Cook did not live to see the book's publication; he was killed in the Hawaiian Islands ten months after recording these impressions at Nootka Sound.

from A VOYAGE TO THE PACIFIC OCEAN

[MARCH 30, 1778] A great many canoes, filled with the natives, were about the ships all day; and a trade commenced betwixt us and them, which was carried on with the strictest honesty on both sides. The articles which they offered to sale were skins of various animals, such as bears, wolves, foxes, deer, rackoons, polecats, martins; and, in particular, of the sea otters, which are found at the islands East of Kamtschatka. Besides the skins in their native shape, they also brought garments made of them, and another sort of clothing made of the bark of a tree, or some plant like hemp; weapons, such as bows, arrows, and spears; fish-hooks, and instruments of various kinds; wooden vizors of many different monstrous figures; a sort of woollen stuff, or blanketing; bags filled with red ochre; pieces of carved work; beads; and several other little ornaments of thin brass and iron, shaped like a horse-shoe, which they hang at their noses; and several chissels, or pieces of iron, fixed to handles. From their possessing which metals, we could infer that they had either been visited before by some civilized nation, or had connections with tribes on their continent, who had communication with them. But the most extraordinary of all the articles which they brought to the ships for sale, were human skulls, and hands not yet quite stripped of the flesh, which they made our people plainly understand they had eaten; and, indeed, some of them had evident marks that they had been upon the fire.

[MARCH 31, 1778] The fame of our arrival brought a great concourse of the natives to our ships in the course of this day. We counted above a hundred canoes at one time, which might be supposed to contain, at an average, five persons each; for few of them had less than three on board; great numbers had seven, eight, or nine; and one was manned with no less than seventeen. Amongst these visitors, many now favoured us with their company for the first time, which we could guess, from their approaching the ships with their orations and other ceremonies. If they had any distrust or fear of us at first, they now appeared to have laid it aside; for they came on board the ships, and mixed with our people with the greatest freedom. We soon discovered, by this nearer intercourse, that they were as light-fingered as any of our friends in the islands we had visited in the course of the voyage. And they were far more dangerous thieves; for, possessing sharp iron instruments, they could cut a hook from a tackle, or any other piece of iron from a rope, the instant that our backs were turned. A large hook, weighing between twenty and thirty pounds, several smaller ones, and other articles of iron, were lost in this manner. And, as to our boats, they stripped them of every bit of iron that was worth carrying away, though we had always men left in them as a guard. They were dextrous enough in effecting their purposes; for one fellow would contrive to amuse the boat-keeper, at one end of a boat, while another was pulling out the iron work at the other. If we missed a thing immediately after it had been stolen, we found little difficulty in detecting the thief, as they were ready enough to impeach one another. But the guilty person generally relinquished his prize with reluctance; and sometimes we found it necessary to have recourse to force.

[APRIL 1778] The sea animals seen off the coast, were whales, porpoises, and seals . . . [The sea otter] abounds here, as it is fully described in different books, taken from the accounts of the Russian adventurers in their expeditions Eastward from Kamtschatka, if there had not been a small difference in one that we saw. We, for some time, entertained doubts, whether the many skins which the natives brought, really belonged to this animal; as our only reason for being of that opinion, was founded on the size, colour, and fineness of the fur; till a short while before our departure, when a whole one, that had been just killed, was purchased from some strangers who came to barter . . . The fur of these animals, as mentioned in the Russian accounts, is certainly softer and finer than that of any others we know of; and, therefore, the discovery of this part of the continent of North America, where so valuable an article of commerce may be met with, cannot be a matter of indifference.

GEORGE VANCOUVER

In 1791 the British government sent Captain George Vancouver on an expedition to survey the Pacific coast between the southern Spanish settlements and the northern Russian outposts, directing him to pay special attention to the Strait of Juan de Fuca. Vancouver was no stranger to the territory, having served under James Cook on the Resolution. *In the warship* Discovery, *Vancouver and his crew spent two months mapping the inland sea named after his lieutenant Peter Puget, and naming many other of the region's most visible landmarks, including Mount Baker, Mount Rainier, and Vancouver Island. Vancouver was one of the first writers to be captivated by the Northwest's natural splendor. "To describe the beauties of this region," he wrote, "will on some future occasion, be a very grateful task to the pen of a skilful panegyrist." In the first entry of these excerpts from his three-volume journal, published in 1798, Vancouver misses the mouth of the Columbia River.*

from A VOYAGE OF DISCOVERY TO THE NORTH PACIFIC OCEAN AND ROUND THE WORLD, 1791–1795

[APRIL 1792] The sea had now changed from its natural, to river coloured water; the probable consequence of some streams falling into the bay, or into the ocean to the north of it, through the low land. Not considering this opening worthy of more attention, I continued our pursuit to the N.W. being desirous to embrace the advantages of the prevailing breeze and pleasant weather, so favourable to our examination of the coast . . .

The country before us presented a most luxuriant landscape, and was probably not a little heightened in beauty by the weather that prevailed. The more interior parts were somewhat elevated, and agreeably diversified with hills, from which it gradually descended to the shore, and terminated in a sandy beach. The whole had the appearance of a continued forest extending as far north as the eye could reach, which made me very solicitous to find a port in the vicinity of a country presenting so delightful a prospect of fertility . . .

[MAY 1792] On landing on the west end of the supposed island [Protection Island], and ascending its eminence which was nearly a perpendicular cliff, our attention was immediately called to a landscape, almost as enchantingly beautiful as the most elegantly furnished pleasure grounds in Europe . . . The summit of this island presented nearly a horizontal surface, interspersed with some inequalities of ground, which produced a beautiful variety on an extensive lawn covered with luxuriant grass, and diversified with an abundance of flowers. To the northwestward was a coppice of pine trees and shrubs of various sorts, that seemed as if it had been planted for the sole purpose of protecting from the N.W. winds this delightful meadow, over which were promiscuously scattered a few clumps of trees, that would have puzzled the most ingenious designer of pleasure grounds to have arranged more agreeably . . .

A light pleasant breeze springing up, we weighed on Wednesday morning the 2d, and steered for the port we had discovered the preceding day . . . The delightful serenity of the weather greatly aided the beautiful scenery that was now presented; the surface of the sea was perfectly smooth, and the country before us exhibited every thing that bounteous nature could be expected to draw into one point of view. As we had no reason to imagine that this country had ever been indebted for any of its decorations to the hand of man, I could not possibly believe that any uncultivated country had ever been discovered exhibiting so rich a picture. The land which interrupted the horizon between the N.W. and the northern quarters, seemed, as already mentioned, to be much broken; from whence its eastern extent round to the S.E. was bounded by a ridge of snowy mountains, appearing to lie nearly in a north and south direction, on which mount Baker rose conspicuously; remarkable for its height, and the snowy mountains that stretch from its base to the north and south. Between us and this snowy range, the land, which on the sea shore terminated like that we had lately passed . . . rose here in a very gentle ascent, and was well covered with a variety of stately forest trees. These, however, did not conceal the whole face of the country in one uninterrupted wilderness, but pleasingly clothed its eminences, and chequered the vallies; presenting, in many directions, extensive spaces that wore the appearance of having been cleared by art, like the beautiful island we had visited the day before . . .

A picture so pleasing could not fail to call to our remembrance certain delightful and beloved situations in Old England.

[LATER MAY 1792] About a dozen [Indians] had attended at our dinner, one part of which was a venison party. Two of them, expressing a desire to pass the line of separation drawn between us, were permitted to do so. They sat down by us, and ate of the bread and fish that we gave them without the least hesitation; but on being offered some of the venison, though they saw us eat it with great relish, they could not be induced to taste it. They received it from us with great disgust, and presented it round to the rest of the party, by whom it underwent a strict examination. Their conduct on this occasion left no doubt in our minds that they believed it to be human flesh, an impression which it was highly expedient should be done away. To satisfy them that it was the flesh of the deer, we pointed to the skins of the animal they had about them. In reply to this they pointed to each other, and made signs that could not be misunderstood, that it was the flesh of human beings, and threw it down in the dirt, with gestures of great aversion and displeasure. At length we happily convinced them of their mistake by shewing them a haunch we had in the boat, by means of which they were undeceived, and some of them ate of the remainder of the pye with a good appetite.

This behaviour, whilst in some measure tending to substantiate their knowledge or suspicions that such barbarities have existence, led us to conclude, that the character given of the natives of North-West America does not attach to every tribe. These people have been represented not only as accustomed inhumanly to devour the flesh of their conquered enemies; but also to keep certain servants, or rather slaves, of their own nation, for the sole purpose of making the principal part of the banquet, to satisfy the unnatural savage gluttony of the chiefs of this country . . . Were such barbarities practised once a month, as is stated, it would be natural to suppose these people, so inured, would not have shewn the least aversion to eating flesh of any description; on the contrary, it is not possible to conceive a greater degree of abhorrence than was manifested by these good people, until their minds were made perfectly easy that it was not human flesh we offered them to eat. This instance must necessarily exonerate at least this particular tribe from so barbarous a practice; and, as their affinity to the inhabitants of Nootka, and of the sea-coast, to the south of that place, in their manners and customs, admits of little difference, it is but charitable to hope those also, on a more minute inquiry, may be found not altogether deserving such a character. They are not, however, free from the general failing attendant on a savage life. One of them having taken a knife and fork to imitate our manner of eating, found means to secrete them under his garment; but, on his being detected, gave up his plunder with the utmost good humour and unconcern.

PETER PUGET

On May 20, 1792, George Vancouver sent Peter Puget, his trusted twenty-eight-year-old second lieutenant, and a company of men in longboats to chart the southern reaches of Puget Sound (the captain thought it too risky to take the Discovery *into shallow waters). With his account of that week-long sojourn, as in previous encounters with the land and its inhabitants, Puget revealed himself as one of the more colorful writers of the exploration era in the Northwest. His journal, still unpublished, is housed in the British Public Records Office in London.*

from PETER PUGET'S JOURNAL

[MAY 11, 1792] The Conduct of these People impressed me with an high Idea of their Honesty, for whatever they had to barter, was suffered to be taken away, without an Exchange & it would be sometimes ten Minutes or a Quarter of an Hour before the person returned from the Boats with the Things he intended to give. yet this Delay did not cause any murmuring or Discontent on the Contrary they appeared perfectly well satisfied of our friendly Intentions. — Surely then, if these People behave with such Confidence to Strangers, may we not infer, that Innate Principles of Honesty actuated their Conduct on this Occasion? Some have attributed that Confidence to Fear of the largeness of the Party, that they were glad to receive whatever we offered in Exchange, as they expected, their Property to be wrested from their Possession. — however I am willing to allow them Credit for Appearances & say they differ in Character from the General Body of their Neighbours, who by Report of former Visitors [seem to be] most arrant Rogues — The Women are not distinguishable by any Effeminacy or Softness of Features, they are nearly in appearance similar to the Men, & those we noticed, were discovered by suckling some Children — They wear their Hair long which is Black & as filthy as the Men's but are more decently covered with Garments as no part of the Body is visible, but the Heads Hands & Feet; some were solicited to grant their favors but they refused I believe for want of more Secret Opportunity, nor did the Men appear at all jealous of the Liberties taken with their Women.

[MAY 20] Two Canoes who had for some time been seen paddling in Shore, One with Four the other with two Indians in them, immediately on our hauling in with an Intention to land, struck off into the Stream & endeavouring to increase their Distance from us — Nor could all the Signs emblematical of Friendship, such as a white Handkerchief — a Green Bough & many other Methods induce them to venture near us, on the Contrary, it appeared to have another Effect, that of redoubling their Efforts in getting away . . .

We left Indian Cove & proceeded along the Continental Shore which Still trended to the Westward & about three Leagues from the Dinner Point at 8 we brought too for the Night where we found the Larboard or Southern Shore composed of Islands. — to this Situation two Canoes had been our Attendants from the last cove & they now lay on their Paddles about One Hundred Yards from the Beach attentively viewing our operations. In the Boats were some fire Arms that in the Course of Day had been found defective & we now wished them to be discharged but the fear of alarming the Indians, prevented me at present doing it: finding however they still kept hovering about the Boats & being apprehensive they would be endeavouring to commit Depredations during the Night I then ordered a Musquett to be fired but so far was it from intimidating or alarming them, that they remained stationary, only exclaiming Pop at every Report in way of Derision.

TRAPPING AND TRADING

1805–1836

WHEN THOMAS JEFFERSON dispatched Meriwether Lewis and William Clark up the Missouri River in 1803, he broke the news gently to the Spanish minister, whose nation owned the soil on which the Corps of Discovery was about to trespass. Not to worry, wrote the President, the expedition was merely "a literary pursuit" to gain scientific and geographic knowledge about the Northwest, a region largely blank on the North American map.

Even as a purely "literary" campaign (which it most definitely was not), the venture must have engendered some misgivings in the Spanish minister. He could not have been unaware of the impact that previous voyagers—especially Cook and Vancouver—had had in strengthening England's claim to the Northwest.

So important were their journals that Jefferson advised Lewis and Clark to duplicate their entries "on the paper of the birch, as less liable to injury from damp" (they did not), and encouraged others in the corps to take notes along the trail. Writing became one of the principal leisure pursuits of the expedition; four sergeants and three privates kept journals, in addition to the main narrative established by Lewis and Clark.

The corps captured the imagination of the American public even before its return home. A letter Lewis sent to Jefferson from Fort Mandan, North Dakota—not yet the halfway point—was used to produce a number of instant histories of the expedition. Sergeant Patrick Gass's journal was published a few months after the completion of the expedition in 1806 and went through a number of editions in Philadelphia, London, and Paris. By the time editor Nicholas Biddle cobbled together an official history from the journals of Lewis and Clark in 1814, the market had run dry. Neither

Biddle, Clark, nor Lewis's widow (the captain died in 1809) saw a dime of the $154.10 profit turned by the publisher.

No profit, but glory: Lewis and Clark inherited Cook's mantle as romantic heroes who fired America's and Europe's imagination about the Northwest. In their wake came a generation of adventurers seeking danger and riches in the wild Northwestern land.

They began arriving in 1810, when New York fur dealer John Jacob Astor sent a company of men by ship, and another by land, to establish a fur-trading post at the mouth of the Columbia River. Astor was one of the Northwest's first literary patrons; three clerks who served at Astoria later wrote accounts of life in the Northwest that found favor with publishers in America, England, and France. Gabriel Franchère's *Narrative of a Voyage to the Northwest Coast of America in the Years 1811, 1812, 1813, and 1814* (published in 1820), Ross Cox's *Adventures on the Columbia River* (1831), and Alexander Ross's *Adventures of the First Settlers on the Oregon or Columbia River* (1849) enthralled readers with tales of Indian massacres (the bloody *Tonquin* incident was always a crowd pleaser), arduous journeys, hellish weather, perilous mountains, roaring rivers, and the occasional wolf or bear desirous of a human repast. They described a landscape at once wild, unforgiving, breathtaking, and glorious.

Astor's clerks were so caught up in their literary pursuits, in fact, that they earned a mild ink-lashing from Washington Irving, who wrote his own account of Astor's folly in *Astoria, or Anecdotes of an Enterprise Beyond the Rocky Mountains* (1836): "Some of the young clerks, who were making their first voyage . . . were, very rationally, in the habit of taking notes and keeping journals. This was a sore abomination to the honest captain [of the *Tonquin*], who held their literary pretensions in great contempt." Irving's complaint flirts with hypocrisy; his own book, for which Astor is said to have paid five thousand dollars, was based in no small degree on the notes taken by those very clerks.

During this period, a layer of the Northwest's mystery was peeled away. The journals of Lewis and Clark overflowed with new information about the geography, flora, fauna, and disposition of the inhabitants of the Northwest. Naturalist David Douglas brought a catalog of the region's brobdingnagian pines and lesser plants home to England. Most reports from the Pacific Northwest were just that—reports, full of objective fact and little introspection. But a few writers began to impart a human meaning to the landscape around them. Ross Cox, the young Astorian clerk, wrote that the "deep and impervious gloom" of the immense Northwest forests "resembles the silence and solitude of death."

Native Americans became less alien and more human in the writing of this time. Scenes of brutal torture and murder at the hands of the indigenous residents continued to spice up many narratives, but were sometimes offset by reports of encounters with more "civilized" tribes. The meetings between Lewis and Clark and the local tribes were almost wholly positive. *The Adventures of John Jewitt,* the story of an American held captive in 1803 by Indians at Nootka, began with a bloody ambush aboard a trading ship but eventually gave way to a well-rounded, humane description of life among the Nootkans. Ross Cox first described the native men at Astoria as "most uncouth-looking objects," but later penned sympathetic portrayals of the inland tribes and recorded the death and misery unleashed upon the native American population by the white man's disease of smallpox.

MERIWETHER LEWIS AND WILLIAM CLARK

Captains Meriwether Lewis and William Clark and their thirty-four-person Corps of Discovery departed St. Louis in May 1804. They paddled to the source of the Missouri River and trekked overland to the Columbia River, which they rode to the Pacific Ocean. After spending a dreadful winter on the coast (only twelve days were without rain), they returned up the Columbia and down the Missouri, arriving in St. Louis in September 1806. Although Nicholas Biddle, a Philadelphia editor, used the diaries of the two leaders to write his 1814 History of the Exploration Under the Command of Captains Lewis and Clark . . . , *their complete journals were not published until 1905. That eight-volume version, edited by Reuben Gold Thwaites (from which these passages are taken), allowed the literary idiosyncrasies of the two leaders to come through. Lewis was the better scholar, Clark the more experienced frontiersman. Each borrowed from the other's observations, with Clark sometimes copying Lewis's entries and embellishing the passages with his own phonetic spelling.*

from THE ORIGINAL JOURNALS OF THE LEWIS AND CLARK EXPEDITION

Meriwether Lewis, September 10, 1805. The party is making its way west across the Bitterroot Mountains and into Idaho via the Lolo Trail:

The morning being fair I sent out all the hunters, and directed two of them to procede down the river as far as it's junction with the Eastern fork which heads near the missouri, and return this evening . . . this evening one of our hunters returned accompanyed by three men of the Flathead nation whom he had met in his excurtion up travellers rest Creek. on first meeting him the Indians were alarmed and prepared for battle with their bows and arrows, but he soon relieved their fears by laying down his gun and advancing towards them. the Indians were mounted on very fine horses of which the Flatheads have a great abundance; that is, each man in the nation possesses from 20 to a hundred head. our guide could not speake the language of these people but soon engaged them in conversation by signs or jesticulation, the common language of all the Aborigines of North America . . . in this manner we learnt from these people that two men which they supposed to be of the Snake nation had stolen 23 horses from them and that they were in pursuit of the theaves. they told us they were in great hast, we gave them some boiled venison, of which the[y] eat sparingly. the sun was now set, two of them departed after receiving a few small articles which we gave them, and the third remained having agreed to continue with us as a guide, and to introduce us to his relations whom he informed us were numerous and resided in the plain below the mountains on the columbia river, from whence he said the water was good and capable of being navigated to the sea; that some of his relation[s] were at the sea last fall and saw an old whiteman who resided there by himself and who had given them some handkerchiefs such as he saw in our possession. he said it would require five sleeps.

William Clark, September 12:

The road through this hilley Countrey is verry bad passing over hills & thro' Steep hollows, over falling timber &c. &c   continued on & passed Some most intolerable road on the Sides of the Steep Stoney mountains, which might be avoided by keeping up the Creek which is thickly covered with under groth & falling timber,   Crossed a Mountain 8 miles with out water & encamped on a hill Side on the Creek after Decending a long Steep mountain, Some of our Party did not get up untill 10 oClock P.M. . . . Party and horses much fatigued.

Clark, September 13:

at 2 miles passed Several Springs which I observed the Deer Elk &c. had made roads to, and below one of the Indians had made a whole to bathe, I tasted this water and found it hot & not bad tasted in further examonation I found this water nearly boiling hot at the places it Spouted from the rocks I put my finger in the water, at first could not bare it in a Second. my guide took a wrong road and took us out of our rout 3 miles through [an] intolerable rout.

Clark, September 14:

in the Valies it rained and hailed, on the top of the mountains Some Snow fell we Set out early and Crossed a high mountain on the right of the Creek for 6 miles to the forks of the Glade Creek (*one of the heads of the Koos koos kee*) . . . I could see no fish, and the grass entirely eaten out by the horses, we proceeded on 2 miles & Encamped opposit a Small Island at the mouth of a branch on the right side of the river . . . here we were compelled to kill a Colt for our men & Selves to eat for the want of meat & we named the South fork Colt killed Creek . . . The Mountains which we passed to day much worst than yesterday the last excessively bad & thickly Strowed with falling timber & Pine Spruce fur Hackmatak & Tamerack, Steep & Stoney our men and horses much fatigued.

Clark, September 15:

proceeded on Down the right Side of (*koos koos kee*) River over Steep points rockey & buschey as usial for 4 miles to an old Indian fishing place, here the road leaves the river to the left and assends a *mountain* winding in every direction to get up the Steep assents & to pass the emence quantity of falling timber which had [been] falling from dift. causes i e fire & wind and has deprived the greater part of the Southerly Sides of this mountain of its green timber, Several horses Sliped and roled down Steep hills which hurt them verry much the one which Carried my desk & Small trunk Turned over & roled down a mountain for 40 yards & lodged against a tree, broke the Desk the horse escaped and appeared but little hurt . . .

Clark, September 16:

began to Snow about 3 hours before Day and continued all day   the Snow in the morning 4 inches deep on the old Snow, and by night we found it from 6 to 8 inches deep,   I walked in front to keep the road and found great dificuelty in keeping it as maney places the Snow had entirely filled up the track, and obliged me to hunt Several minits for the track,   at 12 oClock we halted on the top of the mountain to worm & dry our Selves a little as well as to let our horses rest and graze a little on Some long grass . . .   I have been wet and as cold in every part as I ever was in my life, indeed I was at one time fearfull my feet would freeze in the thin Mockirsons which I wore,   after a Short Delay in the middle of the Day, I took one man and proceeded on as fast as I could about 6 miles to a Small branch passing to the right, halted and built fires for the party agains[t] their arrival which was at Dusk, verry cold and much fatigued,   Killed a Second Colt which we all Suped hartily on and thought it fine meat.

Clark, November 7, 1805. The party has found the Columbia River and is following it to the Pacific Ocean:

Great joy in camp   we are in *view* of the *Ocian*, this great Pacific Octean which we been so long anxious to See. and the roreing or noise made by the waves brakeing on the rockey Shores (as I suppose) may be heard distinctly

Clark, November 8:

A cloudy morning Some rain,   we did not Set out untill 9 oClock, haveing changed our Clothing.   three Indians in a Canoe overtook us, with salmon to Sell,   we came too at the remains of an old village at the bottom of this nitch and dined, here we Saw great numbers of fowl,   Sent out 2 men and they killed a Goose and two *canves back* Ducks   here we found great numbers of flees which we treated with the greatest caution and distance;   after Diner the Indians left us and we took the advantage of a returning tide and proceeded on to the Second point on the Std.   here we found the Swells or Waves so high that we thought it imprudent to proceed; we landed unloaded and drew up our Canoes.

Some rain all day at intervals, we are all wet and disagreeable, as we have been for Several days past, and our present Situation a verry disagreeable one in as much as we have not leavel land Sufficient for an encampment and for our baggage to lie cleare of the tide, the High hills jutting in so close and steep that we cannot retreat back, and the water of the river too Salt to be used, added to this the waves are increasing to Such a hight that we cannot move from this place, in this Situation we are compelled to form our camp between the hite of the Ebb and flood tides, and rase our baggage on logs . . . The Seas roled and tossed the Canoes in such a manner this evening that Several of our party were Sea sick.

Clark, November 9:

at 2 oClock P.M. the flood tide came in accompanied with emence waves and heavy winds, floated the trees and Drift which was on the point on which we Camped and tossed them about in such a manner as to endanger the canoes verry much, with every exertion and the Strictest attention by every individual of the party was scercely sufficient to Save our Canoes from being crushed by those monsterous trees mancy of them nearly 200 feet long and from 4 to 7 feet through. our camp entirely under water dureing the hight of the tide, every man as wet as water could make them all the last night and to day all day as the rain continued all day, at 4 oClock P.M. the wind Shifted about to the S. W. and blew with great violence imediately from the Ocean for about two hours, notwithstanding the disagreeable Situation of our party all wet and cold . . . they are chearfull and anxious to See further into the Ocian, The water of the river being too Salt to use we are obliged to make use of rain water. Some of the party not accustomed to Salt water has made too free a use of it on them it acts as a pergitive.

At this dismal point we must Spend another night as the wind & waves are too high to proceed.

Clark, November 10:

rained verry hard the greater part of the last night & continues this morning, the wind has layed and the swells are fallen. we loaded our canoes and proceeded on,

The wind rose from the N W. and the swells became so high, we were compelled to return about 2 miles to a place where we could unld. our canoes . . . we continued on this drift wood untill about 3 oClock when the evening appearing favourable we loaded & set out in hopes to turn the Point below and get into a better harber, but finding the *waves & swells* continue to rage with great fury below, we got a safe place for our stores & a much beter one for the canoes to lie and formed a campment on Drift logs in the same little Bay under a high hill at the enterence of a small drean, which we found very convt. on account of its water, as that of the river is Brackish. The logs on which we lie is all on flote every high tide. The rain continues all day. we are all wet also our bedding and maney other articles. we are all employed untill late drying our bedding.   nothing to eate but Pounded fish.

Clark, November 11:

A hard rain all the last night,   dureing the last tide the logs on which we lay was all on float,   Sent out Jo Fields to hunt, he Soon returned and informed us that the hills was So high & Steep, & thick with undergroth and fallen Timber that he could not get out any distance;   about 12 oClock 5 Indians came down in a canoe, the wind verry high from the S. W. with most tremendious waves brakeing with great violence against the Shores, rain falling in torrents,   we are all wet as usial—and our Situation is truly a disagreeable one; the great quantites of rain which has loosened the Stones on the hill Sides; and the Small stones fall down upon us, our canoes at one place at the mercy of the waves, our baggage in another; and our selves and party Scattered on floating logs and Such dry Spots as can be found on the hill sides, and crivicies of the rocks. we purchased of the Indians 13 red charr which we found to be an excellent fish. They are badly clad & illy made, Small and Speak a language much resembling the last nation,   one of those men had on a Salors Jacket and Pantiloons. and made Signs that he got those clothes from the white people who lived below the point &c. those people left us and crossed the river (which is about 5 miles wide at this place) through the highest waves I ever Saw a Small vestles ride. Those Indians are certainly the best Canoe navigaters I ever Saw. rained all day.

Clark, November 12:

A Tremendious wind from the S. W. about 3 oClock this morning with Lightineng and hard claps of Thunder, and Hail which Continued untill 6 oClock A.M. when it became light for a Short time,   then the heavens became sudenly darkened by a black cloud from the S. W. and rained with great violence untill 12 oClock, the waves tremendious brakeing with great fury against the rocks and trees on which we were encamped.   our Situation is dangerous.   we took the advantage of a low *tide* and moved our camp around a point to a Small wet bottom, at the Mouth of a Brook, which we had not observed when we came to this cove; from its being verry thick and obscured by drift trees and thick bushes. It would be distressing to See our Situation, all wet and colde our bedding also wet, (and the robes of the party which compose half the bedding is rotten and we are not in a Situation to supply their places) in a wet bottom scercely large enough to contain us our baggage half a mile from us, and Canoes at the mercy of the waves . . .

ROSS COX

The supply ship Beaver *arrived at the year-old trading settlement of Astoria in May 1812. One of those aboard was Ross Cox, a nineteen-year-old Irish clerk for John Jacob Astor's Pacific Fur Company. Cox stayed for five years before returning home to Dublin, where he eventually became a correspondent for the* London Morning Herald. *His two-volume, 760-page book,* Adventures on the Columbia River *(1831), thrilled readers in London and New York. In this excerpt Cox becomes separated from his party while on a trip to the trading post at Spokane and spends fourteen days in the wilderness armed with only a gingham shirt and nankeen "trowsers."*

from ADVENTURES ON THE COLUMBIA RIVER

AFTER WAKING AND RIDING eight hours, I need not say we made a hearty breakfast; after which I wandered some distance along the banks of the rivulet in search of cherries, and came to a sweet little arbour formed by sumach and cherry trees. I pulled a quantity of the fruit, and sat down in the retreat to enjoy its refreshing coolness. It was a charming spot, and on the opposite bank was a delightful wilderness of crimson haw, honeysuckles, wild roses, and currants: its resemblance to a friend's summerhouse in which I had spent many happy days brought back home with all its endearing recollections; and my scattered thoughts were successively occupied with the past, the present, and the future. In this state I fell into a kind of pleasing, soothing reverie, which, joined to the morning's fatigue, gradually sealed my eye-lids; and unconscious of my situation, I resigned myself to the influence of the drowsy god. But imagine my feelings when I awoke in the evening, I think it was about five o'clock, from the declining appearance of the sun! All was calm and silent as the grave. I hastened to the spot where we had breakfasted: it was vacant. I ran to the place where the men had made their fire: all, all were gone, and not a vestige of man or horse appeared in the valley. My senses almost failed me. I called out, in vain, in every direction, until I became hoarse; and I could no longer conceal from myself the dreadful truth that I was alone in a wild, uninhabited country, without horse or arms, and destitute of covering.

. . . The whole of my clothes consisted merely of a gingham shirt, nankeen trowsers, and a pair of light leather moccasins, much worn. About an hour before breakfast, in consequence of the heat, I had taken off my coat and placed it on one of the loaded horses, intending to put it on towards the cool of the evening; and one of the men had charge of my fowling-piece. I was even without my hat; for in the agitated state of my mind on awaking I had left it behind, and had advanced too far to think of returning for it. At some distance on my left I observed a field of high, strong grass, to which I proceeded; and after pulling enough to place under and over me, I recommended myself to the Almighty, and fell asleep. During the night confused dreams of warm houses, feather beds, poisoned arrows, prickly pears, and rattlesnakes, haunted my disturbed imagination.

On the 18th [of August] I arose with the sun, quite wet and chilly, the heavy dew having completely saturated my flimsy covering, and proceeded . . . Late in the evening, I observed about a mile distant two horsemen galloping in an easterly direction. From their dresses I knew they belonged to our party. I instantly ran to a hillock, and called out in a voice to which hunger had imparted a supernatural shrillness; but they galloped on. I then took off my shirt, which I waved in a conspicuous manner over my head, accompanied by the most frantic cries; still they continued on. I ran towards the direction they were galloping, despair adding wings to my flight. Rocks, stubble, and brushwood were passed with the speed of a hunted antelope; but to no purpose: for on arriving at the place where I imagined a pathway would have brought me into their track, I was completely at fault. It was now nearly dark. I had eaten nothing since the noon of the preceding day; and, faint with hunger and fatigue, threw myself on the grass, when I heard a small rustling noise behind me. I turned round, and, with horror, beheld a large rattlesnake cooling himself in the evening shade. I instantly retreated, on observing which he coiled himself. Having obtained a large stone, I advanced slowly on him, and taking a proper aim, dashed it with all my force on the reptile's head, which I buried in the ground beneath the stone.

The late race had completely worn out the thin soles of my moccasins, as my feet in consequence became much swoln. As night advanced, I was obliged to look out for a place to sleep, and, after some time, selected nearly as good a bed as the one I had the first night. My exertions in pulling the long, coarse grass nearly rendered my hands useless by severely cutting all the joints of the fingers.

Seven days later:

About dusk an immense-sized wolf rushed out of a thick copse a short distance from the pathway, planted himself directly before me, in a threatening position, and appeared determined to dispute my passage. He was not more than twenty feet from me. My situation was desperate, and as I knew that the least symptom of fear would be the signal for attack, I presented my stick, and shouted as loud as my weak voice would permit. He appeared somewhat startled, and retreated a few steps, still keeping his piercing eyes firmly fixed on me. I advanced a little, when he commenced howling in a most appalling manner; and supposing his intention was to collect a few of his comrades to assist in making an afternoon repast on my half-famished carcass, I redoubled my cries, until I had almost lost the power of utterance, at the same time calling out various names, thinking I might make it appear I was not alone. An old and a young lynx ran close past me, but did not stop. The wolf remained about fifteen minutes in the same position; but whether my wild and fearful exclamations deterred any others from joining him, I cannot say. Finding at length my determination not to flinch, and that no assistance was likely to come, he retreated into the wood, and disappeared in the surrounding gloom.

The shades of night were now descending fast, when I came to a verdant spot surrounded by small trees, and full of rushes, which induced me to hope for water; but after searching for some time, I was still doomed to bitter disappointment. A shallow lake or pond had been there, which the long drought and heat had dried up. I then pulled a quantity of the rushes and spread them at the foot of a large stone, which I intended for my pillow; but as I was about throwing myself down, a rattlesnake coiled, with the head erect, and the forked tongue extended in a state of frightful oscillation, caught my eye immediately under the stone. I instantly retreated a short distance, but assuming fresh courage, soon dispatched it with my stick. On examining the spot more minutely, a large cluster of them appeared under the stone, the whole of which I rooted out and destroyed. This was hardly accomplished when upwards of a dozen snakes of different descriptions, chiefly dark brown, blue, and green, made their appearance: they were much quicker in their movements than their rattle-tailed brethren; and I could only kill a few of them.

This was a peculiarly soul-trying moment. I had tasted no fruit since the morning before, and after a painful day's march under a burning sun, could not procure a drop of water to allay my feverish thirst. I was surrounded by a murderous brood of serpents, and ferocious beasts of prey, and without even the consolation of knowing when such misery might have a probably termination. I might truly say with the royal psalmist that "the snares of death compassed me round about."

Two days later, and treed overnight by a bear:

On the morning of the 27th, a little after sunrise, the bear quitted the trunk, shook himself, "cast a longing, lingering look" towards me, and slowly disappeared in search of his morning repast. After waiting some time, apprehensive of his return, I descended and resumed my journey through the woods in a north-north-east direction. In a few hours all my anxiety of the preceding night was more than compensated by falling in with a well-beaten horse-path, with fresh traces on it, both of hoofs and human feet . . . About six in the evening I arrived at a spot where a party must have slept the preceding night. Round the remains of a large fire which was still burning were scattered several half-picked bones of grouse, partridges and ducks, all of which I collected with economical industry. After devouring the flesh I broiled the bones. The whole scarcely sufficed to give me a moderate meal, but yet afforded a most seasonable relief to my famished body. I enjoyed a comfortable sleep this night close to the fire, uninterrupted by any nocturnal visitor. On the morning of the 28th I set off with cheerful spirits, fully impressed with the hope of a speedy termination to my sufferings . . . In the evening I arrived at a stagnant pool, from which I merely moistened my lips; and having covered myself with some birch bark, slept by its side. The bears and wolves occasionally serenaded me during the night, but I did not see any of them. I rose early on the morning of the 29th, and followed the fresh traces all day through the wood . . . In the evening I threw a stone at a small animal resembling a hare, the leg of which I broke. It ran away limping, but my feet were too sore to permit me to follow it. I passed the night by the side of a small stream, where I got a sufficient supply of hips and cherries. A few distant growls awoke me at intervals, but no animal appeared. On the 30th the path took a more easterly turn, and the woods became thicker and more gloomy. I had now nearly consumed the remnant of my trowsers in bandages for my wretched feet; and, with the exception of my shirt, was almost naked. The horse-tracks every moment appeared more fresh, and fed my hopes. Late in the evening I arrived at a spot where the path branched off in different directions: one led up rather a steep hill, the other descended into a valley, and the tracks on both were equally recent. I took the higher; but after proceeding a few hundred paces through a deep wood, which appeared more dark from the thick foliage which shut out the rays of the sun, I returned, apprehensive of not procuring water for my supper, and descended the lower path. I had not advanced far when I imagined I heard the neighing of a horse. I listened with breathless attention, and became convinced it was no illusion. A few paces farther brought me in sight of several of those noble animals sporting in a handsome meadow, from which I was separated by a rapid stream. With some difficulty I crossed over, and ascended the opposite bank. One of the horses approached me: I thought him "the prince of palfrey; his neigh was like the bidding of a monarch, and his countenance enforced homage."

On advancing a short distance into the meadow the cheering sight of a small column of gracefully curling smoke announced my vicinity to human beings, and in a moment after two Indian women perceived me: they instantly fled to a hut which appeared at the farther end of the meadow. This movement made me doubt whether I had arrived among friends or enemies; but my apprehensions were quickly dissipated by the approach of two men, who came running to me in the most friendly manner. On seeing the lacerated state of my feet, they carried me in their arms to a comfortable dwelling covered with deer-skins. To wash and dress my own limbs, roast some roots, and boil a small salmon, seemed but the business of a moment. After returning thanks to that great and good Being in whose hands are the issues of life and death, and who had watched over my wandering steps, and rescued me from the many perilous dangers I encountered, I sat down to my salmon, of which it is needless to say I made a hearty supper.

DAVID DOUGLAS

Sponsored by the Hudson's Bay Company and the Royal Horticulture Society, Scottish botanist David Douglas set off in 1824 on an expedition to catalog the flora of the Northwest. During the next three years he covered more than six thousand miles of territory, hunting new species of flowers and trees. He returned to London in 1827 with a remarkable array of new plants and seeds, as well as a glorious scientific reputation (and later his own tree, the Douglas fir). This passage from Douglas's journal describing his hunt for the massive sugar pine— largest of all ninety-six pines known to science—appeared in The Companion to the Botanical Magazine *in London in 1836, two years after his death.*

from DAVID DOUGLAS'S JOURNAL

[OCTOBER 23, 1826] Mr. McLeod has made the desired arrangements, and while Centrenose goes with himself to the coast, one of his sons will accompany me in my researches, which are chiefly directed towards the discovery of the great *Pine* so frequently mentioned.

[OCTOBER 25] Last night was one of the most dreadful I ever witnessed, the rain falling in torrents, was accompanied by so much wind as made it impossible to keep up a fire; and to add to my miseries, the tent was blown about my ears, so that I lay till daylight, rolled in my wet blanket, on *Pteris aquilina* [bracken], with the drenched tent piled above me. Sleep was, of course, not to be procured; every few minutes the falling trees came down with a crash which seemed as if the earth was cleaving asunder, while the peals of thunder and vivid flashes of forky lightning produced such a sensation of terror as had never filled my mind before, for I had at no time experienced a storm under similar circumstances of loneliness and unprotected destitution. Even my poor horses were unable to endure it with-out craving, as it were, protection from their master, which they did, by cowering close to my side, hanging their heads upon me and neighing. Towards daylight the storm abated, and before sunrise the weather was clear, though very cold. I could not stir without making a fire and drying some of my clothes, every thing being soaked through, and I indulged myself with a pipe of tobacco, which was all I could afford. At ten o'clock I started, still shivering with cold, though I had rubbed myself so hard with a handkerchief before the fire that I could no longer endure the pain. Shortly after, I was seized with intense headache, pain in the stomach, giddiness, and dimness of sight. All my medicine being reduced to a few grains of calomel, I felt unwilling, without absolute necessity, to take to this last resource, and therefore threw myself into a violent perspiration by strong exercise, and felt somewhat relieved towards evening, before which time I arrived at three lodges of Indians, who gave me some fish. The food was such as I could hardly have eaten, if my destitution were less; still I was thankful for it, especially as the poor people had nothing else to offer me.

[OCTOBER 26] Weather dull, cold, and cloudy. When my friends in England are made acquainted with my travels, I fear they will think that I have told them nothing but my miseries. This may be very true; but I now know, as they may do also, if they choose to come here on such an expedition, that the objects of which I am in quest can not be obtained without labour, anxiety of mind, and no small risk of personal safety, of which latter statement my this day's adventures are an instance. I quitted my camp early in the morning, to survey the neighboring country, leaving my guide to take charge of the horses until my return in the evening, when I found that he had done as I wished, and in the interval dried some wet paper which I had desired him to put in order. About an hour's walk from my camp, I met an Indian, who on perceiving me, instantly strung his bow . . . and stood on the defensive. Being quite satisfied that this conduct was prompted by fear and not by hostile intentions, the poor fellow having probably never seen such a being as myself before, I laid my gun at my feet, on the ground, and waved my hand for him to come to me, which he did slowly and with great caution. I then made him place his bow and quiver of arrows beside my gun and striking a light gave him a smoke out of my own pipe, and a present of a few beads. With my pencil I made a rough sketch of the Cone and Pine tree which I wanted to obtain, and drew his attention to it, when he instantly pointed with his hand to the hills fifteen or twenty miles distant towards the South; and when I expressed my intention of going thither, cheerfully set about accompanying me. At mid-day I reached my long-wished-for Pines, and lost no time in examining them and endeavouring to collect specimins and seeds . . . Lest I should never again see my friends in England to inform them verbally of this most beautiful and immensely grand tree, I shall here state the dimensions of the largest that I could find among several that had been blown down by the wind. At three feet from the ground its circumference is 57 feet 9 inches; at one hundred and thirty-four feet, 17 feet 5 inches; the extreme length 245 feet. The trunks are uncommonly straight, and the bark remarkably smooth, for such large timber, of whitish or light-brown colour, and yielding a great quantity of bright amber gum. The tallest stems are generally unbranched for two-thirds of the height of the tree; the branches rather pendulous, with cones hanging from their points like sugar-loaves in a grocer's shop. These cones are, however, only seen on the loftiest trees, and the putting myself in possession of three of these (all I could obtain) nearly brought my life to a close. As it was impossible either to climb the tree or hew it down, I endeavoured to knock off the cones by firing at them with ball, when the report of my gun brought eight Indians, all of them painted with red earth, armed with bows, arrows, bone-tipped spears and flint-knives. They appeared anything but friendly . . . To save myself by flight was impossible, so without hesitation I stepped back about five paces, cocked my gun, drew one of the pistols out of my belt, and holding it in my left hand and the gun in my right, showed myself determined to fight for my life. As much as possible I endeavoured to preserve my coolness, and thus we stood looking at one another without making any movement, or utter-ing a word for perhaps ten minutes, when one, at last, who seemed the leader, gave a sign that they wished for some tobacco: this I signified that they should have, if they fetched me a quantity of cones. They went off immediately in search of them, and no sooner were they all out of sight, than I picked up my three cones and some twigs of the trees, and made the quickest possible retreat, hurrying back to camp, which I reached before dusk.

WASHINGTON IRVING

In 1834 fur magnate John Jacob Astor wrote to Washington Irving, the leading man of American letters. Would Irving, he inquired, undertake a history of his ill-fated trading post of Astoria, "something that might take with the reading world," as Irving described the project in a letter to his nephew and research assistant, Pierre, "and secure to him the reputation of having originated the enterprise . . . that [is] likely to have such important results in the history of commerce and colonization." Using Astor's documents and the published journals of adventurers such as Ross Cox and Gabriele Franchère, Irving wrote Astoria, or Anecdotes of an Enterprise Beyond the Rocky Mountains *in nine months. Although his biographer later dismissed the book as "a stupendous piece of hack work," when* Astoria *was published in 1836, the critics raved: "A more finished and exquisite narrative we have never read," wrote one.*

from ASTORIA

THE *TONQUIN* SET SAIL from the mouth of the river on the fifth of June [1811]. The whole number of persons on board amounted to twenty-three. In one of the outer bays they picked up . . . an Indian named Lamazee, who . . . agreed to accompany them as interpreter.

Steering to the north, Captain Thorn arrived in a few days at Vancouver's Island, and anchored in the harbor of Neweetee, very much against the advice of his Indian interpreter, who warned him against the perfidious character of the natives of this part of the coast. Numbers of canoes soon came off, bringing sea-otter skins to sell. It was too late in the day to commence a traffic, but Mr. M'Kay, accompanied by a few of the men, went on shore to a large village to visit Wicananish, the chief of the surrounding territory, six of the natives remaining on board as hostages. He was received with great professions of friendship, entertained hospitably, and a couch of sea-otter skins prepared for him in the dwelling of the chieftain, where he was prevailed upon to pass the night.

In the morning, before Mr. M'Kay had returned to the ship, great numbers of the natives came off in their canoes to trade, headed by two sons of Wicananish. As they brought abundance of sea-otter skins, and there was every appearance of a brisk trade, Captain Thorn did not wait for the return of Mr. M'Kay, but spread his wares upon the deck, making a tempting display of blankets, cloths, knives, beads, and fish-hooks, expecting a prompt and profitable sale. The Indians, however, were not so eager and simple as he had supposed, having learned the art of bargaining and the value of merchandise from the casual traders along the coast. They were guided, too, by a shrewd old chief named Nookamis, who had grown gray in traffic with New England skippers, and prided himself upon his acuteness. His opinion seemed to regulate the market. When Captain Thorn made what he considered a liberal offer for an otter-skin, the wily old Indian treated it with scorn, and asked more than double. His comrades all took their cue from him, and not an otter-skin was to be had at a reasonable rate.

The old fellow, however, overshot his mark, and mistook the character of the man he was treating with. Thorn was a plain, straightforward sailor, who never had two minds nor two prices in his dealings, was deficient in patience and pliancy, and totally wanting in the chicanery of traffic. He had a vast deal of stern, but honest pride in his nature, and, moreover, held the whole savage race in sovereign contempt. Abandoning all further attempts, therefore, to bargain with his shuffling customers, he thrust his hands into his pockets, and paced up and down the deck in sullen silence. The cunning old Indian followed him to and fro, holding out a sea-otter skin to him at every turn, and pestering him to trade. Finding other means unavailing, he suddenly changed his tone, and began to jeer and banter him upon the mean prices he offered. This was too much for the patience of the captain, who was never remarkable for relishing a joke, especially when at his own expense. Turning suddenly upon his persecutor, he snatched the proffered otter-skin from his hands, rubbed it in his face, and dismissed him over the side of the ship with no very complimentary application to accelerate his exit. He then kicked the peltries to the right and left about the deck, and broke up the market in the most ignominious manner. Old Nookamis made for shore in a furious passion, in which he was joined by Shewish, one of the sons of Wicananish, who went off breathing vengeance, and the ship was soon abandoned by the natives.

When Mr. M'Kay returned on board, the interpreter related what had passed, and begged him to prevail upon the captain to make sail, as from his knowledge of the temper and pride of the people of the place, he was sure they would resent the indignity offered to one of their chiefs. Mr. M'Kay, who himself possessed some experience of Indian character, went to the captain, who was still pacing the deck in moody humor, represented the danger to which his hasty act had exposed the vessel, and urged him to weigh anchor. The captain made light of his counsels, and pointed to his cannon and fire-arms as sufficient safeguard against naked savages. Further remonstrances only provoked taunting replies and sharp altercations. The day passed away without any signs of hostility, and at night the captain retired as usual to his cabin, taking no more than the usual precautions.

On the following morning, at daybreak, a canoe came alongside in which were twenty Indians, commanded by young Shewish. They were unarmed, their aspect and demeanor friendly, and they held up otter-skins, and made signs indicative of a wish to trade. The caution enjoined by Mr. Astor, in respect to the admission of Indians on board of the ship, had been neglected for some time past, and the officer of the watch, perceiving those in the canoe to be without weapons, and having received no orders to the contrary, readily permitted them to mount the deck. Another canoe soon succeeded, the crew of which was likewise admitted. In a little while other canoes came off, and Indians were soon clambering into the vessel on all sides.

The officer of the watch now felt alarmed, and called to Captain Thorn and Mr. M'Kay. By the time they came on deck, it was thronged with Indians. The interpreter noticed to Mr. M'Kay that many of the natives wore short mantles of skins, and intimated a suspicion that they were secretly armed. Mr. M'Kay urged the captain to clear the ship and get under way. He again made light of the advice; but the augmented swarm of canoes about the ship, and the numbers still putting off from shore, at length awakened his distrust, and he ordered some of the crew to weigh anchor, while some were sent aloft to make sail.

The Indians now offered to trade with the captain on his own terms, prompted, apparently, by the approaching departure of the ship. Accordingly, a hurried trade was commenced. The main articles sought by the savages in barter were knives; as fast as some were supplied they moved off, and others succeeded. By degrees they were thus distributed about the deck, and all with weapons.

The anchor was now nearly up, the sails were loose, and the captain, in a loud and peremptory tone, ordered the ship to be cleared. In an instant, a signal yell was given; it was echoed on every side, knives and war-clubs were brandished in every direction, and the savages rushed upon their marked victims.

The first that fell was Mr. Lewis, the ship's clerk. He was leaning, with folded arms, over a bale of blankets, engaged in bargaining, when he received a deadly stab in the back, and fell down the companion-way.

Mr. M'Kay, who was seated on the taffrail, sprang on his feet, but was instantly knocked down with a war-club and flung backwards into the sea, where he was despatched by the women in the canoes.

In the meantime Captain Thorn made desperate fight against fearful odds. He was a powerful as well as a resolute man, but he had come upon deck without weapons. Shewish, the young chief, singled him out as his particular prey, and rushed upon him at the first outbreak. The captain had barely time to draw a clasp-knife, with one blow of which he laid the young savage dead at his feet. Several of the stoutest followers of Shewish now set upon him. He defended himself vigorously, dealing crippling blows to right and left, and strewing the quarter-deck with the slain and wounded. His object was to fight his way to the cabin, where there were fire-arms; but he was hemmed in with foes, covered with wounds, and faint with loss of blood. For an instant he leaned upon the tiller wheel, when a blow from behind, with a war-club, felled him to the deck, where he was despatched with knives and thrown overboard.

While this was transacting upon the quarter-deck, a chance-medley fight was going on throughout the ship. The crew fought desperately with knives, handspikes, and whatever weapon they could seize upon in the moment of surprise. They were soon, however, overpowered by numbers, and mercilessly butchered . . .

Thus far the Indian interpreter, from whom these particulars are derived, had been an eye-witness to the deadly conflict. He had taken no part in it, and had been spared by the natives as being of their race. In the confusion of the moment he took refuge with the rest, in the canoes . . .

For the remainder of the day no one ventured to put off to the ship . . . When the [following] day dawned, the *Tonquin* still lay at anchor in the bay, her sails all loose and flapping in the wind, and no one apparently on board of her. After a time, some of the canoes ventured forth to reconnoitre, taking with them the interpreter. They paddled about her, keeping cautiously at a distance, but growing more and more emboldened at seeing her quiet and lifeless. One man at length made his appearance on the deck, and was recognized by the interpreter as Mr. Lewis. He made friendly signs, and invited them on board. It was long before they ventured to comply. Those who mounted the deck met with no opposition; no one was to be seen on board; for Mr. Lewis, after inviting them, had disappeared. Other canoes now pressed forward to board the prize; the decks were soon crowded, and the sides covered with clambering savages, all intent on plunder. In the midst of their eagerness and exultation, the ship blew up with a tremendous explosion. Arms, legs, and mutilated bodies were blown into the air, and dreadful havoc was made in the surrounding canoes. The interpreter was in the mainchains at the time of the explosion, and was thrown unhurt into the water, where he succeeded in getting into one of the canoes. According to his statement, the bay presented an awful spectacle after the catastrophe. The ship had disappeared, but the bay was covered with fragments of the wreck, with shattered canoes, and Indians swimming for their lives, or struggling in the agonies of death; while those who had escaped the danger remained aghast and stupefied, or made with frantic panic for the shore. Upwards of a hundred savages were destroyed by the explosion, many more were shockingly mutilated, and for days afterwards the limbs and bodies of the slain were thrown upon the beach . . .

Such is the melancholy story of the *Tonquin,* and such was the fate of her brave, but headstrong commander, and her adventurous crew . . . The loss of the *Tonquin* was a grievous blow to the infant establishment of Astoria, and one that threatened to bring after it a train of disasters. The intelligence of it did not reach Mr. Astor until many months afterwards. He felt it in all its force, and was aware that it must cripple, if not entirely defeat, the great scheme of his ambition . . . He indulged, however, in no weak and vain lamentation, but sought to devise a prompt and efficient remedy. The very same evening he appeared at the theatre with his usual serenity of countenance. A friend, who knew the disastrous intelligence he had received, expressed his astonishment that he could have calmness of spirit sufficient for such a scene of light amusement. "What would you have me do?" was his characteristic reply; "Would you have me stay at home and weep for what I cannot help?"

POPULATING THE
PROMISED LAND

1832–1853

THE LITERARY IMAGE of the Northwest changed radically in the decade following the publication of Irving's *Astoria*. For a brief time in the 1830s, the savage wilderness of explorers and voyageurs became a holy battleground for missionaries fighting to save the native American population from the clutches of the devil and rival denominations. But within a few years, a more powerful and enduring vision of the Northwest would take hold: that of America's new land of hope and opportunity.

The idea of the Northwest as an American utopia actually took shape in the late 1820s in the mind of a Boston schoolteacher named Hall Jackson Kelley. After reading the 1814 account of the Lewis and Clark expedition, he wrote, "The word came expressly to me to go . . . and promote the propagation of Christianity in the dark and cruel places about the shores of the Pacific." Kelley pursued his obsession with the fervor of an evangelist, lobbying politicians, publishing pamphlets, and enthralling crowds with descriptions of the virtues of a land he had never seen.

About the same time, stories of Northwest Indians starving for the word of God began circulating in Christian newspapers back East. In 1831 a correspondent for a religious paper in Philadelphia recounted his alarming discovery that Northwest coast Indians believed that "a north west crow is the creator of the world" (a conclusion gleaned, most likely, from coastal Raven myths). In 1833 the *Christian Advocate and Journal and Zion's Herald* published a now-legendary tale of the one Flathead and three Nez Percé Indians who traveled a thousand miles to St. Louis to ask William Clark (whom they knew from his Lewis and Clark days) about the Bible, which they had heard was the source of the whites' strong medicine and material wealth. In the American Northeast these reports were heard as the cries of the uncivilized heathen calling out for salvation. In a matter of months missionaries were dispatched westward.

By 1838, Protestant and Catholic clergy had established a handful of outposts, and the war for the Indian soul was on. Though the Bible's tales and theology interested some native Americans, many missionaries believed their task was nothing less than the replacement of the indigenous culture with a European way of life. Reverend Elkanah Walker, who established a station near present-day Spokane, dismissed Indian healing practices as "play medicine" and was appalled at native mythology, which he considered indecent, foolish, and immoral. Those stories were to be replaced by Biblical parables and inspiring hymns such as the following, a composition by Walker's colleague the Reverend Cushing Eells:

Lam-a-lem, one-a-we Je-ho-vah
(Thanks thee Jehovah)
Kain-pa-la tas ka-leel, kait-si-ah wheel-a-wheel
(We not dead, we all alive)
Kain-pe-la ets-in-ko-nam kaits-chow.
(We sing, we pray.)

If the missionaries believed they were preparing souls for the heavenly hereafter, the Oregon Trail immigrants who came in their wake (more than fifty-three thousand new Northwesterners between 1840 and 1860) made their own earthly paradise on 160 acres in Oregon's fertile Willamette Valley. No historic event but the Civil War inspired more Americans to record their experiences in diaries and journals than the overland crossing. Glowing descriptions of Oregon and the great migration were sent home to urge friends and relatives westward. Although most journals contained a strong dose of misery—one 1845 diarist aptly misnamed her book "A Journal of Travails"—the word that reached the East was of paradise found. "Oregon fever" infected would-be Willamette land barons, who endured a four- to six-month journey for the promise of an Eden by the Pacific. Mrs. W. W. Buck, an 1845 immigrant, recalled a typical scene:

> [We] were anxious to hear about the country we were bound for, and our captain said Doctor White, tell us about Oregon. He jumped upon the wagon tongue and all our eyes and ears were open to catch every word. He said: "Friends, you are traveling to the

garden of Eden, a land flowing with milk and honey. And just let me tell you, the clover grows wild all over Oregon, and when you wade through it, it reaches your chin." We believed every word, and for days, I thought that not only our men, but our poor tired oxen, stepped lighter for having met Dr. White.

NARCISSA WHITMAN

It is unfortunate that Narcissa Whitman is known chiefly for her death—at the hands of a Cayuse Indian during the 1847 Whitman Massacre—because she played a noteworthy role in the settlement of the Northwest. In the 1840s the mission she and her husband, Marcus, established at Waiilatpu, near Walla Walla, became a way station for the growing number of immigrants on their way to the Willamette Valley, a development that would ultimately lead to the missionaries' demise. The local Indians felt threatened by the tide of settlers washing over their land, and the bad feelings escalated in 1847 when a virulent strain of measles arrived in Waiilatpu. Marcus Whitman, a doctor, attended to both white and Indian victims, but with little immunity to the disease, Indians perished in much greater numbers than whites. Rumors circulated among the Indians that the doctor practiced two kinds of medicine, one for whites and one for Indians. The tensions culminated in the massacre of November 29, 1847, which claimed the lives of both Whitmans and twelve other white settlers.

from THE LETTERS OF NARCISSA WHITMAN

March 1836:

I should like to tell you how the western people talk . . . Their language is so singular that I could scarcely understand them, yet it was very amusing. In speaking of quantity, they say "heap of man, heap of water, she is heap sick," etc. If you ask, "How does your wife today?" "O, she is smartly better, I reckon, but she is powerful weak; she has been mighty bad. What's the matter with your eye?"

May 1837:

There has been much sickness, both at Vancouver, Walla Walla, and here, and some deaths . . . The old chief Umtippe's wife was quite sick, and came near dying. For a season they were satisfied with my husband's attention, and were doing well; but when they would over eat themselves, or go into a relapse from unnecessary exposure, then they must have their te-wat doctors; say that the medicine was bad, and all was bad. Their te-wat is the same species of juggling as practiced by the Pawnees . . . playing the fool over them, and giving no medicine . . . Umtippe got in a rage about his wife, and told my husband, while she was under his care, that if his wife died that night he should kill him. The contest has been sharp between him and the Indians, and husband was nearly sick with the excitement and care of them. The chief sent for the great Walla Walla te-wat for his wife, at last, who came, and after going through several incantations, and receiving a horse and a blanket or two, pronounced her well; but the next day she was the same again. Now his rage was against the te-wat—said he was bad, and ought to be killed.

April 1838:

The Indians are not easily satisfied. They are so impressed with the idea that all who work are slaves and inferior persons, that the moment they hear of their children doing the least thing they are panic-stricken and make trouble. We have had a school for them for about four months past, and much of the time our kitchen has been crowded, and all seem very much attached . . . We appear to have every encouragement missionaries could possibly expect, for the short time we have been here. We see a very great improvement in them, even in the short space of one year . . . All seem to manifest a deep interest in the instruction given them. Some feel almost to blame us for telling them about eternal realities. One said it was good when they knew nothing but to hunt, eat, drink, and sleep; now it was bad.

October 1838:

A most important transaction during the meeting was the formation of a temperance society for the benefit of the Indians. All of the chiefs and principal men of the tribe who were here, readily agreed to the pledge, and gave in their names to become members of the society. I have recently been informed that two of them have been tempted to drink, but have refused and turned their backs upon it . . .

October 1839:

A Catholic priest has recently been at Walla Walla and held meetings with the Indians and used their influence to draw all the people away from us. Some they have forbidden to visit us again, and fill all of their minds with distraction about truths we teach, and their own doctrine; say we ought to have baptized them long ago, etc., etc. The conflict has begun—what trials await us we know not.

October 1840:

Of late my heart yearns over [the Indians] more than usual. They feel so bad, disappointed, and some of them angry because husband tells them that none of them are Christians; that they are all of them in the broad road to destruction, and that worshipping will not save them. They try to persuade him not to talk such bad talk to them, as they say, but talk good talk, or tell some story, or history, so that they may have some Scripture names to learn. Some threaten to whip him and to destroy our crops, and for a long time their cattle were turned into our potato field every night to see if they could not compel him to change his course of instruction . . .

March 1841:

We are in deep trial and affliction. Our Brother Munger is perfectly insane and we are tried to know how to get along with him. He claims it as a duty we owe him, as the representative of Christ's church, to obey him in all things. He is our lawgiver, as Moses was to the children of Israel.

May 1842:

Mr. Munger . . . has at last killed himself. He—after driving two nails in his left hand—drew out a bed of hot coals and laid himself down upon it, thrusting his hand into the hottest part of the fire and burnt it to a crisp, and died four days after . . .

August 1842:

Romanism stalks abroad on our right hand and on our left, and with daring effrontery boasts that she is to prevail and possess the land. I ask, must it be so? . . . "Is not the Lord on our side?" "If He is, for who can be against us?" The zeal and energy of her priests are without a parallel, and many, both white men and Indians, wander after the beasts . . .

March 1843:

Recently, intelligence has come to us from above that the Indians are talking and making preparations for war. The visit of the government's agent last fall has caused considerable excitement. All decisive measures and language used to them they construe into threats, and say war is declared and they intend to be prepared . . . It is the Kaiuses that cause all trouble. There are no tribes in all the country but what are more quiet and peaceable to live with than they are. If any mischief is going ahead they originate and carry forward. They are more difficult to labour among than the Nez Perces. They are rich, especially in horses, and consequently haughty and insolent.

Letter of Henry Spalding to Narcissa Whitman's parents, April 1848:

Through the wonderful interposition of God in delivering me from the hand of the murderer, it has become my painful duty to apprise you of the death of your beloved daughter, Narcissa, and her worthy and appreciated husband, your honored son-in-law, Dr. Whitman, both my own entirely devoted, ever faithful and eminently useful associates in the work of Christ. They were inhumanly butchered by their own, up to the last moment, beloved Indians, for whom their warm Christian hearts had prayed for eleven years, and their unwearied hands had administered to their every want in sickness and in distress . . . Some of them were members of our church; others candidates for admission; some of them adherents of the Catholic church—all praying Indians. They were, doubtless, urged on to the dreadful deed by foreign influences, which we have felt coming in upon us like a devastating flood for the last three or four years; and we have begged the authors, with tears in our eyes, to desist, not so much on account of our own lives and property, but for the sake of those coming, and the safety of those already in the country. But the authors thought none would be injured but the hated missionaries—the devoted heretics, and the work of hell was urged on, and has ended, not only in the death of three missionaries, the ruin of our mission, but in a bloody war with the settlements, which may end in the massacre of every family.

SIDNEY WALTER MOSS

Authorship of the first novel written in the Northwest was claimed by Oregon City hotelier Sidney Walter Moss, who came west in 1842. The Prairie Flower: or, Adventures in the Far West *was a less than auspicious beginning for indigenous Northwest literature. Moss's book is a poorly written potboiler about two college chums who go west seeking adventure; their sappy, gung-ho spirit and clichéd dialogue are more than most modern readers can bear. The manuscript traveled east with Oregon Trail guide Overton Johnson and found its way into the hands of Cincinnati author Emerson Bennett, who published it in 1849 under his own name as one of a series of western stories.*

from THE PRAIRIE FLOWER

"HO! FOR OREGON—what say you, Frank Leighton?" exclaimed my college chum, Charles Huntly, rushing into my room nearly out of breath. "Come, what say you, Frank?" queried my companion again, as I looked up in some surprise.

"Why, Charley," returned I, "what new notion has taken possession of your brain?"

"Oregon and adventure," he quickly rejoined, with flashing eyes. "You know, Frank, our collegiate course being finished, we must do something for the remainder of our lives. Now, for myself, I cannot bear the idea of settling down to the dry practice of law, without at least having seen something more of the world. You know, Frank, we have often planned together where we would go, and what we would do, when we should get our liberty; and now the Western fever has seized me, and I am ready to exclaim—ho! for Oregon."

"But, Charley," returned I, "consider that we are now in Boston, and that Oregon is thousands of miles away. It is much easier saying, ho! for Oregon, than it is getting to Oregon. Besides, what should we do when there?"

"Hunt, fish, trap, shoot Indians, anything, everything," cried my comrade, enthusiastically, "so we manage to escape ennui, and have plenty of adventure!"

"I must confess," said I, "that I like the idea wonderfully well—but—"

"But me no buts!" exclaimed Huntly; "you will like it—I shall like it—and we will both have such glorious times. College—law—pah! I am heartily sick of hearing of either, and long for those magnificent wilds where a man may throw about his arms without fear of hitting his neighbor. So come, Frank, set about matters—settle up your affairs, if you have any, either in money or love—and then follow me. Faith, man, I'll guide you to a real El Dorado, and no mistake."

AMELIA STEWART KNIGHT

More than eight hundred overland trail diaries are still in existence, although few were published. Most were locked away in trunks and attics, to be discovered by grandchildren (and scholars and archivists) decades later. Amelia Stewart Knight's is one of the finest of the genre. Knight left Iowa in April 1853 with her husband and seven children, bound for the newly created Washington Territory. Her diary is a record of day-to-day matters on the Oregon Trail: the day's mileage, the availability of fresh water and feed for the animals, Indian encounters, and the health of her children. Like many diarists, Knight recorded the sight and smell of dead animals by the side of the trail, but she makes no mention of the grave markers that figure prominently in other journals. Knight and her family arrived in Oregon City on September 17, 1853. The next day she gave birth to her eighth child; she had been pregnant the entire trip.

from AMELIA KNIGHT'S JOURNAL

AUGUST 1ST [1853] MONDAY, Still in camp, have been washing all day, and all hands, have had all the wild currants we could eat, they grow in great abundance along this river, there are three kinds, red, black, and yellow, this evening another of our best milk cows died, cattle are dying off very fast all along this road, we are hardly ever out of sight of dead cattle, on this side of Snake river, this cow was well and fat, an hour before she died.

2ND TUESDAY NOON, traveled 12 miles to day, and have just campt on the bank of Boise river, the boys have all crossed the river, to gather currants, this river is a beautiful clear stream of water running over a stony bottom, I think it the prettiest river I have seen as yet, the timber on it is balm of gilead, made a nice lot of currant pies this afternoon.

5TH FRIDAY, We have just bid the beautiful Boise river with her green timber, and rich currants farewell, and are now on our way to the ferry on Snake river; evening traveled 18 miles to day, and have just reached Fort Boise, and campt, our turn will come to cross, sometime tomorrow, there is one small ferry boat running here, owned by the Hudsons Bay Company have to pay 8 dollars a wagon, our worst trouble at these large rivers, is swimming the stock over, often after swimming nearly half way over, the poor things will turn and come out again, at this place however, there are indians who swim the river from morning till night   it is fun for them, there is many a drove of cattle that could not be got over without their help, by paying them a small sum, they will take a horse by the bridle or halter, and swim over with him, the rest of the horses all follow, and by driving and hurraing to the cattle they will most always follow the horses, sometimes they fail and turn back; this fort Boise is nothing more than three mud buildings, its inhabitants, the Hudsons bay company a few french men, some half naked indians, half breeds &c

7TH SUNDAY EVENING, traveled 15 miles, and have just reached Malheur river and campt, the roads have been very dusty, no water, nothing but dust, and dead cattle all day, the air filled with the odor, from Dead cattle.

AUGST 8TH MONDAY MORN, we have to make a drive of 22 miles, without water to day, have our cans filled to drink, (here we left unknowingly our Lucy behind, not a soul had missed her untill we had gone some miles, when we stopt awhile to rest the cattle; just then another train drove up behind us, with Lucy   she was terribly frightened and so was some more of us, when we found out what a narrow escape she had run, She said she was sitting under the bank of the river, when we started, busy watching some wagons cross and did not know we were ready. And I supposed she was in Mr Carls wagon, as he always took charge of Frances and Lucy and I took care of Myra and Chat, when starting he asked for Lucy, and Frances, says "shes in Mother's wagon," as she often came in there to have her hair combed, — it was a lesson to all of us.) Evening it is nearly dark and we are still toiling on, till we find a camping place   the little ones have curled down, and gone to sleep without supper, wind high, and it is cold enough for a great coat and mittens.

12 FRIDAY, Came 12 miles to day crossed burnt river twice, lost one of our oxen, we were traveling slowly along, when he dropt dead in the yoke unyoked and turned out the odd ox, and drove round the dead one, and so it is all along this road we are continually driving round the dead cattle, and shame on the man who has no pity for the poor dumb brutes that have to travel, and toil month after month, on this desolate road. I could hardly help shedding tears, when we drove round this poor ox who had helped us along thus far, and had even given us his very last step. We have campt on a branch of Burnt river.

16TH TUESDAY, Slow traveling on account of our oxen having sore feet, and the roads being very rocky, passed the Silvery springs . . . we could see a band of Indian horses in the Valley below, and being mostly white, they looked like a flock of chickens, after reaching the bottom of this hill with a good deal of difficulty, we find our selves in a most lovely Valley, and have campt close to a spring, which runs through it, there are also two or three trading posts here, and a great many fine looking Kayuse Indians riding around on their handsome ponies.

17TH WENDSDAY EVENING, crossed the Grand round Valley, which is 8 miles across, and have campt close to the foot of the mountain, good water, and feed plenty, there are 50 or more wagons, campt around us, Lucy, and Myra have their feet and legs poisoned, which gives me a good deal of trouble. bought some fresh Salmon, of the Indians this evening, which is quite a treat to us, it is the first we have seen.

18TH THURSDAY MORN, Commenced the ascent of the Blue Mountains,   it is a lovely morning, and all hands seem to be delighted with the prospect, of being so near the timber again, after weary months of travel, on the dry dusty sage plains, with nothing to relieve the eye; just now the men are holooing, to hear their echo ring through the woods. — Evening travel 10 miles to day up and down steep hills, and have just campt on the bank of Grand round river, in a dense forest of pine Timber, a most beautiful country.

19TH FRIDAY,   quite cold morning, water froze over in the buckets; travel 13 miles, over very bad roads, without water   after looking in vain for water, we were about to give up as it was near night, when husband came across a company of friendly Kayuse Indians about to camp who showed him where to find water, half a mile down a steep mountain, and we have all campt together, with plenty of pine timber all around us. the men and boys have driven the cattle down to water and I am waiting for water to get supper, this fornoon we bought a few potatoes of an Indian, which will be a treat for our supper.

31ST WENDSDAY MORN,   Still in camp, it was too stormy to start out last evening, as intended, the wind was very high, all the afternoon, and the dust and fine sand so bad, we could hardly see   thundered, and rained a little in the evening, it rained and blew very hard all night, is still raining this morning, the air cold and chilly. it blew so hard last night as to blow our buckets and pans from under the wagons, and this morning we found them (and other things which were not secured) scattered all over the valley. one or two pans came up missing. every thing is packed up ready for a start, the men folks are out hunting the cattle. The children, and myself are shivering round and in the wagons, nothing for fires in these parts, and the weather is very disagreeable. Evening got a late start this morning, traveled about a mile and was obliged to stop, and turn the cattle out on account of rain, at noon it cleared off we eat dinner, and started, came up a long, and awful rocky hollow, in danger every moment of smashing our wagons, after traveling 7 miles, we halted in the prairie long enough to cook supper, split up some of the deck boards of our wagons, to make fire, got supper over, and are on our way again . . .

4TH SUNDAY MORNING, Clear and bright. had a fine view of Mount Hood, St Hellens and Jefferson   evening traveled 15 miles to day without water, after descending a long, steep, rocky, and very tedious hill we have campt in a Valley on the bank of Indian creek, near some French men who have a trading post, there are also a good many indians encampt around us   no feed for the cattle to night; 15 miles more will take us to the foot of the mountains.

5TH MONDAY FORENOON, passed a sleepless night last night, as a good many of the indians campt around us were drunk and noisy and kept up a continual racket, which made all hands uneasy, and kept our poor dog on the watch all night, I say poor dog because he is nearly worn out with traveling through the day, and should rest all night, but he hates an Indian and will not let one come near the wagons if he can help it, and doubtless they would have done some mischief but for him. ascended a long steep hill this morning which was very hard on the cattle, and also on myself as I thought I never should get to the top although I rested two or three times. after traveling about two miles over some very pretty rolling prairie, we have turned our cattle out to feed awhile, as they had nothing last night — Evening traveled about 12 miles to day and have encampt on a branch of Deschutes, and turned our cattle and horses out to tolerable good bunch grass.

6TH TUESDAY, Still in camp, washing and overhauling the wagons to make them as light as possible to cross the mountains Evening after throwing away a good many things and burning up most of the deck boards of our wagons so as to lighten them, got my washing and some cooking done, and started on again crossed 2 branches, traveled 3 miles, and have campt near the gate, or foot of the Cascades Mountains, (here I was sick all night caused by my washing and working too hard).

8TH THURSDAY, Traveled 14 miles over the worst road that was ever made. up and down very steep rough and rocky hills, through mud holes, twisting and winding round stumps, logs, and fallen tree. now we are on the end of a log, now bounce down in a mud hole, now over a big root of a tree, or rock, then bang goes the other side of the wagon and woe to be whatever is inside, (there is very little chance to turn out of this road, on account of the timber and fallen trees, for these mountains are a dense forest of pine, fir, white cedar, or redwood, the handsomest timber in the world must be here in these Cascades Mountains) many of the trees are 300 feet high and so dense as to almost excude the light of heaven and for my own part I dare not look to the top of them for fear of breaking my neck . . .

9TH FRIDAY, Came 8½ miles crossed Sandy 4 times, came over cor-duroy roads, through swamps, over rocks and hommochs, and the worst road that could be immagined or thought of, and have encampt about 1 oclock in a little opening near the road, the men have driven the cattle a mile off from the road to try and find grass, and rest them till morning, we hear the road is still worse on ahead; There is a great deal of laurel growing here which will poison the stock if they eat it, (there is no end to the wagons, buggys ox yokes, chains, ect that are lying all along this road some splendid good wagons just left standing, perhaps with the owners name on them; and many are the poor horses, mules, oxen, cows, &c, that are lying dead in these mountains, afternoon, slight shower.

13TH TUESDAY NOON, ascended three very steep muddy hills this morning, drove over some muddy mirey ground, and through mud holes, and have just halted at the first farm to noon, and rest awhile, and buy feed for the stock; paid 1½ dollars per hundred for hay; — price of fresh beef 16 and 18 cts per pound butter ditto 1 dollar, eggs 1 dollar a dozen; onions 4 and 5 dollars per bushel, all too dear for poor folks so we have treated ourselves to some small turnips at the rate of 25 cts per dozen, got rested and are now ready to travel again — Evening traveled 14 miles to day, crossed Deep creek, and have encampt on the bank of it, a very dull look-ing place, grass very scarse, We may now call ourselves through, they say; and here we are in Oregon making our camp in an ugly bottom, with no home, except our wagons and tent,   it is drizzling and the weather looks dark and gloomy.

TREATY TALK

1854–1879

IN 1853 A DELEGATION OF YAKIMA, Cayuse, and Walla Walla Indians told the U.S. Army commander at The Dalles garrison along the Columbia River that they did not object to strangers hunting on their land. What they most dreaded, they said, was "the approach of the whites with ploughs, axes, and shovels in their hands." White settlers had immigrated to the Northwest to own the land, not merely to share its seasonal yield. By the mid-1850s white encroachment and native American reprisals led the federal government to impose a policy of strict and inequitable separation. Whites kept their property in fertile areas such as the Willamette Valley, while Indian leaders signed treaties agreeing to cede their land and move to less desirable areas that held no historic or spiritual significance for them.

The chiefs knew the terms of the treaties were catastrophic, but also knew they had few options. They saw an unending stream of settlers pouring into their country while their own population dwindled from disease. They knew the power of the government's forces, which had defeated the Cayuse in the 1847–1848 war touched off by the Whitman Massacre. And they felt the rising enmity of the settlers, many of whom thought extermination was the best solution to the "Indian problem."

Most ultimately signed agreements with Isaac Stevens (in the Washington Territory, which included present-day Idaho) or General Joel Palmer (in the Oregon Territory), the Indian agents who spent most of 1854 and 1855 on treaty tours of the Northwest. The chiefs did not depart the talks, however, without speaking eloquently of the great injustice being done to their peoples. "How do you show your pity by sending me and my children to a land where there is nothing to eat but wood?" Cayuse chief Camatspelo asked Palmer.

The speeches that survive today, recorded by white translators and jour-nalists, contain classic elements of great oration: history, interpretation, theology, prediction, repetition, anger, and ultimate reconciliation. There are even glimpses of humor—for example, Chief Jo Hutchins's sarcastic remarks about the federal government's unfulfilled promises: "We do not see the things the treaty promised. Maybe they got lost on the way. The President is a long way off. He can't hear us. Our words get lost in the wind before they get there. Maybe his ear is small." The same sort of bitter wit is contained in Chief Joseph's horse-trading analogy:

> Suppose a white man should come to me and say, "Joseph, I like your horses, and I want to buy them." I say to him, "No, my horses suit me, I will not sell them." Then he goes to my neighbor, and says to him: "Joseph has some good horses. I want to buy them, but he refuses to sell." My neighbor answers, "Pay me the money, and I will sell you Joseph's horses." The white man returns to me, and says, "Joseph, I have bought your horses, and you must let me have them." If we sold our lands to the government, this is the way they were bought.

A few treaty speeches have assumed permanent positions of impor-tance in the Northwest conscience. The most famous is Chief Seattle's 1854 address to Isaac Stevens on the shores of Elliott Bay. As the envi-ronmental movement grew in America and other parts of the globe in the 1980s, the chief's message of connection with the earth became world-renowned as a call to the eco-friendly lifestyle. Although what he said has often been bowdlerized to fit the agendas of the late twentieth century, Seattle's original words (or as faithful a version as exists) contain an appeal to conserve and respect the land that seems a century and a half ahead of its time: "Every part of this country is sacred to my people. Every hillside, every valley, every plain and grove has been hallowed by some fond memory or some sad experience of my tribe.

"The soil," Seattle said, "is rich with the life of our kindred."

CHIEF SEATTLE

The following speech by Chief Seattle is one of the most widely quoted documents to come out of the Pacific Northwest. Whether they are entirely Seattle's words, however, is a matter of historical debate. The speech was addressed to Washington Territory Governor Isaac Stevens, who met with Seattle (also translated as Sealth), a leader of the Duwamish and Suquamish tribes, and twelve hundred other Indians in January 1854 to announce treaty negotiations. Henry A. Smith, a local physician and land developer, was on hand to record the chief's words. They did not appear in print until October 29, 1887, when Smith transcribed the speech (with, quite likely, his own embellishments) for a historical article in the Seattle Sunday Star. *After the treaty was signed, many of Seattle's people were removed to the Suquamish, Muckleshoot, Tulalip, and Lummi reservations. Others remained and became off-reservation Indians.*

from CHIEF SEATTLE'S 1854 SPEECH

YONDER SKY THAT HAS WEPT tears of compassion on our fathers for centuries untold, and which, to us, looks eternal, may change. Today it is fair, tomorrow it may be overcast with clouds. My words are like stars that never set. What Seattle says, the great chief, Washington, can rely upon, with as much certainty as our pale-face brothers can rely upon the return of the seasons.

The son of the white chief says his father sends us greetings of friendship and good will. This is kind, for we know he has little need of our friendship in return, because his people are many. They are like the grass that covers the vast prairies, while my people are few, and resemble the scattering trees of a storm-swept plain.

The great, and I presume also good, white chief sends us word that he wants to buy our lands but is willing to allow us to reserve enough to live on comfortably. This indeed appears generous, for the red man no longer has rights that he need respect, and the offer may be wise, also, for we are no longer in need of a great country.

There was a time when our people covered the whole land, as the waves of a wind-ruffled sea cover its shell-paved floor. But that time has long since passed away with the greatness of tribes now almost forgotten.

I will not mourn over our untimely decay, nor reproach my pale-face brothers for hastening it, for we, too, may have been somewhat to blame.

When our young men grow angry at some real or imaginary wrong, and disfigure their faces with black paint, their hearts also are disfigured and turn black, and then their cruelty is relentless and knows no bounds, and our old men are not able to restrain them.

But let us hope that hostilities between the red man and his pale-face brothers may never return. We would have everything to lose and nothing to gain.

True it is, that revenge, with our young braves, is considered gain, even at the cost of their own lives, but old men who stay at home in times of war, and old women, who have sons to lose, know better.

Our great father Washington, for I presume he is now our father as well as yours, since George has moved his boundaries to the north; our great and good father, I say, sends us word by his son, who, no doubt, is a great chief among his people, that if we do as he desires, he will protect us. His brave armies will be to us a bristling wall of strength, and his great ships of war will fill our harbors so that our ancient enemies far to the northward, the Simsiams and Hydas, will no longer frighten our women and old men. Then he will be our father and we will be his children.

But can this ever be? Your God loves your people and hates mine; he folds his strong arms lovingly around the white man and leads him as a father leads his infant son, but he has forsaken his red children; he makes your people wax strong every day, and soon they will fill the land; while my people are ebbing away like a fast-receding tide, that will never flow again. The white man's God cannot love his red children or he would protect them. They seem to be orphans and can look nowhere for help. How then can we become brothers? How can your father become our father and bring us prosperity and awaken in us dreams of returning greatness?

Your God seems to us to be partial. He came to the white man. We never saw Him; never even heard His voice; He gave the white man laws but He had no word for His red children whose teeming millions filled this vast continent as the stars fill the firmament. No, we are two distinct races and must ever remain so. There is little in common between us. The ashes of our ancestors are sacred and their final resting place is hallowed ground, while you wander away from the tombs of your fathers seemingly without regret.

Your religion was written on tables of stone by the iron finger of an angry God, lest you might forget it. The red man could never remember nor comprehend it.

Our religion is the traditions of our ancestors, the dreams of our old men, given them by the great Spirit, and the visions of our sachems, and is written in the hearts of our people.

Your dead cease to love you and the homes of their nativity as soon as they pass the portals of the tomb. They wander far off beyond the stars, are soon forgotten, and never return. Our dead never forget the beautiful world that gave them being. They still love its winding rivers, its great mountains and its sequestered vales, and they ever yearn in tenderest affection over the lonely hearted living and often return to visit and comfort them.

Day and night cannot dwell together. The red man has ever fled the approach of the white man, as the changing mists on the mountainside flee before the blazing morning sun . . .

The Indian's night promises to be dark. No bright star hovers about the horizon. Sad-voiced winds moan in the distance. Some grim Nemesis of our race is on the red man's trail, and wherever he goes he will still hear the sure approaching footsteps of the fell destroyer and prepare to meet his doom, as does the wounded doe that hears the approaching footsteps of the hunter. A few more moons, a few more winters, and not one of all the mighty hosts that once filled this broad land or that now roam in fragmentary bands through these vast solitudes will remain to weep over the tombs of a people once as powerful and as hopeful as your own.

But why should we repine? Why should I murmur at the fate of my people? Tribes are made up of individuals and are no better than they. Men come and go like the waves of the sea. A tear, a tamanawus, a dirge, and they are gone from our longing eyes forever. Even the white man, whose God walked and talked with him, as friend to friend, is not exempt from the common destiny. We may be brothers after all. We shall see.

We will ponder your proposition, and when we have decided we will tell you. But should we accept it, I here and now make this the first condition: That we will not be denied the privilege, without molestation, of visiting at will the graves of our ancestors and friends. Every part of this country is sacred to my people. Every hillside, every valley, every plain and grove has been hallowed by some fond memory or some sad experience of my tribe.

Even the rocks that seem to lie dumb as they swelter in the sun along the silent seashore in solemn grandeur thrill with memories of past events connected with the fate of my people, and the very dust under your feet responds more lovingly to our footsteps than to yours, because it is the ashes of our ancestors, and our bare feet are conscious of the sympathetic touch, for the soil is rich with the life of our kindred.

The sable braves, and fond mothers, and glad-hearted maidens, and the little children who lived and rejoiced here, and whose very names are now forgotten, still love these solitudes, and their deep fastnesses at eventide grow shadowy with the presence of dusky spirits. And when the last red man shall have perished from the earth and his memory among white men shall have become a myth, these shores shall swarm with the invisible dead of my tribe, and when your children's children shall think themselves alone in the field, the store, the shop, upon the highway or in the silence of the woods, they will not be alone. In all the earth there is no place dedicated to solitude. At night, when the streets of your cities and villages shall be silent, and you think them deserted, they will throng with the returning hosts that once filled and still love this beautiful land. The white man will never be alone. Let him be just and deal kindly with my people, for the dead are not altogether powerless.

CHIEF JO HUTCHINS

Following the signing of the 1854–1855 treaties, most Willamette Valley Indians were relocated to the Grande Ronde Reservation, west of Salem, Oregon. Conditions there were not quite what the government had promised, however, as Santiam chief Jo Hutchins made clear in this 1869 speech to A. B. Meacham, Superintendent for Indian Affairs in Oregon. Hutchins's oration appeared in Meacham's 1875 memoir, Wigwam and Warpath, or the Royal Chief in Chains, *a book notable for its author's sharp criticism of the government's mistreatment of native Americans. Although Meacham praised Hutchins ("Here was a man talking to the point. He dodged nothing. He spoke the hearts of the people."), he did not record whether the chief's grievances found redress in Washington, D.C.*

from CHIEF JO HUTCHINS'S 1869 SPEECH

I AM WATCHING YOUR EYE. I am watching your tongue. I am thinking all the time. Perhaps you are making fools of us. We don't want to be made fools. I have heard tyees talk like you do now. They go back home and send us something a white man don't want. We are not dogs. We have hearts. We may be blind. We do not see the things the treaty promised. Maybe they got lost on the way. The President is a long way off. He can't hear us. Our words get lost in the wind before they get there. Maybe his ear is small. Maybe your ears are small. They look big. Our ears are large. We hear everything. Some things we don't like. We have been a long time in the mud. Sometimes we sink down. Some white men help us up. Some white men stand on our heads. We want a school-house built on the ground of the Santiam people. Then our children can have some sense. We want an Indian to work in the blacksmith shop. We don't like half-breeds. They are not Injuns. They are not white men. Their hearts are divided. We want some harness. We want some ploughs. We want a sawmill. What is a mill good for that has no dam? That old mill is not good; it won't saw boards. We want a church. Some of these people are Catholics. Some of them are like Mr. Parish, a Methodist. Some got no religion. Maybe they don't need religion. Some people think Indians got no sense. We don't want any blankets. We have had a heap of blankets. Some of them have been like sail-cloth muslin. The old people have got no sense; they want blankets. The treaty said we, every man, have his land. He have a paper for his land. We don't see the paper. We see the land. We want it divided. When we have land all in one place, some Injun put his horses in the field; another Injun turn them out. Then they go to law. One man says another man got the best ground. They go to law about that. We want the land marked out. Every man builds his own house. We want some apples. Mark out the land, then we plant some trees, by-and-by we have some apples.

Maybe you don't like my talk. I talk straight. I am not a coward. I am chief of the Santiams. You hear me now. We see your eyes; look straight. Maybe you are a good man. We will find out. Sochala-tyee,—God sees you. He sees us. All these people hear me talk. Some of them are scared. I am not afraid. Alta-kup-et,—I am done.

CHIEF JOSEPH

In 1863, Chief Young Joseph, a thirty-one-year-old Nez Percé leader, declined to sign a treaty ceding three-quarters of Nez Percé territory in eastern Washington, Oregon, and central Idaho to white settlers, splitting the tribe between "treaty" and "nontreaty" Nez Percé. Throughout the 1870s the government attempted to move Joseph's band off their native lands; each time they refused. The standoff led to the Nez Percé War in 1877, with Joseph leading a brilliant and ultimately tragic campaign against the U.S. Army. His tactics were so admired that they were later incorporated into an Army ROTC manual: "In 11 weeks, [Joseph] had moved his tribe 1,600 miles, engaged 10 separate U.S. commands in 13 battles and skirmishes, and in nearly every instance had either defeated them or fought them to a standstill." On October 6, 1877, Joseph was stopped forty miles from the Canadian border and freedom. His subsequent speech ran in the North American Review, *under the title "An Indian's View of Indian Affairs," in April 1879. During that year Joseph traveled twice to Washington, D.C., to plead for the return of his people to Idaho, which had been promised under General Howard's terms of surrender. Instead they were sent to Indian Territory in Oklahoma and their leader was held in Kansas. Although his people were eventually allowed to live on an Idaho reservation, Joseph never saw his native land again; he died in 1904 on the Colville Indian Reservation in Washington State.*

from AN INDIAN'S VIEW OF INDIAN AFFAIRS

MY NAME IS IN-MUT-TOO-YAH-LAT-LAT (Thunder traveling over the Mountains). I am chief of the Wal-lam-wat-kin band of Chute-pa-lu, or Nez Percés (nose-pierced Indians). I was born in eastern Oregon, thirty-eight winters ago. My father was chief before me. When a young man, he was called Joseph by Mr. Spaulding, a missionary. He died a few years ago. There was no stain on his hands of the blood of a white man. He left a good name on the earth. He advised me well for my people.

Our fathers gave us many laws, which they had learned from their fathers. These laws were good. They told us to treat all men as they treated us; that we should never be the first to break a bargain; that it was a disgrace to tell a lie; that we should speak only the truth; that it was a shame for one man to take from another his wife, or his property without paying for it. We were taught to believe that the Great Spirit sees and hears everything, and that he never forgets; that hereafter he will give every man a spirit-home according to his deserts: if he has been a good man, he will have a good home; if he has been a bad man, he will have a bad home. This I believe, and all my people believe the same . . .

The first white men of your people who came to our country were named Lewis and Clarke. They also brought many things that our people had never seen. They talked straight, and our people gave them a great feast, as a proof that their hearts were friendly. These men were very kind. They made presents to our chiefs and our people made presents to them. We had a great many horses, of which we gave them what they needed, and they gave us guns and tobacco in return. All the Nez Percés made friends with Lewis and Clarke, and agreed to let them pass through their country, and never to make war on white men. This promise the Nez Percés have never broken. No white man can accuse them of bad faith, and speak with a straight tongue. It has always been the pride of the Nez Percés that they were the friends of the white men. When my father was a young man there came to our country a white man (Rev. Mr. Spaulding) who talked spirit law. He won the affections of our people because he spoke good things to them. At first he did not say anything about white men wanting to settle on our lands. Nothing was said about that until about twenty winters ago, when a number of white people came into our country and built houses and made farms. At first our people made no complaint. They thought there was room enough for all to live in peace, and they were learning many things from the white men that seemed to be good. But we soon found that the white men were growing rich very fast, and were greedy to possess everything the Indian had. My father was the first to see through the schemes of the white men, and he warned his tribe to be careful about trading with them. He had suspicion of men who seemed so anxious to make money. I was a boy then, but I remember well my father's caution. He had sharper eyes than the rest of our people.

Next there came a white officer (Governor Stevens), who invited all the Nez Percés to a treaty council. After the council was opened he made known his heart. He said there were a great many white people in the country, and many more would come; that he wanted the land marked out so that the Indians and white men could be separated. If they were to live in peace it was necessary, he said, that the Indians should have a country set apart for them, and in that country they must stay. My father, who represented his band, refused to have anything to do with the council, because he wished to be a free man. He claimed that no man owned any part of the earth, and a man could not sell what he did not own.

Mr. Spaulding took hold of my father's arm and said, "Come and sign the treaty." My father pushed him away, and said: "Why do you ask me to sign away my country? It is your business to talk to us about spirit matters, and not to talk to us about parting with our land." Governor Stevens urged my father to sign his treaty, but he refused. "I will not sign your paper," he said; "you go where you please, so do I; you are not a child, I am no child; I can think for myself. No man can think for me. I have no other home than this. I will not give it up to any man. My people would have no home. Take away your paper. I will not touch it with my hand . . . "

Eight years later (1863) was the next treaty council. A chief called Lawyer, because he was a great talker, took the lead in this council, and sold nearly all the Nez Percés country. My father was not there. He said to me: "When you go into council with the white man, always remember your country. Do not give it away. The white man will cheat you out of your home. I have taken no pay from the United States. I have never sold our land." In this treaty Lawyer acted without authority from our band. He had no right to sell the Wallowa (*winding water*) country. That had always belonged to my father's own people, and the other bands had never disputed our right to it. No other Indians ever claimed Wallowa.

In order to have all people understand how much land we owned, my father planted poles around it and said:

"Inside is the home of my people—the white man may take the land outside. Inside this boundary all our people were born. It circles around the graves of our fathers, and we will never give up these graves to any man."

The United States claimed they had bought all the Nez Percés country outside of Lapwai Reservation, from Lawyer and other chiefs, but we continued to live on this land in peace until eight years ago, when white men began to come inside the bounds my father had set. We warned them against this great wrong, but they would not leave our land, and some bad blood was raised. The white men represented that we were going upon the war-path. They reported many things that were false.

The United States Government again asked for a treaty council. My father had become blind and feeble. He could no longer speak for his people. It was then that I took my father's place as chief. In this council I made my first speech to white men. I said to the agent who held the council:

"I did not want to come to this council, but I came hoping that we could save blood. The white man has no right to come here and take our country. We have never accepted any presents from the Government. Neither Lawyer nor any other chief had authority to sell this land. It has always belonged to my people. It came unclouded to them from our fathers, and we will defend this land as long as a drop of Indian blood warms the hearts of our men."

The agent said he had orders, from the Great White Chief at Washington, for us to go upon the Lapwai Reservation, and that if we obeyed he would help us in many ways. "You *must* move to the agency," he said. I answered him: "I will not. I do not need your help; we have plenty, and we are contented and happy if the white man will let us alone. The reservation is too small for so many people with all their stock. You can keep your presents; we can go to your towns and pay for all we need; we have plenty of horses and cattle to sell, and we won't have any help from you; we are free now; we can go where we please. Our fathers were born here. Here they lived, here they died, here are their graves. We will never leave them." The agent went away, and we had peace for a little while.

Soon after this my father sent for me. I saw he was dying. I took his hand in mine. He said: "My son, my body is returning to my mother earth, and my spirit is going very soon to see the Great Spirit Chief. When I am gone, think of your country. You are the chief of these people. They look to you to guide them. Always remember that your father never sold his country. You must stop your ears whenever you are asked to sign a treaty selling your home. A few years more, and white men will be all around you. They have their eyes on this land. My son, never forget my dying words. This country holds your father's body. Never sell the bones of your father and your mother." I pressed my father's hand and told him I would protect his grave with my life. My father smiled and passed away to the spirit-land.

I buried him in that beautiful valley of winding waters. I love that land more than all the rest of the world. A man who would not love his father's grave is worse than a wild animal.

For a short time we lived quietly. But this could not last. White men had found gold in the mountains around the land of winding water. They stole a great many horses from us, and we could not get them back because we were Indians. The white men told lies for each other. They drove off a great many of our cattle. Some white men branded our young cattle so they could claim them. We had no friend who would plead our cause before the law councils. It seemed to me that some of the white men in Wallowa were doing these things on purpose to get up a war. They knew that we were not strong enough to fight them. I labored hard to avoid trouble and bloodshed. We gave up some of our country to the white men, thinking that then we could have peace. We were mistaken. The white man would not let us alone. We could have avenged our wrongs many times, but we did not. Whenever the Government has asked us to help them against other Indians, we have never refused. When the white men were few and we were strong we could have killed them all off, but the Nez Percés wished to live at peace.

If we have not done so, we have not been to blame. I believe that the old treaty has never been correctly reported. If we ever owned the land we own it still, for we never sold it. In the treaty councils the commissioners have claimed that our country had been sold to the Government. Suppose a white man should come to me and say, "Joseph, I like your horses, and I want to buy them." I say to him, "No, my horses suit me, I will not sell them." Then he goes to my neighbor, and says to him: "Joseph has some good horses. I want to buy them, but he refuses to sell." My neighbor answers, "Pay me the money, and I will sell you Joseph's horses." The white man returns to me, and says, "Joseph, I have bought your horses, and you must let me have them." If we sold our lands to the Government, this is the way they were bought . . .

I only ask of the Government to be treated as all other men are treated. If I can not go to my own home, let me have a home in some country where my people will not die so fast. I would like to go to Bitter Root Valley. There my people would be healthy; where they are now they are dying. Three have died since I left my camp to come to Washington.

When I think of our condition my heart is heavy. I see men of my race treated as outlaws and driven from country to country, or shot down like animals.

I know that my race must change. We can not hold our own with the white men as we are. We only ask an even chance to live as other men live.

We ask to be recognized as men. We ask that the same law shall work alike on all men. If the Indian breaks the law, punish him by the law. If the white man breaks the law, punish him also.

Let me be a free man—free to travel, free to stop, free to work, free to trade where I choose, free to choose my own teachers, free to follow the religion of my fathers, free to think and talk and act for myself—and I will obey every law, or submit to the penalty.

Whenever the white man treats the Indian as they treat each other, then we will have no more wars. We shall all be alike—brothers of one father and one mother, with one sky above us and one country around us, and one government for all. Then the Great Spirit Chief who rules above will smile upon this land, and send rain to wash out the bloody spots made by brothers' hands from the face of the earth. For this time the Indians race are waiting and praying. I hope that no more groans of wounded men and women will ever go to the ear of the Great Spirit Chief above, and that all people may be one people.

CLOSING THE FRONTIER

1853–1916

UP UNTIL THE 1850S, the Northwest had been defined mostly by writers who were drawn west for reasons other than the creation of great literature. They came to explore the territory, skin its pelted fortune, convert its heathen, and till its soil. The first dedicated writers began arriving at midcentury, when the Northwest remained wild enough to stir the imagination of Eastern and European readers but wasn't so dangerous that a correspondent might actually risk life and limb in pursuit of frontier adventure.

Theodore Winthrop's ten-day journey in 1853 from Port Townsend to The Dalles in what was then the Washington Territory inaugurated a venerable belletristic tradition in the Northwest, that of the highbrowed Easterner taking a literary romp in the American outback. In *The Canoe and the Saddle* the young Yale-educated aristocrat portrayed the Pacific Northwest as a frontier theme park in which one could experience all the excitement and misery of creating civilization anew. Winthrop's ornate language served to emphasize the cultural distance between the civilized New Englander and his barbaric surroundings.

Later literary travelers confirmed Winthrop's picture of a raw territory populated by colorful, rough-and-ready—if not terribly bright or scrupulous—characters. Young national magazines such as *The Atlantic Monthly*, *Scribner's* (which became *The Century*), and *Harper's Monthly* dispatched writers across the continent to bring home descriptions of the majestic land and the people struggling to establish outposts of civilization in Portland, Tacoma, Port Townsend, and The Dalles.

Railroads linking the Pacific Coast to the Midwest ended the ordeal of the Oregon Trail. Passenger trains lured even more immigrants and, for the first time, brought leisure travelers west. The rails also made the Northwest accessible to travel writers of a less intrepid stripe than Winthrop. Remarking upon the great numbers of American, English, French, German, and Swedish writers who roamed the West during this era, a critic for the San Francisco–based *Overland Monthly* wrote, "The field is so new and fresh, and possesses such a living interest, that writers come here in shoals to witness the wonders of the rapid march of Western civilization across those vast tracts which, in the memory of the youngest of them, were marked on the school-maps as 'Unexplored Regions.'"

The prime of the *Overland*, a sort of West Coast *Atlantic*, spanned only seven years (1868–1875), but it had a lasting influence on the literature of the Pacific Coast and the Pacific Northwest. By publishing early work by Mark Twain, Joaquin Miller, Ambrose Bierce, and John Muir, editor Bret Harte forced the Northeastern literary establishment to acknowledge the existence of talented writers west of the Mississippi. The *Overland* regularly published reports from the Northwest, including early articles by Frances Fuller Victor, one of the region's leading historians. Twain's work and Harte's own short stories "The Luck of Roaring Camp" and "The Outcasts of Poker Flat" strengthened the emerging local-color movement, through which American literature escaped the bounds of the Northeast and incorporated the cultural flavor, dialects, and tall-tale traditions of the nation's outlying regions.

This genre predominated among those earliest Northwest novels and stories that found their way to national publication in the 1890s. The most popular novel of the time may have been *The Bridge of the Gods: A Romance of Indian Oregon*, a nearly unreadable melodrama by Frederick Homer Balch, but the best and most enduring work was being created by women whose fiction depicted the gritty reality of homesteading, logging, and mining in the Northwest. In stories for *The Century* and in novels like *The Chosen Valley* (1892) and *Coeur d'Alene* (1894), Mary Hallock Foote described the tough lives of Idaho engineers and miners, sometimes using dialect so thick that the reader is tempted to ask for translation. Ella Higginson (*From the Land of the Snow-Pearls*, 1897) and Anne Shannon Monroe (*Happy Valley*, 1916) depicted a region still full of hope and promise, but not quite as high in clover as the land dreamed of by the overland pioneers. Heroic farmers and good-hearted miners figure heavily in their stories, but so do conniving claim-jumpers, management thugs, and union rabble-rousers. This realistic fiction provided an antidote to the pie-in-the-sky predictions of earlier literary conjurers such as Hall Jackson Kelley, and hinted that those who sought new lives in the Northwest might find themselves trading their old batch of problems and misery for new ones.

THEODORE WINTHROP

After graduating from Yale in 1849, Theodore Winthrop set out to see the world. The young scion of the distinguished New England Winthrops (his ancestor John Winthrop founded Massachusetts in 1630) sailed twice to Europe, then visited Panama before sailing north to San Francisco and the frontier Northwest. He spent the summer of 1853 exploring Oregon and the Puget Sound country, dropping in on such local notables as trail guide Jesse Applegate and Washington Irving's hero Captain Bonneville. From August 21 to August 31, Winthrop traveled from Port Townsend to The Dalles via Fort Nisqually and the northern flank of Mount Rainier. That journey became the basis for The Canoe and the Saddle, *one of the most enduring travelogues of the Northwest. Winthrop's witty, baroque narrative was written in his Staten Island home at least three years after the trip, and was not published until 1862, a year after its author was struck down on a Civil War battlefield.*

from THE CANOE AND THE SADDLE

THE DUKE OF YORK was ducally drunk. His brother, King George, was drunk—royally. Royalty may disdain public opinion, and fall as low as it pleases. But a brother of the throne, leader of the opposition, possible Regent, possible King, must retain at least a swaying perpendicular. King George had kept his chair of state until an angular sitting position was impossible; then he had subsided into a curvilinear droop, and at last fairly toppled over, and lay in his lodge, limp and stertorous.

In his lodge lay Georgius Rex, in flabby insensibility. Dead to the duties of sovereignty was the King of the Klalams. Like other royal Georges, in palaces more regal than this Port Townsend wigwam, in realms more civilized than here, where the great tides of Puget Sound rise and fall, this royal George had sunk in absolute wreck. Kings are but men. Several kings have thought themselves the god Bacchus. George of the Klalams had imbibed this ambitious error, and had proved himself very much lower than a god, much lower than a man, lower than any plebeian Klalam Indian,—a drunken king.

In the great shed of slabs that served them for a palace sat the Queen,— sat the Queens,—mild-eyed, melancholy, copper-colored persons, also, sad to say, not sober. Etiquette demanded inebriety. The stern rules of royal indecorum must be obeyed. The Queen Dowager had succumbed to ceremony; the Queen Consort was sinking; every lesser queen,—the favorites for sympathy, the neglected for consolation,—all had imitated their lord and master.

Courtiers had done likewise. Chamberlain Gold Stick, Black Rod, Garter King at Arms, a dozen high functionaries, were prostrate by the side of prostrate majesty. Courtiers grovelled with their sovereign. Sardanapalus never presided, until he could preside no longer, at a more tumble-down orgie.

King, royal household, and court all were powerless, and I was a suppliant here, on the waters of the Pacific, for means of commencing my homeward journey across the continent toward the Atlantic. I needed a bark from that fleet by which King George ruled the waves. I had dallied too long at Vancouver's Island, under the hospitable roof of the Hudson's Bay Company, and had consumed invaluable hours in making a detour from my proper course to inspect the house, the saw-mill, the bluff, and the beach, called Port Townsend. These were the last days of August, 1853. I was to meet my overland comrades, a pair of roughs, at the Dalles of the Columbia on the first of September. Between me and the rendezvous were the leagues of Puget's Sound, the preparation for an ultra-montane trip, the passes of the Cascades, and all the dilatoriness and danger of Indian guidance. Moments now were worth days of common life.

Therefore, as I saw winged moments flit away unharnessed to my chariot of departure, I became wroth, and, advancing where the king of all this region lay, limp, stertorous, and futile, I kicked him liberally.

Yes, I have kicked a king!

Proudly I claim that I have outdone the most radical regicide. I have offered indignities to the person of royalty with a moccasined toe. Would that that toe had been robustly booted! In his Sans Souci, Oeil de Boeuf, his Brighton Pavilion, I kicked so much of a first gentleman of his realm as was George R., and no scalping-knife leaped from greasy seal-skin sheath to avenge the insult. One bottle-holder in waiting, upon whose head I had casually trodden, did indeed stagger to his seat, and stammer truculently in Chinook jargon, "Potlatch lum!—Give me to drink," quoth he, and incontinently fell prone again, a poor, collapsed bottle-holder.

But kicking the insensible King of the Klalams, that dominant nation on the southern shores of Puget Sound, did not procure me one of his canoes and a crew of his braves to paddle me to Nisqually, my next station, for a blanket apiece and gratuities of sundries. There was no help to be had from that smoky barn or its sorry inmates, so regally nicknamed by British voyagers. I left them lying upon their dirty mats, among their fishy baskets, and strode away, applying the salutary toe to each dignitary as I passed.

Fortunately, without I found the Duke of York, only ducally drunk. A duke's share of the potables had added some degree to the arc of vibration of his swagger, but had not sent it beyond equilibrium. He was a reversed pendulum, somewhat spasmodic in swing, and not constructed on the compensation principle,—when one muscle relaxed, another did not tighten. However, the Duke was still sober enough to have speculation in his eyes, and as he was Regent now, and Lord High Admiral, I might still by his favor be expedited.

It was a chance festival that had intoxicated the Klalams, king and court. There had been a fraternization, a powwow, a wahwah, a peace congress with some neighboring tribe,—perhaps the Squaksnamish, or Squallyamish, or Sinahomish, or some other of the Whulgeamish, dwellers by Whulge,—the waters of Puget's Sound. And just as the festival began, there had come to Port Townsend, or Kahtai, where the king of the Klalams, or S'Klalams, now reigned, a devilsend of a lumber brig, with liquor of the fieriest. An orgie followed, a nation was prostrate.

The Duke was my only hope. Yet I must not betray eagerness. A dignitary among Indians does not like to be bored with energy. If I were too ardent, the Duke would grow coy. Prices would climb to the unapproachable. Any exhibition of impatience would cost me largess of beads, if not blankets, beyond the tariff for my canoe-ride. A frugal mind, and, on the other hand, a bent toward irresponsible pleasure, kept the Duke palpably wavering. He would joyfully stay and complete his saturnalia, and yet the bliss of more chattels, and consequent consideration, tempted him.

Which shall it be, "lumoti" or "pississy,"—bottle or blanket? revel and rum, or toil and toilette?—the great alternative on which civilization hinges, as well among Klalams as elsewhere. Sunbeams are so warm, and basking such dulcet, do-nothing bliss, why overheat one's self now for the woollen raiment of future warmth? Not merely warmth, but wealth,— wives, chiefest of luxuries, are bought, and to a royal highness, blankets are purple, ermine, and fine linen.

Calling the Duke's attention to these facts, I wooed him cautiously, as craft wooes coyness; I assumed a lofty indifference of demeanor, and negotiated with him from a sham vantage-ground of money-power, knowing what trash my purse would be, if he refused to be tempted. A grotesque jargon called Chinook is the lingua-franca of the whites and Indians of the Northwest. Once the Chinooks were the most numerous tribe along the Columbia, and the first, from their position at its mouth, to meet and talk with strangers. Now it is all over with them; their bones are dust; small-pox and spirits have eliminated the race. But there grew up between them and the traders a lingo, an incoherent coagulation of words,—as much like a settled, logical language as a legion of centrifugal, marauding Bashi Bazouks, every man a Jack-of-all-trades, a beggar and blackguard, is like an accurate, unaminous, disciplined battalion. It is a jargon of English, French, Spanish, Chinook, Kallapooga, Haida, and other tongues, civilized and savage. It is an attempt on a small scale to nullify Babel by combining a confusion of tongues into a confounding of tongues,—a witches' caldron in which the vocable that bobs up may be some old familiar Saxon verb, having suffered Procrustean docking or elongation, and now doing substantive duty; or some strange monster, evidently nurtured within the range of tomahawks and calumets. There is some danger that the beauties of this dialect will be lost to literature.

"Carent quia vate sacro."

The Chinook jargon still expects its poet. As several of my characters will use this means of conveying their thoughts to my readers, and employ me only as an interpreter, I have thought it well to aid comprehension by this little philological preface.

My big talk with the Duke of York went on in such a lingo, somewhat as follows:—"Pottlelum mitlite King Jawge; Drunk lieth King George," said I. "Cultus tyee ocook; a beggarly majesty that. Hyas tyee mika; a mighty prince art thou,—pe kumtux skookum mamook esick; and knowest how robustly to ply paddle. Nika tikky hyack katawah copa Squally, copa canim; I would with speed canoe it to Squally. Hui pississy nika potlatch pe hui ikta; store of blankets will I give, and plenteous sundries."

"Nawitka siks; yea, friend," responded the Duke, grasping my hand, after two drunken clutches at empty air. "Klosche nika tum tum copa hyas Baasten tyee; tender is my heart toward thee, O great Yankee don. Yaka pottlelum—halo nika—wake cultus mann Dookeryawk; he indeed is drunk—not I—no loafer-man, the Duke of York. Mitlite canim; got canoe. Pe klosche nika tikky klatawah copa Squally; and heartily do I wish to go to Squally."

JAMES G. SWAN

James G. Swan settled on Shoalwater (now Willapa) Bay at a time when fewer than two dozen white Americans populated the coast north of the Columbia River. The prosperous Boston shipfitter had abandoned his wife, family, and business to seek California gold in 1849, but moved north a few years later on the advice of two friends, one of whom happened to be a S'Klallam Indian named Chetzamakha—aka the Duke of York. Unlike Theodore Winthrop, Swan saw the Duke and his people as more than figures of comic relief, and over the next forty-eight years he became one of the leading experts on Northwest native culture. His memoir of his early years on Shoalwater Bay, from which the following was excerpted, was published in 1857.

from THE NORTHWEST COAST

AFTER MY RETURN FROM CHENOOK, nothing of any particular interest transpired till toward the first of July, when it was announced to me that the boys, as the oystermen were termed, intended celebrating the 4th of July at my tent; and accordingly, as the time drew near, all hands were engaged in making preparations; for it was not intended that I should be at the expense of the celebration, but only bear my proportionate part. The day was ushered in by a tremendous bonfire, which Baldt and myself kindled on Pine Island, which was answered by every one who had a gun and powder blazing away. Toward two o'clock they began to assemble, some coming in boats, others in canoes, and a few by walking round the beach, which they could easily do at any time after the tide was quarter ebb.

Each one brought something: one had a great oyster pie, baked in a milk-pan; another had a boiled ham; a third brought a cold pudding; others had pies, doughnuts, or loaves of bread; and my neighbor Russell came, bringing with him a long oration of his own composing, and a half a dozen boxes of sardines. When all were assembled, the performances were commenced by the reading of the Declaration of Independence by Mr. St. John, extracts from Webster's oration at Boston on Adams and Jefferson, then Russell's oration, which was followed by the banquet, and after that a feu-de-joie by the guns and rifles of the whole company.

These ceremonies over, it was proposed to close the performance for the day by going on top of the cliff opposite, and make a tremendous big blaze. This was acceded to, and some six or eight immediately crossed the creek and soon scrambled to the top of the hill, where we found an old hollow cedar stump about twenty feet high. We could enter this on one side, and found it a mere shell of what had once been a monster tree.

I had with me a little rifle, which measured, stock and all, but three feet long. With this I measured across the space, and found it was just six lengths of my rifle, or eighteen feet, and the tree undoubtedly, when sound, must have measured, with the bark on, at least sixty feet in circumference.

We went to work with a will, and soon had the old stump filled full of dry spruce limbs, which were lying about in great quantities, and then set fire to the whole. It made the best bonfire I ever saw; and after burning all night and part of the next day, finally set fire to the forest, which continued to burn for several months, till the winter rains finally extinguished it. The party broke up at an early hour, and all declared that, with the exception of the absence of a cannon, they never had a pleasanter "fourth."

The winter was now wearing away, and the snow had all disappeared, although January had not quite gone, and every pleasant day the sun shone out warm and bright, giving token of an early spring. While we were thus engaged in clearing up land and burning trees, a party of Indians from Chenook arrived, consisting of old Carcumcum (sister of the celebrated

Comcomly, the Chenook chief mentioned in Irving's *Astoria,* and also by Ross Cox), and her son Ellewa, the present chief of the Chenooks, with his wife and two or three slaves. They made a camp on the beach near the house, where they lived under a little old tent. They had been to the wrecks, and among other things was found an India-rubber pillow, which Ellewa had filled with some kind of spirits he had also procured at the same place. He and his squaw, Winchestoh, managed to keep drunk for three or four days, when, their liquor giving out, they were obliged to get sober. As it commenced to rain, they were very miserable, and Ellewa requested Russell to allow the squaw to lie down by the fire in the house, which he did, and the same day Ellewa, with old Carcumcum, returned to Chenook. At supper-time I gave the squaw some tea and toast, and remarked that her face and neck were covered with little spots like flea-bites. I said to Russell, "This woman has either got the small-pox or measles." "Oh!" said he, "don't say that, for I would never have had her in the house if I suspected any such thing." "Well," said I, "we shall see."

Soon after supper I went to bed, as did Joe and the captain, leaving Russell writing. About nine o'clock he called me to come down, for he thought the woman was dying; and, sure enough, when I got down stairs she was entirely dead. We laid her in the store, and the next morning the captain and Joe made her a coffin, and after we had put her in we carried her about five hundred rods from the house, and, having dug a grave, buried her in a Christian manner.

Some ten or twelve days after this Russell was taken with a violent pain in his head and back, and had to take to his bed. Joe and the captain also were attacked, but very slightly, however. They all attributed their sickness to severe colds, but I knew that in Russell's case it was something more serious. I did not dare tell him, as I knew it would only frighten him; nor did I dare tell my fears either to the captain or Joe, or any of the other settlers; there was such a panic in the minds of all, that I knew the bare mention of small-pox would drive them all away from the house, if not from the Bay. I could not leave, as there was no vessel in the Bay at the time, nor would I leave during his illness, although I could easily have gone to Astoria; so I made up my mind to do what I could and keep my own counsel, which I did so effectually that Russell did not know what was the matter till the fever had passed and he was nearly blind, and the captain and Joe did not know what ailed him till he was nearly well and all danger had passed. Joe was so scared that he ran off the same day, but the old man complimented me on my caution, and said that he could then account for the violent attack he had experienced, and which he thought was a severe cold.

As soon as Russell was able, he went to San Francisco, leaving me in charge of his affairs. His cousin, Walter Lynde, had insisted on seeing him while he was sick, and he was taken next, and I nursed him through, but his attack was very slight.

Several cases occurred among the other settlers, but mostly Indians in their employ, and several of the Indians died. I thought my hospital duties were at an end, but the hardest case was yet to come off. Poor Que-a-quim was taken with the unmistakable symptoms, and, rather than have him in the lodge with the other Indians, where I was afraid the infection would spread, I had him brought over and placed in a comfortable position in the chamber near my bed, where the captain and myself did all we could to make him easy. During his sickness, Old Cartumhays, whose wife had just died of the small-pox, sent for me to go to his house on the Palux, as he had the same complaint. I accordingly went, and found the old fellow in his bed making great lamentations. After a little time he pulled out from the chest a package of about a dozen different kinds of medicine, that he had either begged, borrowed, or, more probably, stolen. He said he was very sick, and wished me to help him.

Judging, however, from the presence of five or six empty whisky bottles that his complaint was not a very dangerous one, I recommended him a dose of salts, to be followed up with half a cupful of sulphur and molasses, to be taken instead of preserves or sweetmeats. The prescription in his case was happily effective, and in two days he was well.

Poor Que-a-quim, however, grew worse. He had, besides the small-pox, an affection of his liver, which had troubled him a long time. He knew he should die, and told me so. His brother, to whom I told this, remarked, "Well, if he wants to die, he will die." He then brought into the house, from the lodge, all the little property of his brother, consisting of a few shirts, a blanket or two, and some few trinkets, with a request that they might be buried with him. The day Que-a-quim died, we felt satisfied, from appearances, that such must be the case, and the captain remarked, "He will die this evening at high water;" and at nine o'clock, just as the tide began to ebb, he died.

Now, then, was a job before us. The Indians would not have any thing to do with the body, nor would we let them, for fear of their taking the infection, neither did we feel disposed to remain all night with the corpse; so the captain procured a piece of old canvas, and, wrapping the body up in several blankets, taking care to inclose all the things which had been brought in from the lodge, the whole was then sewed up in the canvas, and the corpse lashed on to a board, and launched out of the chamber window by the captain, while I received the body from below, and laid it on a barrel till the captain came with a lantern and two shovels, when we took up the corpse, resting the board on our shoulders. Poor Que-a-quim! he was not very heavy, and we soon reached the spot where but a few weeks before we had buried the squaw. It did not take us long to dig a grave in the soft sand, and we soon laid him beside the wife of Ellewa.

"We buried him darkly at dead of night."

The little clock in Russell's house struck twelve as we closed the door on our return.

The time, the place, and the occasion gave rise to the most solemn feelings; neither of us could speak a word. But the old captain, who had seen many a scene of death, and assisted often in launching the bodies of his shipmates into the blue waters of the ocean, could not refrain from shedding a tear to the memory of the poor Indian lad, a tribute of sympathy in which I most heartily joined. This was the last case of small-pox I was called on to attend, and I trust I may not be obliged to pass through such another trial, feeling perfectly satisfied with my acquaintance with that most disgusting and contagious disease.

FITZ HUGH LUDLOW

In the spring of 1863, with the Civil War raging in the East, painter Albert Bierstadt and his friend Fitz Hugh Ludlow left New York for a year-long tour of the Western frontier. Both were already men of reputation—Bierstadt for his romantic, breathtaking portrayals of the Rocky Mountain region, Ludlow for his daring autobiography, The Hasheesh Eater. *They traveled by train and stagecoach, one taking measure of the land in sketches, the other in journals.*

Back in his New York studio, Bierstadt would use that material to create some of the great paintings of the American West. History has looked less favorably upon Ludlow, who published four articles on the journey in The Atlantic Monthly *but whose book-length account,* Heart of the Continent, *has been out of print for decades. This article appeared in* The Atlantic *in December 1864.*

from ON THE COLUMBIA RIVER

"THE DALLES" IS A TOWN of one street, built close along the edge of a bluff of trap thirty or forty feet high, perfectly perpendicular, level on the top as if it had been graded for a city, and with depth of water at its base for the heaviest draught boats on the river. In fact, the whole water-front is a natural quay,—which wants nothing but time to make it alive with steam-elevators, warehouses, and derricks. To Portland and the Columbia it stands much as St. Louis to New Orleans and the Mississippi. There is no reason why it should not some day have a corresponding business, for whose wharfage-accomodation it has even greater natural advantages.

Architecturally, the Dalles cannot be said to lean very heavily on the side of beauty. The houses are mostly two-story structures of wood, occupied by all the trades and professions which flock to a new mining-entre-pot. Outfit-merchants, blacksmiths, printing-office (for there is really a very well-conducted daily at the Dalles,) are cheek by jowl with doctors, tailors, and Cheap Johns—the latter being only less merry and thrifty over their incredible sacrifices in everything, from pins to corduroy, than that predominant class of all, the barkeepers themselves. The town was in a state of bustle when our steamer touched the wharf; it bustled more and more from there to the Umatilla House, where we stopped; the hotel was one organized bustle in bar and dining-room; and bedtime brought no hush. The Dalles, like the Irishman, seemed sitting up all night to be fresh for an early start in the morning.

We found everybody interested in gold. Crowds of listeners, with looks of incredulity or enthusiasm, were gathered around the party in the bar-room which had last come in from the newest of the new mines, and a man who had seen the late Fort-Hall discoveries was "treated" to that extent that he might have become intoxicated a dozen times without expense to himself. The charms of the interior were still further suggested by placards posted on every wall, offering rewards for the capture of a person who on the great gold route had lately committed some of the grimmest murders and most talented robberies known in any branch of Newgate enterprise. I had for supper a very good omelet, (considering its distance from the culinary centres of the universe,) and a Dalles editorial debating the claims of several noted cut-throats to the credit of the operations ascribed to them—feeling that in the *ensemble* I was enjoying both the exotic and the indigenous luxuries of our virgin soil.

After supper and a stroll I returned to the ladies' parlor of the Umatilla House, rubbed my eyes in vain to dispel the illusion of a piano and a carpet at this jumping-off place of civilization, and sat down at a handsome centre-table to write up my journal. I had reviewed my way from Portland as far as Fort Vancouver, when another illusion happened to me in the shape of a party of gentlemen and ladies, in ball-dresses, dress-coats, white kids, and elaborate hair, who entered the parlor to wait for further accessions from the hotel. They were on their way with a band of music to give some popular citizen a surprise-party. The popular citizen never got the fine edge of that surprise. I took it off for him. If it were not too much like a little Cockney on Vancouver's Island who used the phrase on all occasions, from stubbing his toe to the death of a Cabinet Lord, I should say, "I never was more astonished in me life!"

None of them had ever seen me before,—and with my books and maps about me, I may have looked like some public, yet mysterious character. I felt a pleasant sensation of having interest taken in me, and, wishing to make an ingenuous return, looked up with a casual smile at one of the party. Again to my surprise, this proved to be a very charming young lady, and I timidly became aware that the others were equally pretty in their several styles. Not knowing what else to do under the circumstances, I smiled again, still more casually. An equal uncertainty as to alternative set the ladies smiling quite across the row, and then, to my relief, the gentlemen joined them, making it pleasant for us all. A moment later we were engaged in general conversation,—starting from the bold hypothesis, thrown out by one of the gentlemen, that perhaps I was going to Boisé, and proceeding, by a process of elimination, to the accurate knowledge of what I was going to do, if it wasn't that. I enjoyed one of the most cheerful bits of social relaxation I had found since crossing the Missouri, and nothing but my duty to my journal prevented me, when my surprise-party left, from accompanying them, by invitation, under the brevet title of

Professor, to the house of the popular citizen, who, I was assured, would be glad to see me. I certainly should have been glad to see him, if he was anything like those guests of his who had so ingenuously cultivated me in a far land of strangers, where a man might have been glad to form the acquaintance of his mother-in-law. This is not the way people form acquaintances in New York; but if I had wanted that, why not have stayed there? As a cosmopolite, and on general principles of being, I prefer the Dalles way. I have no doubt I should have found in that circle of spontaneous recognitions quite as many people who stood wear and improved on intimacy as were ever vouchsafed to me by social indorsement from somebody else. We are perpetually blaming our heads of Government Bureaus for their poor knowledge of character,—their subordinates, we say, are never pegs in the right holes. If we understood our civilized system of introductions, we could not rationally expect anything else. The great mass of polite mankind are trained *not* to know character, but to take somebody else's voucher for it. Their acquaintances, most of their friendships, come to them through a succession of indorsers, none of whom may have known anything of the goodness of the paper. A sensible man, conventionally introduced to his fellow, must always wonder why the latter does not turn him around to look for signatures in chalk down the back of his coat; for he knows that Brown indorsed him over to Jones, and Jones negotiated him with Robinson, through a succession in which perhaps two out of a hundred took pains to know whether he represented metal. You do not find the people of new countries making mistakes in character. Every man is his own guaranty,—and if he has no just cause to suspect himself bogus, there will be true pleasure in a frank opening of himself to the examination and his eyes for the study of others. Not to be accused of intruding radical reform under the guise of belles-lettres, let me say that I have no intention of introducing this innovation at the East.

HAZARD STEVENS

As a young boy Hazard Stevens accompanied his father, Washington Territory Governor Isaac I. Stevens, on expeditions to negotiate treaties with Northwest Indian tribes, riding two thousand miles across the territory and fighting in the

*Indian Wars of 1855–1856 before reaching his fifteenth birthday. The younger
Stevens was decorated for valiant service in the Union Army and after the
Civil War, settled in Portland and Olympia. There he hired on as an attorney
for the Northern Pacific Railroad Company, for which his chief assignment
was to nab wildcat loggers poaching trees on company land. In 1870 he and
P. B. Van Trump became the first men to reach the summit of Mount Takhoma
(Rainier). They were nearly among the first to die there, too; forced by darkness
to sleep at the summit, they stayed alive by warming themselves in the steam of
the volcano's crater. This excerpt was published in* The Atlantic Monthly *in
November 1876.*

from THE ASCENT OF TAKHOMA

NOTHING CAN CONVEY an idea of the grandeur and ruggedness of the
mountains. Directly in front, and apparently not over two miles distant,
although really twenty, old Takhoma loomed up more gigantic than ever.
We were far above the level of the lower snow-line on Takhoma. The
high peak upon which we clung seemed the central core or focus of all the
mountains around, and on every side we looked down vertically thousands of feet, deep down into vast, terrible defiles, black and fir-clothed,
which stretched away until lost in the distance and smoke. Between them,
separating one from another, the mountain-walls rose precipitously and
terminated in bare, columnar peaks of black basaltic or volcanic rock, as
sharp as needles. It seemed incredible that any human foot could have
followed out the course we came, as we looked back upon it.

After a few hours more of this climbing, we stood upon the summit of
the last mountain-ridge that separated us from Takhoma. We were in a
saddle of the ridge; a lofty peak rose on either side. Below us extended a
long, steep hollow or gulch filled with snow, the farther extremity of which
seemed to drop off perpendicularly into a deep valley or basin. Across this
valley, directly in front, filling up the whole horizon and view with an
indescribable aspect of magnitude and grandeur, stood the old leviathan of
mountains. The broad, snowy dome rose far among and above the clouds.
The sides fell off in vertical steeps and fearful black walls of rock for a
third of its altitude; lower down, vast, broad, gently sloping snow-fields
surrounded the mountain, and were broken here and there by ledges or
masses of the dark basaltic rock protruding above them . . .

We camped, as the twilight fell upon us, in an aromatic grove of balsam firs . . . After supper we reclined upon our blankets in front of the bright, blazing fire, well satisfied. The Indian, when starting from Bear Prairie, had evidently deemed our intention of ascending Takhoma too absurd to deserve notice . . . But his views had undergone a change with the day's march. The affair began to look serious to him, and now in Chinook, interspersed with a few words of broken English and many signs and ges-ticulations, he began a solemn exhortation and warning against our rash project.

Takhoma, he said, was an enchanted mountain, inhabited by an evil spirit, who dwelt in a fiery lake on its summit. No human being could ascend it or even attempt its ascent, and survive. At first, indeed, the way was easy. The broad snow-fields, over which he had so often hunted the mountain goat, interposed no obstacle, but above them the rash adventurer would be compelled to climb up steeps of loose, rolling rocks, which would turn beneath his feet and cast him headlong into the deep abyss below. The upper snow-slopes, too, were so steep that not even a goat, far less a man, could get over them. And he would have to pass below lofty walls and precipices whence avalanches of snow and vast masses of rock were continually falling; and these would inevitably bury the intruder beneath their ruins. Moreover, a furious tempest continually swept the crown of the mountain, and the luckless adventurer, even if he wonderfully escaped the perils below, would be torn from the mountain and whirled through the air by this fearful blast. And the awful being upon the summit, who would surely punish the sacrilegious attempt to invade his sanctuary,—who could hope to escape his vengeance? Many years ago, he continued, his grandfather, a great chief and warrior, and a mighty hunter, had ascended part way up the mountain, and had encountered some of these dangers, but he fortunately turned back in time to escape destruction; and no other Indian had ever gone so far.

Finding that his words did not produce the desired effect, he assured us that, if we persisted in attempting the ascent, he would wait three days for our return, and would then proceed to Olympia and inform our friends of our death; and he begged us to give him a paper (a written note) to take to them, so that they might believe his story. Sluiskin's manner during this harangue was earnest in the extreme, and he was undoubtedly sincere in his forebodings. After we had retired to rest, he kept up a most dismal chant, or dirge, until late in the night. The dim, white, spectral mass towering so near, the roar of the torrents below us, and the occasional thunder of avalanches, several of which fell during the night, added to the weird effect of Sluiskin's song.

Two days later, on the summit:

The wind blew so violently that we were obliged to brace ourselves with our Alpine staffs and use great caution to guard against being swept off the ridge. We threw ourselves behind the pinnacles or into the cracks every seventy steps, for rest and shelter against the bitter, piercing wind. Hastening forward in this way along the dizzy, narrow, and precarious ridge, we reached at length the highest point. Sheltered behind a pinnacle of ice we rested a moment, took out our flags and fastened them upon the Alpine staffs, and then, standing erect in the furious blast, waved them in triumph with three cheers. We stood a moment upon that narrow summit, bracing ourselves against the tempest to view the prospect . . . On every side of the mountain were deep gorges falling off precipitously thousands of feet, and from these the thunderous sound of avalanches would rise occasionally. Far below were the wide-extended glaciers already described. The wind was now a perfect tempest, and bitterly cold; smoke and mist were flying about the base of the mountain, half hiding, half revealing its gigantic outlines; and the whole scene was sublimely awful.

It was now five p.m. We had spent eleven hours of unremitted toil in making the ascent, and, thoroughly fatigued, and chilled by the cold, bitter gale, we saw ourselves obliged to pass the night on the summit without shelter or food, except our meagre lunch. It would have been impossible to descend the mountain before nightfall, and sure destruction to attempt it in darkness. We concluded to return to a mass of rocks not far below, and there pass the night as best we could, burrowing in the loose débris.

The middle peak of the mountain, however, was evidently the highest, and we determined first to visit it. Retracing our steps along the narrow crest of Peak Success, as we named the scene of our triumph, we crossed an intervening depression in the dome, and ascended the middle peak, about a mile distant and two hundred feet higher than Peak Success. Climbing over a rocky ridge which crowns the summit, we found ourselves within a circular crater two hundred yards in diameter, filled with a solid bed of snow, and inclosed with a rim of rocks projecting above the snow all around. As we were crossing the crater on the snow, Van Trump detected the odor of sulphur, and the next instant numerous jets of steam and smoke were observed issuing from the crevices of the rocks which formed the rim on the northern side. Never was a discovery more welcome! Hastening forward, we both exclaimed, as we warmed our chilled and benumbed extremities over one of Pluto's fires, that here we would pass the night, secure against freezing to death, at least.

JOHN MUIR

John Muir's essays on the Sierra Nevada, published in the Overland Monthly, Harper's, *and* Scribner's *in the 1870s, earned him a reputation as America's foremost nature writer. But Muir's pen ran dry in the 1880s; he spent most of the decade overseeing his northern California fruit orchard. In 1888 he contracted to write a book,* Picturesque California, *that reinvigorated both his writing and his fighting preservationist spirit. Despite its title, the book included many scenes from the Northwest. The contrast between Oregon's and Washington's virgin forests and his own beloved Sierra Nevada—which he saw being despoiled by domestic sheep ("hoofed locusts" he called them), fire, and rapacious lumber companies—brought home the need to protect America's wilderness. The next year Muir led the fight to establish Yosemite National Park, and in 1892 he founded the Sierra Club, which remains one of the most powerful conservationist groups in the country. Muir climbed Mount Rainier during his 1888 journey and in 1899 led the fight to establish Mount Rainier National Park.*

from PICTURESQUE CALIFORNIA

THE TOWNS OF PUGET SOUND are of a very lively, progressive, and aspiring kind, fortunately with abundance of substance about them to warrant their ambition and make them grow. Like young sapling sequoias, they are sending out their roots far and near for nourishment, counting confidently on longevity and grandeur of stature. Seattle and Tacoma are at present far in the lead of all others in the race for supremacy, and these two are keen, active rivals, to all appearances well matched. Tacoma occupies near the head of the Sound a site of great natural beauty. It is the terminus of the Northern Pacific Railroad, and calls itself the "City of Destiny." Seattle is also charmingly located about twenty miles down the Sound from Tacoma, on Elliott Bay. It is the terminus of the Seattle, Lake-Shore, and Eastern Railroad, now in process of construction, and calls itself the "Queen City of the Sound" and the "Metropolis of Washington" . . . They are probably about the same size and they each claim to have about twenty thousand people; but their figures are so rapidly changing, and so often mixed up with counts that refer to the future that exact measurements of either of these places are about as hard to obtain as measurements of the clouds of a growing storm. Their edges run back for miles into the woods which hide a good many of the houses and the stakes which mark the lots; so that, without being as yet very large towns, they seem to fade away into the distance.

But, though young and loose-jointed, they are fast taking on the forms and manners of old cities, putting on airs, as some would say, like boys in haste to be men. They are already towns "with all modern improvements, first-class in every particular," as is said of hotels. They have electric motors and lights, paved broadways and boulevards, substantial business blocks, schools, churches, factories, and foundries. The lusty, titanic clang of boilermaking may be heard there, and plenty of the languid music of pianos mingling with the babel noises of commerce carried on in a hundred tongues. The main streets are crowded with bright, wide-awake lawyers, ministers, merchants, agents for everything under the sun; ox-drivers and loggers in stiff, gummy overalls; back-slanting dudes, well-tailored and shiny; and fashions and bonnets of every feather and color bloom gayly in the noisy throng and advertise London and Paris. Vigorous life and strife are to be seen everywhere. The spirit of progress is in the air. Still it is hard to realize how much good work is being done here of a kind that makes for civilization—the enthusiastic, exulting energy displayed in the building of new towns, railroads, and mills, in the opening of mines of coal and iron and the development of natural resources in general. To many, especially in the Atlantic States, Washington is hardly known at all. It is regarded as being yet a far wild west—a dim, nebulous expanse of woods—by those who do not know that railroads and steamers have brought the country out of the wilderness and abolished the old distances. It is now near to all the world and is in possession of a share of the best of all that civilization has to offer, while on some of the lines of advancement it is at the front.

———————

In general views the western section [of Oregon] seems to be covered with one vast, evenly planted forest, with the exception of the few snow-clad peaks of the Cascade Range, these peaks being the only points in the landscape that rise above the timber-line. Nevertheless, embosomed in this forest and lying in the great trough between the Cascades and coast mountains, there are some of the best bread-bearing valleys to be found in the world . . .

The climate of this section, like the corresponding portion of Washington, is rather damp and sloppy throughout the winter months, but the summers are bright, ripening the wheat and allowing it to be garnered in good condition. Taken as a whole, the weather is bland and kindly, and like the forest trees the crops and cattle grow plump and sound in it. So also do the people; children ripen well and grow up with limbs of good size and fiber and, unless overworked in the woods, live to a good old age, hale and hearty.

But, like every other happy valley in the world, the sunshine of this one is not without its shadows. Malarial fevers are not unknown in some places, and untimely frosts and rains may at long intervals in some measure disappoint the hopes of the husbandman. Many a tale, good-natured or otherwise, is told concerning the overflowing abundance of the Oregon rains. Once an English traveler, as the story goes, went to a store to make some purchases and on leaving found that rain was falling; therefore, not liking to get wet, he stepped back to wait till the shower was over. Seeing no signs of clearing, he soon became impatient and inquired of the store-keeper how long he thought the shower would be likely to last. Going to the door and looking wisely into the gray sky and noting the direction of the wind, the latter replied that he thought the shower would probably last about six months, an opinion that of course disgusted the fault-finding Briton with the "blawsted country," though in fact it is but little if at all wetter or cloudier than his own.

———————

No lover of trees will ever forget his first meeting with the sugar pine. In most coniferous trees there is a sameness of form and expression which at length becomes wearisome to most people who travel far in the woods. But the sugar pines are as free from conventional forms as any of the oaks. No two are so much alike as to hide their individuality from any observer. Every tree is appreciated as a study in itself and proclaims in no uncertain terms the surpassing grandeur of the species. The branches, mostly near the summit, are sometimes nearly forty feet long, feathered richly around with short, leafy branchlets, and tasselled with cones a foot and a half long. And when these superb arms are outspread, radiating in every direction, an immense crown-like mass is formed which, poised on the noble shaft and filled with sunshine, is one of the grandest forest objects conceivable. But though so wild and unconventional when full-grown, the sugar pine is a remarkably regular tree in youth, a strict follower of coniferous fashions, slim, erect, tapering, symmetrical, every branch in place. At the age of fifty or sixty years this shy, fashionable form begins to give way. Special branches are thrust out away from the general outlines of the trees and bent down with cones. Henceforth it becomes more and more original and independent in style, pushes boldly aloft into the winds and sunshine, growing ever more stately and beautiful, a joy and inspiration to every beholder.

Unfortunately, the sugar pine makes excellent lumber. It is too good to live, and is already passing rapidly away before the woodman's axe. Surely out of all of the abounding forest-wealth of Oregon a few specimens might be spared to the world, not as dead lumber, but as living trees. A park of moderate extent might be set apart and protected for public use forever, containing at least a few hundreds of each of these noble pines, spruces, and firs. Happy will be the men who, having the power and the love and benevolent forecast to do this, will do it. They will not be forgotten. The trees and their lovers will sing their praises, and generations yet unborn will rise up and call them blessed.

RUDYARD KIPLING

Twenty-three-year-old Rudyard Kipling arrived in San Francisco in the spring of 1889, dispatched by his editor at the Allahabad (India) Pioneer *to write a series of feature articles on American society. Kipling toured the West for four months before sailing to London, where he would rise to fame with works such as* Wee Willie Winkie *and* The Jungle Book. *Armed with "keen powers of observation, numerous clever and original tricks of expression, and a genuine prejudice against anything American" (as one reviewer quipped), Kipling visited Portland, Tacoma, Vancouver, and Victoria before heading east to the Rockies. His letters to the* Pioneer *were collected in* American Notes, *an unauthorized 1891 American edition.*

from AMERICAN NOTES

I HAVE LIVED!

The American Continent may now sink under the sea, for I have taken the best that it yields, and the best was neither dollars, love, nor real estate.

Hear now, gentlemen of the Punjab Fishing Club, who whip the reaches of the Tavi, and you who painfully import trout to Ootacamund, and I will tell you how "old man California" and I went fishing, and you shall envy.

We returned from The Dalles to Portland by the way we had come, the steamer stopping en route to pick up a night's catch of one of the salmon wheels on the river, and to deliver it at a cannery downstream.

When the proprietor of the wheel announced that his take was two thousand two hundred and thirty pounds' weight of fish, "and not a heavy catch, neither," I thought he lied. But he sent the boxes aboard, and I counted the salmon by the hundred—huge fifty-pounders, hardly dead, scores of twenty and thirty-pounders, and a host of smaller fish . . .

We reached Portland, California and I, crying for salmon, and the real-estate man, to whom we had been intrusted by "Portland" the insurance man, met us in the street saying that fifteen miles away, across country, we should come upon a place called Clackamas where we might perchance find what we desired. And California, his coat-tails flying in the wind, ran to a livery stable and chartered a wagon and team forthwith. I could push the wagon about with one hand, so light was its structure. The team was purely American—that is to say, almost human in its intelligence and docility. Some one said that the roads were not good on the way to Clackamas and warned us against smashing the springs. "Portland," who had watched the preparations, finally reckoned "he'd come along too," and under heavenly skies we three companions of a day set forth; California carefully lashing our rods into the carriage, and the bystanders over-whelming us with directions as to the sawmills we were to pass, the ferries we were to cross, and the sign-posts we were to seek signs from. Half a mile from this city of fifty thousand souls we struck (and this must be taken literally) a plank-road that would have been a disgrace to an Irish village.

Then six miles of macadamized road showed us that the team could move. A railway ran between us and the banks of the Willamette, and another above us through the mountains. All the land was dotted with small townships, and the roads were full of farmers in their town wagons, bunches of tow-haired, boggle-eyed urchins sitting in the hay behind. The men generally looked like loafers, but their women were all well dressed. Brown hussar-braiding on a tailor-made jacket does not, however, consort with hay-wagons. Then we struck into the woods along what California called a *"camina reale,"* —a good road,—and Portland a "fair track." It wound in and out among fire-blackened stumps, under pine trees, along the corners of log-fences, through hollows which must be hopeless marsh in the winter, and up absurd gradients. But nowhere throughout its length did I see any evidence of road-making. There was a track,—you couldn't well get off it,—and it was all you could do to stay on it. The dust lay a foot thick in the blind ruts, and under the dust we found bits of planking and bundles of brushwood that sent the wagon bounding into the air. Sometimes we crashed through bracken; anon where the blackberries grew rankest we found a lonely little cemetery, the wooden rails all awry, and the pitiful stumpy headstones nodding drunkenly at the soft green mulleins. Then with oaths and the sound of rent underwood a yoke of mighty bulls would swing down a "skid" road, hauling a forty-foot log along a rudely made slide . . .

. . . That was a day to be remembered, and it had only begun when we drew rein at a tiny farmhouse on the banks of the Clackamas and sought horse-feed and lodging ere we hastened to the river that broke over a weir not a quarter of a mile away.

Imagine a stream seventy yards broad divided by a pebbly island, run-ning over seductive riffles, and swirling into deep, quiet pools where the good salmon goes to smoke his pipe after meals. Set such a stream amid fields of breast-high crops surrounded by hills of pine, throw in where you please quiet water, log-fenced meadows, and a hundred-foot bluff just to keep the scenery from growing too monotonous, and you will get some faint notion of the Clackamas.

Portland had no rod. He held the gaff and the whisky. California sniffed, upstream and downstream across the racing water, chose his ground, and let the gaudy spoon drop in the tail of a riffle. I was getting my rod together when I heard the joyous shriek of the reel and the yells of California, and three feet of living silver leaped into the air far across the water. The forces were engaged. The salmon tore up stream, the tense line cutting the water like a tide-rip behind him, and the light bamboo bowed to breaking. What happened after I cannot tell. California swore and prayed and Portland shouted advice and I did all three for what appeared to be half a day but was in reality a little over a quarter of an hour, and sullenly our fish came home with spurts of temper, dashes head-on, and sarabands in the air; but home to the bank came he, and the remorseless reel gathered up the thread of his life inch by inch. We landed him in a little bay, and the spring-weight checked at eleven and a half pounds. Eleven and one-half pounds of fighting salmon! We danced a war-dance on the pebbles, and California caught me round the waist in a hug that went near to breaking my ribs while he shouted: "Partner! Partner! This is glory! Now you catch your fish! Twenty-four years I've waited for this!"

FRANCES FULLER VICTOR

Frances Fuller Victor was one of the Northwest's most versatile early journalists and historians. She published stories, poems, and reportage in the Overland Monthly, *and spent twelve years writing for Hubert Howe Bancroft in his San Francisco "history factory," where she and other writers helped Bancroft publish thirty-nine volumes of Western American history. Although the two-volume* History of Oregon *(1886, 1888) and the* History of Washington, Idaho, and Montana *(1890) were credited to Bancroft, the books were in fact written by Victor. In later years she exhibited the histories at literary fairs, naming herself as author. "That is her way of claiming her own," wrote Ambrose Bierce, "and it is to be hoped that the same thing will be done . . . [by] every living writer whose work Mr. Bancroft claims as 'his' because he paid for it." The Oregon-based writer did publish a number of books under her own* name, including The New Penelope *(stories and poems, 1877) and the travelogue* Atlantis Arisen; or, Talks of a Tourist about Oregon and Washington *(1891).*

from ATLANTIS ARISEN

THE SECOND TOWN in the Yakima Basin is North Yakima. Why *North* Yakima? Only because when some people of their own accord had laid off a town two or three miles south of them, then came the Northern Pacific Railroad Company, and in 1885 laid off a town of its own, on the most approved plan, north of them, and drew to itself the trade of the country of Yakima. This proceeding naturally was greatly irritating to the South Yakimas, who complained of the treatment of the railroad company. The company as a corporation could not be expected to have a soul, but it had a fair-to-middling kind of brain, and made a proposition to the residents of the South Yakima to come over and dwell in the tents of the north town, or, in other words, to let the railroad company remove them, houses and inhabitants, on the railroad town site, where they were to be given lots for those they left behind, and made welcome. As the business of the place had already departed, the majority felt forced to accept the proposition, and the company accordingly had the south town removed, house by house, and set down on its town-site. This procedure increased the value of North Yakima real property. History is silent as to the financial and mental condition of real-estate dealers in the old town, but they probably threw themselves off a rock into the sea.

"Keep your eye on Pasco!" is the injunction which meets you in newspaper and hand-bill advertisements, making you curious to behold it, as if it were the What Is It. When you arrive, you look about you for something on which to keep your eye, which being blown full of sand refuses to risk more than the briefest glimpses thenceforward. There is a hotel, of brick, and some houses scattered about, built, I am told, by the Pasco Land Company, which has also in contemplation a large irrigating canal with which to make cultivable the wastes of sand and sage-brush owned by it. A Chinaman, it is said, has a small patch of ground behind his cabin which he sprinkles with a watering-pot, thereby being enabled to grow flowers and

vegetables in luxuriant beauty and proportions. From this it is inferred that the irrigation of these wastes will redeem them from their present sterility; but in the interim, keeping one's eyes on Pasco is a painful experience.

MARY HALLOCK FOOTE

"No girl ever wanted less to 'go West' with any man," wrote Mary Hallock Foote, a native of upstate New York, before leaving for California in 1876 to join her husband, a mining engineer. Yet the West proved to be the source of her many stories and novels. From California the Footes moved to Colorado and then to Idaho, where Mary Hallock Foote became a leading voice in the local color movement. She drew on her own experiences to write two of Idaho's earliest novels, The Chosen Valley *(1892) and* Coeur d'Alene *(1894).*

from COEUR D'ALENE

"MIKE," SAID DARCIE, looking up from the table, where he had cleared a space for his writing-materials, "I am telling my people at home about the labor troubles here, but upon my life I don't know how to put the thing fairly. I can't see the need of union intervention in the Coeur d'Alene. Do you know what the miners' grievances are?"

"I'll be domned if I do," Mike replied without hesitation. "We was doin' *well*. Every man was gettin' his three dollars, or his three and a half, or his four dollars, a day, accordin' to what he could 'arn, and we knew no betther than be fri'n's with the men that ped us our wages. That's how it was whin first I come. 'T was the age av innocence with us: the lion an' the lamb was lyin' down together, and there was n't a man av us suspicioned what a set of robbers and iron-heeled oppressors thim mine-owners was till the brotherhood in Butte cast their eye on us in the par'lous shtate we was in.

" 'Luk at thim sons av toil over there,' says they, 'in darkest Idyho, sellin' themselves for what wages the monop'lists chooses to fling them, and not a dollar comin' into the union! We'll attind to that,' they says. And they put up a convarsion fund for to carry the goshpel into Idyho; yes, and a good thing they med av it, too. They set up the union in our midst, and they med themselves the priests, and gev out the law, and gethered the off'rin's. They cursed us this wan, and they cursed us that wan, and most partic'ler they cursed him that would n't put up his money and come into the tint av meetin'."

Darcie began to laugh. "It's the trut' I'm tellin' ye," Mike insisted hotly, "though ye'll get a different tale off o' them. But y're askin' me, and I'm givin' it straight, the way I hare it. 'T is the game they've worked in every new camp betuxt the Black Hills an' the coast.

"There was n't a miner come into the Cor de 'Lane but they nabbed him for a convart; and if he belonged to no union, an' would n't be pershuaded, they put their shpite on him, and med his bread bitter to him by ivery mane parsecution they could lay their hand to. There was moighty few stud out against them. I dunno fwhere I'd be now an I had n't been me own mine-owner, workin' a contrac' wid meself. But they ped me more than wan visit, an' they toiled and shweated wid me for to jine them.

"'Fwhat do I want wid a union?' I says. 'I'm me own union, head and hands as God made me. And I niver yet seen the time whin me head could n't set me hands to work, and me hands could n't keep me head whilst I was doin' it. And if I can't find work in the Cor de 'Lane,' says I, 'I'll lay me two feet to the road till I'll come where it is.'

OWEN WISTER

Owen Wister is best known for The Virginian *(1902), one of the most popular Westerns ever published, but he also wrote nearly eighty short stories about the American West. Most were set in Wyoming or the Southwest, but Wister sought out stories in all parts of the region, visiting every Western state in the course of fifteen sojourns from his Philadelphia home between 1885 and 1914. Despite the sloppy romantic reputation of the genre, Wister was a stickler for accuracy. "I don't care how effective [stories may be], if they're false, they're spoiled for me," he wrote in his journal. That preoccupation with historical accuracy can be seen in the following excerpt from "The Second Missouri Compromise," which appeared in Wister's first story collection,* Red Men and White *(1896). In the story, set in the post–Civil War Idaho Territory, the Union-appointed governor plans to force Confederate-sympathizing legislators to swear loyalty to the Union by withholding their per diem pay. The story is based on the real 1867 showdown between Idaho's pro-Union governor, David W. Ballard, and the Dixie transplants serving in the territorial legislature.*

from THE SECOND MISSOURI COMPROMISE

THE LEGISLATURE HAD SAT UP all night, much absorbed, having taken off its coat because of the stove. This was the fortieth and final day of its first session under an order of things not new only, but novel. It sat with the retrospect of forty days' duty done, and the prospect of forty days' consequent pay to come. Sleepy it was not, but wide and wider awake over a progressing crisis. Hungry it had been until after a breakfast fetched to it from the Overland at seven, three hours ago. It had taken no intermission to wash its face, nor was there just now any apparatus for this, as the tin pitcher commonly used stood not in the basin in the corner, but on the floor by the Governor's chair; so the eyes of the Legislature, though earnest, were dilapidated. Last night the pressure of public business had seemed over, and no turning back the hands of the clock likely to be necessary. Besides Governor Ballard, Mr. Hewley, Secretary and Treasurer, was sitting up too, small, iron-gray, in feature and bearing every inch the capable, dignified official, but his necktie had slipped off during the night. The bearded Councillors had the best of it, seeming after their vigil less stale in the face than the member from Silver City, for instance, whose day-old black growth blurred his dingy chin, or the member from Big Camas, whose scantier red crop bristled on his cheeks in sparse wandering arrangements, like spikes on the barrel of a musical box. For comfort, most of the pistols were on the table with the Statutes of the United States. Secretary and Treasurer Hewley's lay on his strong-box immediately behind him. The Governor's was a light one, and always hung in the armhole of his waistcoat. The graveyard of Boisé City this year had twenty-seven tenants, two brought there by meningitis, and twenty-five by difference of opinion . . .

"I'll take a hun'red mo', Gove'nuh," said the member from Silver City, softly, his eyes on space. His name was Powhattan Wingo.

The Governor counted out the blue, white, and red chips to Wingo, penciled some figures on a thickly ciphered and cancelled paper that bore in print the words "Territory of Idaho, Council Chamber," and then filled up his glass from the tin pitcher, adding a little sugar.

"And I'll trouble you fo' the toddy," Wingo added, always softly, and his eyes always on space. "Raise you ten, suh." This was to the Treasurer. Only the two were playing at present. The Governor was kindly acting as bank; the others were looking on.

"And ten," said the Treasurer.

"And ten," said Wingo.

"And twenty," said the Treasurer.

"And fifty," said Wingo, gently bestowing his chips in the middle of the table.

The Treasurer called.

The member from Silver City showed down five high hearts, and a light rustle went over the Legislature when the Treasurer displayed three twos and a pair of threes, and gathered in his harvest. He had drawn two cards, Wingo one; and losing to the lowest hand that could have beaten you is under such circumstances truly hard luck. Moreover, it was almost the only sort of luck that had attended Wingo since about half after three that morning. Seven hours of cards just a little lower than your neighbor's is searching to the nerves.

"Gove'nuh, I'll take a hun'red mo'," said Wingo; and once again the Legislature rustled lightly, and a new deal began.

Treasurer Hewley's winnings flanked his right, a pillared fortress on the table, built chiefly of Wingo's misfortunes. Hewley had not counted them, and his architecture was for neatness and not ostentation; yet the Legislature watched him arrange his gains with sullen eyes. It would have pleased him now to lose; it would have more than pleased him to be able to go to bed quite a long time ago. But winners cannot easily go to bed . . .

"Five better," said Hewley, winner again four times in the last five.

"Ten," said Wingo.

"And twenty," said the Secretary and Treasurer.

"Call you."

"Three kings."

"They are good, suh. Gove'nuh, I'll take a hun'red mo'."

Upon this the wealthy and weary Treasurer made a try for liberty and bed. How would it do, he suggested, to have a round of jack-pots, say ten—or twenty, if the member from Silver City preferred—and then stop? It would do excellently, the member said, so softly that the Governor looked at him. But Wingo's large countenance remained inexpressive, his black eyes still impersonally fixed on space. He sat thus till his chips were counted to him, and then the eyes moved to watch the cards fall. The Governor hoped he might win now, under the jack-pot system. At noon he should have a disclosure to make; something that would need the most cheerful and contented feelings in Wingo and the Legislature to be received with any sort of calm. Wingo was behind the game to the tune of—the Governor gave up adding as he ran his eye over the figures of the bank's erased and tormented record, and he shook his head to himself. This was inadvertent.

"May I inquah who yo're shakin' yoh head at, suh?" said Wingo, wheeling upon the surprised Governor.

"Certainly," answered that official. "You." He was never surprised for very long. In 1867 it did not do to remain surprised in Idaho.

"And have I done anything which meets yoh disapprobation?" pursued the member from Silver City, enunciating with care.

"You have met my disapprobation."

Wingo's eye was on the Governor, and now his friends drew a little together, and as a unit sent a glance of suspicion at the lone bank.

"You will gratify me by being explicit, suh," said Wingo to the bank.

"Well, you've emptied the toddy."

"Ha-ha, Gove'nuh! I rose, suh, to yoh little fly. We'll awduh some mo'."

"Time enough when he comes for the breakfast things," said Governor Ballard, easily.

"As you say, suh. I'll open for five dollahs." Wingo turned back to his game. He was winning, and as his luck continued his voice ceased to be soft, and became a shade truculent. The Governor's ears caught this change, and he also noted the lurking triumph in the faces of Wingo's fellow-statesmen. Cheerfulness and content were scarcely reigning yet in the Council Chamber of Idaho as Ballard sat watching the friendly game. He was beginning to fear that he must leave the Treasurer alone and take some precautions outside. But he would have to be separated for some time from his ally, cut off from giving him any hints. Once the Treasurer looked at him, and he immediately winked reassuringly, but the Treasurer failed to respond. Hewley might be able to wink after everything was over, but he could not find it in his serious heart to do so now. He was wondering what would happen if this game should last till noon with the company in its present mood. Noon was the time fixed for paying the Legislative Assembly the compensation due for its services during this session; and the Governor and the Treasurer had put their heads together and arranged a surprise for the Legislative Assembly. They were not going to pay them . . .

Until lately the Western citizen has known one every-day experience that no dweller in our thirteen original colonies has had for two hundred years. In Massachusetts they have not seen it since 1641; in Virginia not since 1628. It is that of belonging to a community of which every adult was born somewhere else. When you come to think of this a little it is dislocating to many of your conventions. Let a citizen of Salem, for instance, try to imagine his chief-justice fresh from Louisiana, his mayor from Arkansas, his tax-collector from South Carolina, and himself recently arrived in a wagon from a thousand-mile drive. To be governor of such a community Ballard had travelled in a wagon from one quarter of the horizon; from another quarter Wingo had arrived on a mule. People reached Boisé in three ways: by rail to a little west of the Missouri, after which it was wagon, saddle, or walk for the remaining fifteen hundred miles; from California it was shorter; and from Portland, Oregon, only about five hundred miles, and some of these more agreeable, by water up the Columbia. Thus it happened that salt often sold for its weight in gold-dust. A miner in the Bannock Basin would meet a freight teamster coming in with the staples of life, having journeyed perhaps sixty consecutive days through the desert, and valuing his salt highly. The two accordingly bartered in scales, white powder against yellow, and both parties content. Some in Boisé to-day can remember these bargains. After all, they were struck but thirty years ago. Governor Ballard and Treasurer Hewley did not come from the same place, but they constituted a minority of two in Territorial politics because they hailed from north of Mason and Dixon's line. Powhattan Wingo and the rest of the Council were from Pike County, Missouri. They had been Secessionists, some of them Knights of the Golden Circle; they had belonged to Price's Left Wing, and they flocked together. They were seven—two lying unwell at the Overland, five now present in the State-House with the Governor and Treasurer. Wingo, Gascon Claiborne, Gratiot des Péres, Pete Cawthon, and F. Jackson Gilet were their names. Besides this Council of seven were thirteen members of the Idaho House of Representatives, mostly of the same political feather with the Council, and they too would be present at noon to receive their pay. How Ballard and Hewley came to be a minority of two is a simple matter. Only twenty-five months had gone since Appomattox Court-House. That surrender was presently followed by Johnson's to Sherman, at Durhams Station, and following this the various Confederate armies in Alabama, or across the Mississippi, or wherever they happened to be, had successively surrendered—but not Price's Left Wing. There was the wide open West under its nose, and no Grant or Sherman infesting that void. Why surrender? Wingos, Claibornes, and all, they melted away. Price's Left Wing sailed into the prairie and passed below the horizon. To know what it next did you must, like Ballard or Hewley, pass below the horizon yourself, clean out of sight of the dome at Washington to remote, untracked Idaho. There, besides wild red men in quantities, would you find not very tame white ones, gentlemen of the ripest Southwestern persuasion, and a Legislature to fit. And if, like Ballard or Hewley, you were a Union man, and the President of the United States had appointed you Governor or Secretary of such a place, your days would be full of awkwardness, though your difference in creed might not hinder you from playing draw-poker with the unreconstructed. These Missourians were whole-souled, ample-natured males in many ways, but born with a habit of hasty shooting. The Governor, on setting foot in Idaho, had begun to study pistolship, but acquired thus in middle life it could never be with him that spontaneous art which it was with Price's Left Wing. Not that the weapons now lying loose about the State-House were brought for use there. Everybody always went armed in Boisé, as the gravestones impliedly testified. Still, the thought of the bad quarter of an hour which it might come to at noon did cross Ballard's mind, raising the image of a column in the morrow's paper: "An unfortunate occurrence has ended relations between esteemed gentlemen hitherto the warmest personal friends . . . They will be laid to rest at 3 P.M. . . . As a last token of respect for our lamented Governor, the troops from Boisé Barracks . . . " The Governor trusted that if his friends at the post were to do him any service it would not be a funeral one.

ELLA HIGGINSON

Ella Higginson was one of the most popular turn-of-the-century Northwestern writers. But she was not universally loved in her own hometown; several Belling-ham, Washington, women threatened Higginson after reading too much of them-selves into an unflattering character in her 1904 novel, Mariella; of Out West. *According to a story in the* San Francisco Sunday Examiner Magazine, *"Hatred of the novelist runs . . . so high that she is not allowed to venture upon the streets at any time unprotected." Higginson was an editor for the Portland-based* West Shore *magazine and published three books of poetry. This story appeared in her first fiction collection,* From the Land of the Snow Pearls *(1897).*

THE BLOW-OUT AT JENKINS'S GROCERY

THE HANDS OF THE BIG, round clock in Mr. Jenkins's grocery store pointed to eleven. Mr. Jenkins was tying a string around a paper bag con-taining a dollar's worth of sugar. He held one end of the string between his teeth. His three clerks were going around the store with little stiff prances of deference to the customers they were serving. It was the night before Christmas. They were all so worn out that their attempts at smiles were only painful contortions.

Mr. Jenkins looked at the clock. Then his eyes went in a hurried glance of pity to a woman sitting on a high stool close to the window. Her feet were drawn up on the top rung, and her thin shoulders stooped over her chest. She had sunken cheeks and hollow eyes; her cheek-bones stood out sharply.

For two hours she had sat there almost motionless. Three times she had lifted her head and fixed a strained gaze upon Mr. Jenkins and asked, "D'yuh want to shet up?" Each time, receiving an answer in the negative, she had sunk back into the same attitude of brute-like waiting.

It was a wild night. The rain drove its long, slanting lances down the window-panes. The wind howled around corners, banged loose shutters, creaked swinging sign-boards to and fro, and vexed the telephone wires to shrill, continuous screaming. Fierce gusts swept in when the door was opened.

Christmas shoppers came and went. The woman saw nothing inside the store. Her eyes were set on the doors of a brightly lighted saloon across the street.

It was a small, new "boom" town on Puget Sound. There was a saloon on every corner, and a brass band in every saloon. The "establishment" opposite was having its "opening" that night. "At home" cards in square envelopes had been sent out to desirable patrons during the previous week. That day, during an hour's sunshine, a yellow chariot, drawn by six cream-colored horses with snow-white manes and tails, had gone slowly through the streets, bearing the members of the band clad in white and gold. It was followed by three open carriages, gay with the actresses who were to dance and sing that night on the stage in the rear of the saloon. All had yellow hair and were dressed in yellow with white silk sashes, and white ostrich plumes falling to their shoulders. It was a gorgeous procession, and it "drew."

The woman lived out in the Grand View addition. The addition consisted mainly of cabins built of "shakes" and charred stumps. The grand view was to come some ten or twenty years later on, when the forests surrounding the addition had taken their departure. It was a full mile from the store.

She had walked in with her husband through the rain and slush after putting six small children to bed. They were very poor. Her husband was shiftless. It was whispered of them by their neighbors that they couldn't get credit for "two bits" except at the saloons.

A relative had sent the woman ten dollars for a Christmas gift. She had gone wild with joy. Ten dollars! It was wealth. For once the children should have a real Christmas—a good dinner, toys, candy! Of all things, there should be a wax doll for the little girl who had cried for one every Christmas, and never even had one in her arms. Just for this one time they should be happy—like other children; and she should be happy in their happiness—like other mothers. What did it matter that she had only two calico dresses and one pair of shoes, half-soled at that, and capped across the toes?

Her husband had entered into her childish joy. He was kind and affectionate—when he was sober. That was why she had never had the heart to leave him. He was one of those men who are always needing, pleading for—and, alas! receiving—forgiveness; one of those men whom their women love passionately and cling to forever.

He promised her solemnly that he would not drink a drop that Christmas—so solemnly that she believed him. He had helped her to wash the dishes and put the children to bed. And he had kissed her.

Her face had been radiant when they came into Mr. Jenkins's store. That poor, gray face with its sunken cheeks and eyes! They bought a turkey—and with what anxious care she had selected it, testing its tenderness, balancing it on her bony hands, examining the scales with keen, narrowed eyes when it was weighed; and a quart of cranberries, a can of mince meat and a can of plum pudding, a head of celery, a pint of Olympia oysters, candy, nuts—and then the toys! She trembled with eagerness. Her husband stood watching her, smiling good-humoredly, his hands in his pockets. Mr. Jenkins indulged in some serious speculation as to where the money was coming from to pay for all this "blow-out." He set his lips together and resolved that the "blow-out" should not leave the store, under any amount of promises, until the cash paying for it was in his cash-drawer.

Suddenly the band began to play across the street. The man threw up his head like an old war-horse at the sound of a bugle note. A fire came into his eyes; into his face a flush of excitement. He walked down to the window and stood looking out, jingling some keys in his pocket. He breathed quickly.

After a few moments he went back to his wife. Mr. Jenkins had stepped away to speak to another customer.

"Say, Molly, old girl," he said affectionately, without looking at her, "yuh can spare me enough out o' that tenner to git a plug o' tobaccer for Christmas, can't yuh?"

"W'y—I guess so," said she slowly. The first cloud fell on her happy face.

"Well, jest let me have it, an' I'll run out an' be back before yuh're ready to pay for these here things. I'll only git two bits' worth."

She turned very pale.

"Can't yuh git it here, Mart?"

"No," he said in a whisper; "his'n ain't fit to chew. I'll be right back, Molly—honest."

She stood motionless, her eyes cast down, thinking. If she refused, he would be angry and remain away from home all the next day to pay her for the insult. If she gave it to him—well, she would have to take the chances. But oh, her hand shook as she drew the small gold piece from her shabby purse and reached it to him. His big, warm hand closed over it.

She looked up at him. Her eyes spoke the passionate prayer that her lips could not utter.

"Don't stay long, Mart," she whispered, not daring to say more.

"I won't, Molly," he whispered back. "I'll hurry up. Git anything yuh want."

She finished her poor shopping. Mr. Jenkins wrapped everything up neatly. Then he rubbed his hands together and looked at her, and said: "Well, there now, Mis' Dupen."

"I—jest lay 'em all together there on the counter," she said hesitatingly. "I'll have to wait till Mart comes back before I can pay yuh."

"I see him go into the s'loon over there," piped out the errand boy shrilly.

At the end of half an hour she climbed upon the high stool and fixed her eyes upon the saloon opposite and sat there.

She saw nothing but the glare of those windows and the light streaming out when the doors opened. She heard nothing but the torturing blare of the music. After awhile something commenced beating painfully in her throat and temples. Her limbs grew stiff—she was scarcely conscious that they ached. Once she shuddered strongly, as dogs do when they lie in the cold, waiting.

At twelve o'clock Mr. Jenkins touched her kindly on the arm. She looked up with a start. Her face was gray and old; her eyes were almost wild in their strained despair.

"I guess I'll have to shet up now, Mis' Dupen," he said apologetically. "I'm sorry—"

She got down from the stool at once. "I can't take them things," she said, almost whispering. "I hate to of put yuh to all that trouble of doin' 'em up. I thought—but I can't take 'em. I hope yuh won't mind—very much." Her bony fingers twisted together under her thin shawl.

"Oh, that's all right," said Mr. Jenkins in an embarrassed way. She moved stiffly to the door. He put out the lights and followed her. He felt mean, somehow. For one second he hesitated, then he locked the door, and gave it a shake to make sure that it was all right.

"Well," he said, "good night. I wish you a mer—"

"Good night," said the woman. She was turning away when the doors of the saloon opened for two or three men to enter. The music, which had ceased for a few minutes, struck up another air—a familiar air.

She burst suddenly into wild and terrible laughter. "Oh, my Lord," she cried out, "they're a-playin' 'Home, Sweet Home!' *In there!* Oh, my Lord! *Wouldn't that kill yuh!*"

ANNE SHANNON MONROE

Anne Shannon Monroe grew up in Yakima and Tacoma but left for Chicago as a young woman. There she sold her first novel, Eugene Norton *(1900), and wrote columns and features for the* Daily News *and the* Tribune. *In 1913 she returned to the Northwest—as a farmer. She "proved up" on a three-hundred-acre homestead in Harney County, Oregon, and used the experience to write* Happy Valley, *her 1916 novel about frontier life in Oregon's Inland Empire.*

from HAPPY VALLEY

OUR OLD MAN SIZED UP our first settlers well enough for all practical purposes: "They ain't very pretty and they got odd ways about 'em, but they'll do."

They certainly weren't pretty. An old man drove the first outfit that drew up before the Clark tent. He was no older, perhaps, than our old man, but oh, so sad. His eyes were big and mournful and mostly on the outside of his face . . . He wanted to know, before getting down, how much we charged for meals. Our old man took it as a huge joke, and slapped his stout thighs and laughed till I thought he would explode, while the settler solemnly chewed on, working his jaw and his nose.

On the seat beside him sat a man who had not lifted his head from a book he was reading. He seemed bent on finishing the chapter. He was clean shaven, small, dark, slick, and neat in spite of the dust. I could imagine him near the entrance of the Emporium at home, saying, "This way, ladies." At last he lifted his head, and apparently discovered for the first time that the team had stopped, that a tent was before him, and that a group of human beings had some way been belched up from the earth to a spot within the focus of his eyes. He took us in without surprise or question, carefully marked the place in his book, laid the book beside him on the wagon seat, and asked, "Have we, then, arrived?"

"Yes; conductor a little slow about callin' the station," our old man answered, chuckling. "Alight, friends; get down and come right in; mother'll give you some hot coffee and fresh bread, and I guess there's some ham and potatoes that won't go bad, eh, mother? Get down, friends; get down."

The old driver chewed on. "First, I want to know what it's going to cost me. Food for self and one-half the team. My friend here pays for himself and the other half."

"Not a copper, friend; not a copper. Get down, get down; you must be stiff with settin'."

The old man climbed out with a spryness of which I would not have believed him capable. His companion took another look at his book, then got down reluctantly.

"My name's Sneed; Sol Sneed. And this is Mr. Howard, who I fell in with at Ossing. We joined forces and shared expenses. I'm from up Vermont way, and Howard's from Boston. We're here to take up your offer to be located, free; you understand, free! I'd like it in writing."

Again our old man went off into a spasm of laughter, while Mrs. Clark's head went up stiffly, and Susie looked to me with a twinkle in her eyes.

"Come, Susie," said her mother, starting down the steps. "We'll get dinner goin'."

I offered to peel the potatoes, but Susie shook her head. "You'd peel 'em too thick; we have to almost scrape 'em; my goodness, but I'll be glad when the new ones come and we can have enough potatoes at any rate." She ran down the steps.

I turned to the man from Boston, who had again picked up his book and was deep into it. I think he had not cast a solitary glance at the country, the tent—not even at Susie. "Good yarn?"

He lifted his small, steady, black eyes, and regarded me as the dirt under his feet; no, he had not looked at the dirt under his feet. I must find another figure. Never mind; he looked at me, and after a long stare vouchsafed the information: "It is *Bledstoe on Dry Farming*. I am told that this section has thirteen inches of rainfall; Bledstoe says thirteen inches is enough for dry farming; I am told that this is mostly sagebrush land with

very little greasewood; Bledstoe says that is the proper land for dry farming; I am told small grains will do well here; according to Bledstoe—."

"Why, yes; they'll do fine; we have enough samples coming on to
demonstrate that. Come on out and see our little experimental station.
The rabbits have taken a good deal of it, but you can see that everything
is coming on thriftily, even the vegetables."

He followed me rather regretfully, his finger still keeping his place in
Bledstoe. He gazed at the garden ruefully, and the fence bothered him.

"Bledstoe says nothing about fencing of this peculiar nature."

He seemed to want to dispute the fence, and yet it was there. I turned
away to hide a smile, and saw Susie watching us from the back of the
tent. Throwing her wicked hands to her wicked mouth, she ran on around
the tent, out of sight, to hide her amusement. I sobered as best I could and
gave my attention to our settler.

"Bledstoe possibly has left out many of the facts of pioneering," I
suggested.

"Nevertheless, I shall be governed by Bledstoe!" he defied me. "I think
I have read everything written on dry farming. You possibly do not know
the advantages of Boston's public library."

"Possibly not," I murmured, and followed him, for he had turned away
from our fence and headed back toward the tent . . .

The Book-farmer, for such Susie called him—and such he remained—
ate absent mindedly, after having asked politely for a napkin. Once, some
time afterward, he said to me, "It's peculiar, isn't it, what a fondness all
these people have for cream gravy. I find it—I might also say—indigenous
to the country. Everywhere, they are eating this peculiar thickened substance known as cream gravy. I would like to look it up—that's the draw-
back of being so far from a library; I would like to look up the foods of
pioneer peoples, and see if there is anything about pioneering that makes
the stomach crave this odd dish."

"It's just possible," I suggested, "that the fact of one cow to supply
thirteen people, including six children, to say nothing of guests, has
some bearing on the butter supply, and that cream gravy thus becomes a
substitute not so much chosen as thrust on the pioneer."

He looked at me doubtingly, and said, "Possibly," but without a flicker
of light in his face.

WAGE WORKERS, WOBBLIES, AND BINDLE STIFFS

1917–1919

"SAY IKE WHAT DO YOU THINK we oughta do?" asks Mac, a working-man down on his luck, in *The 42nd Parallel,* the first book in John Dos Passos's *U.S.A.* trilogy about America in the early twentieth century. "I think we oughta go down on the boat to Seattle Wash like a coupla dude passengers. I wanta settle down an get a printin job, there's good money in that. I'm goin to study to beat hell this winter. What do you think Ike? I want to get out of this limejuicy hole an get back to God's country."

Mac's plan to light out for Seattle matched the schemes of thousands of other young working stiffs who came to the Pacific Northwest looking for employment in the decades leading up to the end of the First World War. The Northwest was the workingman's land of opportunity, but when that opportunity turned sour, it sparked fights between those earning the wages and those paying them out.

In 1880, Portland's population stood at a respectable 17,500; Seattle was a relative hamlet with only 3,500 citizens. Over the next thirty years, the region's cities exploded with growth, none more so than Seattle, which by 1910 counted more than 250,000 residents. Legions of young single men rode the rails west looking for wage work. The jobs were plentiful but rarely steady. A man might work one season as a harvest hand in Eastern Washington and another as a logger or sawmill worker on the wet side of the state, or he might try his luck in the Idaho mines. Mobile laborers were often called "bindle stiffs" for the blanket rolls, or bindles, they carried on their backs. Many were lured to the Northwest by the same sort of promotions that had brought the homesteaders of a previous generation. Railroad pamphlets and immigration bureaus promised a land of class harmony, a place from which the strike and lockout had been banished forever.

Those promises, like most promotional come-ons, weren't worth the paper they were printed on. The Pacific Northwest's first prominent union, the Knights of Labor, is remembered today for leading the infamous anti-Chinese crusades of 1885 in Tacoma and Seattle. The Idaho mining conflicts of 1892 and 1899 resulted in violence that claimed eight lives. The Northwest's reputation for labor radicalism was made between the turn of the century and the end of World War I, a time that included the Wobbly wars and the Seattle General Strike.

Although the Industrial Workers of the World was never the most powerful or important union in the Northwest, it is the focus of much of the era's best writing. The romance that surrounds the IWW grew out of its flair for dramatic action and creative propaganda, which gave it a louder voice than its following truly warranted. Better wages and working conditions were small potatoes for the IWW; the Wobblies aimed at nothing less than a workers' revolution. The union's radical worldview was written into the preamble to its constitution—"The working class and the employing class have nothing in common"—and it was most popular among workers who experienced the greatest disparity between the wageworker's Western idealism and the harsh reality of physical labor in the Northwest. Loggers, who lived for months at a stretch in cold, wet, and thoroughly miserable logging camps, were prime recruiting targets. So were the harvest hands, miners, and construction workers who floated from job to job.

One of the union's favorite tactics was the free-speech fight, in which a Wob would stump noisily on a busy street-corner until a local constable arrested him. Once he was cuffed, the call went out and IWW sympathizers poured into town, each taking his turn on the soapbox and in the pokey until the jail was too crowded to handle them all.

The Wobblies may not have had the brightest tacticians (free-speech fights tended to rile the local citizenry, which was inclined to be short on temper and long on brick and buckshot), but they knew how to broadcast their message. Wobbly songbooks and newspapers floated around the logging camps or wherever workers gathered; IWW political cartoons and graphics were among the best of the era; and sympathetic writers such as Walker Smith produced volumes of books, pamphlets, and satirical plays aimed at winning the hearts and minds of the working class.

WALTER V. WOEHLKE

In 1916 the bloodiest episode of labor violence in Northwest history broke out in Everett, Washington. A shingle-weavers' strike that began in May was bolstered by the Seattle IWW, which opened an Everett office and began a free-speech campaign in support of the strikers. The conflict exploded on November 5, when more than two hundred Seattle Wobblies who had traveled by boat to stage a demonstration were met at the Everett dock by the sheriff and a crowd of armed citizens. Five Wobblies and two deputies were shot dead, fifty were wounded, and five others are believed to have jumped ship and drowned. In this excerpt from his February 1917 Sunset *magazine article "The I.W.W. and the Golden Rule: Why Everett Used Club and Gun on the Red Apostles of Direct Action," Walter V. Woehlke describes the working conditions that started it all.*

from THE I.W.W. AND THE GOLDEN RULE

SHINGLE-WEAVING IS NOT A TRADE; it is a battle. For ten hours a day the sawyer faces two teethed steel disks whirling around two hundred times a minute. To the one on his left he feeds heavy blocks of cedar, reaching over with his left hand to remove the rough shingles it rips off. He does not, cannot stop to see what his left hand is doing. His eyes are too busy examining the shingles for knot holes to be cut out by the second saw whirling in front of him.

The saw on his left sets the pace. If the singing blade rips fifty rough shingles off the block every minute, the sawyer must reach over to its teeth fifty times in sixty seconds; if the automatic carriage feeds the odorous wood sixty times into the hungry teeth, sixty times he must reach over, turn the shingle, trim its edge on the gleaming saw in front of him, cut out the narrow strip containing the knot hole with two quick movements of his right hand and toss the completed board down the chute to the packers, meanwhile keeping eyes and ears open for the sound that asks him to feed a new block into the untiring teeth. Hour after hour the shingle weaver's hands and arms, plain unarmored flesh and blood, are staked against the screeching steel that cares not what it severs. Hour after hour the steel sings its crescendo note as it bites into the wood, the sawdust cloud thickens, the wet sponge under the sawyer's nose fills with fine particles. If "cedar asthma," the shingle weaver's occupational disease, does not get him, the steel will. Sooner or later he reaches over a little too far, the whirling blade tosses drops of deep red into the air and a finger, a hand or part of an arm comes sliding down the slick chute.

That is the case of the Everett shingle weaver. "I want all I can get," he says, "because I earn every penny I can squeeze out of the mill owners."

WALKER C. SMITH

It is a tribute to the literary talent of Walker C. Smith that his 1918 book, The Everett Massacre, *continues to be quoted as the most comprehensive account of that incident despite the pro-IWW bias of its author. Smith was one of the Wobblies' most indefatigable leaders and propagandists on the West Coast, taking on roles ranging from office boy to stump speaker to head of the Northwest organization. In addition to the Everett history he turned out numerous pamphlets, including* Sabotage: Its History, Philosophy, and Function *(1913) and* Was It Murder? The Truth About Centralia *(1922), and wrote skits satirizing the trials of IWW members in Everett and Centralia. Smith's documents were often meant to raise money as well as emotions; the Everett book includes a call for donations to offset the legal fees of the men accused (and acquitted) of murder during the* Verona *incident.*

from THE EVERETT MASSACRE

AS THE *VERONA* CLEAVED the placid, sunlit waters of the Bay and swung up to the City Dock at Everett, shortly before two o'clock, the men were merrily singing the English Transport Workers' strike song,

> *HOLD THE FORT!*
> We meet today in Freedom's cause
> And raise our voices high;
> We'll join our hands in union strong,
> To battle or to die.

(chorus)
Hold the fort for we are coming,
Union men be strong.
Side by side we battle onward,
Victory will come!

Look, my comrades, see the union,
Banners waving high.
Reinforcements now appearing,
Victory is nigh . . .

From a hillside overlooking the scene thousands upon thousands of Everett citizens sent forth cheer after cheer as a hearty welcome to the "invading army." High up on the flag-pole of the *Verona* clambered Hugo Gerlot, a youthful free speech enthusiast, to wave a greeting to the throng that lined the shore. Passenger Oscar Carlson and his friend Ernest Nordstrom, from their position on the very bow of the boat, caught the spirit of the party and endeavored to join in the song that resounded louder and clearer as many of the men left the cabins to go out upon the deck . . .

Waiting until Captain Ramwell's wharfinger, William Kenneth, had made fast the bowline to prevent the boat from backing out, Sheriff Donald McRae gave his belt holster a hitch to bring his gun directly across his middle and then lurched forward to the face of the dock. Holding up his left hand to check the singing, he yelled to the men on board:

"Who is your leader?"

Immediate and unmistakable was the answer from practically every member of the Industrial Workers of the World:

"We are all leaders!"

Angrily jerking his gun from his holster and flourishing it in a threatening manner, McRae cried:

"You can't land here!"

"The hell we can't!" came the reply as the men stepped toward the partly thrown-off gang plank.

A shot rang out from the immediate vicinity of deputy W. A. Bridges, then another, closely followed by a volley that sent them staggering backward. Many fell to the deck. Evidently the waving of McRae's revolver was the prearranged signal for the carnage to commence. The long months of lumber trust lawlessness had culminated in cowardly, deliberate, premeditated and foul murder!

Young Gerlot crumpled up and slid part way down the flag pole, then suddenly threw out both arms and crashed lifeless to the deck, his bullet-torn and bleeding body acting as a shield for several who had thrown themselves prostrate. Passenger Oscar Carlson threw himself flat upon the forward deck and while in that position seven bullets found their way into his quivering flesh, life clinging to the shattered form by a strange vagary of fate. With a severe bullet wound in his abdomen, Ed Roth swayed back and forth for a moment and then toppled forward on his face.

When a bullet whistled past the head of Captain Chauncey Wiman, and another tore a spoke as thick as a man's wrist from the pilot wheel beneath his hand, he deserted his post to barricade himself behind the safe with a mattress, remaining in that position until the close of the hostilities.

At the first shot and during the first volley the unarmed men wildly sought cover from the deadly leaden hail. Those who had not dropped to the deck, wounded or seeking shelter, surged to the starboard side of the boat, causing it to list to an alarming degree, the fastened bowline alone preventing it from capsizing. Several men lost their footing on the blood-slimed decks and were pitched headlong overboard. There, struggling frantically in the water—by no possible chance combatants—a storm of rifle bullets churning little whirlpools around their heads, one by one they were made the victims of lumber trust greed by the Hessianized deputies stationed at the shore end of the City Dock and upon the dock to the south. The bay was reddened with their blood. Of all who went overboard, James Hadley alone regained the deck, the rest disappearing beneath the silent waters to be dragged by the undertow out to an unknown and nameless ocean grave.

Young Joe Ghilezano seized the rail preparatory to jumping overboard, but seeing two men shot dead while they were in the water he lay down on the deck instead. While there a bullet pierced his hip, another went thru his back close to the spine, and a third completely tore off his left knee cap. Harry Parker slipped over the starboard side in order to gain the lower deck, and a rifle bullet from the vicinity of the tug Goldfinch, along the Everett Improvement Company Dock, ranged thru his back from left to right, just as his friend, Walter Mulholland, also wounded, pulled him in thru a hole torn in the canvas wind shield. An abdominal wound laid Felix Baran low. The thud of bullets as they struck the prostrate men added to the ghastly sound caused by the firing of rifles and revolvers, the curses of the deputies and the moans of the wounded men.

Following the first volley the deputies who had been out in the open scuttled into the warehouses on either side. Thru their scattering ranks the scabs on the tug Edison poured their rifle fire toward the men on the *Verona*. Lieutenant C. O. Curtis pitched forward and fell dead upon the dock—the victim of a rifle bullet. One of the fleeing deputies paused behind the corner of the waiting room just long enough to flinchingly reach out his hand and, keeping his head under cover, emptied his revolver without taking aim. Deputy Sheriff Jefferson Beard fell mortally wounded as he turned to run, and was dragged into the warehouse by some of the less panic stricken murderers. Sheriff McRae, with a couple of slight wounds in his left leg and heel, was forced to his knees by the impact of bullets against the steel jacket which he wore, remaining in a supplicating attitude for a few seconds while he sobbed out in a quavering tone, "O-o-oh! I'm hit! I–I'm hit!! I–I–I'm hit!!!" . . .

Inside the waiting room and the warehouses the drink-crazed deputies ran amuck, shooting wildly in all directions, often with some of their own number directly in the line of fire—bullet holes in the floor and a pierced clock case high up on the waiting room wall giving mute evidence of their insane recklessness. One deputy fled from the dock in terror, explaining to all who would listen that a bullet hole in his ear was from the shot of one of his associates on the dock.

"They've gone crazy in there!" he cried excitedly. "They're shootin' every which way! They shot me in the ear!"

Thru the loopholes already provided, and even thru the sides of the warehouses they blazed away in the general direction of the boat, using revolvers and high powered rifles with steel and copper-jacketed missiles. Dum-dums sang their deadly way to the *Verona* and tore gaping wounds in the breasts of mere boys—an added reward by the industrial lords for their first season of hard labor in the scorching harvest fields. John Looney was felled by a rifle bullet and even as he fell shuddering to the deck another leaden missile shattered the woodwork and impaled one of his eyeballs upon a spear of wood, gouging it from the socket.

At the foot of the dock, protected by the Klatawa slip, (Indian name for runaway) C. R. Schweitzer, owner of a scab plumbing establishment, fired time after time with a magazine shotgun, the buckshot scattering at the long range and raking the forward deck with deadly effect. The pilot house was riddled and the woodwork filled with hundreds of the little leaden messengers that carried a story of "mutual interest of Capital and Labor." Deputy Russell and about ten others assisted in the dastardly work at that point, pouring shot after shot into the convulsive struggling heaps of wounded men piled four and five deep on the deck. One boy in a brown mackinaw suddenly rose upright from a tangled mass of humanity, the blood gushing from his wounds, and with an agonized cry of "My God! I can't stand this any longer!" leaped high in the air over the side of the boat, sinking from sight forever, his watery resting place marked only by a few scarlet ripples.

ZANE GREY

Although best known for his Westerns set in Arizona, New Mexico, and Texas, Zane Grey wrote a handful of novels about the Pacific Northwest, including The Border Legion, Thunder Mountain, Rogue River Feud, *and* Horse Heaven Hill. *In 1919, Grey wove his strong anti-German sentiments into a novel of eastern Washington,* The Desert of Wheat. *The villains of the piece are IWW saboteurs, as Wobbly conspirators set fire to wheat fields to undermine the food supply of American forces fighting in France. Grey's Western heroes take care of the no-goods by lynching their leader on a railroad bridge and shipping the rest of the gang out of town in boxcars.*

from THE DESERT OF WHEAT

LATE IN JUNE THE VAST northwestern desert of wheat began to take on a tinge of gold, lending an austere beauty to that endless, rolling, smooth world of treeless hills, where miles of fallow ground and miles of waving grain sloped up to the far-separated homes of the heroic men who had conquered over sage and sand.

These simple homes of farmers seemed lost on an immensity of soft gray and golden billows of land, insignificant dots here and there on distant hills, so far apart that nature only seemed accountable for those broad squares of alternate gold and brown, extending on and on to the waving horizon-line. A lonely, hard, heroic country, where flowers and fruit were not, nor birds and brooks, nor green pastures. Whirling strings of dust looped up over fallow ground, the short, dry wheat lay back from the wind, the haze in the distance was drab and smoky, heavy with substance.

A thousand hills lay bare to the sky, and half of every hill was wheat and half was fallow ground; and all of them, with the shallow valleys between, seemed big and strange and isolated. The beauty of them was austere, as if the hand of man had been held back from making green his home site . . .

Here was grown the most bounteous, the richest and finest wheat in all the world. Strange and unfathomable that so much of the bread of man, the staff of life, the hope of civilization in this tragic year 1917, should come from a vast, treeless, waterless, dreary desert!

This wonderful place was an immense valley of considerable altitude called the Columbia Basin, surrounded by the Cascade Mountains on the west, the Coeur d'Alene and the Bitter Root Mountains on the east, the Okanogan range to the north, and the Blue Mountains to the south . . . The Columbia River, making a prodigious and meandering curve, bordered on three sides what was known as the Bend country. South of this vast area, across the range, began the fertile, many-watered region that extended on down into verdant Oregon. Among the desert hills of this Bend country, near the center of the Basin, where the best wheat was raised, lay widely separated little towns, the names of which gave evidence of the mixed population. It was, of course, an exceedingly prosperous country, a fact manifest in the substantial little towns, if not in the crude and unpretentious homes of the farmers.

Upon a morning in early July, exactly three months after the United States had declared war upon Germany, a sturdy young farmer strode with darkly troubled face from the presence of his father. At the end of a stormy scene he had promised his father that he would abandon his desire to enlist in the army.

Kurt Dorn walked away from the gray old clapboard house, out to the fence, where he leaned on the gate. He could see for miles in every direction, and to the southward, away on a long yellow slope, rose a stream of dust from a motor-car.

"Must be Anderson—coming to dun father," muttered young Dorn.

This was the day, he remembered, when the wealthy rancher of Ruxton was to look over old Chris Dorn's wheat-fields. Dorn owed thirty-thousand dollars and the interest for years, mostly to Anderson. Kurt hated the debt and resented the visit, but he could not help acknowledging that the rancher had been lenient and kind. Long since Kurt had sorrowfully realized that his father was illiterate, hard, grasping, and growing worse with the burden of years.

"If we had rain now—or soon—that section of Bluestem would square father," soliloquized young Dorn, as with keen eyes he surveyed a vast field of wheat, short, smooth, yellowing in the sun. But the cloudless sky, the haze of heat rather betokened a continued drought . . .

"You're in for a dry spell?" inquired Anderson, with interest that was keen, and kindly as well.

"Father says so. And I fear it, too—for he never makes a mistake in weather or crops."

"A hot, dry spell! . . . This summer? . . . Hum! . . . Boy, do you know that wheat is the most important thing in the world to-day?"

"You mean on account of the war," replied Kurt. "Yes, I know. But father doesn't see that. All he sees is—if we have rain we'll have bumper crops. That big field there would be a record—at war prices . . . And he wouldn't be ruined!"

"Ruined . . . Oh, he means I'd close on him . . . Hum! . . . Say, what do you see in a big wheat yield—if it rains?"

"Mr. Anderson, I'd like to see our debt paid, but I'm thinking mostly of wheat for starving peoples. I—I've studied this wheat question. It's the biggest question in this war" . . .

"Are you an—American?" queried Anderson, slowly, as if treading on dangerous ground.

"I am," snapped Kurt. "My mother was American. She's dead. Father is German. He's old. He's rabid since the President declared war. He'll never change."

"That's hell. What're you going to do if your country calls you?"

"Go!" replied Kurt, with flashing eyes. "I wanted to enlist. Father and I quarreled over that until I had to give in. He's hard—he's impossible . . . I'll wait for the draft and hope I'm called."

"Boy, it's that spirit Germany's roused, an' the best I can say is, God help her! . . . Have you a brother?"

"No. I'm all father has."

"Well, it makes a tough place for him, an' you, too. Humor him. He's old. An' when you're called—go an' fight. You'll come back."

"If I only knew that—it wouldn't be so hard."

"Hard? It sure is hard. But it'll be the makin' of a great country. It'll weed out the riffraff . . . See here, Kurt, I'm goin' to give you a hunch. Have you had any dealin's with the I.W.W.?"

"Yes, last harvest we had trouble, but nothing serious. When I was in Spokane last month I heard a good deal. Strangers have approached us here, too—mostly aliens. I have no use for them, but they always get father's ear. And now! . . . To tell the truth, I'm worried."

"Boy, you need to be," replied Anderson, earnestly. "We're all worried. I'm goin' to let you read over the laws of that I.W.W. organization. You're to keep mum now, mind you. I belong to the Chamber of Commerce in Spokane. Somebody got hold of these by-laws of this so-called labor union. We've had copies made, an' every honest farmer in the Northwest is goin' to read them. But carryin' one around is dangerous, I reckon, these days. Here."

Anderson hesitated a moment, peered cautiously around, and then, slipping folded sheets of paper from his inside coat pocket, he evidently made ready to hand them to Kurt.

"Lenore, where's the driver?" he asked.

"He's under the car," replied the girl.

Kurt thrilled at the sound of her voice. It was something to have been haunted by a girl's face for a year and then suddenly to hear her voice.

"He's new to me—that driver—an' I ain't trustin' any new men these days," went on Anderson. "Here now, Dorn. Read that. An' if you don't get red-headed—"

Without finishing his last muttered remark, he opened the sheets of manuscript and spread them out to the young man.

Curiously, and with a little rush of excitement, Kurt began to read. The very first rule of the I.W.W. aimed to abolish capital. Kurt read on with slowly growing amaze, consternation, and anger. When he had finished, his look, without speech, was a question Anderson hastened to answer.

"It's straight goods," he declared. "Them's the sure-enough rules of that gang. We made certain before we acted. Now how do they strike you?"

"Why, that's no labor union!" replied Kurt, hotly. "They're outlaws, thieves, blackmailers, pirates. I—I don't know what!"

"Dorn, we're up against a bad outfit an' the Northwest will see hell this summer. There's trouble in Montana and Idaho. Strangers are driftin' into Washington from all over. We must organize to meet them—to prevent them gettin' a hold out here. It's a labor union, mostly aliens, with dishonest an' unscrupulous leaders, some of them Americans. They aim to take advantage of the war situation. In the newspapers they rave about shorter hours, more pay, acknowledgment of the union. But any fool would see, if he read them laws I showed you, that this I.W.W. is not straight."

"Mr. Anderson, what steps have you taken down in your country?" queried Kurt.

"So far all I've done was to hire my hands for a year, give them high wages, an' caution them when strangers come round to feed them an' be civil an' send them on."

"But we can't do that up here in the Bend," said Dorn, seriously. "We need, say, a hundred thousand men in harvest-time, and not ten thousand all the rest of the year."

"Sure you can't. But you'll have to organize somethin'. Up here in this desert you could have a heap of trouble if that outfit got here strong enough. You'd better tell every farmer you can trust about this I.W.W."

Thirty masked men sat around a long harvest mess-table. Two lanterns furnished light enough to show a bare barnlike structure, the rough-garbed plotters, the grim set of hard lips below the half-masks, and big hands spread out, ready to draw from the hat that was passing.

The talk was low and serious. No names were spoken. A heavy man, at the head of the table, said: "We thirty, picked men, represent the country. Let each member here write on his slip of paper his choice of punishment for the I.W.W.'s—death or deportation . . . "

The members of the band bent their masked faces and wrote in a dead silence. A noiseless wind blew through the place. The lanterns flickered;

huge shadows moved on the walls. When the papers had been passed back to the leader he read them.

"Deportation," he announced. "So much for the I.W.W. men . . . Now for the leader . . . But before we vote on what to do with Glidden let me read an extract from one of his speeches. This is authentic. It has been furnished by the detective lately active in our interest. Also it has been published. I read it because I want to bring home to you all an issue that goes beyond our own personal fortunes here."

Leaning toward the flickering flare of the lantern, the leader read from a slip of paper: "If the militia are sent out here to hinder the I.W.W. we will make it so damned hot for the government that no troops will be able to go to France . . . I don't give a damn what this country is fighting for . . . I am fighting for the rights of labor . . . American soldiers are Uncle Sam's scabs in disguise."

The deep, impressive voice ended. The leader's huge fist descended upon the table with a crash. He gazed up and down the rows of sinister masked figures. "Have you anything to say?"

"Pass the slips," said another.

And then a man, evidently on in years, for his hair was gray and he looked bent, got up. "Neighbors," he began, "I lived here in the early days. For the last few years I've been apologizing for my home town. I don't want to apologize for it any longer."

He sat down. And a current seemed to wave from him around that dark square of figures. The leader cleared his throat as if he had much to say, but he did not speak. Instead he passed the hat. Each man drew forth a slip of paper and wrote upon it. The action was not slow. Presently the hat returned round the table to the leader. He spilled its contents, and with steady hand picked up the first slip of paper.

"Death!" he read, sonorously, and laid it down to pick up another. Again he spoke that grim word. The third brought forth the same, and likewise the next, and all, until the verdict had been called out thirty times.

"At daylight we'll meet," boomed out that heavy voice. "Instruct Glidden's guards to make a show of resistance . . . We'll hang Glidden to the railroad bridge. Then each of you get your gangs together. Round up all the I.W.W.'s. Drive them to the railroad yard. There we'll put them aboard a railroad train of empty cars. And that train will pass under the bridge where Glidden will be hanging . . . We'll escort them out of the country."

ANNA LOUISE STRONG

Anna Louise Strong often wrote under the pen name Anise, but she was hardly anonymous in Seattle. In 1918 she covered the Everett massacre trial for the New York Evening Post; *the next year her stirring front-page editorial in the* Seattle Union Record *provided a manifesto for the city's famous General Strike and became one of the best-known documents of the American labor movement. The piece reprinted here is the product of a jailhouse interview with Britt Smith, one of the Wobblies tried for killing four World War I veterans in the Centralia Armistice Day massacre of 1919. Smith was ultimately convicted of second-degree murder. Although written in the free-verse style of reportage that Strong often employed in her* Union Record *columns, the poem did not appear in the Seattle paper. It was discovered in an IWW archive by historian Joyce Kornbluh and published in her collection* Rebel Voices: An IWW Anthology. *The original place of publication is unknown.*

BRITT SMITH

The weight of the world
Seemed resting
On his shoulders,
He was thirty-eight
And had followed the woods
For twenty years.
He knew to the full
The lumber camps of Washington
And he had no more
ILLUSIONS
He sawed the timbers
To build the great flume
At Electron,
Where the mountain waters
Come pouring down
To give, light and power
In Tacoma,
And to carry

The LUXURIOUS Olympian
Over the Cascades,
Softly and smoothly,
With passengers warm
And COMFORTABLE.
But he and his fellows
Had slept in a SWAMP
On cedar PLANKS,
And had no place
To WASH
After their day's labor.
He said: "I have slept
WEEKS at a time
In WET CLOTHES,
Working
All day in the rain,
Without any place,
To DRY OUT.

I have washed my clothes
By tying them
To a stake in the river,
Letting the current
Beat them partly clean.
It was often the only place
We had for washing."
It was HE
The LYNCHERS sought
That night of terror
When the lights went out
And they broke into the jail
And dragged forth Everest
To torture
And mutilation

And hanging,
Crying: "We've got Britt
Smith!"
For he was secretary
Of the I.W.W.s
And lived in a little room
At the back of the hall
Which he tried to defend
In the RAID,—
It was his only HOME
He had spent his strength
And used his youth
Cutting LUMBER
For the homes of others!

A HOMEGROWN
LITERATURE
1920–1945

THE MODERN ERA in Northwest letters began with a startling *cri de coeur.* "Something is wrong with Northwestern literature," wrote H. L. Davis and James Stevens in their scathing 1927 polemic, *Status Rerum: A Manifesto upon the Present Condition of Northwestern Literature, Containing Several Near-Libelous Utterances, upon Persons in the Public Eye.* The region's authors, they charged, had produced "a vast quantity of bilge, so vast, indeed, that the few books which are entitled to respect are totally lost in the general and seemingly interminable avalanche of tripe." In their eight-page pamphlet, of which no more than two hundred were privately printed, Davis and Stevens blasted the fashionable writers of the day as inept and contemptible mental weaklings. They named names in their determined effort to alienate themselves from the Northwest's cozy society of literary backscratchers.

The rage of the angry young men was wholly warranted. In 1927, Frederick Homer Balch's sappy *The Bridge of the Gods* remained the most popular work on the Northwest (in its twenty-seventh printing!), and the region was awash in literary Balchism. Sentimental novels were peopled with heroic pioneers, noble savages, and tragic half-breeds. Poetry tended toward light verse full of vapid phrasing and empty metaphor. Students in Professor Glenn Hughes's University of Washington poetry classes turned out, Stevens and Davis wrote, "a banquet of breath-tablets, persistently and impotently violet." (A trip to the stacks of the UW library, where one of Hughes's collections has gone unmolested for the past quarter-century, confirms their judgment.)

Stevens singled out the Northwest's most notorious poetry mill, Colonel E. Hofer's *Lariat,* based in Salem, for special condemnation in a *Rerum*-style essay that appeared in *The American Mercury* in 1929. The Colonel insisted on clean poetry in the *Lariat*—no jazz, no sex, no psychology. Titles like "Old Horse": *Are you glad to see me, old horse? / If you answer with a rub of your nose, / I'll know you mean, 'of course.'* " Nothing that couldn't be read aloud in mixed company or understood by a class of kindergarteners. Above all, none of that modern free-verse bunk.

"It lies with us, and with the young and yet unformed spirits, to cleanse the Augean stables which are poisoning the stream of Northwestern literature at the source," concluded Stevens and Davis. Over the next twenty years, they and their contemporaries—writers who came of age in a fully settled Northwest—would do just that, creating work that not only captured the region's folklore, vernacular, humor, dirt, sweat, pride, and shame, but broke the bounds of "regional" literature to create lasting contributions to American letters. James Stevens's *Paul Bunyan* (1925) and Stewart Holbrook's *Holy Old Mackinaw* (1938) recorded the culture and lore of the American lumberjack, who chopped his way west from Maine to the Great Lakes and made his last stand in the Northwest's old-growth timber. H. L. Davis's first novel, *Honey in the Horn* (1935), is an American classic, one of only two novels (the other being Ken Kesey's *Sometimes a Great Notion*) that attempt to swallow the Northwest whole. Books like Vardis Fisher's *Toilers of the Hills* (1928) and Davis's later *Winds of Morning* (1952) sought to portray the lives of pioneers in a more honest light. In the latter, an Oregon pioneer who came seeking Eden realizes late in life that the sins of civilization were part of the provisions packed in his wagon. Fisher's *Toilers* conveys the anxiety and loneliness of a woman whose husband has dragged her off to a life of tremendous hardship dry-farming (no irrigation) in Idaho.

The modernism that Colonel Hofer so despised arrived decisively in 1934 with the publication of Robert Cantwell's remarkable novel *The Land of Plenty*. Cantwell used techniques of shifting narration, stream-of-consciousness prose, and *Rashomon*-style replayings of the same scene from different points of view to produce a classic proletarian novel of the 1930s—about sawmill workers who strike after being pushed to the brink by the mill's managers—an unjustly neglected book in the social reform tradition of Upton Sinclair and John Dos Passos.

In the years leading up to the Second World War, a second-generation myth-breaker arrived on the scene. Though Wallace Stegner was always a Western, not Northwestern, writer, his early novel *The Big Rock Candy Mountain* depicted the sort of true Northwestern experience— the life of a loose-rooted family always struggling and hoping for better prospects in the next town—that had rarely been seen in print. Eastern writers kept coming west for a dose of nature's majesty, but with the literary works of Stevens and Davis's generation, the Northwest began to shape its own identity from within.

JAMES STEVENS

James Stevens left his native Iowa to travel alone to Idaho at the age of ten. From there he worked his way around the West, taking turns as a logger, soldier, poet, singer, milker, and muleteer. His most famous role, however, was that of novelist. Alfred A. Knopf published his Paul Bunyan *collection in 1925 and his novel* Brawnyman *the following year; his best work would come more than twenty years later with the novel* Big Jim Turner, *the story of an itinerant worker in Idaho. Stevens's name remains inextricably linked with Bunyan, even though Bunyan's authenticity as a regional folk hero has been challenged by Western folklorists such as Barre Toelken. Toelken claimed that Stevens sanitized the relatively few Bunyan stories that were really told around the bunkhouse stove, "such as the one where Bunyan gets scared of heights while topping a tree in winter, and to get down quickly urinates and slides down the icicle." In this excerpt, Bunyan has moved his band of hearty loggers to the Pacific Northwest ("He-Man Country") from New Iowa, where they had been infected with an insidious love for poetry.*

from PAUL BUNYAN

IN PAUL BUNYAN'S TIME the He Man country was far from its present tame and safe condition. It was then a high, smooth valley which lay between the Cascade Mountains and the Rockies. The highest peaks towered only a few hundred feet above it. Down the center of the valley Moron River flowed, and on each side of this amazing stream the sage trees grew, the wild horses roved, and the long-eared, stub-tailed high-behinds sat with lifted front feet and savagely sniffed the air for the scent of their hereditary enemy, the blond wolf . . .

Paul Bunyan moved to this region after his disastrous experience in New Iowa, when his loggers all turned poets. He depended on the He Man country to make plain, honest men of them again. The super-masculine sage trees, he was sure, would inspire them to anything but poetry; and the logging off of these hard forests would be a historical achievement. But the great logger left nothing to chance. He remembered a species of animal which his former boss, John Shears, had originated, and he ordered a herd of them to be brought West. John Shears had proved to him that the virility of buffalo milk was incomparable. So Paul Bunyan planned to stuff his loggers with buffalo milk hot cakes as an antidote to any poison of poetry that might remain in them.

Thus the great logger's first move in the He Man country was to build a great buffalo corral and milking pen. When it was completed the buffalos were brought from the old home camp, and a gang of scissor-bills came along to herd and milk them. After their first breakfast of the new man food the loggers got some of their old swagger back, and Paul Bunyan was a picture of cheerfulness as he cruised the sage trees and planned the work of his men.

Moron River offered a chance for the most eventful and picturesque drive of logging history. From its source above the Border to its mouth on the Oregon coast it was like a huge child of a river, for it flowed ridiculously in every mile of its course. Here it ran smoothly for a short distance, then it would flow jerkily, making spasmodic waves; again, its surface would form into vast eddies that whirled like merry-go-rounds, and from these the waters rushed in heaving rolls of foam; there were quicksands where the river played hide and seek, nearly disappearing in places, miles where it turned and ran back and then curved into its course again, making a perfect figure eight. Moron River flowed everywhere in zigzags and curlicues, cutting all manner of capers and didos. Any man but Paul Bunyan would have admitted the impossibility of making a drive on it. But he only smiled when he saw it and said: "If my rivermen will forget poetry they can drive it easily."

The timber in this high, wide valley reached from the Eastern slopes of the Cascade Hills to the Western slopes of the Rockies. These sage trees resembled the desert sagebrush of to-day. They were not large; few of them were over two hundred feet in height, and not one of them could give a butt log over nine feet in diameter. But they all had many massive limbs which were crowded with silver gray leaves, each leaf being the size of a No. 12 shoe. The brown bark of the sage trees was thick, loose and stringy; it would have to be peeled from the logs before they were snaked to the landings by the blue ox.

"Splendid work for the swampers and limbers," said Paul Bunyan, as he cruised the timber. "What a noble logging land is the He Man country! Surely my loggers will be re-born here into even better men than they were before they fell into an illness of poetry and ideas!"

The first day of logging in the He Man country seemed to justify the great logger's best hopes. The men came out from breakfast with a swinging, swaggering tramp, loudly smacking their lips over the lingering flavors of buffalo milk hot cakes. This potent food made them vigorously he in every action. Each man chewed at least three cans of Copenhagen and a quarter-pound of fire cut during his first twelve hours in the woods. "P-tt-tooey! P-tt-tooey! P-tt-tooey!" sounded everywhere among shouted oaths and coarse bellowing. Every ax stroke buried the bit deeply in the tough sage wood, and brown dust spurted and gushed constantly from every singing saw. Crash! Crash! Crash! The thunder of falling trees sounded like a heavy cannonade. On all the loggers' backs gray sweat stains spread from under their suspenders, and their hair hung in dripping strings over their red, wet faces. They had got up steam for the first time since leaving the Hickory Hill country, and they were rejoicing in it. Even after the eleventh hour had passed their eyes were bright, though red-rimmed from stinging sweat, though wrinkles of weariness had formed around them. The men were tired indeed; the fallers and swampers were now panting through open mouths, and they were chewing nervously on their tongues, as is the habit of men when they are wearied out; but they never missed a lick, and when Paul Bunyan called them home they could still walk springily.

When they were back in camp they did not even complain of the smeared, sticky feeling which always follows great sweats. No one spoke delicately of bathing; the loggers all washed and combed carelessly; and soon they made a trampling, growling host around the cookhouse door.

The rafters and beams of the great cookhouse shook at this supper, so savagely did the loggers tackle the platters of bear meat. Even the bones were crushed, ground, and devoured; and Hot Biscuit Slim and his helpers were delighted when all the dishes were left slick and clean.

That night no poems were recited in the bunkhouses, but the loggers roared out "The Jam on Garry's Rock" and other plain old songs. The loggers all crawled into their blankets at an early hour, and every one of them emitted gruff snores as soon as he went to sleep.

Paul Bunyan listened to them, and he praised the saints for the He Man country. Had it not been for this region there was no telling what continuous plagues of poetry would have afflicted his simple men. Now they were back to normalcy.

The loggers continued to improve as summer passed and the short autumn of the He Man country ran its course. The first snow of the cold season fell on a redeemed camp. That snow flew in on a thundering wind; its flakes quickly made masses of dry snow around the bunkhouse doors; and these were swept into huge drifts that were window-high in places when the breakfast gong rang. The loggers roared and cheered when they rushed out for their buffalo milk hot cakes. Paul Bunyan listened to their basso growls of hunger, their rumbling jovial cursing, their bellows of laughter, and he chuckled so heartily that the snow which had gathered on his beard was shaken over a crowd of loggers, burying them. They dug themselves out, whooping their appreciation of the humorous happening, and they jestfully shook their fists at their chuckling leader. Then, without stopping to dig the snow from their shirt collars, they galloped on for the steaming cookhouse.

The stamping and banging, the clatter and crash, the smoking, sucking and grinding of meal time had never sounded with more vigor and power than on this wild winter morning. Breakfast done, the loggers came forth wiping their mouths with flourishing swipes of their fists, and with much snorting thumb-blowing of noses. When they were back in the bunkhouses, they laced up their boots, arguing loudly the while as to whether true savages, real tough bullies, would wear mackinaws when it was only forty below zero.

"Mackinaws?" yelled the majority. "Where's your red bully blood, you Hunyoks? Mackinaws! Hell, no, burlies; we won't even button the collars of our shirts!"

And then Ford Fordsen, camp tinker, bunkhouse handyman, and prophet, got an idea which swiftly ran through all the bunkhouses.

"Real rough, red-blooded, burly, bully, savage, dirt-stomping, ear-chewing, tobacco-loving, whisker-growing, hell-roaring He Men are not going to wear their boots and pants like we've been doing," said he. "Look you now: here's a ten-inch boot top, here are two inches of wool sock above it; and there's a pants' leg all tucked down nice and pretty inside of it. Mates, it looks too delicate. It is no way for a fire-eating logger to wear his duds. Here now; watch me and do as I do, and be a real band of honest-to-God bullies. This way—look!"

He jerked open his horn-handled old knife, and he slashed off the legs of his tin breeches, his mackinaw pants and his overalls, just below his knees. He bit off a jaw-full of fire cut and then stood up, his fists on his hips, an unshaven cheek bulging with pepper-flavored tobacco, shapeless hat down over one eye, collar unbuttoned, suspenders stretching over his expanded chest, and—high mark of all high marks, distinction of distinctions—his pants ending in ragged edges below his knees. An inch of red drawers' legs showed below them, there followed bands of green wool socks, then black boot tops. Stagged pants! The finishing touch! Poetry was crushed to earth, never to rise triumphantly again in Paul Bunyan's camp.

HATHAWAY JONES

Known as the "Münchhausen of the Rogue," Hathaway Jones came from a long line of tall-tale tellers. His grandfather, Ike Jones, and father, Sampson Jones, were renowned Oregon liars, and they passed on the tradition to Hathaway, who would spin his yarns to folks he met along the U.S. Mail route that he walked through the wild Rogue River country in southwestern Oregon from 1898 to 1937. "Hathaway's speech was most peculiar—a cross between a hare-lip and a tongue-tie," recalled one listener. "His pronunciation of some words was intriguing, and he always seemed in dead earnest." Earnest is the key word— Jones once threatened to sue the Oregonian *when he got word that the paper had called someone else the biggest liar in the state. The following selection is from the collection* Tall Tales from Rogue River: The Yarns of Hathaway Jones.

THE YEAR OF THE BIG FREEZE

THE YEAR OF THE BIG FREEZE, ice on the Rogue at Battle Bar was so thick cattle and horses crossed the river upon it. It turned cold so suddenly, some wild creatures were surprised. Scattered here and there were salmon lying on the ice which quickly froze under them when they jumped into the air for the purpose of discovering how they were progressing upon their journey to the creek of their nativity. A big blue heron pecked at a frog which was sitting upon a rock under the water, and before it could withdraw its bill the ice froze around it and held the bird fast. Hathaway Jones chopped the ice away from the heron's bill with an ax, and when it straightened up it still had the frog, which it swallowed.

Thin ice on standing water, which is common on frosty mornings, was all Hathaway had ever before seen. His grandfather, Ike, had told him of thick ice which forms on some eastern lakes and rivers; how the people skate, and drive wagon trains upon it. Testing the ice on the Rogue, he discovered it would support him, so he decided to take a walk.

He was having a grand time sliding around, and sometimes sitting down abruptly, never dreaming the ice might not be thick enough all along the river to stand his weight. Suddenly he broke through into the swift, cold river which carried him under the ice.

Swimming downstream with all his might in the hopes of seeing a hole in the ice through which he could crawl out, he was very glad he had practiced holding his breath. It was cold under the ice, and his heavy clothing and shoes weighted him down to the bottom of the river. There he saw a big Chinook salmon and grabbed it by the tail, knowing it would, when scared, swim downstream.

The salmon darted away like an arrow from a long bow, towing Hathaway through the water so fast the friction warmed him. He enjoyed the speed and the warm glow which suffused him, but was at a loss to know how he would breathe after tiring of holding his breath.

Now Hathaway knew that salmon desiring to rid themselves of hooks or other undesirable obstacles usually leap high out of the water and shake their heads. He was thinking of that very thing when the fish whose tail he was holding saw a hole in the ice and leaped with all its strength. It was a big salmon, and a strong one. It leaped so high it landed upon the ice beyond the hole, dragging Hathaway out with it.

Whereupon he threw the salmon across his shoulders and carried it home for supper, helping himself along with a straight stick which he found by the trail. Arriving at the cabin, he leaned the stick against the wall back of the stove where the heat thawed it, and it turned out to be a snake.

VARDIS FISHER

The early novels of Vardis Fisher, Idaho's favorite literary son, represent some of the most autobiographical "fiction" the region has produced. His first published work, Toilers of the Hills *(1928), tells the story of two Idaho pioneers who struggle to scratch a living out of the state's dry, unforgiving soil. The main characters, Dock and Opal Hunter, are based on Dock and Opal Fisher, the author's uncle and aunt. As the real Dock's neighbor Cal McMurtrey recalled in the Fisher biography* Tiger on the Road, *Dock wasn't pleased at first with his newfound fame. "He had hell in his eye," said McMurtrey. "Someone had told him that Vardis had said some things about him in the book. I asked him what he was going to do, and he said he was going down there and kill the son of a bitch." Fisher survived the encounter. "Three hours later, Dock came back all smiles," according to McMurtrey. "I asked him what happened and he said, 'The son of a bitch made a hero outa me.'"*

from TOILERS OF THE HILLS

THE HOMESTEAD WHICH Dock Hunter chose from Antelope's fifty square miles of Idaho benchland was bare, except in one corner, of everything but sagebrush and dwarfed mountain mahogany and scraggy serviceberry bushes, dry weeds of many kinds and tall wheat grass and smaller grasses and ragweed. In one corner was a tiny cove, opening to the north, in which snow lay longer in the spring of the year. It had a few stunted aspens, some willows, and serviceberry bushes which always blossomed and never bore fruit. "This-here's where our house will be," he told Opal, and he climbed down from the wagon and shook off his coating of white dust. "Them trees'll maken it a little cooler for you."

While he unhitched and tethered his sweaty team, Opal sat and looked over her new home, but in her eyes there was none of her husband's glad eagerness. Here, as elsewhere in this Antelope country, everything that grew was hard and dry and looked brittle in the hot sunlight—everything on this choked desert of earth, over these hills with their resting clouds of dust. She saw no birds, nothing alive but squirrels, gray like the earth, and some hawks far above, circling around and around. In her dooryard, even where she imagined her front step might be, were tall sagebrush and scraggy bushes, full of dust and the forgotten nests of former years. The few aspen trees were short and gnarled and twisted, not straight and lovely like the ones she had known; and she could see black scars on their trunks, and she could see their naked roots in still writhing shapes. Of all things around her on these hills, as far as the eye could see, the only tender green thing was a willow in the wettest part of the cove; and it seemed to be, when Opal looked at its trunk, an old thing strangely topped with youth.

And when she looked westward, along the way they had come, she saw only gray rolling slopes, gray round-backed hills, and a sky hung like a gray curtain at their far end. She looked at the tarpaulin, now white with dust, covering their belongings, at two curved plow handles, at something prodding up which she knew was the leg of a chair. She watched her husband, stripping off the wet harness, examining with gentle hands a patch of raw flesh on a horse's shoulder, stroking the dust from their manes. When he came toward her, smiling, brushing his clothes, Opal stared at his teeth. He had two very large teeth on top with a space between, and on either side, not close by, was a small sharp-pointed tooth. Never before had she observed his teeth with such acuteness. She imagined that his ears stuck out farther from his head to-day, that there was more bow in his legs; and when he came near, she saw a drop of water hanging from the point of his nose. "Here," she said, and wiped the drop away and kissed him lightly.

"You like this-here place a ourn, don't you?" he asked, and he turned around to see all of it. "Let's go outen and look it over."

And hand in hand they took their way among sagebrush, around buckbrush that clawed at their legs, up to the highest point of all. "Looken at all that, will you?" said Dock, and, circling her waist with one arm, he pointed with his other at all of the things he saw here, at the sagebrush growing as tall as a man's shoulder, at a little pasture of lush pine grass down low at one side. "Where them-there stuff'll grow, why, wheat will just jump up liken rabbits, Ope. See that-air patch a grass far over there?

That ground must a-been wettern all this-here rest. All that big of stuff must find water somewheres, without it wouldn't be a-growun like it is. We can have a garden over there, potatoes and a sight a green truck and mebbe even an orchard."

And while Opal stared with eyes that ached from the heat and seeing so much that was only gray and lonely, Dock strove to make her see their home as it would be soon, as it would be in next year or in the next. There would be fields of grain, acres and acres of it, rolling slopes and hills of green in June, in July, and sheets of white and gold in August. Oats, he explained, would be white when ripe, wheat would be golden. He would get busy at once. He would build a house first, and perhaps he would get out the logs for a barn; and then he would set to and plow up at least a hundred acres for winter wheat. It would be hard work, breaking this stubborn sod, uprooting the big sagebrush, the buckbrush and the mahogany. But he would do it. His hands were itching for the handles of a plow; he wanted to feel again the reins around his waist, the pull upon them by horses eager to go; he wanted to feel his feet sinking in plowed earth, to smell a field of broken sod. And Opal would not have much to do, not till he had built chicken coops and bought chickens, not till next spring when there would be a garden to tend, hens to set, chicks to be kept away from weasels and skunks and hawks; and so she could come out and sit on a furrow and follow him around the field now and then, or she could sit in the shade of a mahogany and read a book. And during the months when snow lay deep and winter wheat slept, he would get out posts for a fence, cedar posts, if he could find any, because, he explained, "quakun asp posts ain't worth a tinker's damn nohow, without you set them every year. They rot plumb off in a year." Too, he would get out logs for a chicken house, and possibly he would build an underground cellar in which they would keep their eggs and cream cool and fresh for a long time.

"My idea," said Dock, "is to keepen our eggs all summer long, when eggs ain't worth a little, and sell them in the fall. My mother always done it that way and she never had no rotten eggs to say about. They always candled her eggs and they was fresh as the day they was borned. And I guess we could keepen cream a long while, too. Stir it good every day, that's all of the trouble it would be."

And as he talked eagerly of his plans, of all the things he would do, of the great sums of money he would make and of the fine homes he would some day build, Opal felt warmly happy and very proud of him. She pulled his head down and kissed him and patted his cheek.

"But I don't see," she told him, "how you can plow all them brush out with just a hand plow. It looks like they would just bust your plow to splinters."

Dock dug into a rear pocket and fetched out a plug of tobacco. He picked some dirt off the place where he had last bitten and looked at the chaparral over the hills. "No," he said, and bit deep into his plug. "I'll take them out, roots and all, liken they was only twigs. I'll sharpen my old plow and whack them-there off cleanern a whistle. They won't bother me worth a mention, Ope. I'll take them out liken they was never there and pile them up and burn them. That's all of the big them-there things is in my figgerun."

With Dock's arm around her waist, her left hand in his, they went back down the slope to the wagon. On their slow way back he would stop and look about him, or he would kick his toe into the earth. "It's dryern all hell on top, ain't it? But down under, them roots gets water somewheres. Them sage and hogany ain't a-burnun that a man can see." And for a little while he looked over the gray hills, now flowing away through a deepening twilight.

ROBERT CANTWELL

No writer captured the sights, sounds, and smells of a Northwest lumber mill better than did Robert Cantwell in his 1934 novel, The Land of Plenty. *Using shifting points of view, the book explores a conflict between bosses and workers that culminates in a violent strike. Although critics argued over his blue-collar sympathies, none could fault the accuracy of Cantwell's vision of a dark industrial nightmare.* "The Land of Plenty *puts you right in the shoes of the men and women who exploit the lumber business,"* wrote John Dos Passos in The New Republic. *"Some of it is not too hellishly agreeable to go through."*

from THE LAND OF PLENTY

SUDDENLY THE LIGHTS went out. He was standing in a cleared space toward the head end of the mill, trying to decide what he should do, when the lights went out and left him groping for the wall behind him. There was no warning fading or flickering of the bulbs; there was only a swift blotting out of the visible world. At one moment there were things he could see, there were familiar objects and people and walls; and at the next there was nothing, nothing but darkness streaming from the empty bulbs.

For a time he stood motionless, waiting for the light to come back. He was conscious of a dull, growing exasperation, a feeling like that he experienced if he was kept waiting by someone he did not like. He said "Hell," somewhat plaintively, and then waited, occasionally turning his head to see if somewhere a flare of light would not break out in a signal that the brief night was over. In the darkness the motors began whining down to silence. The operators could no longer see, but they moved blindly and automatically to stop the machines that were already stopping. No current was passing through the switch boxes, but at each machine the operator stepped back to press the switch that stopped his motor, finding it at once in spite of the darkness. When no current was passing through the wires the sound of the switch releasing was hollow, a dull throb, somewhat like the sound of a rock dropped into a well. For a time this was the only sound in the factory, this dull throb of switches cutting a current that had already ceased to flow.

Then the voices began to bubble up in the darkness, faint and wordless at first, growing to a slight shuffle of release . . . At the far end of the factory someone shouted, *Yahoo! Yahoo!* over and over again. Listen to that, he thought. Listen to that.

He stepped back indecisively, feeling his way to the wall he knew was not far behind him. He knew where he was. He knew that all around him the floor was clear and solid. But as soon as he started to move he could not be sure; he could not remember whether there wasn't a drop through the floor somewhere near him, or whether he wasn't nearer the sloping walls of a conveyor than he had thought. So he shuffled along uneasily, his feet sliding and testing each plank before he placed his weight upon it. He was skating along with great caution when he heard someone running past him.

He stopped incredulously. He heard the steps coming a long way off, long steps coming down hard on the fragile plank floor, leaping over the pits and gullies where the refuse was spilled, the sound splashing up from the leather meeting the wood. He stood listening in amazement with his own feet still delicately testing the planks that the darkness had turned to tissue-paper.

You crazy fool, he said silently. Do you want to get killed?

The movement passed him as he reached the wall.

He reached the wall and held it for its sightless guidance, waiting now for the lights to come back . . . He leaned against the wall to get his breath, listening to the darkness without wondering what he should do or what had happened, without expecting anything except the light to come back, and in the blindness of no light he could only wait helplessly and believe that the miracle that had robbed him of his sight would soon give it back to him again.

Outside, the tideflat on which the factory stood was almost as dark. There was no moon and the summer sky was clouded with the film of smoke drifting toward the sea from the forest fires in the mountains. In this part of the country, at the edge of the last great forests between the mountains and the Pacific, the hills burn each summer between the rains, the fires starting in the logged-off land and spreading into the green timber where nothing can stop them but a river or a patch of bare ground or a storm. A fire had broken out and in two days was out of human control. Before that the weather had been fine and dry, rare for the Northwest where there is a saying that it is a lucky year if summer comes on a Sunday, and the timber, the last great forest that stretches for a hundred miles to the north and fifty miles to the east, was seasoned and waiting. The loggers had had to stop work because the woods were so inflammable. A cable might grind against a stump, or a spark fly from a donkey-engine, and in an instant an area a hundred feet across would be in flames, almost as though the underbrush had exploded. Two weeks before, the fire had started. It could be seen from town, looking at first like a new mountain pushing its way up beyond the nearer hills. The great glaciers of smoke piled up and rolled in silent avalanches down its sides. As the days passed the peak dissolved and the rolls of smoke, heavier and thicker than clouds, drifted behind the wind. At night an indefinite red light showed somewhere behind the smoke, coloring it dimly; sometimes the fire itself rose over the hills. During the hot days the smoke seemed like a great tan canvas stretched tight from one horizon to the other, and underneath it the world looked dull and strange, the sharp colors and outlines disappearing or running into one another like objects under water.

This film of smoke covered the sky. The factory was a good mile from town and there were no lights on the tideflat. There were a few lights marking the ship channels in the harbor, and the reflection of the lights over the main streets of the town, but that was all. Once the tideflat around the factory had been a marsh, until bulkheads had been built around it and mud from the bottom of the harbor pumped in behind the bulkheads. Gradually the tideflat had been drained and packed, and as the bunch grass and bulrushes had taken root in it, and the scrub willows that grew beside the drainage canals had spread, a small prairie had formed around the factory. Only one road connected it with the highway, and a spur with the main line of the railroad. There were a few empty freight cars on the siding, and a few automobiles huddled in the parking space at the entrance of the factory.

All the way across the tideflat and across town there was felt an accident at the power house. One of the men moving behind the switchboard, for some reason that was never known, brushed against the deadly wires and in an instant half the town was dark. The street cars ran blindly for a few feet and stopped; the people looked toward their companions who had so suddenly become invisible. In the houses the darkness settled like a weight. At the factory the very nerves and muscles of the machines were cut, the motors began whining down to silence, the men moved automatically to press the control buttons. Thousands of great and small precautions were taken, thousands of dangers avoided, casually, as part of the moment's work, and then the men settled themselves to wait. The crew on the presses worked feverishly in the dark trying to save the doors that were partly finished. The electricians hurried through the building, trying to find the break; in the fireroom the fireman cut the steam that was going to the kilns. In the factory a man climbed under the roof, feeling his way up a ladder that seemed to lean outwards, crawled over a shaky plank bridge to set a valve, finding it by burning his hands along the pipe. And out at the head end of the mill, where the logs were lifted from the steam vats, a man was hurt when the hoist that lifted the logs suddenly stopped.

The factory was a large rectangular building with a long peninsula thrust out from it, to the edge of the water, like the handle of a frying pan. The long peninsula was a relic of its early days, when the logs had been moved in from the vats on trucks that ran on a narrow-gauge track. The logs were sawed into lengths while they still floated in the water of an inlet, lifted into vats and steamed for two days under pressure. Then they were taken into the mill through the long corridor that thrust out from the factory, washed and cleaned and peeled into veneer; moving on, then, through the complicated processes that transformed them into doors and desks, into panels for walls and furniture.

The man who was hurt worked at the far end of the peninsula, where he was running the hoist that lifted the logs into the factory. He was a new man and, since he worked off by himself and the accident happened swiftly and silently, it was a long time before anyone found him. When the lights went out the log had lifted enough to be free to swing. It was a large log, six feet through and nine feet long, the butt log of an enormous fir. It lifted very slowly, for the motor of the hoist was geared down to give it greater power. There was a strained singing sound from the motor as the cable tightened and the hooks buried themselves in the wood at each end of the log, and the sap and water spurted out around the hooks as they sank into the wood. Then the log stirred in the shadow of its own steam, rising like some great awkward beast awakened at night, rising and swaying until it was almost clear of the ground.

The motor stopped when the power was cut. A brake prevented the log from dropping back, but it began to swing, very slowly, until the uneven track let it go. Slowly and silently it moved through the darkness to where the hoist man was staring at the darkened lights, picked him up and pressed him against the foundations. For a time it held him there, crushing through the brief defense he made against it, breaking through his arms, his clothing, the frail protection of his flesh. Then it settled back slightly, leaving him jammed against the piling.

This happened in the instant that Carl was groping his way toward the wall. He did not know it. He knew only that there was a tremendous amount of work that had to be done and that it could not be done as long as the factory was dark. When he realized that the lights were not coming on again a wave of despair, almost of physical sickness, swept over him, and when he thought of how he was going to answer the manager about the orders that had to be got out, his hands clenched and unclenched nervously. He was a new foreman. A year before he had come to the factory as an efficiency engineer with a contract to cut operating costs and power to weed out the incompetent men, and before the year was over he had been given charge of the night shift to show what he could do. Nothing like this had happened since he came into the factory. He knew what to do in case of a fire, and he had learned what men to give the cutting orders to when the shift started and where to check up when the stock seemed to be running short, but nothing had ever happened to make him wonder what to do when the lights went out.

He shifted his hold on the wall and wiped his moist palm on his overalls. The factory rocked when he released the wall. He grabbed it again, his fingers clamping on one of the cross-pieces. He felt the sweat on his forehead.

Oh, Christ, he said silently. Come back on.

H. L. DAVIS

Harold Lenoir Davis intended his first novel, he once said, to be "representative of every calling that existed in Oregon during the homesteading period." With Honey in the Horn *he came mighty close. The novel, which won both the Harper Award and the Pulitzer Prize following its 1935 publication, might best be described as the* Huckleberry Finn *of the Northwest. Forced on the lam after a botched jailbreak, Davis's hero Clay Calvert roams the Northwest in search of the woman he loves and a community he can settle in. Along the way he meets horse traders, farmers, loggers, homesteaders, storekeepers, and outlaws, most of whom seem to be looking for a better situation; they're either on the move or aiming to be. In this excerpt Calvert has settled, for the time being, with a group of hop pickers in southern Washington.*

from HONEY IN THE HORN

THEY PICKED A CAMP-SITE a couple of hundred yards off from the main scramble of hop-pickers' tents and wagons and clothes-drying rigs, on the bank of a spring branch under big alder trees, adjoining somebody's winter stock of high-class oak cordwood. There was no grass; the alder leaves had killed it all out; but it was clean and convenient to water, the woodpile was handy to borrow from, and across the spring branch was an old orchard with a good rail fence and a meadow-grass pasture under the unpruned old fruit-trees. It wasn't extra-good feed, being seed-less and badly fouled up with acrid dog-fennel, but it was sustaining enough for horses that didn't have to work, and it was easy to watch against thieves. They turned all the horses into it except the horse-trader's sorrel stallion, keeping him up on account of a childish notion of the horse-trader's that he had to be fed twice a day on grain. Then they pitched the tent and made camp, which was easy, and then they circu-lated around where the picking was going on, sizing up the pickers and the work.

There was plenty of sportiveness and high spirits around the hop-fields that fall. Hops were fetching thirty-five cents a pound at the drier, and the hundred-acre patch where they were camped stood to return its owner a profit of sixty thousand dollars, clear of all expenses for planting, plowing, poling, stringing, picking, drying, and baling. The owner walked around between the rows, looking solemn and responsible about it, though that may have been due to his wearing all his best clothes, including a stiff-bosomed shirt and a funeral-model stand-up collar. His hops were going to make him rich, and since they couldn't be cashed in on till they got picked, he felt bound to tog himself out uncomfortably by way of showing his pickers how much he appreciated their being there. He had even taken care to see that everybody got camped decently. All the campsites were laid off with shade, clean water, brick fireplaces, straw for bedding, and free clotheslines out in the open pasture where the women could hang their washing. There was a small commissary store handling fresh meat and common groceries and gloves and work clothes, at which Clay bought a pair of new overalls to replace Zack Wall's ten-acre pants. There was a little clearing in the brush beyond the hop-yard fence where the men could get action on their day's earnings at chuckaluck, which, according to the long-chinned old Civil War veteran who ran the table, was the game that had been used to put down the Rebellion; and there were lanes and trails in the deep dog-fennel of the old orchard where young couples could go walking after work to watch the moon come up and go down.

Both the gambling and the moon-watching ought to have done busi-ness to an extensive clientele. Picking hops was not grinding toil, and a young man could easily get through several weeks at it without having his emotional reflexes worn down a particle. Also, it was fairly profitable. A man with his mind on it could weigh in from three to five dollars' worth of picked hops in a day. But the men among the hop-pickers didn't show much interest in getting a play either on their emotions or on their earnings. Mostly they preferred to sit around camp and gas while the women flagged to and fro, doing up the camp chores for the evening. To the general way of thinking, of course, hop-picking was a kind of squaw's job, and though the men did get out and work at it, they kept their dignity by letting on not to be interested in it or anything connected with it. They were disappointing when you came to know them, for there wasn't enough adventurousness in the whole bunch to kick a breachy hog through a hole in the fence. They lived on the move, all right, but it wasn't the kind of moving that people did who sashayed out into unknown country to see whether it could be lived in or not. They followed the same line of travel year in and year out, from the California prune-orchards up the Coast to the Calgary wheat-fields and back again as regular and undeviating as a man tending a suburban milk route. A lot of them let on to have been blooded gamblers in their time, and some of them had a good deal to say about fights they had been in and towns they had left where women followed them several miles down the road, bawling and begging them not to leave. Some of them even claimed reputations in other sections of the country as dangerous desperadoes, and allowed that a common short-pod hell-raiser like Wade Shiveley might look pretty mean to a hayseed community, but that he wouldn't constitute over one mouthful for them if they ever took a notion to cut loose. None of them ever did cut loose. The nearest they ever got to it was sitting around the fire, devouring tobacco and blowing about what they had been through, as if the old Civil War veteran's chuckaluck board and the couples in the dog-fennel had worn off all interest for them about the time they stopped crawling under the barn to smoke cigarettes . . .

. . . When he got a couple of rows distant from the weighing-stand, [Clay] set the basket down to rest and change holds, and saw that he was about to bump into visitors. There was a wagon at the gate with two men in it. They hadn't called out of neighborliness, for one of them showed a star on his suspender and then covered it with his coat. He was after somebody among the hop-pickers, because he handed down a paper with printing on it and the hop-yard owner read it and asked, indignantly, why the damnation he had come bothering a man's hired help right in the middle of the picking-season.

"You got the right place for this, I reckon, but you certainly played hell pickin' a time for it," he complained. "I can't have you wavin' your star and your papers around these camps. You'd scatter these pickers of mine like a bunch of quail, and I'd have this crop left on my hands till January. If you'll wait right here a few minutes, this criminal you're doggin' will be down to weigh up, and you can do your arrestin' and be on your way without stampedin' anybody. Damned if I don't believe this is a rannikaboo them Forty-Gallon church people down the valley has got up to rob my pickers away from me, anyhow. It's a wonder the blamed hymn-shoutin' robbers wouldn't hire somebody to put strychnine in my coffee and be done with it."

He was really outraged. Stampeding a man's hop-pickers in a big season was almost as mean as dogging his milk-cows. The offending clatter of his Adam's apple against his stand-up collar was distinctly audible. The sheriff's deputy said the hymn-shouters had nothing to do with his warrant, because it had come in from another county. He wouldn't mind waiting if it didn't take too long. In that hop-raising country, hindering a man's hop-harvest was serious trespass. He pulled his wagon in against the fence and asked how long it was likely to be.

"A few minutes at the outside," the owner said, unsociably. "You can see most of the hands has gone to camp already. They all fetch their hops down here the last thing, and this desperado you're drawin' the taxpayers' money for trailin' is almost the only one we've still got to hear from." He clacked his stiff collar and repeated the word desperado to make sure they got the sarcasm. "You certainly do hump down to work when it's some fool mail-order case that nobody gives a damn about, don't you? You all set around the office with your feet on the stove when that Wade Shiveley raises hell in another county, but when it's some measly family row or other, out you rip to fetch the mallyfactor to justice if it wears out every horse in the livery-stable. Are any of your men out helpin' to catch Shiveley? No, you're damn right they ain't!"

It had taken Clay very little time to decide that the warrant was for him. He was backing cautiously away when the mention of Wade Shiveley froze him in his tracks. If an out-of-the-way farmer in the far corner of another county was keeping tab on that case, it was more serious than he had thought. If Wade Shiveley had killed somebody since the jailbreak—For the first time, Clay cussed Uncle Preston to himself for not letting his blamed son stay in jail and be hung. But he was premature, for no more killings had been reported. The deputy remarked lightly that Wade Shiveley didn't amount to much these days, and they were sort of saving him around for seed.

"They'll haul him in when they need him," he said. "With his nerve broke and all his hide-outs stopped on him, he'll be easy to head. He was layin' out on his old man's ranch in the mountains last week, we heard, and a sixteen-year-old girl on the place run him through the fence with a kittle of hot water and dared him to come back and fight. She hit him in the face with it, kittle and all, and scalded hell out of him. He took to the brush, but she like to burnt his eyes out and he ain't got any gun, so he won't git far. Your pickers' camps are over by them fires, ain't they?"

One reason Clay had not felt very uneasy about being caught before was that he had seen and sized up all the sheriff's men whose job it was to catch him. He couldn't see these men except as shadows in the lantern-light. They sounded most infernally like business, and that and the narrowness with which he had missed walking right into their laps scared him. If he had been three minutes earlier they would have caught him getting his hops weighed. If they had been ten minutes later they would have walked in on him in camp, with Luce standing by to watch them haul him away. Nothing had saved him but plain luck. His smartness, on which he had depended with such confidence, had failed him completely. He hesitated, wondering how he could ever trust it again and knowing that he could trust nothing else, and the hop-yard owner put the finisher to his scare by giving careful directions about where he was camped.

"Them fires is the main camp," he explained. "You have to go through that and past it till you strike that belt of big alders. Foller them up the branch, and it's the last camp this side of the woodpiles. If you let on to any of them other pickers that you've come to arrest anybody, you'll have 'em boilin' out of here like bees a-swarmin'. Damn, if I was sure that church outfit had started this to git my pickers away from me—"

Clay backed cautiously till he could no longer hear the owner's lament over his endangered livestock, and then ran. Nearing the main camp, he swung wide and waded the spring branch to the orchard where the horses were pasturing. For a piece of luck, no couples were out in it so early, and for another the feed was poor and unnourishing. He could never have caught the buckskin mare in the dark if it had been a question of pulling her off decent grass to go to work. But she was tired of weed stalks and choky dog-fennel, and she nickered and came to him of her own accord on the chance that he might be fixing to take her where the rations were better. He strapped his belt around her nose to hold her, sneaked back across the spring branch, and eased his saddle and bridle down from the tree under the bank. His camp-ground was about two feet from his head, and he could see the fire and hear the woman putting wood on it. It was mean to slope without telling her, but he knew that he looked scared and that she would be sure to notice it and ask why, and he didn't want Luce to see him at all. The wagon rattled across plowed ground, coming between the hop-rows, and he backed away from that place and all thoughts about it for good. He saddled and bridled the mare and got on at a trot, took her over the rail fence at a jump, and racked out on the road in the dark toward the low timbered ridge of the Coast Range Mountains where the sun set and all the rainstorms came from. The one thought in his head was that he must not let himself get caught, and it was not entirely a selfish one. His arrest, he knew, would humiliate the guitar-playing woman before the other hop-pickers. He didn't much mind leaving without notice, because there was something wistful and desperate about the way she hung on his company that made him feel embarrassed around her; but she had been good to him and he didn't want her humiliated any more than he wanted himself arrested.

STEWART HOLBROOK

"When Stewart Holbrook wrote about a Pacific Northwest logging camp," wrote an Oregonian *editorialist upon Holbrook's death in 1964, "you could fairly smell the smoke from the crooked stove pipe of the cookhouse." Holbrook came west as a young man to work in the logging camps, and acquired a reputation as the "Lumberjack Boswell" with the publication of* Holy Old Mackinaw, *his 1938 history of the American logger. He was a prolific writer, authoring forty-one books, editing countless others, and contributing to magazines ranging from*

The American Scholar *to* Startling Detective. *Because magazine editors often turned to him when they needed a story from the Northwest, he became the region's de facto literary ambassador to the nation; when readers pictured the Northwest, the scene was often set by Holbrook.*

from HOLY OLD MACKINAW

WHEN THE FIRST LOGGERS saw the fir that grew along the banks of the Columbia around Puget Sound they said there couldn't be timber that big and tall. It took, so they told each other, two men and a boy to look to the top of one of these giants.

And thick? Holy Old Mackinaw, the great trunks stood so close that the boys wondered how a tree could be felled at all! And between the trunks grew a jungle of lush growth that no Maine or Michigan logger had ever imagined. You actually had to swamp out a path to a tree and to clear a space around it before there was room to swing an ax . . . It would take some doing, mister, to let any daylight into *this* swamp.

The first loggers couldn't know it, but it becomes increasingly apparent, in 1938, that they will never be able to let daylight into all of the Western timber. The boys didn't know what manner of forest they were facing—or, forests, rather, for there were two of them.

The forest that hugs the Pacific shore is the outstanding timber zone of the United States or the world, then or now. It is rather narrow, running from thirty to one hundred and fifty miles wide, but it ranges north and south for a thousand miles. It grows very fast. And one acre of it contains more timber than did five acres of the biggest, thickest stuff Maine or Michigan could offer. In the southern part of this forest grows the redwood. North of the redwood the dominant species is the Douglas fir, named for David Douglas, young Scotch botanist who took some of it back to London when his stay with the Hudson's Bay Company at Vancouver, in the Oregon country, was done . . .

The early loggers saw at once there could be no quick yanking and twitching around, with a team of horses, such big stuff as grew in the coast fir country. What was needed was a lot of power and a strong, steady pull. So the boys reverted to the loggers' ancient beast of burden, the ox. Only here, they called oxen "the bulls," and for half a century bulls did most of the logging west of the Cascade Range.

Sleighs wouldn't do to handle these big logs, and there was seldom much snow, anyway. The ground was too rough and too soft to think of using the Big Wheels of Michigan. And only here and there was a stream deep and powerful enough to do much river driving. Faced with such new conditions the boys quickly adapted themselves. They built skidroads.

The skidroad was the Western loggers' first and greatest contribution to the science of moving timber. They first cleared a path in the forest. At suitable intervals they felled trees across this path, cut them free of limbs, then buried them half-deep in the soft ground. These were the skids that made a skidroad, a sort of track that would keep moving logs from hanging up on rocks or miring in mud. The completed job looked not unlike ties laid for a gargantuan railroad.

It was crude, but it worked beautifully. They hitched the bulls to the logs—five, six, even ten yokes of them, in charge of the bullwhacker, the teamster, undoubtedly the master of all profane men, and they pulled long turns of the big sticks, held together by hooks, over the skids.

It was something to see, this skidroad logging on the West Shore. First, you heard the loud, clear call of the bullwhacker's voice echoing down the forest road that was more like a deep green canyon, so tall and thick stood the fir; and the clank of chains and the wailing of oxbows as the heavy animals got into the pull and "leaned on her." And then the powerful line of red and black and spotted white would swing by with measured tread, the teamster, sacred goadstick over his shoulder, walking beside the team, petting and cursing them to high heaven by turns, the huge logs coming along behind with a dignified roll. Back of the oxen, but ahead of the logs, walked the skid greaser, daubing thick oil on the skid poles that smoked from friction.

Gray old men, sitting around bunkhouse stoves, still cackle in their high voices that it was the noblest sight they ever saw; and they curse the steam that relegated the bull teams to the murals of Western hotels and barrooms.

Skidroads always had one end in deep timber. The other end might be a sawmill, or it might be the waters of Puget Sound or the Columbia or one of its tributaries. If the sawmill wasn't handy, the logs went into booms for towing by steamboats.

By all odds the most important man of a woods crew in the bull-team era was the bullwhacker. He was paid three times as much as an axman, and his opinions on all subjects from oxshoes to the cosmos were considered weighty. He ruled the skidroad, man and beast, with a firm and practiced hand, and his badge of authority was his goadstick, a slim piece of wood some five feet long with a steel brad in one end.

The bullwhacker's profanity long ago became legendary in the Western woods. When he raised his voice in blasphemous obscenity, the very bark of the smaller fir trees was said to have smoked a moment, then curled up and fallen to the ground. No sailor, no truck driver, nor logger who hadn't driven bulls, could hope to touch its heights of purple fluidity. And when both goadstick and profanity failed to rouse the plodding oxen to their best, the bullwhacker might leap upon an animal's back and walk the entire length of the team, stepping heavy with his calked boots and yelling like all the devils in hell.

Migrating lumberjacks found the whoopee districts of Western lumber towns a bit different from anything they had known before. Basically, of course, the bowery-like skidroads were composed of the same things as elsewhere. But these Western joints were wilder, tougher, and more openly sinful than ever Haymarket Square in Bangor, Water Street in Saginaw, or even the Sawdust Flats of Muskegon. In spots they were gaudier; everywhere they were "bigger, wider, and more of it"—in keeping with the bigger, taller timber.

Skidroads were where you blew her in. A skidroad might be one, two, or a dozen streets of a lumber city. You didn't have to ask how to find it, for it had a character of its own. It was usually handy to the waterfront, whether of river or ocean, and not far from the railroad depot. Its places of business catered to loggers, miners, cowhands, fishermen, and sailors, and construction workers, but on the West Coast loggers were the most numerous customers.

Saloons, restaurants, and lodginghouses were in greatest number, and many of them had names with a timber flavor. "The High-Lead" was popular for saloons. Restaurants ran the gamut from "The Loggers Waldorf" to "The Cookhouse." There was generally a "Hotel Michigan," a "Saginaw Rooms," and a "Bangor House."

Next in number were the chippy establishments, and cheap-john stores which seem to have always been stocked with Sunday suits of a particularly bilious and offensive purple-blue color. On the Skidroad, too, one would find the slave markets, employment offices, like Hicks' Loggers Agency in Vancouver, British Columbia, and Archie McDougal's in Seattle. Somewhere along the stem would be an open-front "demonstration room" of Dr. Painless Parker, the eminent chain-dentist, with one of Dr. Parker's men ballyhooing the dangers of decayed teeth, while a stooge dressed like a logger sat in a dentist chair, a bib around his neck.

A tattooing parlor might be next to a show window in which were displayed perhaps a basket of China tea, a bottle of American ink, a carton of soap, and some advertising cigarette cards. Any logger could tell by this display of unrelated wares that here was a Chinese lottery.

There might be a combined shooting gallery and penny arcade, and here and there a mission place where you could get free soup if you would sit through a lecture or a sermon. There would surely be, after 1906, an I.W.W. hall, and always a barber shop with lady barbers, and a barber college where bums could get free shaves and haircuts. And there might be a secondhand book store, like Raymer's in Tacoma and Seattle, or a place that defies definition like Tom Burns' Timeshop in Portland.

Until well into the present century open gambling was a feature of Western skidroads. When pioneer realism faded, the gaming joints were driven under cover by civilized hypocrisy where they still flourish. But gambling, like food, clothing, dentistry, and other minor needs, was of secondary importance to loggers. Saloons and fancyhouses got their stakes.

RICHARD NEUBERGER

Richard Neuberger wrote his first article, a warning about Hitler's rise to power, for The Nation *in 1933. He was nineteen years old. Between then and his death in 1960, the lifelong Oregonian wrote on the Northwest seemingly without cease for national magazines and local papers. In 1954 he ran for and won a seat in the U.S. Senate, a feat unheard of for a Democrat in a then-notoriously conservative state. He continued to write even as a senator—it was his way of relaxing. Neuberger was known to set up a typewriter in the Democratic cloakroom and tap out an article while his colleagues argued over legislation in the next room. His early work was collected in the 1938 book* Our Promised Land, *from which the following selection on the construction of the Grand Coulee Dam is excerpted.*

from THE BIGGEST THING ON EARTH

TO MOST AMERICANS, Grand Coulee is merely another of the ten or fifteen dams Mr. Roosevelt is building about the country to confound the private power companies and relieve unemployment. Completely lost in the five-year political hurly-burly between the New Deal and its antagonists has been the fact that Grand Coulee is the most elaborate and expensive engineering development ever undertaken by any government. When the Panama Canal was dug, the world marveled at the magnitude of the enterprise. Grand Coulee will cost approximately $25,000,000 more than the Panama Canal. All of us have heard a good deal about the hugeness of Boulder Dam; Grand Coulee will contain more than three times as much concrete. Yet the average citizen is not even certain of its location, or for what purpose it is being constructed. Persons entirely familiar with the Tennessee Valley Authority are unaware that Grand Coulee will produce more hydroelectric power than all seven dams in the TVA combined. The Passamaquoddy fiasco in Maine has been a *bête noire* of Republican budget balancers; yet the total proposed Passamaquoddy appropriation would scarcely finance the cement plant at Grand Coulee. The undertaking is so Brobdingnagian that Waldemar Borquist, the director of Sweden's Royal Board of Waterfalls, was astounded. "Our projects in Sweden are only one-tenth, or one-twentieth as large as this one," he said. "I am amazed by Grand Coulee. It is gigantic . . ."

Mason City is a typical company town. The contractors operate the theater, the pool hall, the barber shop, the general store, and virtually all other concessions. Prices are fairly high, and the workers grumble that most of their earnings are spent with the company. "They get us going and coming. By golly! President Roosevelt wouldn't stand for that if he knew about it," a number of them told me. The President is definitely the hero of at least three-fourths of the laborers on the dam, and over a majority of the bunks are pasted "F.D.R." stickers or newspaper photographs of Mr. Roosevelt.

A surprising feature is the preponderant number of young men employed at Grand Coulee. Waiting in line to eat in the mess hall, I noticed dozens of tall lads wearing football sweaters from nearby colleges and universities. The work is dangerous, and scarcely a day passes without some one's being injured; fifty-four men have already been killed. I talked with some of the older men engaged in specialized tasks, and discovered that a considerable proportion of them had drifted to Coulee after the completion of the giant Boulder Dam on the Colorado River. They were unanimous in agreeing there was no comparison between the magnitude of the undertakings. "I thought Boulder Dam was the biggest thing on earth," one stoop-shouldered steel riveter said. "Hell! This outfit makes it look like nothin' at all." He swept a long arm down to where a temporary cofferdam as long as Muscle Shoals was beginning to hold back the hitherto unshackled fury of the Columbia. White water breaking with a subdued roar around the pier of the bridge connecting Coulee Dam and Mason City indicated the speed and force of the stream.

The best way to appreciate the vastness of this engineering enterprise is to look at it from the river itself—from a motorboat, riding downstream on the Columbia. The motorboat sticks its prow round a bluff at the water's edge. And there it is—Grand Coulee! Between cliffs nearly a mile apart, steam shovels scrape down to bedrock. From these cliffs protrude trestles almost two hundred feet high. Along the trestles move chains of flatcars carrying buckets of concrete. Cranes reach out slowly like stork bills to empty the buckets into pits far below the trestles. Hard against the granite walls of the canyon are peaked cement silos which suggest the sentry towers on the battlements of some medieval fortress. Cofferdams—steel cells backed by earth and lumber—flank each side of the river. They have diverted the second largest waterway in the United States from its course—an engineering feat never before attempted. On the summit of the cliffs above Mason City the pointed roofs of the world's largest gravel plant look no bigger than chalets clinging to a crag in the Alps.

On every side of the Columbia's horseshoe bend, naked escarpments of rock and shale tower against the sky. The only break is above the Bureau of Reclamation's bungalow village, where the cliffs part at the head of the Coulee. Far up the canyon wall is a sign "SAFETY PAYS." This marks where the crest of the dam will be. One looks from cliff to cliff. The granite bluffs are separated by nearly a mile of slope and water, yet in the not distant future they will be connected by a bulwark of concrete forty-three hundred feet long, five hundred feet high, and five hundred feet thick at the base. Knock off the tower of the Empire State Building, chink up the windows, lengthen the structure almost three-fourths of a mile, pour over its center a waterfall more than twice as high as Niagara, and you have an improvised conception of the government's greatest construction undertaking.

WALLACE STEGNER

"Why haven't Westerners ever managed to get beyond the celebration of the heroic and mythic frontier?" asked Wallace Stegner in his 1964 essay "Born a Square." If the West ever does leave the mythic frontier behind, it will be due in no small part to the writings of Stegner. In his novels and essays he changed the very idea of the West, challenging the romantic cowboy-and-Indian vision with hard truths about the place's people and its sometimes grand, sometimes shameful history. As his friend James Hepworth wrote a few months after Stegner's death in 1993, he saw the West as "a region that embodies the national culture at its most energetic, rootless, complex, reactionary, subdivided, wild, half-baked, comic, tragic, and hopeful." As a boy Stegner roamed the West with his family, moving from Iowa to North Dakota to Washington State to Saskatchewan to Salt Lake City. He used that personal history as the framework for his first major novel, The Big Rock Candy Mountain *(1943). Ostensibly the story of one family chasing the American Dream, the novel served as a microcosm of the settlement of the West. In this scene Elsa Mason, the proprietor of a Midwestern hotel, watches her husband, Bo, succumb to the lure of Klondike gold. A few months later, Elsa and Bo head west, but like many Northwest immigrants, they stop short of Alaska and settle for a while in Washington State.*

from THE BIG ROCK CANDY MOUNTAIN

[A]S SHE SAT BEHIND THE DESK the screen door of the lobby opened and a little hatless baldheaded man came in. His face was a fiery rose-pink, and his bald red scalp was scrawled with bluish veins above the temples. His breath, when he leaned confidentially toward her, almost knocked her down. His voice was a whiskey voice. She had learned to recognize that. "I was told," said his hoarse whisper, "that a man could get a drink in here."

She jingled the bell for Bo, not even bothering to deny that they served liquor, as she ordinarily would have. This man was obviously no officer, but only a tramp or barfly wandering in on his way through town. Bo came hurriedly to the door, looked the man over, and motioned him inside. The door he left ajar.

She heard the clump of a bottle on the bar, and a low mutter of talk. Shortly the whiskey voice rose. "I'll have another'n of those."

Altogether he ordered five drinks in the course of an hour, in his hoarse, commanding whisper. The dead summer afternoon drifted on. A boy going past opened and slammed the screen door just to hear the noise. "Gimme another'n," said the whiskey voice from the bar.

Drowsily, without much interest but with nothing else to occupy her attention, she heard Bo come over and set one up for the stranger as he always did when anyone was buying freely. After a time the whiskey voice said, "How much, barkeep?"

Jud's voice said, "One seventy-five," and change clinked on the bar.

"Ain't got the change," the whiskey voice said. "You got a gold scale?"

"Hell no," Jud said, and laughed. "What for?"

"This's all I got with me." There was a sodden thump on the wood, and for once Elsa heard excitement and haste in Jud's voice. "I'll be damned," he said. "Hey, Bo, this guy wants to pay off in gold dust."

But the rapid steps, the noise of crowding, the exclamations, were at the bar almost as soon as he started to speak. "Where in hell did you get that?" Bo said.

"Klondike," said the superior, bored whiskey voice, "if that's any-a your business."

"No offense, no offense," Bo said. "We just don't see any of that around here. Pan it yourself?"

"Right out of the gravel, boys."

He must have poured some into his palm, for there were whistles and exclamations. Elsa strained her ears, but she needn't have. The men in the pig were almost shouting. "Jumping Jesus," a drummer said. "How much is that poke worth?"

"Oh—five, six hundred."

"Quite a slug to be lugging around," Bo said.

"More where that came from," the stranger said. "Plennnty more salted away, boys. Never carry more than I need."

"I'll go try the drugstore for a scale," Bo said. "How much an ounce?"

"Eighteen bucks."

Bo laughed, a short, incredulous chop of sound. "You have to spend your money with an eyedropper at that rate."

Pinky Jordan stayed all afternoon to soak up the admiration he had aroused. After she had brought the baby down in his buggy and set Chester to playing with his blocks, Elsa heard scraps of the tales he was holding his listeners with. Three more men had come back with Bo from the drugstore, and all afternoon others kept dropping in to have a beer and listen to stories of hundreds of miles of wild timberland, hundreds of thousands of caribou, hundreds of millions of salmon in suicidal dashes up the rivers; of woods full of bear and deer and otter and fox and wolverine and mink; of fruit salads on every tree in berry time. You didn't need to work for a living. You picked it off the bushes, netted it out of the river, shot it out of the woods, panned it out of the gravel in your front yard.

"You know how much a frenna mine got for one silver fox skin?" the whiskey voice was saying as she drew near the door once with the broom as an excuse. "For one, leetle, skin?" The voice was confidential and dramatic. "Four hunnerd dollahs."

There were whistles, clickings against teeth. "Four hunnerd dollahs," Pinky Jordan said, "an' he traded it out of a halfbreed for a flannel shirt and a sheath knife. You wanna make your fortune, genlemen, you go on up to God's country. Flowin'th milk and honey."

It was nearly supper time when Pinky Jordan, drunk on his own eloquence and the uncounted drinks his listeners had poured for him, wobbled out of the lobby. Bo was at his elbow, telling him confidentially that sometimes they got up a little game in the evenings. Be glad to have him drop in. Just a friendly little game, no high stakes, but pleasant. They'd be glad to have him.

Pinky Jordan nodded owlishly, winked both eyes so that his naked red scalp pulled down over his brows like a loose slipping skullcap. From the desk Elsa watched him in the horizontal light of evening hesitating on the front sidewalk, a little man with a red bald head and a nick out of his right ear as if someone had taken a neat bite from it. Then he started up the walk, kicking at a crumpled piece of paper. Each time he came up behind it, measured his kick, booted it a few feet, and staggered after it to measure and kick again. On the fourth kick he stubbed his toe and fell into the street, and the men who had been looking after him from lobby and sidewalk ran to set him straight again. He jerked his kingly elbows out of their hands and staggered out of sight.

Pinky Jordan never returned for the poker game, though Bo tried all the next day to locate him around town. But he had done his work. He left behind a few dollars' worth of gold dust in a shot glass behind Bo Mason's bar. He also left behind him a vision of clean wilderness, white rivers and noble mountains, forests full of game and fabulously valuable fur, sand full of glittering grains. And he left in Bo, fretted by hard times and the burden of an unpaid mortgage and the worry and wear of keeping his nose too long to an unprofitable grindstone, a heightened case of that same old wandering itch that had driven him from town to town and job to job since he was fourteen.

He was born with the itch in his bones, Elsa knew. He was always telling stories of men who had gone over the hills to some new place and found a land of Canaan, made their pile, got to be big men in the communities they fathered. But the Canaans toward which Bo's feet had turned had not lived up to their promise. People had been before him. The cream, he said, was gone. He should have lived a hundred years earlier.

Yet he would never quite grant that all the good places were filled up. There was somewhere, if you knew where to find it, some place where money could be made like drawing water from a well, some Big Rock Candy Mountain where life was effortless and rich and unrestricted and full of adventure and action, where something could be had for nothing. He hadn't found it in Chicago or Milwaukee or Terre Haute or the Wisconsin woods or Dakota; there was no place and no business where you took chances and the chances paid off, where you played, and the play was profitable. Ball playing might have been it, if he had hit the big time, but hard luck had spoiled that chance. But in the Klondike . . . the Klondike, Elsa knew as soon as he opened his mouth to say something when Pinky Jordan was gone, was the real thing, the thing he had been looking for for a lifetime.

BETTY MACDONALD

American children know Betty MacDonald as the creator of the popular "Mrs. Piggle-Wiggle" books, but in the Northwest, MacDonald will forever be identified as the author of The Egg and I, *a whimsical 1945 memoir of life on a chicken ranch in the foothills of the Olympic Mountains. In the book, MacDonald and her husband, Bob, cope with lunatics in the hen run, irascible neighbors, skunks, loggers, cougars, and an adversarial appliance known as Stove.* The Egg and I *was made into a movie in 1947 starring Claudette Colbert and Fred MacMurray. Two supporting characters in the book and film, MacDonald's fictional neighbors Ma and Pa Kettle (no relation to Stove), inspired a series of successful cornball movies in the 1950s.*

from THE EGG AND I

DESPITE ITS LOCATION, I never had the feeling that our small ranch was nestled on the protective lap of the Olympic Mountains. There was nothing protective about them. Each time I looked out of a window or stepped out of doors, I was confronted by great, white, haughty peaks staring just above my head and doing their chilly best to make me realize that that was once a very grand neighborhood and it was curdling their blood to have to accept "trade." We were there with our ugly little buildings and livestock, but, by God, they didn't have to associate with us or make us welcome. They, no doubt, would have given half their timber if they could have changed the locale to Switzerland and brushed us off with a nice big avalanche.

All that first spring and summer they were obviously hostile but passive. With the coming of September they pulled mists down over their heads like Ku-Klux hoods and began giving us the old water cure.

It rained and rained and rained and rained. It drizzled—misted—drooled—spat—poured—and just plain rained. Some mornings were black and wild, with a storm raging in and out and around the mountains. Rain was driven under the doors and down the chimney, and Bob went to the chicken house swathed in oilskins like a Newfoundland fisherman and I huddled by the stove and brooded about inside toilets. Other days were just gray and low hanging with a continual pit-pat-pit-pat-pitta-pattapitta-patta which became as vexing as listening to baby talk. Along about November I began to forget when it hadn't been raining and became as one with all the characters in all of the novels about rainy seasons, who rush around banging their heads against the walls, drinking water glasses of straight whiskey and moaning, "The rain! The rain! My God, the rain!"

In case you are wondering why I didn't take a good book, settle down by the stove and shut-up, I would like to explain that Stove, as we called him, had none of the warm, friendly qualities ordinarily associated with the name. In the first place he was too old and, like some terrible old man, he had a big strong frame, a lusty appetite and no spirit of cooperation. All attempts to get Stove to crackle and glow were as futile as trying to get the Rock of Gibraltar to giggle and cavort. I split pure pitch as fine as horsehair and stuffed his ponderous belly full, but there was no sound and no heat. Yet, when I took off the lids the kindling had burned and only a few warm ashes remained. It was as mysterious as the girl in high school who ate enormous lunches without apparently chewing or swallowing.

Incongruously, things did boil on Stove. This always came as a delightful shock, albeit I finally stopped rushing to the back door and shouting hysterically to Bob, quietly and competently at work, "The water is BOILING!" as I had done for the first few hundred times I had witnessed this miracle.

I put my first cake into the oven with such a sense of finality that I almost added a Rest-in-Peace wreath, and I felt like Sarah Crewe when I came in from the chicken house and the air was vibrant with the warm spicy smell of baking.

On the coldest dreariest mornings Stove sulked all over his end of the kitchen. He smoked and choked and gagged. He ate load after load of my precious live bark and by noon I could have sat cross-legged on him and read *Pilgrim's Progress* from cover to cover in perfect comfort.

Stove was actually a sinister presence and he was tricky. The day we first looked at the place, I remarked that he seemed rather defiantly backed up against the wall, but such an attitude could come from neglect, I thought, and so when we moved in the first thing I did was to clean his suit, take all the rust off his coat and vest, blacken every inch of him, except his nickel which I polished brightly, and then I built my first fire, which promptly went out. I built that fire five times and then Bob came in and poured about a gallon of kerosene on top of the kindling and Stove began balefully to burn a little. I learned by experience that it took two cups of kerosene to get his blood circulating in the morning and that he would only digest bark at night. In the summer and spring I didn't care how slow he was or how little heat he gave out. Bob and I were out doors from dawn to dark and we allowed plenty of time for cooking things and all of the wood was dry and the doors were open and there was plenty of draught. But with the first rainy day I realized that Stove was my enemy and would require the utmost in shrewd, cautious handling.

WAR STORIES

1948–1957

JOBS IN THE BOOMING WARTIME economy brought a new generation of immigrants to the Northwest during the Second World War. Mil-
itary bases sprang up all over the Northwest, including the top-secret
atomic facility at Hanford, Washington. More than two hundred thousand workers turned out Navy vessels in shipyards in Puget Sound and
along the Columbia and Willamette rivers. The Boeing Company began
1939 with four thousand employees; five years later the company had
more than fifty thousand workers building airplanes. Those planes were
built with aluminum from smelters constructed in the Northwest to take
advantage of the cheap hydroelectric power supplied by dams on the
Columbia.

But the war's literary legacy has nothing to do with all that. The
wartime literary legacy has to do with racism, ignorance, and fear.

Anti-Asian sentiment had been a part of the Pacific Northwest since
the anti-Chinese riots of the 1880s. Japanese immigrants were prohib-
ited from owning land and living in desirable areas, and could not become
naturalized citizens. Caucasian farmers and businessmen formed the Anti-
Japanese League in 1919, and in 1921 the Washington State legislature
passed a law prohibiting Japanese farmers from even leasing or renting
land. Strong Asian-American communities, especially in Seattle and Portland, flourished despite the laws.

News of the Japanese attack on Pearl Harbor on December 7, 1941,
"hit like a blockbuster, paralyzing us," recalled Monica Sone in *Nisei
Daughter,* her memoir of life before and during the war. "An old wound
opened up again, and I found myself shrinking inwardly from my Japanese blood, the blood of an enemy. I knew instinctively that the fact that

I was an American by birthright was not going to help me escape the consequences of this unhappy war."

Within 24 hours of the attack, FBI agents began arresting prominent Asian-Americans, including Buddhist priests and Japanese-language teachers. Japanese were warned to keep their distance from railroad tunnels and highway bridges. The racist notion that Asians were inscrutable foreigners who could never assimilate into American society suddenly was taken for a proven fact. "The Japanese race is an enemy race and while many second and third generation Japanese born on United States soil, possessed of United States citizenship have become 'Americanized,' the racial strains are undiluted," wrote Lieutenant General John DeWitt, head of the Western Defense Command, in his February 1942 recommendation to evacuate the Nikkei (people of Japanese ancestry) from the Western states.

DeWitt's memo was followed within days by President Roosevelt's Executive Order 9066, which forcibly removed 110,000 Japanese-Americans—two-thirds of whom were American citizens—from their West Coast homes and sent them to ten inland detention camps. Most Northwestern Nikkei were sent to Camp Minidoka, in south-central Idaho, or to Tule Lake in northern California. Although the government excused the internment camps on grounds of national security, no Japanese-American was ever charged with or convicted of espionage or sabotage, and many young Nikkei men served with distinction in the American armed forces.

Out of that experience came the best literary depictions of the Northwest during and after wartime—Monica Sone's *Nisei Daughter* and John Okada's *No-No Boy*. Sone and Okada's books are poignant evocations of life in Seattle's International District in the 1940s, exploring both the racial tensions of the Northwest and the conflict between first-, second-, and third-generation Japanese-American immigrants.

MONICA SONE

"All Japanese Americans talk of themselves and their history in three epochs," wrote novelist and playwright Frank Chin: "Before the war . . . Camp . . . After Camp." In her 1952 memoir, Nisei Daughter, *Monica Sone portrayed all*

three eras in the life of Seattle's Asian-American community. Born the daughter of Japanese immigrants (the terms issei, nisei, *and* sansei *refer to first-, second-, and third-generation immigrants), Sone grew up in the International District in the 1930s and was sent with her family to Camp Minidoka in Idaho during World War II. She left the camp in 1943 to attend college in Indiana.*

from NISEI DAUGHTER

ON A PEACEFUL SUNDAY morning, December 7, 1941, Henry, Sumi and I were at choir rehearsal singing ourselves hoarse in preparation for the annual Christmas recital of Handel's "Messiah." Suddenly Chuck Mizuno, a young University of Washington student, burst into the chapel, gasping as if he had sprinted all the way up the stairs.

"Listen, everybody!" he shouted. "Japan just bombed Pearl Harbor . . . in Hawaii! It's war!"

The terrible words hit like a blockbuster, paralyzing us. Then we smiled feebly at each other, hoping this was one of Chuck's practical jokes. Miss Hara, our music director, rapped her baton impatiently on the music stand and chided him, "Now Chuck, fun's fun, but we have work to do. Please take your place. You're already half an hour late."

But Chuck strode vehemently back to the door. "I mean it, folks, honest! I just heard the news over my car radio. Reporters are talking a blue streak. Come on down and hear it for yourselves."

With that, Chuck swept out of the room, a swirl of young men following in his wake. Henry was one of them. The rest of us stayed, rooted to our places like a row of marionettes. I felt as if a fist had smashed my pleasant little existence, breaking it into jigsaw puzzle pieces. An old wound opened up again, and I found myself shrinking inwardly from my Japanese blood, the blood of an enemy. I knew instinctively that the fact that I was an American by birthright was not going to help me escape the consequences of this unhappy war.

One girl mumbled over and over again, "It can't be, God, it can't be!" Someone else was saying, "What a spot to be in! Do you think we'll be considered Japanese or Americans?"

A boy replied quietly, "We'll be Japs, same as always. But our parents are enemy aliens now, you know."

A shocked silence followed. Henry came for Sumi and me. "Come on, let's go home," he said.

We ran trembling to our car. Usually Henry was a careful driver, but that morning he bore down savagely on the accelerator. Boiling angry, he shot us up Twelfth Avenue, rammed through the busy Jackson Street intersection, and rocketed up the Beacon Hill bridge. We swung violently around to the left of the Marine Hospital and swooped to the top of the hill. Then Henry slammed on the brakes and we rushed helter-skelter up to the house to get to the radio. Asthma skidded away from under our trampling feet.

Mother was sitting limp in the huge armchair as if she had collapsed there, listening dazedly to the turbulent radio. Her face was frozen still, and the only words she could utter were, *"Komatta neh, komatta neh.* How dreadful, how dreadful."

Henry put his arms around her. She told him she first heard about the attack on Pearl Harbor when one of her friends phoned her and told her to turn on the radio.

We pressed close against the radio, listening stiffly to the staccato out-bursts of an excited reporter: "The early morning sky of Honolulu was filled with the furious buzzing of Jap Zero planes for nearly three hours, raining death and destruction on the airfields below . . . A warship anchored beyond the Harbor was sunk . . . "

We were switched to the White House. The fierce clack of teletype machines and the babble of voices surging in and out from the background almost drowned out the speaker's terse announcements.

With every fiber of my being I resented this war. I felt as if I were on fire. "Mama, they should never have done it," I cried. "Why did they do it? Why? Why?"

Mother's face turned paper white. "What do you know about it? Right or wrong, the Japanese have been chafing with resentment for years. It was bound to happen, one time or another. You're young, Ka-chan, you know very little about the ways of nations. It's not as simple as you think, but this is hardly the time to be quarreling about it, is it?"

"No, it's too late, too late!" and I let the tears pour down my face.

Father rushed home from the hotel. He was deceptively calm as he joined us in the living room. Father was a born skeptic, and he believed nothing unless he could see, feel and smell it. He regarded all newspapers and radio news with deep suspicion. He shook his head doubtfully,

"It must be propaganda. With the way things are going now between America and Japan, we should expect the most fantastic rumors, and this is one of the wildest I've heard yet." But we noticed that he was firmly glued to the radio. It seemed as if the regular Sunday programs, sounding off relentlessly hour after hour on schedule, were trying to blunt the catastrophe of the morning.

The telephone pealed nervously all day as people searched for comfort from each other. Chris called, and I told her how miserable and confused I felt about the war. Understanding as always, Chris said, "You know how I feel about you and your family, Kaz. Don't, for heaven's sake, feel the war is going to make any difference in our relationship. It's not your fault, nor mine! I wish to God it could have been prevented." Minnie called off her Sunday date with Henry. Her family was upset and they thought she should stay close to home instead of wandering downtown.

Late that night Father got a shortwave broadcast from Japan. Static sputtered, then we caught a faint voice, speaking rapidly in Japanese. Father sat unmoving as a rock, his head cocked. The man was talking about the war between Japan and America. Father bit his lips and Mother whispered to him anxiously, "It's true, then, isn't it, Papa? It's true?"

Father was muttering to himself, "So they really did it!" Now having heard the news in their native tongue, the war had become a reality to father and mother.

"I suppose from now on, we'll hear about nothing but the humiliating defeats of Japan in the papers here," Mother said, resignedly.

Henry and I glared indignantly at Mother, then Henry shrugged his shoulders and decided to say nothing. Discussion of politics, especially Japan versus America, had become taboo in our family for it sent tempers skyrocketing. Henry and I used to criticize Japan's aggressions in China and Manchuria while Father and Mother condemned Great Britain and America's superior attitude toward Asiatics and their interference with Japan's economic growth. During these arguments, we had eyed each other like strangers, parents against children. They left us with a hollow feeling at the pit of the stomach.

———————

It made me positively hivey the way the FBI agents continued their raids into Japanese homes and business places and marched the Issei men away into the old red brick immigration building, systematically and efficiently, as if they were stocking a cellarful of choice bottles of wine. At first we noted that the men arrested were those who had been prominent in community affairs, like Mr. Kato, many times president of the Seattle Japanese Chamber of Commerce, and Mr. Ohashi, the principal of our Japanese language school, or individuals whose businesses were directly connected with firms in Japan; but as time went on, it became less and less apparent why the others were included in these raids.

We wondered when Father's time would come. We expected momentarily to hear strange footsteps on the porch and the sudden demanding ring of the front doorbell. Our ears became attuned like the sensitive antennas of moths, translating every soft swish of passing cars into the arrival of the FBI squad.

Once when our doorbell rang after curfew hour, I completely lost my Oriental stoicism which I had believed would serve me well under the most trying circumstances. No friend of ours paid visits at night anymore, and I was sure that Father's hour had come. As if hypnotized, I walked woodenly to the door. A mass of black figures stood before me, filling the doorway. I let out a magnificent shriek. Then pandemonium broke loose. The solid rank fell apart into a dozen separate figures which stumbled and leaped pell-mell away from the porch. Watching the mad scramble, I thought I had routed the FBI agents with my cry of distress. Father, Mother, Henry and Sumi rushed out to support my wilting body. When Henry snapped on the porch light, one lone figure crept out from behind the front hedge. It was a newsboy who, standing at a safe distance, called in a quavering voice, "I . . . I came to collect for . . . for the *Times.*"

Shaking with laughter, Henry paid him and gave him an extra large tip for the terrible fright he and his bodyguards had suffered at the hands of the Japanese. As he hurried down the walk, boys of all shapes and sizes crawled out from behind trees and bushes and scurried after him.

We heard all kinds of stories about the FBI, most of them from Mr. Yorita, the grocer, who now took twice as long to make his deliveries. The war seemed to have brought out his personality. At least he talked more, and he glowed, in a sinister way. Before the war Mr. Yorita had been uncommunicative. He used to stagger silently through the back door with a huge sack of rice over his shoulders, dump it on the kitchen floor and silently flow out of the door as if he were bored and disgusted with food and the people who ate it. But now Mr. Yorita swaggered in, sent a gallon jug of soy sauce spinning into a corner, and launched into a comprehensive report of the latest rumors he had picked up on his route, all in chronological order. Mr. Yorita looked like an Oriental Dracula, with his triangular eyes and yellow-fanged teeth. He had a mournfully long sallow face and in his excitement his gold-rimmed glasses constantly slipped to the tip of his long nose. He would describe in detail how some man had been awakened in the dead of night, swiftly handcuffed, and dragged from out of his bed by a squad of brutal, tight-lipped men. Mr. Yorita bared his teeth menacingly in his most dramatic moments and we shrank from him instinctively. As he backed out of the kitchen door, he would shake his bony finger at us with a warning of dire things to come. When Mother said, "Yorita-san, you must worry about getting a call from the FBI, too," Mr. Yorita laughed modestly, pushing his glasses back up into place. "They wouldn't be interested in anyone as insignificant as myself!" he assured her.

But he was wrong. The following week a new delivery boy appeared at the back door with an airy explanation. "Yep, they got the old man, too, and don't ask me why! The way I see it, it's subversive to sell soy sauce now."

The Matsuis were visited, too. Shortly after Dick had gone to Japan, Mr. Matsui had died and Mrs. Matsui had sold her house. Now she and her daughter and youngest son lived in the back of their little dry goods store on Jackson Street. One day when Mrs. Matsui was busy with the family laundry, three men entered the shop, nearly ripping off the tiny bell hanging over the door. She hurried out, wiping sudsy, reddened hands on her apron. At best Mrs. Matsui's English was rudimentary, and when she became excited, it deteriorated into Japanese. She hovered on her toes, delighted to see new customers in her humble shop. "Yes, yes, something you want?"

"Where's Mr. Matsui?" a steely-eyed man snapped at her.

Startled, Mrs. Matsui jerked her thumb toward the rear of the store and said, "He not home."

"What? Oh, in there, eh? Come on!" The men tore the faded print curtain aside and rushed into the back room. "Don't see him. Must be hiding."

They jerked open the bedroom doors, leaped into the tiny bathroom, flung windows open and peered down into the alley. Tiny birdlike Mrs.

Matsui rushed around after them. "No, no! Whatsamalla, whatsamalla!"

"Where's your husband? Where is he?" one man demanded angrily, flinging clothes out of the closet.

"Why you mix 'em all up? He not home, not home." She clawed at the back of the burly men like an angry little sparrow, trying to stop the holocaust in her little home. One man brought his face down close to hers, shouting slowly and clearly, "WHERE IS YOUR HUSBAND? YOU SAID HE WAS HERE A MINUTE AGO!"

"Yes, yes, not here. *Mah, wakara nai hito da neh.* Such stupid men."

Mrs. Matsui dove under a table, dragged out a huge album and pointed at a large photograph. She jabbed her gnarled finger up toward the ceiling, saying, "Heben! Heben!"

The men gathered around and looked at a picture of Mr. Matsui's funeral. Mrs. Matsui and her two children were standing by a coffin, their eyes cast down, surrounded by all their friends, all of whom were looking down. The three men's lips formed an "Oh." One of them said, "We're sorry to have disturbed you. Thank you, Mrs. Matsui, and good-by." They departed quickly and quietly.

Having passed through this baptism, Mrs. Matsui became an expert on the FBI, and she stood by us, rallying and coaching us on how to deal with them. She said to Mother, "You must destroy everything and anything Japanese which may incriminate your husband. It doesn't matter what it is, if it's printed or made in Japan, destroy it because the FBI always carries off those items for evidence."

In fact all the women whose husbands had been spirited away said the same thing. Gradually we became uncomfortable with our Japanese books, magazines, wall scrolls and knickknacks. When Father's hotel friends, Messrs. Sakaguchi, Horiuchi, Nishibue and a few others vanished, and their wives called Mother weeping and warning her again about having too many Japanese objects around the house, we finally decided to get rid of some of ours. We knew it was impossible to destroy everything. The FBI would certainly think it strange if they found us sitting in a bare house, totally purged of things Japanese. But it was as if we could no longer stand the tension of waiting, and we just had to do something against the black day. We worked all night, feverishly combing through bookshelves, closets, drawers, and furtively creeping down to the basement furnace for the burning. I gathered together my well-worn Japanese language schoolbooks which I had been saving over a period of ten years with the thought that they might come in handy when I wanted to teach Japanese to my own children. I threw them into the fires and watched them flame and shrivel into black ashes.

NARD JONES

*Seattle native Nard Jones sold his first story in 1926 and went on to publish more than three hundred by the late 1950s. His twelve novels were all set in the Northwest; most dealt with life in small wheat-farming towns (*Oregon Detour, *1930, and* Wheat Women, *1933), on cattle ranches (*All Six Were Lovers, *1934), and along the Columbia River (*Swift Flows the River, *1940, and* Scarlet Petticoat, *1941). All drew heavily on the history of the region. The Island, Jones's 1948 novel about a Seattle reporter who works as a public relations officer for the Navy during World War II (as Jones did himself), was his only fictional, book-length depiction of modern life in the Northwest.*

from THE ISLAND

AILEEN MADCLIFF TELEPHONED me halfway through the week to say that the party was still on for the next Sunday. "I was going to call it off," she said, "but then Jack and I talked about it and decided to go ahead. You'll come, won't you? I mean, you don't think it's wrong to go ahead with it, do you?"

I didn't know what I thought about it. I had forgotten the party completely. "I'll come," I said.

"That's wonderful, Lou. And will you pick up Carol Bundy? I've telephoned her. It may not be very gay, but we decided we ought to get together anyhow. While we can. I don't suppose there'll be many parties now."

Aileen did not sound like herself, and her uncertainty was a reflection of the vague partial paralysis that had crept over Seattle in those first few days. This was not the way it was to have been at all. Something had gone wrong somewhere. We were to have acted as the arsenal of democracy and Seattle was to have been one of the cities that sends fighting implements all over the world. We were to have shown our position clearly, and then worked, willingly but safely, behind our great shores. In that way we were to have liberated the world, and in that way we were to have saved ourselves without the need of shedding blood.

But that had turned out to be an unfulfilled part of the American dream, which was both puzzling and shocking. The head of the Army's Western Defense Command and the three Navy commandants stationed along the coast, appeared to be the only ones not puzzled or shocked. What had they known that the public hadn't known? Or was it simply that their training protected them from shock at a time like this? We were proud of their attitude, of the calm that framed their public orders and pronouncements. But most of us were a little miffed, too, because the orders and pronouncements carried a definite implication that this was what they had expected, that really nothing else could have occurred at the end of our hopes and fears.

Because it was the Army that had to look to land defense in the air raid that was quite possible, even probable, the responsibility for ordering our lives fell most quickly on General DeWitt. Within a few hours he set the pattern for us from his headquarters in San Francisco. We blacked out our windows, or sat in darkness at night behind soundless radios. We covered the lenses of our flashlights with blue cellophane and fixed our automobile headlights so that only slits of light shone through.

It was a strange new world, a strange new way of living, in a city that had changed its shape and coloring, between a quiet morning and a bleak and fearful evening. It seemed that half of Seattle had gone into uniform. We had not realized how many officers in mufti were among us. The Reserves looked self-conscious, and the older regulars were sad-faced men. Even in the top ranks there was no real knowledge of what had happened, in detail, at Pearl Harbor. But there were horrible suspicions; rumors licked like little flames along the streets of the city.

Seattle knew it was unprotected. It had not been told by so much as an official whisper, but the truth was in the air that we breathed. The high sounds from Washington, D.C., did not deceive the West Coast towns and cities. And gradually there set in a new fear over the first fear. We began to suspect that the enemy must know of our helplessness, know it in greater detail than we did. There had been so many Japs among us, and suddenly we remembered that some of them had returned to Japan not long ago. Like Manabe, the "Number One Boy" at the Ivy Club. Like

Oboe, a bar boy at the University Club. Like Mr. J. Matsuo, who was not a "boy" because he had not been a servant. Mr. Matsuo had resigned as second vice-president of the Yokohama American warehouse to visit, so he said, his ailing parents in Japan. What did men like these know, what had they gathered in their friendly smiling years among us, and how much of it had they carried home with them? And, we began to ask ourselves, what was their rank in Japan?

"Lou, what about Bill Mokosato?" Aileen had asked me when she telephoned about the party. "Do you think it would be all right to ask him? He's often here, you know, and I feel if we don't now . . . "

The advice I gave her came quickly, and was against asking Bill. I knew Bill, who was American born, and I had known him for years. But suddenly I remembered that Bill had returned to Japan soon after his graduation from the university and had stayed a year. Bill had an unusual talent for water colors. He had won some prizes and had had shows in New York galleries. His parents were comfortably fixed—his father ran an importing shop.

When Aileen asked about inviting Bill Mokosato to her party I realized there was considerable that Bill and I had never talked about. He had been one of my best leads on Japanese stories for the paper, and whenever I got stuck on a Jap story I'd telephone Bill. It was usually a business story or a human interest piece, for the Japs rarely got into the kind of trouble that makes news. After Aileen called I remembered that about three weeks before Pearl Harbor he had opened up the subject of American-Japanese relations. The negotiations in Washington appeared to be getting nowhere, and it seemed natural that Bill should bring up the subject. I think all he said was that he hoped the people in this country would not get too disturbed over some of the stories in the newspapers. It was now that I recalled that he had said "the people in this country" instead of "we," and that irritated me in retrospect, in the glare of the shame of Pearl Harbor.

I had not been very adult in answering him. I said that I did not understand international relations, which was true, but I added that they gave me a pain, which was a foolish remark. "It's only City Hall finagling in striped pants," I said to Bill. "Suppose our City Hall finaglers had Dorothy Thompsons and Walter Lippmanns to write about them, instead of a Lou Benedict. We'd begin to think of them as great men. But they'd still be only power jockeys."

"It is more serious than that," said Bill Mokosato.

"Certainly. It's damned serious. But it is still jockeying for power, just like down at our dirty old City Hall."

"Japan and this country will not go to war," Bill said then. "We understand each other. All that jingoism of twenty or thirty years ago is gone. There will be a settlement satisfactory to both countries."

That night he had marked some articles for me to read in a couple of English-language periodicals printed in Japan. He had never done that before. "What are you trying to do, Bill?" I asked him. "Are you trying to sell me a bill of goods?" I meant nothing by it, but after December 7 I wondered. I wondered whether he had been trying to educate me, or throw me off, or convince himself, or whether he was just hoping everything would be all right. Perhaps he guessed the truth, if he did not have an inkling of it, and only hoped against it.

He had telephoned me the day after the attack in Hawaii. "You can imagine I feel like hell," he said. Somehow it did not ring true for me. It couldn't. How in the name of common sense could Bill Mokosato help but feel, somewhere inside him, a tiny exaltation at the confusion of the white race, which had treated Japanese as odd little people, studious but imitative, and wonderful servants?

I don't know if it was right to give Aileen the answer I gave her about Bill Mokosato. I do know this—if you lived on the West Coast that day you had to decide something about the Japanese, one way or the other.

"I wouldn't invite Bill," I told Aileen. "It would only make him unhappy if he came, and there's the chance some guy will get too much to drink and punch him in the nose because he is Japanese." That was not a nice way to put it, but it was the truth. I might have said that it was not yet the time for such tolerance, that we were not yet ready to take our places in the brotherhood of the world, and that first we would have to go through our bath of blood. But that would not have sounded very nice, either; besides, nobody talks like that in America until after the war is over. And after a war is over we stand self-conscious and ashamed because we won.

So Bill Mokosato did not come to the party, and a few days later he was gone. I have never seen him since, and I think he did not come back to Seattle. There are stories about him: that when he saw his father and mother moved from their home and business he became bitter and troublesome and was transferred to Tule Lake, where they kept the bad ones.

JOHN OKADA

The story of John Okada's novel No-No Boy *is the stuff of great tragedy and triumph. The book went virtually unnoticed when it was published in 1957. Thirteen years later writer Jeff Chan discovered a used copy of the novel in a San Francisco bookshop and began passing it among his friends, who included the writers Lawson Fusao Inada, Frank Chin, and Shawn Wong. They reprinted a small edition in 1976, and three years later the University of Washington Press picked up the book. By 1981 it was in its second printing, and John Okada was being recognized as one of America's finest Asian-American writers. The novel tells the story of Ichiro, labeled a "no-no boy" for refusing to serve the country that had imprisoned his parents in internment camps. Okada himself served in the Pacific during the war. He died in 1971, five years before his novel was revived.*

from NO-NO BOY

TWO WEEKS AFTER his twenty-fifth birthday, Ichiro got off a bus at Second and Main in Seattle. He had been gone four years, two in camp and two in prison . . .

He walked toward the railroad depot where the tower with the clocks on all four sides was. It was a dirty looking tower of ancient brick. It was a dirty city. Dirtier, certainly, than it had a right to be after only four years.

Waiting for the light to change to green, he looked around at the people standing at the bus stop. A couple of men in suits, half a dozen women who failed to arouse him even after prolonged good behavior, and a young Japanese with a lunch bucket. Ichiro studied him, searching his mind for the name that went with the round, pimply face and the short-cropped hair. The pimples were gone and the face had hardened, but the hair was still cropped. The fellow wore green, army-fatigue trousers and an Eisenhower jacket—Eto Minato. The name came to him at the same time as did the horrible significance of the army clothes. In panic, he started to step off the curb. It was too late. He had been seen.

"Itchy!" That was his nickname.

Trying to escape, Ichiro urged his legs frenziedly across the street.

"Hey, Itchy!" The caller's footsteps ran toward him.

An arm was placed across his back. Ichiro stopped and faced the other Japanese. He tried to smile, but could not. There was no way out now.

"I'm Eto. Remember?" Eto smiled and extended his palm. Reluctantly, Ichiro lifted his own hand and let the other shake it.

The round face with the round eyes peered at him through silver-rimmed spectacles. "What the hell! It's been a long time, but not that long. How've you been? What's doing?"

"Well . . . that is, I'm . . . "

"Last time must have been before Pearl Harbor. God, it's been quite a while, hasn't it? Three, no, closer to four years, I guess. Lotsa Japs coming back to the Coast. Lotsa Japs in Seattle. You'll see 'em around. Japs are funny that way. Gotta have their rice and saké and other Japs. Stupid, I say. The smart ones went to Chicago and New York and lotsa places back east, but there's still plenty coming back out this way." Eto drew cigarettes from his breast pocket and held out the package. "No? Well, I'll have one. Got the habit in the army. Just got out a short while back. Rough time, but I made it. Didn't get out in time to make the quarter, but I'm planning to go to school. How long you been around?"

Ichiro touched his toe to the suitcase. "Just got in. Haven't been home yet."

"When'd you get discharged?"

A car grinding its gears started down the street. He wished he were in it. "I . . . that is . . . I never was in."

Eto slapped him good-naturedly on the arm. "No need to look so sour. So you weren't in. So what? Been in camp all this time?"

"No." He made an effort to be free of Eto with his questions. He felt as if he were in a small room whose walls were slowly closing in on him. "It's been a long time, I know, but I'm really anxious to see the folks."

"What the hell. Let's have a drink. On me. I don't give a damn if I'm late to work. As for your folks, you'll see them soon enough. You drink, don't you?"

"Yeah, but not now."

"Ahh." Eto was disappointed. He shifted his lunch box from one arm to the other.

"I've really got to be going."

The round face wasn't smiling any more. It was thoughtful. The eyes confronted Ichiro with indecision which changed slowly to enlightenment and then to suspicion. He remembered. He knew.

The friendliness was gone as he said: "No-no boy, huh?"

Ichiro wanted to say yes. He wanted to return the look of despising hatred and say simply yes, but it was too much to say. The walls had closed in and were crushing all the unspoken words back down into his stomach. He shook his head once, not wanting to evade the eyes but finding it impossible to meet them. Out of his big weakness the little ones were branching, and the eyes he didn't have the courage to face were ever present. If it would have helped to gouge out his own eyes, he would have done so long ago. The hate-churned eyes with the stamp of unrelenting condemnation were his cross and he had driven the nails with his own hands.

"Rotten bastard. Shit on you." Eto coughed up a mouthful of sputum and rolled his eyes around it: "Rotten, no-good bastard."

Surprisingly, Ichiro felt relieved. Eto's anger seemed to serve as a release to his own naked tensions. As he stooped to lift the suitcase a wet wad splattered over his hand and dripped onto the black leather. The legs of his accuser were in front of him. God in a pair of green fatigues, U.S. Army style. They were the legs of the jury that had passed sentence upon him. Beseech me, they seemed to say, throw your arms about me and bury your head between my knees and seek pardon for your great sin.

"I'll piss on you next time," said Eto vehemently.

He turned as he lifted the suitcase off the ground and hurried away from the legs and the eyes from which no escape was possible.

Jackson Street started at the waterfront and stretched past the two train depots and up the hill all the way to the lake, where the houses were bigger and cleaner and had garages with late-model cars in them. For Ichiro, Jackson Street signified that section of the city immediately beyond the railroad tracks between Fifth and Twelfth Avenues. That was the section which used to be pretty much Japanese town. It was adjacent to Chinatown and most of the gambling and prostitution and drinking seemed to favor the area.

Like the dirty clock tower of the depot, the filth of Jackson Street had increased. Ichiro paused momentarily at an alley and peered down the passage formed by the walls of two sagging buildings. There had been a door there at one time, a back door to a movie house which only charged a nickel. A nickel was a lot of money when he had been seven or nine or eleven. He wanted to go into the alley to see if the door was still there.

Being on Jackson Street with its familiar store fronts and taverns and restaurants, which were somehow different because the war had left its mark on them, was like trying to find one's way out of a dream that seemed real most of the time but wasn't really real because it was still only a dream. The war had wrought violent changes upon the people, and the people, in turn, working hard and living hard and earning a lot of money and spending it on whatever was available, had distorted the profile of Jackson Street. The street had about it the air of a carnival without quite succeeding at becoming one. A shooting gallery stood where once had been a clothing store; fish and chips had replaced a jewelry shop; and a bunch of Negroes were horsing around raucously in front of a pool parlor. Everything looked older and dirtier and shabbier.

He walked past the pool parlor, picking his way gingerly among the Negroes, of whom there had been only a few at one time and of whom there seemed to be nothing but now. They were smoking and shouting and cussing and carousing and the sidewalk was slimy with their spittle.

"Jap!"

His pace quickened automatically, but curiosity or fear or indignation or whatever it was made him glance back at the white teeth framed in a leering dark brown which was almost black.

"Go back to Tokyo, boy." Persecution in the drawl of the persecuted.

The white teeth and brown-black leers picked up the cue and jigged to the rhythmical chanting of "Jap-boy, To-ki-yo; Jap-boy, To-ki-yo . . . "

Friggin' niggers, he uttered savagely to himself and, from the same place deep down inside where tolerance for the Negroes and the Jews and the Mexicans and the Chinese and the too short and too fat and too ugly abided because he was Japanese and knew what it was like better than did those who were white and average and middle class and good Democrats or liberal Republicans, the hate which was unrelenting and terrifying seethed up.

Then he was home. It was a hole in the wall with groceries crammed in orderly confusion on not enough shelving, into not enough space. He knew what it would be like even before he stepped in. His father had described the place to him in a letter, composed in simple Japanese characters because otherwise Ichiro could not have read it. The letter had been purposely repetitive and painstakingly detailed so that Ichiro should not have any difficulty finding the place. The grocery store was the same one the Ozakis had operated for many years. That's all his father had had to say. Come to the grocery store which was once the store of the Ozakis. The Japanese characters, written simply so that he could read them, covered pages of directions as if he were a foreigner coming to the city for the first time.

Thinking about the letter made him so mad that he forgot about the Negroes. He opened the door just as he had a thousand times when they had lived farther down the block and he used to go to the Ozakis' for a loaf of bread or a jar of pickled scallions, and the bell tinkled just as he knew it would. All the grocery stores he ever knew had bells which tinkled when one opened the door and the familiar sound softened his inner turmoil.

"Ichiro?" The short, round man who came through the curtains at the back of the store uttered the name preciously as might an old woman. "Ya, Ichiro, you have come home. How good that you have come home!" The gently spoken Japanese which he had not heard for so long sounded strange. He would hear a great deal of it now that he was home, for his parents, like most of the old Japanese, spoke virtually no English. On the other hand, the children, like Ichiro, spoke almost no Japanese. Thus they communicated, the old speaking Japanese with an occasional badly mispronounced word or two of English; and the young, with the exception of a simple word or phrase of Japanese which came fairly effortlessly to the lips, resorting almost constantly to the tongue the parents avoided.

THE POSTWAR
NORTHWEST

1950–1976

WHEN THEODORE ROETHKE arrived in Seattle to teach at the University of Washington in the autumn of 1947, the chairman of the English department told him, "Ted, we don't know quite what to do with you; you're the only serious practicing poet within fifteen hundred miles." Roethke saw himself stepping into a cultural backwater, a friendly but unsophisticated province. "This town is pleasant enough, but I'm afraid I'm going to be overwhelmed by nice people," he wrote to Kenneth Burke. "It's a kind of vast Scarsdale, it would seem. Bright, active women, with blue hair, and well-barbered males. The arts and the 'East' seem to cow them . . ."

By the time Roethke died sixteen years later, the Northwest had become a thriving literary outpost. With his Pulitzer Prize– and National Book Award–winning collections, Roethke joined T. S. Eliot, W. H. Auden, Dylan Thomas, and others in the highest echelons of modern poetry. Leading national poets contributed to the UW's literary journal *Poetry Northwest,* reversing the traditional eastward course of the literary mails. Roethke's students—Richard Hugo, David Wagoner, Carolyn Kizer, and Richard Wright among them—earned strong reputations in their own right, and the next generation of poets flocked to the university from all over the country. In Oregon, William Stafford was creating the poems that would go into the 1966 collection *Traveling Through the Dark* (another National Book Award winner). Seattle hosted readings by Marianne Moore, William Snodgrass, W. S. Merwin, Louise Bogan, and other literary figures, "all of them come to Seattle or detoured there en route down or up the coast," recalled UW English professor Kermit Vanderbilt, "because Roethke had made the Northwest a vital corner of American poetry."

This was a Northwest renaissance, but it was never a "Northwest school." The phrase risks tarring the poetry with a second-rate regionalism, as if the meaning of the work would melt away as it crossed the Rockies or entered California. Roethke used scenes from the Northwest in his later work, especially in the North American Sequence that opens his posthumously published collection, *The Far Field* (1964). "My imagery is coming more out of the Northwest rather than the whole of America," he told a reporter for an English newspaper in 1960. But his images were never intended to be read as sunny seashore descriptions; they contain the poet's ruminations on the searching journey of the human spirit and strengthen the language of the poem itself. After nearly a century of vapid posies-and-teacups verse, the Northwest landed in Roethke a poet who finally connected the region's misty atmosphere and raw landscape to the weather and topography of the soul. When he wrote, "In a bleak time, when a week of rain is a year," in "The Longing," he captured in a single line the crushing grayness of a Pacific Northwest winter and a corresponding inner spiritual despair.

The native territory had a much greater influence on the work of the generation after Roethke. Many of Richard Hugo's best poems draw on his childhood in the working-class Seattle suburb of White Center and on his adult love for rivers like the Duwamish, Skagit, and Hoh. David Wagoner's poems are as rooted in the forests of the Northwest as an old-growth Douglas fir. Gary Snyder worked as a logger and fire lookout in the North Cascades while vagabonding up and down the West Coast in the 1950s, and even convinced his friend Jack Kerouac to give tree-perching a try. Kerouac nearly went nutty in the silent woods, but later wrote the experience into his Beat novel *The Dharma Bums*.

Snyder's experiences in the Northwest woods are chronicled in some of his better-known early poems, including "Mid-August at Sourdough Mountain Lookout," "The Late Snow & Lumber Strike of the Summer of Fifty-Four," and the section "Logging" of his *Myths & Texts* collection. Whereas George Vancouver compared the region's "most luxuriant landscape" to the sylvan grounds of England and Theodore Winthrop relied on a Northeastern United States frame of reference for his descriptions, Snyder executed an about-face and stepped across the ocean, marrying the wild spirit of the far-western wilderness to the farther-western myths and beliefs of the Asian Buddhist tradition.

A new sense of connection with the natural world emerged in the post-war period, one that had lain virtually dormant since John Muir first floated the idea of sparing a few trees from the ax back in the 1880s. In the poetry of Roethke—and especially Hugo, Wagoner, and Snyder—the Northwest's mountains, rivers, and forests are sources of wisdom and spiritual renewal, not ominous forces to be whipped and tamed in the name of civilization.

Before this eco-pluralism overran Northwest literature, however, Ken Kesey came along and gave the old man-against-nature theme one last yawp. Like Snyder, Kesey is often associated with the Beat generation. Both had good friends inside the Beat core: Snyder turned Kerouac on to Buddhism, Kesey teamed up with Neal Cassady on the famous Merry Prankster road trips. But the characters in Kesey's 1964 epic *Sometimes a Great Notion* would scoff at Snyder's yin/yang model of the universe. In Hank Stamper, Kesey created the greatest ax-swinging he-man since Paul Bunyan. An independent logger who tramps into the forest every morning to slay the monstrous trees, Hank comes home every night to battle the river, which is eating away at the bank that is the foundation of his home and life. Hank Stamper proved to be the last of the frontiersmen—within and without Kesey's novel. After his passing, the Pacific Northwestern hero was more likely to join nature than beat it.

WILLIAM O. DOUGLAS

During his long tenure on the United States Supreme Court, William O. Douglas wrote thirty books and numerous articles on civil liberties, foreign policy, wilderness conservation, and his personal history. In his autobiography, Go East, Young Man *(1974), Douglas described his early years growing up in Yakima, Washington. But an earlier book,* Of Men and Mountains *(1950), better captures the judge's love of the Northwest wilderness and the homesickness he suffered while working the halls of justice in New York and Washington, D.C.*

from OF MEN AND MOUNTAINS

MOUNT ADAMS HAS ALWAYS had a special lure for me. Its memory has been the most haunting of all. Adams is more intimate than Rainier. Its lines are softer; it is more accessible. It has always been my favorite snow-capped mountain. My long ambition was to climb it. It was a mountain of mystery. It had been at one time, as I shall relate, a brave Indian chief named Klickitat. It had exhibited recent volcanic activity. High on its shoulders are crevasses that spout sulfur fumes. The Indians would not go up to its glaciers. There in the fastness of the mountain lived the Tomanows, the spirit chiefs of the Indians.

This mountain was so legendary I might not have believed it existed had I not lived in its shadow and seen it in sun and storm for twenty years. The vision of it would come back to me in dusty law libraries as I searched for the elusive thing called the law. High in an office building on New York's Wall Street I would be lost in the maze of a legal problem, forgetful of my bearings, and then suddenly look from the window to the west, thinking for a second that I might see Mount Adams, somber in its purplish snow at sunset. I have done the same thing while sitting deep in meditation in a canoe on a Maine lake or in a boat in Florida's Everglades . . .

[T]he most vivid recollections have reached me in environments that have been bleak and dreary and oppressive. I remember a room in New York City on West 120th Street that overlooked an air well.

The sun reached that room but a scant two hours a day. There was no other outlook. The whole view was a dull brick wall, pierced by dingy panes of glass. In one of these windows some poor soul had set a tiny, scrawny geranium. There were lively zoological specimens around—such as cockroaches. But the only botanical specimen in sight was the geranium. I would see it in the morning when I arose and on rainy Sundays when I stayed indoors. In the poverty of that view the memories of the Cascades would come flooding back.

Lush bottom lands along the upper Naches, where the grass grows stirrup high—succulent grass that will hold a horse all night.

A deer orchid deep in the brush off the American River Trail.

A common rock wren singing its heart out on a rock slide above Bumping Lake.

Clusters of the spring beauty in the damp creek beds along the eastern slopes of Hogback Mountain.

The smell of wood smoke, bacon, and onions at a camp below Meade Glacier.

Indian paintbrush and phlox on the high shoulders of Goat Rocks.

The roar of the northwesters in the treetops in Tieton Basin.

Clumps of balsam fir pointed like spires to the sky in Blankenship Meadows.

The cry of a loon through the mist of Bumping Lake.

A clump of whitebark pine atop Darling Mountain—gnarled and tough, beaten by a thousand gales.

A black, red-crested woodpecker attacking in machine-gun style a tree at Goose Prairie.

The scrawny geranium across the rooming house court in New York City brought back these nostalgic memories and many more. The glories of the Cascades grew and grew in the desolation of the bleak view from my window. New York City became almost unbearable. I was suffocated and depressed. I wanted to flee the great city with its scrawny geraniums and bleak courtyards. The longing for the silences of the Cascades, the smell of fir boughs at night, the touch of the chinook as it blew over the ridges— these longings were almost irresistible in the oppressiveness of my New York City rooming house.

I had had a similar experience on my way east to law school. I had left on a freight train from Wenatchee, Washington, with 2000 sheep. That was in September, 1922 . . .

I knew the freight trains well. Hitchhikers of the period prior to the First World War chose them as a matter of necessity, because the great flow of highway traffic had not yet started. Like many others, I had ridden the rods up and down the Yakima Valley and to points east, to work in the hay- and wheatfields and in the orchards . . .

On this trip through Minnesota I paid toll to the crew of the freight train—fifty cents apiece, as I recall. When we came to a new division point, I discovered that the new crew was also collecting fares. I was easy prey, for I was on a flatcar—the only available space, except the rods and the top of the boxcars. This was a loaded and sealed train, carrying for the most part fruit in refrigerator cars. When the new brakeman came along he asked for a dollar and I paid him. Nothing more happened for a long time. Then along came the conductor. We were on the outskirts of Chicago. It was three or four o'clock in the morning on a clear, cold night. The conductor asked for a dollar; he said there were yard bulls ahead, he did not want me to get into trouble, and he would see that the yard bulls did not arrest me. It was the same old story.

I was silent for a while, trying to figure out how I could afford to part with another dollar. I had only a few left. I had not had a hot meal for seven days; I had not been to bed for thirteen nights; I was filthy and without a change of clothes. I needed a bath and a shave and food; above all else I needed sleep. Even flophouses cost money. And the oatmeal, hot cakes, ham and eggs and coffee—which I wanted desperately—would cost fifty or seventy-five cents.

"Why should I pay this guy and become a panhandler in Chicago?" I asked myself.

He shook me by the shoulder and said, "Come on, buddy. Do you want to get tossed off the train?"

"I'm broke," I said.

"Broke?" he retorted. "You paid the brakeman and you can pay me."

"Have a heart," I said. "I bet you were broke some time. Give a guy a break."

He roared at me to get off or he would turn me over to the bulls. I was silent.

"Well, jump off or I'll run you in."

I watched the lights of Chicago come nearer. We were entering a maze of tracks. There were switches and sidetracks, boxcars on sidings, occasional loading platforms. And once in a while we roared over a short highway bridge. It was dark and the train was going about thirty miles an hour. The terrain looked treacherous. A jump might be disastrous. But I decided to husband my two or three remaining dollars. I stood poised on the edge of the flatcar, searching the area immediately ahead for a place to jump.

Suddenly in my ear came the command, "Jump!" I jumped.

Something brushed my left sleeve. It was the arm of a switch. Then I fell clear, hitting a cinder bank. I lost my footing, slid on my hands and knees for a dozen feet down the bank, and rolled to the bottom.

I got slowly to my feet as the last cars of the freight roared by and disappeared with a twinkling of lights into the east. My palms were bleeding and full of cinders. My knees were skinned. I was dirty and hungry and aching. I sat on a pile of ties by the track, nursing my wounds.

A form came out of the darkness. It proved to be an old man who also rode the rods. He put his hand on my shoulder and said, "I saw you jump, buddy. Are you hurt?"

"No, thank you," I replied. "Not much. Just scratched."

"Ever been to Chicago?"

"No."

"Well," he said, "don't stay here. It's a city that's hard on fellows like us."

"You mean the bulls?"

"Yes, they are tough," he said. "Maybe they have to be. But it's not only that. Do you smell the stockyards?"

I had not identified the odor, but I had smelled it even before I jumped.

"So that's it?"

"Yeah. I've worked there. The pay ain't so bad. But you go home at night to a room on an alley. There's not a tree. There's no grass. No birds. No mountains."

"What do you know of mountains?" I ventured.

It led to his story. He had come, to begin with, from northern California. He had worked in the harvests, and as he worked he could look up and see the mountains. Before him was Mount Shasta. He could put his bedroll on the ground and fall asleep under the pines. There was dust in the fields of northern California, but it was good clean dirt. People were not packed together like sardines. They had elbow room. A man need not sit on a Sunday looking out on a bleak alley. He could have a piece of ground, plant a garden, and work it. He might even catch a trout, or shoot a grouse or pheasant, or perhaps kill a deer.

I listened for about an hour as he praised the glories of the mountains of the West and related his experiences in them. Dawn was coming, and as it came I could see the smoke and some of the squalor of which my friend spoke.

I asked what brought him to the freight yards at this hour of the morning. He said he came to catch a west-bound freight—back to God's own land, back to the mountains. Lonesomeness swept over me. I never had loved the Cascades as much as I did that early morning in the stockyards of Chicago. Never had I missed a snow-capped peak as much. Never had I longed more to see a mountain meadow filled with heather and lupine and paintbrush. As dawn broke I could see smokestacks everywhere, and in the distance to the east the vague outlines of tall buildings. But there lay before me nothing higher, no ridge or hill or meadow—only a great monotony of cinders, smoke, and dingy factories with chimneys pouring out a thick haze over the landscape.

The old man and I sat in silence a few moments. He said, "Do you know your Bible, son?"

"Pretty well."

"Then you will remember what the psalmist said about the mountains." I racked my brain. "No, I don't recall."

Then the old man said with intonations worthy of the clergy, "I will lift mine eyes unto the hills from whence cometh my help. My help cometh from the Lord who made heaven and earth."

There was a whistle in the east. A quarter-mile down the track a freight was pulling onto the main line.

"That's my train," he said. "That train takes me to the mountains." He took my hand. "Good luck, son. Better come back with me. Chicago's not for us."

MURRAY MORGAN

After earning a degree from the Columbia School of Journalism in the late 1940s, Murray Morgan turned down job offers from Time, *the* New York Herald-Tribune, *and CBS News to return to the Northwest, where prospects for a writer were not nearly so promising. In 1951 Viking Press published his enduringly popular* Skid Road: An Informal Portrait of Seattle, *which established his reputation as the region's leading historical chronicler. Morgan's books provide a virtual historical tour of the Northwest; his works include* The Dam *(1954),* Puget's Sound *(1979), and* The Mill on the Boot *(1982). The following is from his 1955 history of the Olympic Peninsula.*

from THE LAST WILDERNESS

IT WAS RAINING, OF COURSE. It rained nearly all that summer and fall on the Northwest Coast. The wind from the south, strong and steady and cold, fanned across the swell, kicking up a nasty chop around our lifeboat. There were no whitecaps. The water was heavy green. Four miles to the east we could see the hulk of the mainland, its cliff green-black under the claylike clouds. To the west the ocean stretched unbroken for four thousand miles. The thirty-six-foot boat seemed small.

We were making the once-every-three-weeks run from LaPush, the Quillayute fishing village where the Coast Guard maintains a life-saving station, to Destruction Island, the bleak rock which many Coast Guardsmen consider the most remote and forlorn spot in the United States.

The boy from Los Angeles ducked out of the forward compartment. He was nineteen years old, just a few weeks out of Coast Guard boot camp. This was his first trip to Destruction, where he was to be stationed. He held his lips carefully against his teeth. "Pretty rough," he said, gulping.

"I didn't think you'd stay in that compartment long," said the bos'n. His name was Roberts. He had a rugged, uncomplicated face and looked, I thought, rather like Wallace Beery. "You feel the weather down in there plenty." He pointed ahead. "See your new home?"

The boy turned and looked. Some miles ahead, low and bleak and ominous, lay Destruction Island. He stared at it for a long time, and then he said, "Well, it's only eighteen months."

The bos'n grinned. "You know the difference between Destruction and Alcatraz?"

"What's the difference?"

"On Alcatraz you get time off for good behavior."

"Very funny." The boy tried to light a cigarette. The wind blew out the matches as he raised them toward his face. He gave up and tossed the cigarette overboard.

"Actually," said the bos'n, "most guys get transferred after a year."

"No time at all," said the boy. "Well, I asked for it. Forty-two on, nineteen off. In nineteen days I can drive home and have a couple weeks with my folks. I couldn't do that on shore with just weekends."

He turned and studied the mainland. The waves broke lacy-white and dangerous at the base of a cliff crested with dark evergreens. The tops of the firs and cedars scraped the bottom of the leaden clouds. Somewhere behind the clouds lay the mountains.

"Some country," said the boy.

"It's not bad," said the bos'n. "It's one place you can still get away from people."

"I'll say," the boy replied, not without bitterness.

"I've fished places in there no one ever fished before, far as I could tell," said the bos'n. "There are spots where you can limit on trout in fifteen minutes." He spun the wheel delicately, and the boat curved westward. "You can't beat that, being first to see a piece of your own country. It's a privilege."

"I'll settle for L.A."

"Don't fight it, kid. Relax and enjoy it."

The lifeboat droned southward through the chop.

The landing on Destruction, on a narrow channel known as The Hole, is on the southeast tip of the island. Roberts made his approach along the western shore. Since the highway around the peninsula skirts the shore opposite Destruction, I had often seen the island from the east—a long, low, black rock lying in the breakers like some enormous and menacing whale. But the western shore was as unfamiliar as the far side of the moon . . .

Bos'n Roberts stopped our lifeboat just off the Hole. "Pretty quiet in there today," he remarked, studying the narrow channel between the rock cliffs. "You should see it when there's a good wind from the south. We get a real surge. Kill a boat in a minute in there."

An outboard nosed out of the Hole and worked toward us through a bed of iodine-colored kelp streamers. "Thought you were coming all the way in," the seaman in the outboard said to Roberts as he came alongside. He was a slight, brown-haired young man with a fluffy mustache.

"Thought I was nuts," said Roberts. "This rig costs forty thousand dollars. It'd take all my pay for a year to buy the Uncle a new one."

The boy from Los Angeles and I clambered down into the outboard. "See you this evening," said Roberts to me. "If the wind holds out, that is." The boats moved apart.

"If that wind does shift," the young seaman said, "you've found a home. You could be with us quite a while."

The outboard took us up The Hole to a cove barely fifteen feet across. The cliff rose forty or fifty feet, then folded into a steep, brush-covered hill. Three men stood on the break of the cliff, working the boom arm of a derrick. A square box at the end of a cable came swinging down; we got in and were hauled up, spinning slowly. Opening my eyes, I could see the lifeboat, very white against the dull green water, moving away. The box came to rest gently on the platform.

A lean man in green fatigues came from the winch and stuck out his hand. "I'm Hagen," he said. "I'm in charge here."

We climbed a long flight of gray steps up the hill and came out on an oval of tableland. The island is overgrown with a shoulder-high tangle of salmonberry and salal, impossible to walk through. A path tunnels through the brush to a clearing in which are clustered the quarters, the oil house, and the blunt pillar of the lighthouse. Near the quarters we passed a concrete tennis court, netless, the slabs awry, grass bunched in the cracks.

"Play much tennis?" I asked.

Hagen shook his head. "No time," he said. "We're busy as hell out here—painting, keeping the place up, fighting the bushes. Besides, we get rain half the year, and when it isn't raining it's foggy or the wind is blowing. Get a good wind in winter, and it blows the tops of the waves clear over the island. I've seen spray hit the top of the lighthouse. This place isn't set up to be any Forest Hills."

OLIVE BARBER

While James Stevens, Stewart Holbrook, and other writers lionized the Northwest's he-man logging culture, the women who often kept the logging camps running were virtually ignored. That silence ended when Olive Barber's memoir, The Lady and the Lumberjack, *was published in 1952. Barber, who wrote a popular local newspaper column in the 1940s and 1950s, followed her husband, Curly, to logging camps in Oregon and Alaska, but never lost her loathing for the dangerous work, or her respect for the women in the camps. "Loggers' wives," she once said, "have more dignity than most women. They always wear dresses. You almost never see them in slacks or Levi's. They are feminine, the way their men want them to be."*

from THE LADY AND THE LUMBERJACK

I LEARNED THE REAL MEANING of the word morale, that winter—learned it from those camp women who took each day as it came. They did not work at being good sports—they just were. When it was time for the men to come home at night, they went into a dither of preparation. Noses were freshly powdered; heads, bumpy with curlers through the day, at homecoming time were bewitchingly curled and waved. When they heard the shay come down the hill, they whisked off soiled aprons and put on clean ones. Babies were "dried," the other children told to wash-up, Daddy would be home any minute.

Too, these women had a practical knowledge of psychology. And they applied it. If the potatoes were not quite done, if the meat still had to be fried, then a little camouflage was necessary, men being what they are. So the women set the table. As Minnie, wife of Old Joe, said, "Supper can be all ready to dish up but if the table ain't set, Joe just knows he's to be let starve to death. But if I've just put the spuds on the stove and the table is set, Joe feels as good as though he already had his feet under the table. So if he's early, or I'm late, I whisk some dishes on the table before Joe gets in the house and the poor goof never notices it's a good half hour before he's actually eating."

I, too, adopted the "set-the-table" technique and to watch Curly's face light up as he entered the door and saw me freshly aproned with as far as he knew, supper waiting, always did things to me. That I had the power to bring such complete contentment to him was a humbling experience. What small return, I thought, men asked of life. They worked day after day in wet and cold and mud and felt fully repaid if, at night, they returned to a lighted home and found it fragrant with food and their women waiting.

I was learning, that winter, other things besides marital technique. I learned how untrained men may die in the woods because of their inexperience. Over on Blue Ridge a choker setter tried to outrun a log instead of lying in a ground depression and letting the log roll over him. An experienced logger would have done this and survived the accident all in one piece. But the log caught up with this youngster, carried him against a ledge, and crushed him. It was his first day in the rigging. And his last, for he died that night.

Although the Martin Slough camp settlement was some distance from the actual seat of logging operations, yet we women heard every whistle, subconsciously waiting for the five which would mean "man hurt," dreading most of all the six which meant a call for the stretcher.

Then one day we did hear that ominous chatter of sound. Women poured out of cabin doors, white faced, some crying, some in a sort of frozen stillness. Whose man was it! Oh, God, not mine! *Please*, God, not *mine!*

The shay came shrieking down the incline and soon we could see the stretcher on the flat car, see a form lying on it. Four men stood upright, swaying perilously as the engine attached flatcar reeled by on its way to the log dump. The standing men knew the terror that was in our hearts, the question in our faces; and, as they flew by, one shouted,

"Bart Jones!"

One woman said, "Thank God!" then looked strickenly at us, asking our understanding for such a seeming lack of feeling. And we did understand, for all of us had experienced that same upsurge of relief. Though grieving for both the victim and his loved ones, yet he was not *our* man. Again we had been spared.

Not until the men came in from the woods did we get the particulars of the accident. Bart was a loader; two logs had rolled and pinched his legs. Instantly, the six-whistle call for a stretcher had been sent to the donkey. But Bart had been hurt at the outermost rim of operations and it took time to get the stretcher to him. I sensed something of how the men doing this work must have felt when that night Curly said, his voice a cry of frustration and grief,

"Oh, God, Hon, we were so *slow!* I wanted to get down and tear at those logs with my bare hands."

But the work of removing those timbers had to be gone at slowly, cautiously, lest a shift in weight change the balance and perhaps bring about even greater pressure on the victim. Even after the rigging crew got him free, there was still the long trip out of the woods. So it was two hours from the time of the accident until Bart was put in the ambulance at the log dump. Both legs had to be amputated.

After such an accident as this, it would not have surprised me if every man in camp had left and gone in search of safer jobs. But that idea never even entered their heads. It entered Curly's all right for I put it there—but could not make it stick. He met every argument with that ingrained philosophy of all loggers—"you go when your time comes and not until." The camp women shared this belief and I could tell they felt that I was being disloyal when I vocally disagreed. Sensing this, I learned to keep such ideas to myself. But I think it was at this time that I really began to hate logging.

JACK KEROUAC

Three months before the publication of Allen Ginsberg's Howl, *and a year before his own novel* On the Road *would make him a literary celebrity, Jack Kerouac spent eight weeks as a fire lookout on Desolation Mountain in the North Cascades. The 1956 sojourn was inspired by his friend Gary Snyder, who spent many summers meditating and writing poetry in the lookout towers. "I'm one of the few people I know who at the end of a season on lookouts really didn't want to come down," Snyder once said. Although Kerouac found the mountain interminably boring, he used scenes from that summer in his 1958 novel,* The Dharma Bums, *in which Snyder appears as the character Japhy Ryder.*

from THE DHARMA BUMS

AT MORNING I could see the mighty beginnings of the Cascade Range, the northernmost end of which would be my mountain on the skirt of Canada, four hundred more miles north. The morning brook was smoky because of the lumber mill across the highway. I washed up in the brook and took off after one short prayer over the beads Japhy had given me in the Matterhorn camp: "Adoration to emptiness of the divine Buddha bead."

I immediately got a ride on the open highway from two tough young hombres to outside Junction City where I had coffee and walked two miles to a roadside restaurant that looked better and had pancakes and then walking along the highway rocks, cars zipping by, wondering how I'd ever get to Portland let alone Seattle, I got a ride from a little funny lighthaired housepainter with spattered shoes and four pint cans of cold beer who also stopped at a roadside tavern for more beer and finally we were in Portland crossing vast eternity bridges as draws went up behind us to allow crane barges through in the big smoky river city scene surrounded by pine ridges. In downtown Portland I took the twenty-five-cent bus to Vancouver Washington, ate a Coney Island hamburger there, then out on the road, 99, where a sweet young mustached one-kidney Bodhisattva Okie picked me up and said, "I'm s'proud I picked you up, someone to talk to," and everywhere we stopped for coffee he played the pinball machines with dead seriousness and also he picked up all hitchhikers on the road, first a big drawling Okie from Alabama then a crazy sailor from Montana who was full of crazed intelligent talk and we balled right up to Olympia

Washington at eighty m.p.h. then up Olympic Peninsula on curvy woods-roads to the Naval Base at Bremerton Washington where a fifty-cent ferry ride was all that separated me from Seattle!

We said goodbye and the Okie bum and I went on the ferry, I paid his fare in gratitude for my terrific good luck on the road, and even gave him handfuls of peanuts and raisins which he devoured hungrily so I also gave him salami and cheese.

Then, while he sat in the main room, I went topdeck as the ferry pulled out in a cold drizzle to dig and enjoy Puget Sound. It was one hour sailing to the Port of Seattle and I found a half-pint of vodka stuck in the deck rail concealed under a *Time* magazine and just casually drank it and opened my rucksack and took out my warm sweater to go under my rain jacket and paced up and down all alone on the cold fogswept deck feeling wild and lyrical. And suddenly I saw that the Northwest was a great deal more than the little vision I had of it of Japhy in my mind. It was miles and miles of unbelievable mountains grooking on all horizons in the wild broken clouds, Mount Olympus and Mount Baker, a giant orange sash in the gloom over the Pacific-ward skies that led I knew toward the Hokkaido Siberian desolations of the world. I huddled against the bridge-house hearing the Mark Twain talk of the skipper and the wheelman inside. In the deepened dusk fog ahead the big red neons saying: PORT OF SEATTLE. And suddenly everything Japhy had ever told me about Seattle began to seep into me like cold rain, I could feel it and see it now, and not just think it. It was exactly like he'd said: wet, immense, timbered, mountainous, cold, exhilarating, challenging. The ferry nosed in at the pier on Alaskan Way and immediately I saw the totem poles in old stores and the ancient 1880-style switch goat with sleepy firemen chug chugging up and down the waterfront spur like a scene from my own dreams, the old Casey Jones locomotive of America, the only one I ever saw that old outside of Western movies, but actually working and hauling boxcars in the smoky gloom of the magic city.

I immediately went to a good clean skid row hotel, the Hotel Stevens, got a room for the night for a dollar seventy-five and had a hot tub bath and a good long sleep and in the morning I shaved and walked out First Avenue and accidentally found all kinds of Goodwill stores with wonderful sweaters and red underwear for sale and I had a big breakfast with five-cent coffee in the crowded market morning with blue sky and clouds scudding overhead and waters of Puget Sound sparkling and dancing under old piers. It was real true Northwest. At noon I checked out of the hotel, with my new wool socks and bandanas and things all packed in gladly, and walked out to 99 a few miles out of town and got many short rides.

Now I was beginning to see the Cascades on the northeast horizon, unbelievable jags and twisted rock and snow-covered immensities, enough to make you gulp. The road ran right through the dreamy fertile valleys of the Stilaquamish and the Skagit, rich butterfat valleys with farms and cows browsing under that tremendous background of snow-pure heaps. The further north I hitched the bigger the mountains got till I finally began to feel afraid. I got a ride from a fellow who looked like a bespectacled careful lawyer in a conservative car, but turned out he was the famous Bat Lindstrom the hardtop racing champion and his conservative automobile had in it a souped-up motor that could make it go a hundred and seventy miles an hour. But he just demonstrated it by gunning it at a red light to let me hear the deep hum of power. Then I got a ride from a lumberman who said he knew the forest rangers where I was going and said "The Skagit Valley is second only to the Nile for fertility." He left me off at Highway 1-G, which was the little highway to 17-A that wound into the heart of the mountains and in fact would come to a dead-end as a dirt road at Diablo Dam. Now I was really in the mountain country. The fellows who picked me up were loggers, uranium prospectors, farmers, they drove me through the final big town of Skagit Valley, Sedro Woolley, a farming market town, and then out as the road got narrower and more curved among cliffs and the Skagit River, which we'd crossed on 99 as a dreaming belly river with meadows on both sides, was now a pure torrent of melted snow pouring narrow and fast between muddy snag shores. Cliffs began to appear on both sides. The snow-covered mountains themselves had disappeared, receded from my view, I couldn't see them any more but now I was beginning to feel them more.

GARY SNYDER

"I'll do a new long poem called 'Rivers and Mountains Without End' and just write it on and on on a scroll and unfold on and on with new surprises and always what went before forgotten, see, like a river," says Japhy Ryder, né Gary

Snyder, in Kerouac's The Dharma Bums. *The poem is real; Snyder has been creating it since 1956. And though it has never been published in its entirety, part of it appeared in Snyder's 1965 collection* Six Sections from Mountains and Rivers Without End. *Included in that collection was "Night Highway Ninety-Nine," which describes a hitchhiking trip from Bellingham to San Francisco.*

from NIGHT HIGHWAY NINETY-NINE

I

We're on our way

         man

         out of town

         go hitching down

         that highway ninety-nine

Too cold and rainy to go out on the Sound

Sitting in Ferndale drinking coffee

Baxter in black, been to a funeral

Raymond in Bellingham—Helena Hotel—

Can't go to Mexico with that weak heart

Well you boys can go south. I stay here.

Fix up a shack—get a part-time job—

         (he disappeared later

         maybe found in the river)

In Ferndale & Bellingham

Went out on trailcrews

Glacier and Marblemount

There we part.

            tiny men with moustaches

            driving ox-teams

            deep in the cedar groves.

            wet brush, tin pants, snoose

Split-shake roof barns

       over berryfields

            white birch chickencoop

Put up in Dick Meigs cabin

            out behind the house—

Coffeecan, PA tin, rags, dirty cups,

Kindling fell behind the stove
              miceshit
      old magazines,
           winter's coming in the mountains
           shut down the show
           the punks go back to school
           & the rest hit the road
     strawberries picked, shakeblanks split
     fires all out and the packstrings brought
     down to the valleys
              set to graze

Gray wharves and hacksaw gothic homes
Shingle mills and stump farms
              overgrown.

II

Fifty drunk Indians   *Mt. Vernon*
Sleep in the bus station
Strawberry pickers speaking Kwakiutl
        turn at Burlington for Skagit
            & Ross Dam

     under appletrees by the river
     banks of junkd cars

        B. C. drivers give hitch-hikers rides

"The sheriff's posse stood in double rows   *Everett*
        flogged the naked Wobblies down
        with stalks of Devil's Club
        & run them out of town"

While shingle-weavers lost their fingers
     in the tricky feed and take
      of double saws.
Dried, shrimp   *Seattle*
      smoked,   salmon
    —before the war old indian came

& sold us hard-smoked Chinook
From his truck-bed model T
                    Lake City,

        waste of trees & topsoil, beast, herb,
        edible roots, Indian field-farms & white men
        dances   washed, leached, burnt out
        Minds blunt, ug! talk twisted
                A night of the long poem
                and the mined guitar . . .
                "Forming the new society
                within the shell of the old"
                        mess of tincan camps and littered roads

The Highway passes straight through
                            every town
At Matsons washing bluejeans
                hills and saltwater
                        ack, the woodsmoke in my brain

High Olympics—can't go there again

                East Marginal Way the hitch-hike zone
                Boeing down across Duwamish slough
& angle out
                & on.

Night rain wet concrete headlights
                            blind   *Tacoma*

Salt air/   Bulk cargo/   Steam cycle

                AIR REDUCTION

        eating peanuts I don't give a damn
        if anybody ever stops   I'll walk
        to San Francisco   what the hell

"that's where you're going?
"why you got that pack?
Well man I just don't feel right
Without something on my back

    & this character in milkman overalls
    "I have to come out here
    every once in a while, there's a guy
    blows me here"

        way out of town.

Stayed in Olympia with Dick Meigs
   —this was a different year & he had moved—
   sleep on a cot in the back yard
   half the night watch falling stars

These guys got babies now
        drink beer, come back from wars
     "I'd like to save up all my money
     get a big new car, go down to Reno
     & latch onto one of those rich girls—
     I'd fix their little ass"—nineteen yr old
      N. Dakota boy fixing to get married next month
To Centralia in a purple ford.

      carstruck dead doe
      by the Skookumchuck river

Fat man in a Chevrolet
        wants to go back to L.A.
        "too damnd poor now"
Airbrakes on the log trucks hiss and whine
Stand in the dark by the stoplight.
      big fat cars tool by
Drink coffee, drink more coffee
        brush teeth back of Shell

hot shoes
                stay on the rightside of that
                        yellow line

Marys Corner, turn for Mt. Rainier
            —once caught a ride at night for Portland here
Five Mexicans, ask me "chip in on the gas"
                I never was more broke & down.
                got fired that day by the USA
                (the District Ranger up at Packwood
                thought the wobblies had been dead for
                                        forty years
                but the FBI smelled treason
                            —my red beard)

That Waco Texas boy
            took A. G. & me through miles of snow
            had a chest of logger gear
            at the home of an Indian girl
            in Kelso, hadn't seen since Fifty-four

Toledo, Castle Rock, free way
                four lane
            no stoplights & no crossings, only cars
            & people walking, old hitch-hikers
            break the law. How do I know.
                        the state cop
                            told me so.

Come a dozen times into
                    Portland
            on the bum or
                    hasty lover
                late   at   night

BERNARD MALAMUD

New Yorker Bernard Malamud came west in 1949 to teach composition at Oregon State College. While in Corvallis, he wrote his first four works of fiction, including The Natural *(1952) and* The Magic Barrel *(1958). In 1961, Farrar, Straus & Cudahy released* A New Life, *a biting satire of life at a Northwestern college based partly on Malamud's experience at OSC. In the novel, English professor Seymour Levin leaves New York to take a position at Cascadia College and, he hopes, shed his former life. Instead, he finds himself an uncomfortable outsider, a New York intellectual dropped into a magnificent Western wilderness populated by small-minded philistines. Perhaps anticipating the book's local reception, Malamud left OSC for Bennington College in Vermont the same year that* A New Life *was published.*

from A NEW LIFE

S. LEVIN, FORMERLY a drunkard, after a long and tiring transcontinental journey, got off the train at Marathon, Cascadia, toward evening of the last Sunday in August, 1950. Bearded, fatigued, lonely, Levin set down a valise and suitcase and looked around in a strange land for welcome. The small station area—like dozens he had seen en route—after a moment's activity, was as good as deserted, and Levin after searching around here and there, in disappointment was considering calling a taxi, when a man and woman in sports clothes appeared at the station. They stared at Levin—the man almost in alarm, the woman more mildly—and he gazed at them. As he grasped his bags and moved towards them they hurried to him. The man, in his forties, tall, energetic, with a rich head of red hair, strode forward with his hand outstretched.

"Sorry I'm late. My name's Dr. Gilley."

"S. Levin," Levin said, removing his black fedora, his teeth visible through his beard. "From the East."

"Good," beamed Gilley, his voice hearty. He indicated the tall, flat-chested woman in a white linen dress. "My wife."

"I'm pleased—" Levin said.

"I'm Pauline Gilley." She was like a lily on a long stalk.

"Let me help you with your bags," Gilley said.

"No, thanks, I—"

"No trouble at all."

He had grabbed both bags and now carried them around to the car, parked in front of the station, his wife and Levin hurrying after him. Unlocking the trunk, where two golf bags lay, one containing a brand new set of clubs, he deposited Levin's things.

Levin had opened the rear door but Pauline said there was room for all in front. He shyly got in and she sat between them.

"We were delayed at the golf course," she explained.

"Do you play?" Gilley asked Levin.

"Play?"

"Golf."

"Oh, no."

They drove a while in silence.

"I hope to learn some day," Levin said with a broken laugh.

"Good," said Gilley.

Levin relaxed and almost enjoyed the ride. They were driving along an almost deserted highway, in a broad farm-filled valley between distant mountain ranges laden with forests, the vast sky piled high with towering masses of golden clouds. The trees softly clustered on the river side of the road were for the most part deciduous; those crawling over the green hills to the south and west were spear-tipped fir.

My God, the West, Levin thought. He imagined the pioneers in covered wagons entering this valley for the first time, and found it a moving thought. Although he had lived little in nature Levin had always loved it, and the sense of having done the right thing in leaving New York was renewed in him. He shuddered at his good fortune.

"The mountains on the left are the Cascades," Pauline Gilley was saying. "On the right is the Coastal Range. They're relatively young mountains, whatever that means. The Pacific lies on the other side of them, about fifty miles."

"The Pacific Ocean?"

"Yes."

"Marvelous."

The Gilleys laughed. "We could drive over to the coast some time before Registration Week," Dr. Gilley said.

He went on amiably, "Seymour shortens to Sy—isn't that right?"

Levin nodded.

"My first name's Gerald and you already know Pauline's. People aren't too formal out this way. One of the things you'll notice about the West is its democracy."

"Very nice."

"And we're curious about everybody," Pauline said. "One can't help be in a small town. Have you any pictures of your family in your wallet? Or perhaps a sweetheart?" She laughed a little.

Levin blushed. "No pictures, no sweetheart."

He said after a minute, "No wallet."

They laughed, Pauline merrily, Gilley chuckling.

"Oh, look there!" She pointed toward the eastern mountains.

In the distance, a huge snow-capped peak rising above the rosy clouds reflecting the setting sun, floated over the darkish blue mountain range.

"Extraordinary," muttered Levin.

"Mt. Chief Joseph," Pauline said. "I knew you'd like it."

"Overwhelming. I—"

His heart was still racing from the sight when Pauline said, "We're almost in town. Would you like us to drive through the campus?"

"Tomorrow," Gilley said. He pointed under the setting sun. "That's Eastchester we're coming to. The college is over there to the southwest. That tall building just over those trees is Chem Engineering. That one is the new Ag building. You can't see Humanities Hall, where we hang out, but it's in that direction there. We live about half a mile from the campus, about that way. You'll be living close in if you like Mrs. Beaty's house, about three blocks from the office, very convenient."

Levin murmured his thanks.

They were driving through downtown, and were, before he could get much of an impression, out of it and into a residential section of lovely tree-lined streets and attractive wooden houses. The many old trees and multitudes of green leaves excited Levin pleasantly. In a few minutes they had arrived in front of a two-story frame house, painted an agreeable brown, with a slender white birch on the lawn, its lacy branches moving in the summer breeze. What surprised Levin was the curb-strip planted thick with flowers the whole length of the house, asters, marigolds, chrysanthemums, he guessed; in his valise was a copy of *Western Birds, Trees, and Flowers,* a fat volume recently purchased.

"This is our house," said Pauline, "although Gerald would prefer a ranch type."

"Someday we'll build," said Gerald. "She'd have a lot less housework," he said to Levin.

Though Levin liked the house, birch tree, and flowers, to enter a house after so long a time traveling slightly depressed him; he hid this as he followed Gilley along the flagstone path and through the door.

Pauline said she would whip up something for supper, nothing elaborate, as soon as the sitter had finished feeding the children in the kitchen.

"Care for a drink after your long journey?" Gilley asked Levin, winking.

Levin thanked him, no.

"Not even a short one?" He measured an inch with long thumb and forefinger.

"No, I really—"

"All right. Mind if I do?"

"Please, I—"

"How about beer?" Pauline asked. "Or if not that I can open an orange drink, or give you a glass of water?"

"Beer is fine," Levin said.

"I'd be just as happy to bring you water."

"I'll take the beer."

"There's a blue towel for you in the bathroom if you wish to wash."

She returned to the kitchen and Gilley drew the shade at the side window before he mixed martinis. Through the open blinds of the front window Levin admired a small purple-leaved tree in front of the house diagonally to the left across the wide street.

"Plum tree," Gilley said. "Pink flowers every spring."

"Beautiful." Levin, out of the corner of his eye, watched the man watching him.

When Pauline returned with the beer her husband raised his martini glass. "To a successful career for Sy."

"Cheers," said Pauline.

"Thank you." Levin's hand trembled as he held the glass aloft.

They drank, Levin drinking to himself before he knew he was doing it.

"Do you mind eating early?" Pauline asked. "It makes a longer evening. We've had to do that since the children."

"Please, as you desire."

He was sitting on the couch enjoying the beer and the room. It was a long room, tastefully furnished and curtained. On the wall hung a black and white print of a hunter shooting at a bird, and a Vermeer reproduction of a young woman. The shelved right wall was filled with books. On the kitchen side, the room was apparently for dining, and an old-fashioned round table stood there with three place settings and four chairs.

"TV?" Gilley asked. "The set's in my den."

"Later, Gerald," Pauline said. "I'm sure Mr. Levin has seen television."

"I didn't say he hadn't, but there won't be much time later. He's got to get settled."

"Don't have any worries on my account," Levin said.

"I'll drive you over to Mrs. Beaty's right after supper," Gilley said, pouring another martini. "She's got a good-sized room with a private entrance by way of the back yard. And there are kitchen privileges if you want them, Sy, damn convenient for eight o'clocks, which I can tell you you will have. She's a widow—nice woman, former grade-school teacher married to a carpenter; he died almost two years ago, I'd say—came from South Dakota, my native state. Funny thing, I spent my first week in this town, just eighteen years ago, in the same room she's offering you."

"You don't say," said Levin.

Gilley nodded.

"I'll be glad to have a look at it."

"If you don't like it you can come back here tonight," Pauline suggested.

Gilley seemed to be considering that but Levin hastily said, "That's so kind but I won't trouble you any more. The hotel is fine. You wrote me they have one here, as I remember?"

"Two—moderate prices."

"Fine," said Levin.

"Good. Let me freshen your beer."

"This is fine."

Pauline finished her drink and went into the kitchen.

"You're our twenty-first man, the most we've ever had full-time in the department," Gilley said to Levin. "Professor Fairchild will meet you tomorrow afternoon at two. He's a fine gentleman and awfully considerate head of department, I'm sure you'll like him, Sy. He kept us going at full complement for years under tough budgetary conditions. Probably you've heard of his grammar text, *The Elements of Grammar*? God knows how many editions it's been through. The department's been growing again following the drop we took after the peak load of veterans, though we've still got plenty of them around. We put on three men last year and we plan another two or three, next. College registration is around forty-two hundred now, but we figure we'll double that before ten years.

He smiled happily at Levin and Levin smiled at him. Nice chap, very friendly. He put you at your ease.

"We've been hearing from people from every state in the Union. For next year I already have a pile of applications half a foot high."

"I'm grateful for—"

"You won't miss New York? This is a small town, Sy, ninety-seven hundred, and there isn't much doing unless you get outdoors or are interested in football and such. Season tickets for athletic events are modestly priced for faculty."

"No, I won't miss it," Levin said with a sigh.

"Pauline's been talking for years about visiting New York City."

"Yes?"

"I wouldn't want to stay too long. I don't take to cities well, I get jumpy after a while."

"I know what you mean."

"You seem pretty glad to leave?"

"I lived there all my life."

"I should say. Eight million people, that's seven more than we have in the entire state of Cascadia."

"Imagine," muttered Levin.

"We're growing, though, about three thousand a year."

Pauline set glasses on the table, then came out of the kitchen, carrying a casserole.

"Tuna fish and mashed potatoes," she said apologetically. "I hope you like it."

"Perfect," Levin said. He was abruptly very hungry. They sat down at the round table, for which he felt a surprising immediate affection. Pauline had forgotten the salad bowl and went in to get it. When she returned she served the casserole, standing. A child called from the kitchen. Distracted, she missed Levin's plate and dropped a hot gob of tuna fish and potato into his lap.

He rose with a cry.

"I'm so dreadfully sorry." She hastily wiped at his pants with a cloth but Levin grabbed it from her and did it himself. The operation left a large wet stain.

"I'd better change," he said, shaken. "My other suit is in my bag."

"I'll get it," Gilley said, his face flushed. "It's still in the trunk."

"Everything will get stone cold," Pauline said. "Gerald, why don't you lend Mr. Levin a pair of your slacks? That'll be quicker."

"I'd rather get my own," Levin said.

"Let him do what he wants," Gilley told his wife.

"There's no need for him to be uncomfortable till we get his suitcase in. Your gray slacks will go nicely with his jacket. They're hanging in your closet."

"Please—" Levin was perspiring.

"Maybe she's right," Gilley said. "It'd be quicker."

"I'll change in a minute once I have my suitcase."

"Gerald's pants will be less trouble."

"They won't fit. He's taller than I am."

"Roll up the cuffs. By the time you're ready to leave I'll have your trousers spot-cleaned and ironed. It was my fault and I'd feel much better if you both please let me work it out my own way."

Gilley shrugged and Levin gave up. He changed into Gerald's slacks in the bathroom.

While he was there Pauline tapped on the door.

"I forgot about your shorts, they must be damp. I have a clean pair of Gerald's here."

He groaned to himself, then said quietly, "I don't want them."

"Are you sure?"

"Positive."

Before leaving the bathroom Levin soaped his hands and face, dried them vigorously and combed his damp whiskers. When he came out he felt momentarily foolish in Gilley's baggy pants but the food, kept hot, was delicious, and he ate heartily.

_____

JOHN STEINBECK

John Steinbeck and his wife, Carol, escaped the public furor surrounding the 1939 publication of The Grapes of Wrath *by driving up the coast to the Northwest and spending a few days in Seattle, then continuing on to Vancouver. Twenty-one years later, Steinbeck returned to Seattle and recorded his impressions in his final full-length book.* Travels with Charley *was published in 1962, a few months before the author was awarded the Nobel Prize for literature.*

from TRAVELS WITH CHARLEY

THE PACIFIC IS MY HOME OCEAN; I knew it first, grew up on its shore, collected marine animals along the coast. I know its moods, its color, its nature. It was very far inland that I caught the first smell of the Pacific. When one has been long at sea, the smell of land reaches far out to greet one. And the same is true when one has been long inland. I believe I smelled the sea rocks and the kelp and the iodine and the under odor of washed and ground calcareous shells. Such a far-off and remembered odor comes subtly so that one does not consciously smell it, but rather an electric excitement is released—a kind of boisterous joy. I found myself plunging over the roads of Washington, as dedicated to the sea as any migrating lemming.

I remembered lush and lovely eastern Washington very well and the noble Columbia River, which left its mark on Lewis and Clark. And, while there were dams and power lines I hadn't seen, it was not greatly changed from what I remembered. It was only as I approached Seattle that the unbelievable change became apparent.

Of course, I had been reading about the population explosion on the West Coast, but for West Coast most people substitute California. People swarming in, cities doubling and trebling in numbers of inhabitants, while the fiscal guardians groan over the increasing weight of improvements and the need to care for a large new spate of indigents. It was here in Washington that I saw it first. I remembered Seattle as a town sitting on hills beside a matchless harborage—a little city of space and trees and gardens, its houses matched to such a background. It is no longer so. The tops of hills are shaved off to make level warrens for the rabbits of the present. The highways eight lanes wide cut like glaciers through the uneasy land. This Seattle had no relation to the one I remembered. The traffic rushed with murderous intensity. On the outskirts of this place I once knew well I could not find my way. Along what had been country lands rich with berries, high wire fences and mile-long factories stretched, and the yellow smoke of progress hung over all, fighting the sea winds' efforts to drive them off.

This sounds as though I bemoan an older time, which is the preoccupation of the old, or cultivate an opposition to change, which is the currency of the rich and stupid. It is not so. This Seattle was not something changed that I once knew. It was a new thing. Set down there not knowing it was Seattle, I could not have told where I was. Everywhere frantic growth, a carcinomatous growth. Bulldozers rolled up the green forests and heaped the resulting trash for burning. The torn white lumber from concrete forms was piled beside gray walls. I wonder why progress looks so much like destruction.

Next day I walked in the old port of Seattle, where the fish and crabs and shrimps lay beautifully on white beds of shaved ice and where the washed and shining vegetables were arranged in pictures. I drank clam juice and ate the sharp crab cocktails at stands along the waterfront. It was not much changed—a little more run-down and dingy than it was twenty years ago. And here a generality concerning the growth of American cities, seemingly true of all of them I know. When a city begins to grow and spread outward, from the edges, the center which was once its glory is in a sense abandoned to time. Then the buildings grow dark and a kind of decay sets in . . . The district is still too good to tear down and too outmoded to be desirable. Besides, all the energy has flowed out to the new developments, to the semi-rural supermarkets, the outdoor movies, new houses with wide lawns and stucco schools where children are confirmed in their illiteracy. The old port with narrow streets and cobbled surfaces, smoke-grimed, goes into a period of desolation inhabited at night by the vague ruins of men, the lotus eaters who struggle daily toward unconsciousness by way of raw alcohol. Nearly every city I know has such a dying mother of violence and despair where at night the brightness of the street lamps is sucked away and policemen walk in pairs. And then one day perhaps the city returns and rips out the sore and builds a monument to its past.

HORACE CAYTON

Horace Cayton was the grandson of Hiram Revels, the first African American elected to the U.S. Senate, and the son of Horace Cayton, Sr., the publisher of the Seattle Republican *in the early 1900s and an early black leader in the Northwest. The younger Cayton grew up on Seattle's Capitol Hill, and by the time he graduated from the University of Washington in the late 1920s, he had served as a messman on a freighter, a handyman in an Alaskan bordello, a longshoreman, and a King County sheriff's deputy. In later life Cayton served as an assistant to the Secretary of the Interior, taught at several universities, and covered the United Nations as a reporter and columnist. This account of Seattle in the 1920s is taken from his autobiography, published in 1963.*

from LONG OLD ROAD

I DIDN'T HAVE AN EASY TIME when I first went on the force. There were three strikes against me—I was the youngest man in the outfit, a college student, and the first Negro ever to be appointed a deputy in our rough-and-tumble city. It was hard for me to figure out on which grounds I was most disliked.

The fact that I was young certainly weighed heavily against me. Men who had been on the force for twenty or thirty years found it hard to accept the fact that new recruits had to be taken on to keep the department running. And my being a college student doubled the felony. As long as I was on the force this was referred to with varying degrees of sarcasm. Even when we became friendly, they condescendingly called me "high school boy."

Being a Negro helped least of all. They were not so much prejudiced against Negroes as surprised and confused to find one suddenly in their midst. They were accustomed to Negroes as bootblacks or as suspects, but to ride a prowl car with one was a new experience. They looked upon me as an unfortunate experiment that should and would fail, or at least they were not going out of their way to help it succeed. I was more nervous about the whole thing than they but I attended to my duties as best I could. There was no training program, and as none of them gave me a hint about what to do I had to pick up the trade as best I could.

My first assignment was in the fingerprint room, where each prisoner was printed and mugged soon after he was arrested. My boss was a man named Rosenfelds, who at first acted the martyr for having been given a Negro assistant. But when he found that I could type and saw how quickly I learned to take prints, he became quite friendly. I was fascinated with the work, because we processed every individual who was arrested. The prisoners, incidentally, paid no attention to my being a Negro . . .

Occasionally when work was slack, Rossie and I would talk about the old days when he was a working deputy. He wasn't a bad guy, and I got the impression he talked tougher than he really was. But there was a streak of sadistic cruelty, or perhaps cowardliness, which came out in many of his stories. He loved to reminisce about the massacre of the I.W.W.'s at Everett. The Wobblies had ridden the freights in from all over the Northwest to set up a picket line for the strike. The Seattle police got wind of the fact that some of them had assembled in Seattle and hired a small, unseaworthy boat to sail up to Everett. They didn't try to stop them but notified the Everett police, who met the little ship with gunfire. It shoved off immediately to return to Seattle.

Rossie and a car full of deputies met it along the coast highway with high-powered rifles and shot at every man who came on deck. Since the leaky old boat couldn't venture too far out, the deputies were able to pick them off like clay pigeons.

"What was the big idea?" I asked. "You could have got them in Seattle when they landed."

"They were Wobblies!" Rossie shouted with indignation.

"Why shoot a man when you know you can arrest him in a few hours?"

"The goddamn Reds deserved to be shot."

"Why?" I asked. "I met one, and he wasn't a bad guy. Besides, they can't do anything, they're just a handful of workers who want to make things better for their kind."

"What the hell are you talking about? They want to overthrow the government. They sided with Germany during the war, they don't believe in God. They even got a plan to nationalize women."

"Like that little girl you said I could screw for free if I flashed my buzzer?"

Rossie's face had turned purple. He shouted, "If you love them so much you must be a Red yourself. And let me tell you something for your own good—I'd advise you not to go sleeping around with white women if you want to get along in this office."

"Go fuck yourself, Rossie," I replied with contempt.

Nothing came of the incident; apparently he didn't even repeat it to the rest of the boys.

After I had worked in the fingerprint room for about a year, there was a break at the jail, and we worked around the clock for three days. We got most of the prisoners back, but as a result of the break Captain Bunker from Walla Walla State Penitentiary was brought in as the new jail superintendent . . .

[Bunker] had the reputation of being a tough prison man and had started out as a hangman. When he took over the prisoners were wary and the guards frightened and angry; the sheriff, however, was pleased, for he knew Bunker would run a tight, honest jail.

The very first day Captain Bunker took over, I unwittingly had a minor brush with him. We had a set order in which we called for prisoners to be mugged. First the women, then the men held for petty crimes—vagrancy, petty larceny, liquor violations, nonsupport, and the like. Next came the lesser felonies—breaking and entering, taking an automobile without the owner's permission. Finally the serious, and perhaps dangerous prisoners, whom we mugged one at a time. I would turn my list over to whomever was in charge of the cell block, he'd turn the prisoner or prisoners over to me, and I'd take them to the mug room, or Hollywood, as some of them called it. When we were finished I'd return them to the cell block.

This particular morning, before I had a chance to present my list, Captain Bunker announced that he had the prisoners lined up and ready for me. Without thinking I said, "We don't take them that way, Captain."

I doubt if Captain Bunker had ever had anyone refuse to obey any suggestion he made. He looked confused but seemed unaware that I had defied him, so I simply smiled and went for my prisoners. Nothing came of it for two or three days, then when I was coming back from lunch one day he came out of his office and motioned for me to go in.

As I sat across the table from him, his piercing, cold eyes penetrated me. "You're colored, aren't you, Cayton?"

"Yes," I replied. "Can't you tell?"

"Just answer the questions," he said, hard and cold. "I hear that you go to school."

"Yes."

"Tell me about it."

"What is there to tell? I'm majoring in sociology."

"Do you study about crime?" he asked.

"Yes, I do take one course in criminology."

"I'd like to see some of your books. Maybe they might want a speech. I'd be glad to talk to the students." He relaxed, became confidential. "As a matter of fact, I like colored people. Of course, the only ones I've known have been prisoners, but they make good prisoners after you break them a little. I hung one colored fellow in Walla Walla, gave him a nice hanging. I kept the rope under my desk and greased it with talcum powder. Didn't even burn his skin. But I've never known a colored deputy."

"I do my work," I said.

"I'll transfer you to the cell block, then you can study your books at night."

"But I like it in the fingerprint room."

"That's all, Cayton," he replied. "Report for the midnight shift. You can do all your studying until feeding time at seven in the morning. Come and talk to me if you need any help in your criminology class."

I was annoyed, but knew I had made a good although rather puzzling friend. I didn't like what he stood for, and his cool brutality dismayed me, yet there was a childlike innocence about this ex-hangman. Soon everyone in the jail was aware that I was his pet, although he barked orders at me like anyone else. But in all our relations Bunker gave me what I most wanted—a sense of dignity.

In our formal contacts, I was a man and a deputy and was treated as such. When he came around on an unexpected tour of the cell block, he would make a strict inspection, then relax. If he thought that I was not being attentive enough he would pinion me against the wall with his massive stomach so that it was impossible for me to move away. He talked about his children, one of whom was taking tap dancing; sometimes he went into exquisite detail about the finer techniques of hanging . . .

My only escape, when such moods were on him, was to say, "Cap, I've got to punch my time clock or the sheriff's office will call."

As I made my rounds . . . I began to be aware of Klondike, a Negro prisoner who was in a cell by himself. The others were kept in tanks, each a group of cells connected to a dayroom. But Klondike was by himself, and since he never seemed to sleep I began to talk to him occasionally in order to stay awake myself.

I knew about Klondike. He was a drug addict who had been convicted of murder and would probably hang. A dangerous man. But in spite of this, one night I stopped and smoked a cigarette with him. He was middle-aged, brown-skinned, short, stocky, physically a powerful man. But he was one of the most soft-spoken, gentle-looking men I have ever seen and looked strangely like our Baptist minister.

I offered him a cigarette, and he thanked me, neither humbly nor arrogantly. The man had great dignity. Every night about three or four o'clock, when the hours grew intolerably long, I would stop by his cell to smoke and talk. He told me all about himself, how he had gone to Alaska to mine gold, which was where he had gotten his nickname. After that he had come back to the States and worked as a longshoreman and a sailor. He bought himself a little house; then, just when everything seemed to be going well, someone on the waterfront talked him into walking some dope off a ship. Step by step he had been introduced to morphine and soon became a heavy user.

One night when he was broke he tried to get some morphine from the man who had made him an addict, and was refused. He went away but came back later, taped the man's mouth shut, and tied him to a chair, cutting him thirty times before he finally died. He then walked to the police station and gave himself up.

Weeks went by, and Klondike and I became more and more friendly. Finally, against all the rules, I let him out of his cell nights so we could play checkers in the corridor where no one from the front office could see us. I even used to bring coffee and sandwiches from the kitchen.

After he was tried, convicted, and sentenced to be hanged, I stopped letting Klondike out of his cell for a while. He kidded me about it one night. "I'm the same fellow," he said. "Just because I got sentenced don't mean I want to start anything."

After a week or so I started taking Klondike out again.

We never spoke about his crime or his sentence. I wanted to, but his natural dignity prevented me. I was curious to know how a man felt who had killed another in cold blood. How it felt, knowing that you had to die on a certain day. By this time his appeal had been turned down, and the governor also had refused to honor his plea for executive clemency.

Nothing happened, that is nothing until the week before he was to be executed. There is an odd belief among prisoners that any man about to be hanged will start feeling the rope as his time grows shorter. A sure sign of this is that he will begin to scratch his neck.

I had just made a very good move, and Klondike was trying to figure out how to counter it. He was studying the board intently; I was watching him just as closely. In addition to helping keep myself awake, I had another secret reason for letting Klondike out of his cell and playing checkers with him. I was taking abnormal psychology and I had thought that perhaps I might write my term paper on him. An actual case study of a man who was going to be hanged; I figured it would be a sensation, a sure-fire A. With this in mind, I had been watching Klondike more closely than I had the game. But he was so intent on beating me, which he usually did, that he hadn't noticed.

Now I had him in a tight corner, and he didn't want to lose. Suddenly, as he thought he had found a way out, his hand moved slowly to his neck and started to scratch. Slowly and methodically he scratched his neck on both sides, then he began to caress it. I watched, fascinated. There was the sign. Up until now he had given no indication either by word or expression that he realized that in a week he would be hanged.

He looked up, a half-smile on his face, about to say, "Well, I got out of that one." I was so fascinated by his preoccupation with his neck that I couldn't look away—even though I realized he had caught me staring at him. Puzzled, he glanced down to see what I was looking at and then he realized what he had been doing.

Slowly his expression changed. He had been smiling, happy, when he first looked up from the board. Now his facial muscles began to tighten; his lips drew back, baring his white teeth, and his nostrils seemed to widen. He no longer looked like a Baptist preacher but exactly like a man who had tied somebody in a chair and cut him thirty times before he died.

He started to get to his feet; I automatically rose with him. We stood staring into each other's eyes, not four feet apart. I don't know how I looked, but Klondike's face was a picture of cold fury and hatred. It is difficult to describe the quality of his voice when he spoke. It was still soft but no longer gentle. It was shot through with hostility, hate, and the threat to kill. "It really itched, copper."

Klondike had never called me copper before. At first it had been guard, and later, when we got to know each other better, Cayton. But now I had challenged his manhood, intimating that he was afraid to die. I was on the other side now. I wasn't even a Negro like him; I was the law.

I had the sudden realization that there had never been any real friendship between Klondike and myself. I was the law; he was the convicted prisoner awaiting execution. I understood emotionally, perhaps for the first time, that Klondike was a brutal murderer, a killer who had shown no remorse or guilt over his crime. I was afraid of Klondike as a man; I was afraid of him as a prisoner.

Sometimes, not from courage but out of a strange inner necessity, we act in spite of our fears. I don't know if it was my being the youngest deputy on the force and the only Negro who had ever been thus appointed which caused me to muster some inner strength, strength I certainly did not feel. I had known for some time that most of my fellow deputies had wanted me to fail; they still said I was too young and that I would favor Negro prisoners over white. This may have influenced me, or perhaps it was merely a case of one man against another; but I saw then that it was either Klondike or me. I was armed with my keys and knew I could get in one hard blow. But I didn't want to, not so much out of any personal feeling for Klondike—it was too late for that—but for fear of starting something.

Then I heard a voice—firm and steady and unbelievably calm. "Back into your cell, Klondike."

We stood facing each other. The seconds passed. The tension was intolerable. It was a sheer contest of wills, as intense as physical combat.

Suddenly I acted. I didn't think it out, it was impulsive. I took one slow step forward, my face not a foot from his. "Back in your cell, Klondike."

He had to do something, hit me or give in. My hand tightened on the bunch of heavy keys, waiting. He stood the tension for at least ten seconds, then stepped backward. Step by step we moved, he backward and I forward, until we had covered the five or six feet to his cell. I locked him in, gathered up the checkers, and left without a word.

For the next few nights I avoided Klondike, using another route to make my rounds. On about the fifth evening I made a point of walking past his cell; it was he who broke the ice.

"Got a cigarette, Cayton?" he called.

"Sure, Klondike."

I was anxious to make up for my callow curiosity and the stupid insensibility I had shown toward this man who was about to face death.

We smoked together in silence for a while, then he spoke. "I want you to know," he said, "it really itched."

"I know it did."

"I wouldn't have done anything the other night," he continued. "After all, we're both colored, we got to stick together."

"Sure, Klondike," I said. "Take another cigarette, I've got to make my rounds."

KEN KESEY

After completing One Flew Over the Cuckoo's Nest *in 1961, Ken Kesey spent two years researching and writing the greatest novel to come out of the Northwest,* Sometimes a Great Notion *(1964). The story of a logging family's fight for independent survival in the Oregon woods, the novel did not garner the popular acclaim of* Cuckoo's Nest, *although it is in many ways superior. The book's ambitious scope gave its own author pause: he wrote to a friend, "My book is trying maybe too goddamn much, trying to encompass a man, a family, a town, a country, and a time—all at once . . . Awful much, Awful much."*

from SOMETIMES A GREAT NOTION

THE OREGON BEARS, Jonas Stamper found, were well fed on clams and berries, and fat and lazy as old house cats. The Indians, nourished on the same two limitless sources of food, were even fatter and a damn sight lazier than the bears. Yes. They were peaceful enough. So were the bears. In fact the whole country was more peaceful than he had expected. But there was this odd . . . *volatile* feeling about the new country that struck him the very day he arrived, struck him and stuck, and never left him all the three years he lived in Oregon. "What's so hard about this country?" Jonas wondered when they arrived. "All it needs is somebody to whip it into shape."

No, it wasn't such as bears or Indians that got stern and stoic Jonas Stamper.

"But I wonder how come it's still as unsettled as it is?" Jonas wondered when he arrived; others wondered when he left. "Tell me, weren't they a Jonas Stamper hereabouts?"

"He was here, but he's gone."

"Just up and scoot."

"What come of his family?"

"They're still around, her'n' the three boys. Folks here are kinda helpin' keep their heads above water. Old Foodland Stokes sends 'em a bit of grocery every day or so, back up river. They got a sort of house—"

Jonas started the big frame house a week after they settled in Wakonda. He divided three years, three short summers and three long winters, between his feed-and-seed store in town and his building site across the river—eight acres of rich riverbank land, the best on the river. He had homesteaded his lot under the 1880 Land Act before he left Kansas— "Live on the Highway of Water!"—homesteaded it sight unseen, trusting to the pamphlets that a riverbank site would be a good site for a patriarch to do the Lord's work. It had sounded good on paper.

"Just scooted out, huh? That sure don't sound like Jonas Stamper. Didn't he leave anything?"

"Family, feed store, odds and ends, and a whole pisspot of shame."

He had sold a feed store in Kansas, a good feed store with a rolltop desk full of leatherbound ledgers to finance the move, then had sent the money ahead so it was already waiting for him when he arrived, waiting bright green and growing, like everything else in the rich new land, the rich new promising frontier he'd read about in all the pamphlets his boys had brought him from the post office back in Kansas. Pamphlets sparkling red and blue, ringing with wild Indian names like bird-call signals in the forest: Nakoomish, Nahailem, Chalsea, Silcoos, Necanicum, Yachats, Siuslaw, and Wakonda, at Wakonda Bay, on the Peaceful and Promising Wakonda Auga River, Where (the pamphlets had informed him) A Man Can Make His Mark. Where A Man Can Start Anew. Where (the pamphlets said) The Grass Is Green And The Sea Is Blue And The Trees And Men Grow Tall And True! Out In The Great Northwest, Where (the pamphlets made it clear) There Is Elbow Room For A Man To Be As Big And Important As He Feels It Is In Him To Be!

Ah, it had sounded *right* good on paper, but, as soon as he saw it, there was something . . . about the river and the forest, about the clouds grinding against the mountains and the trees sticking out of the ground . . . something. Not that it was a hard country, but something you must go through a winter of to understand.

But that's what you did not know. You knew the cursed look of wanderlust but you did not know the hell that lust was leading you into. You must go through a winter first . . .

"I'll be switched. Just gone. It sure don't sound like old Jonas."

"I wouldn't be too tough on him; for one thing, you got to go through a rainy season or so to get some idee."

You must go through a winter to understand.

For one thing, Jonas couldn't see all that elbow room that the pamphlets had talked about. Oh, it was there, he knew. But not the way he'd imagined it would be. And for another thing, there was nothing, *not a thing!* about the country that made a man feel Big And Important. If anything it made a man feel dwarfed, and about as important as one of the fish-Indians living down on the clamflats. Important? Why, there was something about the whole blessed country that made a soul feel whipped before he got started. Back home in Kansas a man had a *hand* in things, the way the Lord *aimed* for His servants to have: if you didn't water, the crops died. If you didn't feed the stock, the stock died. As it was ordained to be. But there, in that land, it looked like our labors were for naught. The flora and fauna grew or died, flourished or failed, in *complete* disregard for man and his aims. A Man Can Make His Mark, did they tell me? Lies, lies. Before God I tell you: a man might struggle and labor his livelong life and make *no* mark! None! No permanent mark at all! I say it is true.

You must go through at least a year of it to have some notion.

———————

Teddy, the part-time bartender and full-time owner of the Snag, though he might have been compelled to take open issue with the woodcarver's choice of cocktails, would have been, of all the men in Wakonda, the man most likely to believe in the woodcarver's principle. For the town's leanest days were inordinately Teddy's fattest, the town's darkest nights his brightest. He turned more liquor Halloween night at the crowd's disappointment than he would have sold if Big Newton had knocked Hank Stamper's head off . . . and the Halloween rain that brought a deluge of despair down on the striking loggers the following day brought a jingle of joy from Teddy's till.

Floyd Evenwrite's reaction to the rain was somewhat different. "Oh me, oh me, oh me." He woke late Sunday morning, hung over and suspicious of the effect of last night's beer on his bowels. "Look at it come down out there. Dirty motherin' rain! An' what was that dream I had? Something bound to be awful . . . "

"This country will rot a man like a corpse," was Jonathan Draeger's response when he looked from his hotel window onto a Main Street running an inch of black water.

"Rain," was all Teddy had to say, watching the falling texture of the sky through his bedside lace curtains. "Rain."

Those Halloween clouds had continued to roll in off the sea all the rumbling night—a surly multitude, angry at being kept waiting so long, and full of moody determination to make up for time lost. Pouring out rain as they went, they had rolled over the beaches and town, into the farmlands and low hills, finally piling headlong up against the wall of the Coastal Range mountains with a soft, massive inertia. All night long. A few piled to the mountaintops and over into the Willamette Valley with their overloads of rain, but the majority, the great bulk of that multitude gathered and blown from the distant stretches of the sea, came rebounding heavily back into the other clouds. They exploded above the town like colliding lakes.

The garrison of speargrass that picketed the edges of the dunes was beaten flat by the clouds' advance guard; with the fallen green spearpoints pointing the way the attack had gone by graying dawn.

A torrent of water that ran from the dunes back to the sea, in measured sweeps, as though enormous waves were combing overhead and breaking far inland . . . swept the beaches clean of a whole summer's debris by gray daylight.

And along parts of the Oregon coast there are clusters of seaside trees permanently bent by a wind that blows everlastingly landward across all the Oregon beaches—whole groves of strangled cedars and spruce bent in an attitude of paralyzed recoil, as though frozen by a midmorning of that first day after October, the little short-tailed mice that dwelt between the roots of these trees had crept from their homes and, for the first time in local remembrance, were moving in droves east, toward higher ground, afraid that such a rain would surely raise the sea and flood their burrows . . .

"Oh me, oh me; the mice are leavin' their holes. We're in for a bad one," was the way Evenwrite viewed the migration.

The hillside rang with the tight whine of cutting; the sound of work in the woods was like insects in the walls. Numb clubs of feet registered the blow against the cold earth only by the pained jarring in the bones. Henry dragged a screwjack to a new log. Joe Ben sang along with his radio:

"Leaning, leaning,
Safe and secure from all alarms . . . "

The forest fought against the attack on its age-old domain with all the age-old weapons nature could muster: blackberries strung out barbed barricades; the wind shook widow-makers crashing down from high rotted snags; boulders reared silently from the ground to block sides that had looked smooth and clear a moment before; streams turned solid trails into creeping ruts of icy brown lava . . . And in the tops of the huge trees, the very rain seemed to work at fixing the trees standing, threading the million green needles in an attempt to stitch the trees upright against the sky.

But the trees continued to fall, gasping long sighs and ka-whumping against the spongy earth. To be trimmed and bucked into logs. To be coaxed and cajoled downhill into the river with unflagging regularity. In spite of all nature could do to stop it.

Leaning on the ev-ver-last-ting arms.

As the trees fell and the hours passed, the three men grew accustomed to one another's abilities and drawbacks. Few words actually passed between them; they communicated with the unspoken language of labor toward a shared end, becoming more and more an efficient, skilled team as they worked their way across the steep slopes; becoming almost one man, one worker who knew his body and his skill and knew how to use them without waste or overlap.

Henry chose the trees, picked the troughs where they would fall, placed the jacks where they would do the most good. And stepped back out of the way. *Here she slides!* See? A man can whup it god-dammit with nothin' but his experience an' stick-to-'er, god*dam* if he can't . . . Hank did the falling and trimming, wielding the cumbersome chain saw tirelessly in his long, cable-strong arms, as relentless as a machine; working not fast but steadily, mechanically, and certainly far past the point where other fallers would have rested, pausing only to refuel the saw or to place a new cigarette in the corner of his mouth when his lips felt the old one burning near—taking the pack from the pouch of his sweat shirt, shaking a cigarette into view, withdrawing it with his lips . . . touching the old butt for the first time with his muddy gloves when he removed it to light the new smoke. Such pauses were brief and widely separated in the terrible labor, yet he almost enjoyed returning to work, getting back in the groove, not thinking, just doing the work like it was eight to five and none of that other crap to worry about, just letting somebody turn me on and aim me at what and where is just the way I like it. The way it used to be. Peaceful. And simple. (*And I ain't thinking about the kid, not in hours I ain't wondered where he is.*) . . . And Joe Ben handled most of the screwjack work, rushing back and forth from jack to jack, a little twist here, a little shove there, and whup! she's turnin', tippin', heading out downhill! Okay—get down there an' set the jacks again, crank and uncrank right back an' over again. Oh yeah, that's the one'll do it. *Shooooom*, all the way, an' here come another one, Andy ol' buddy, big as the ark . . . feeling a mounting of joyous power collecting in his back muscles, an exhilaration of faith rising with the crash of each log into the river. Whosoever believes in his heart shall cast *mountains* into the sea an' Lord knows what other stuff . . . then heading back up to the next log—running, leaping, a wingless bird feathered in leather and aluminum and mud, with a transistor radio bouncing and shrill beneath his throat:

> *Leaning on Jee-zus, leaning on Jee-zus*
> *Safe an' secure from all alarms . . .*

Until the three of them meshed, dovetailed . . . into one of the rare and beautiful units of effort sometimes seen when a jazz group is making it completely, swinging together completely, or when a home-town basketball squad, already playing over its head, begins to rally to overtake a superior opponent in a game's last minute . . . and the home boys can't miss; because everything—the passing, the dribbling, the plays—every tiny *piece* is clicking perfectly. When this happens everyone watching *knows* . . . that, be it five guys playing basketball, or four blowing jazz, or three cutting timber, that *this bunch—right* now, right *this* moment—is the best of its kind in the world! But to become this kind of perfect group a team must use *all* its components, and use them in the slots best suited, and use them all with the pitiless dedication to victory that drives them up to their absolute peak, and past it.

Joe felt this meshing. And old Henry. And Hank, watching his team function, was aware only of the beauty of the team and of the free-wheeling thrill of being a part of it. Not of the pitiless drive. Not of the three of them building toward a peak the way a machine running too fast too long accelerates without actually speeding up as it reaches a breaking point, accelerating *past* it and *toward* it at the same time and at the same immutable rate . . .

Then, as though the fuse had burned away, the forest ended its brief hush.

And a wind, heavy with rain, came up from the river through the fern and huckleberry like a deep-drawn breath; and *"as you go through life make this your goal . . . "* and Hank feels the air about him swell with that wind, gathering with it, just as he rocks the saw free from a limb he is bucking off the fallen fir, looking up, frowning to himself before he even hears it listen! the maddened snapping of bark someplace else moving, he turns back to the log in time to see a bright yellow-white row of teeth appear splintering over the mossy lips to gnash the saw from his hands fling it furiously to the ground it claws screaming machine frenzy and terror trying to dig escape from the vengeful wood just above where old Henry drops his screwjack *Gaw* when mud and pine needles spray over him like black *damn!* rain an' even if I don't *see* so clear as I used to there's still time to get *down* the hill Joe Ben hears the metal scream behind a curtain of fern but if you never *doubt* in your mind where's *Hank* spins away leaving his log and turn me on and aim me is all I want still peaceful, relaxed like sleep from eight to five without thinking or I'd said *Nothing doing* to see the log springing suddenly massive upright pivots on Henry's ARM GOD my good one goddammit GOD GOD just leave the old nigger enough to whup it enough arm that he'd been using to fix his screwjack it waves limp then disappears a second beneath the row of teeth before the log springs on downhill massive upright like the bastard is trying to stand up again and find its *stump!* a swinging green fist slams Hank's shoulder goes somersaulting past upright like the bastard is so mad getting chopped down it jumps up chews off the old man's arm clubs me one now tearing off downhill after "Joe! Joby!" the last of us and Joe Ben's hand parts the fern there's this *blunted* white circle fanged jagged spreading toward him larger and larger down the mud-trough *oop* springs backward from the fern over the bank not really scared or startled or anything but *light* like the mud on my boots turned to *wings* . . . and hangs in the air over the bank for an instant . . . a jack-in-the-box, bobbling . . . sprung up from his box and dangling backward above the tangle of vines . . . face sudden clown red the color of the old man's arm now crushed flowing all the way to the boogerin' *bone* . . . hangs, sprung up, for an instant, with that ugly little goblin face red and still merry grinning to me that it's okay Hankus okay that you couldn't of been thinkin' that limb you cut off would of done this then falls cut loose slapping back to the muddy bank outa the way if it wasn't "Look out!" for that screwjack "Look out!" don't worry Hankus face still red like the old man's GOD you booger, leave me *somethin'* to fight with the ARM GOD my one good ARM *Look out!* just don't worry Hankus just never doubt slaps against the muddy bank right in the path LOOK OUT JOBY slaps and rolls as the runaway log thunks the log he'd been working with his screwjack jolts sideways rearing above ROLL rolls still light-feeling confident almost safe half into the river almost but slamming down, the log, across both legs, and stopping.

THEODORE ROETHKE

When Theodore Roethke accepted a position in the English department at the University of Washington in 1947, he was already marked as a promising young poet, having published the collection The Open House *to strong reviews six years before. During his sixteen years in Seattle, he created the body of work that established him as one of the most respected American poets of the twentieth century, including the Pulitzer Prize–winning collection* The Waking *(1953) and two National Book Award winners,* Words for the Wind *(1958) and* The Far Field *(published in 1964, a year after his death). "The Rose" is the final poem in Roethke's North American Sequence, published in* The Far Field. *He wrote it in 1962 during a stay in the San Juan Islands.*

THE ROSE

1

There are those to whom place is unimportant,
But this place, where sea and fresh water meet,
Is important—
Where the hawks sway out into the wind,
Without a single wingbeat,
And the eagles sail low over the fir trees,
And the gulls cry against the crows
In the curved harbors,
And the tide rises up against the grass
Nibbled by sheep and rabbits.

A time for watching the tide,
For the heron's hieratic fishing,
For the sleepy cries of the towhee,
The morning birds gone, the twittering finches,
But still the flash of the kingfisher, the wingbeat of the scoter,
The sun a ball of fire coming down over the water,
The last geese crossing against the reflected afterlight,
The moon retreating into a vague cloud-shape
To the cries of the owl, the eerie whooper.
The old log subsides with the lessening waves,
And there is silence.

I sway outside myself
Into the darkening currents,
Into the small spillage of driftwood,
The waters swirling past the tiny headlands.
Was it here I wore a crown of birds for a moment
While on a far point of the rocks
The light heightened,
And below, in a mist out of nowhere,
The first rain gathered?

2

As when a ship sails with a light wind—
The waves less than the ripples made by rising fish,
The lacelike wrinkles of the wake widening, thinning out,
Sliding away from the traveler's eye,
The prow pitching easily up and down,
The whole ship rolling slightly sideways,

The stern high, dipping like a child's boat in a pond—
Our motion continues.

But this rose, this rose in the sea-wind,
Stays,
Stays in its true place,
Flowering out of the dark,
Widening at high noon, face upward,
A single wild rose, struggling out of the white embrace of the
        morning-glory,
Out of the briary hedge, the tangle of matted underbrush,
Beyond the clover, the ragged hay,
Beyond the sea pine, the oak, the wind-tipped madrona,
Moving with the waves, the undulating driftwood,
Where the slow creek winds down to the black sand of the
        shore
With its thick grassy scum and crabs scuttling back into their
        glistening craters.

And I think of roses, roses,
White and red, in the wide six-hundred-foot greenhouses,
And my father standing astride the cement benches,
Lifting me high over the four-foot stems, the Mrs. Russells,
        and his own elaborate hybrids,
And how those flowerheads seemed to flow toward me, to
        beckon me, only a child, out of myself.
What need for heaven, then,
With that man, and those roses?

3

What do they tell us, sound and silence?
I think of American sounds in this silence;
On the banks of the Tombstone, the wind-harps having their
      say,
The thrush singing alone, that easy bird,
The killdeer whistling away from me,
The mimetic chortling of the catbird
Down in the corner of the garden, among the raggedy lilacs,
The bobolink skirring from a broken fencepost,
The bluebird, lover of holes in old wood, lilting its light
      song,
And that thin cry, like a needle piercing the ear, the insistent
      cicada,
And the ticking of snow around oil drums in the Dakotas,
The thin whine of telephone wires in the wind of a Michigan
      winter,
The shriek of nails as old shingles are ripped from the top of
      a roof,
The bulldozer backing away, the hiss of the sandblaster,
And the deep chorus of horns coming up from the streets in
      early morning.
I return to the twittering of swallows above water,
And that sound, that single sound,
When the mind remembers all,
And gently the light enters the sleeping soul,
A sound so thin it could not woo a bird,

Beautiful my desire, and the place of my desire.

I think of the rock singing, and light making its own silence,
At the edge of a ripening meadow, in early summer,
The moon lolling in the close elm, a shimmer of silver,
Or that lonely time before the breaking of morning
When the slow freight winds along the edge of the ravaged
      hillside,

And the wind tries the shape of a tree,
While the moon lingers,
And a drop of rain water hangs at the tip of a leaf
Shifting in the wakening sunlight
Like the eye of a new-caught fish.

4

I live with the rocks, their weeds,
Their filmy fringes of green, their harsh
Edges, their holes
Cut by the sea-slime, far from the crash
Of the long swell,
The oily, tar-laden walls
Of the toppling waves,
Where the salmon ease their way into the kelp beds,
And the sea rearranges itself among the small islands.
Near this rose, in this grove of sun-parched, wind-warped
    madronas,
Among the half-dead trees, I came upon the true ease of
    myself,
As if another man appeared out of the depths of my being,
And I stood outside myself,
Beyond becoming and perishing,
A something wholly other,
As if I swayed out on the wildest wave alive,
And yet was still.
And I rejoiced in being what I was:
In the lilac change, the white reptilian calm,
In the bird beyond the bough, the single one
With all the air to greet him as he flies,
The dolphin rising from the darkening waves;

And in this rose, this rose in the sea-wind,
Rooted in stone, keeping the whole of light,
Gathering to itself sound and silence—
Mine and the sea-wind's.

RICHARD HUGO

Born and raised in a tough White Center neighborhood, Richard Hugo attended the University of Washington and studied poetry under Theodore Roethke. After graduation he took a job at Boeing but continued to write. Hugo produced two of his best-known collections, A Run of Jacks *(1961) and* Death of the Kapowsin Tavern *(1965) while working as a technical writer. In 1965 he moved to Missoula and helped create a thriving writing program at the University of Montana. A poet of landscapes, towns, and places, Hugo described his poetic sensibility as often "triggered" by the local geography of the Northwest.*

from THE REAL WEST MARGINAL WAY: A POET'S AUTOBIOGRAPHY

WEST MARGINAL WAY parallels the Duwamish River for several miles, but the part I used in my poems is a stretch of about three miles from the foot of Boeing Hill (now renamed Highland Park Way) north to Spokane Street where it ends, a half mile or so from the river mouth. This stretch runs along the base of a high steep hill thickly wooded with alders, maples and evergreens. The north end of this hill, that part near Spokane Street, is called Pigeon Hill. Traveling on West Marginal Way, just before you reach Spokane Street, you come to Riverside, a cluster of drab frame houses. Many immigrants lived there in the '30s, Slavs and Greeks mostly. The homes huddle together and climb the east side of Pigeon Hill, up into alders and ivy. The names, Popick, Zuvela, Petrapolous, were exotic, and the community, more European in appearance than any other in Seattle, always seemed beautiful to me.

I was ready to believe all stories I heard about Riverside. The Greeks who distrusted banks and kept huge amounts of cash in their houses. The Slavs who bought cheap bourbon in the liquor store, then mixed it with pieces of raw fruit in mason jars which they put on their roofs all summer for the sun to work on. The results were said to be staggering. Succulent dishes the immigrant women prepared with eels, cod and sole the river provided. Old John, the Greek fisherman, whose feats of strength had become legend along the river. He had killed a bear in an exhibition wrestling match in Alaska. He could throw the bow rope over his shoulder and walk away from the river hauling his twenty-foot fishing skiff onto the dry land. He had once knocked two thieves senseless, then carried them, one over each shoulder, a quarter of a mile to the rundown Riverside grocery on Spokane Street where he called the police.

BETWEEN THE BRIDGES

These shacks are tricks. A simple smoke
from wood stoves, hanging half-afraid
to rise, makes poverty in winter real.
Behind unpainted doors, old Greeks
are counting money with their arms.
Different birds collect for crumbs
each winter. The loners don't
but ought to wear red shawls.
Here, a cracked brown hump
of knuckle caved a robber's skull.
That cut fruit is for Slavic booze.
Jars of fruit-spiked bourbon bake
on roofs throughout July; festive tubs
of vegetables get wiser in the sun.
All men are strong. Each woman knows
how river cod can be preserved.
Money is for life. Let the money
pile up thirty years and more.
Not in banks, but here, in shacks
where green is real: the stacks of tens
and twenties and the moss on broken piles
big ships tied to when the river
and the birds ran painted to the sea.

. . . The boys of Youngstown-Riverside and the boys of White Center shared at least one concern. Many of us felt socially inferior to children of West Seattle. If the girls of our district felt that, I never heard them express it but then I seldom spoke with girls. There, directly west of Youngstown, sat the castle, the hill, West Seattle where we would go to high school. What a middle class paradise. The streets were paved, the homes elegant, the girls well groomed and simply by virtue of living in West Seattle, far more beautiful and desirable than the girls in our home districts. Gentility and confidence reigned on that hill. West Seattle was not a district. It was an ideal. To be accepted there meant one had become a better person. West Seattle was too far to be seen from White Center, but for the children of Youngstown and Riverside, it towered over the sources of felt debasement, the filthy, loud belching steel mill, the oily slow river, the immigrants hanging on to their odd ways, Indians getting drunk in the unswept taverns, the commercial fishermen, tugboat workers and mill workers with their coarse manners.

When people from White Center applied for work in the '20s and '30s, they seldom mentioned White Center, either in the interview or on the application form. The smart ones said they lived in West Seattle. White Center had the reputation of being just outside the boundary of the civilized world. This stigma remains and as recently as ten years ago a movement started but failed to change the name to Delridge Heights or something equally offensive in its sorry try for respectability.

The reputation was not without reason. White Center was tough. Roxbury Street, the city limits, splits White Center, and following the repeal of prohibition, drinking laws were far more lenient outside the city. Just south of Roxbury Street the taverns flourished. People came to White Center from miles around to have a good time and a good time often involved a good brawl. When I was fourteen, I would go to the roller rink, not to skate but to wait for a fight to start. I had my heroes, Bill Gavin, Tommy Silverthorn. Many of the White Center toughs, like Gavin, came from Youngstown or Riverside. Fights started in the rink with a challenge by someone who had suffered insult enough to serve as an excuse, and ended outside with somebody senseless and bloody on the gravel. I idolized those tough guys but I was too frightened to fight. I stood outside that brutal world, a fascinated witness, winning vicariously. Those battlers from Youngstown and Riverside seemed super masculine, and I wanted to be one of them.

I had two direct connections with West Marginal Way. One was with the Duwamish Slough where I often went fishing when I was nine, ten, eleven, twelve. Duwamish Slough, long ago filled in by progress, sat along West Marginal Way at the foot of Boeing Hill . . . What fishing that was. Porgies, shiners we called them, were so numerous there that after the out-tide drained the slough, we continued to catch them out of the small puddles left standing in the mud flats. I remember vividly the bloated dogs we used to find in those flats, gunnysacks of rocks around their swollen necks. During the Depression, people killed their pets to save the expense of feeding them. An old shingle mill stood beside the slough, but it was seldom operating when we fished there beside it. A cat lived at that mill, a mascot of the mill crew. He was so tough he used to dive into the slough and catch shiners for his meals. I make reference to him in the last stanza of a poem called Duwamish Head. West Marginal Way bridged the slough just south of where it crossed Boeing Hill. Someone, probably the mill crew, had built an outhouse that hung over the slough under the bridge. Sometimes we fished through the toilet down into the water. It made no difference. Shiners nibbled wherever we fished. Along the back part of the slough stood an abandoned brickmill. It was a large low red brick building, and when we were bored catching fish we, chums from White Center and I, explored the mill. We never got far. There were only a few small openings, doorways a grown man had to hunch down to pass through, and little light got inside.

But that is not the West Marginal Way of my poems. My speaker, I, whoever, was downstream at least a mile, alone on the bank with the reeds, birds, the ponderous tugs towing huge logs upstream, the usual gray sky of Seattle turning the river gray. I saw people who never were, in a place I had never been . . .

WEST MARGINAL WAY

One tug pounds to haul an afternoon
of logs up river. The shade
of Pigeon Hill across the bulges
in the concrete crawls on reeds
in a short field, cools a pier
and the violence of young men
after cod. The crackpot chapel,
with a sign erased by rain, returned
before to calm and a mossed roof.

A dim wind blows the roses
growing where they please. Lawns
are wild and lots are undefined

as if the payment made in cash
were counted then and there.
These names on boxes will return
with salmon money in the fall,
come drunk down the cinder arrow
of a trail, past the store of Popich,
sawdust piles and the saw mill
bombing air with optimistic sparks,
blinding gravel pits and the brickyard
baking, to wives who taught themselves
the casual thirst of many summers
wet in heat and taken by the sea.

Some places are forever afternoon.
Across the road and a short field
there is the river, split and yellow
and this far down affected by the tide.

DAVID WAGONER

*No poet has been more profoundly influenced by the natural environment of
the Northwest than David Wagoner, a Midwesterner who came to Seattle in
1954 to teach at the University of Washington. Beginning with his second book,*
A Place to Stand *(1958), and continuing with thirteen other award-winning
collections, Wagoner established himself as the poet of the Northwest woods.
"Where I grew up, between Gary, Indiana, and Chicago, there was no natural world," Wagoner once said. "My father worked all his life in the steel mills
in Gary. So when I came out here in the 1950s, it was a great shock; I thought
I was in Eden." This work appeared in his* Collected Poems, 1956–1976.

ELEGY FOR A FOREST CLEAR-CUT BY THE WEYERHAEUSER COMPANY

Five months after your death, I come like the others
Among the slash and stumps, across the cratered
Three square miles of your graveyard:

Nettles and groundsel first out of the jumble,
Then fireweed and bracken
Have come to light where you, for ninety years,
Had kept your shadows.

The creek has gone as thin as my wrist, nearly dead
To the world at the dead end of summer,
Guttering to a pool where the tracks of an earth-mover
Showed it the way to falter underground.
Now pearly everlasting
Has grown to honor the deep dead cast of your roots
For a bitter season.

Those water- and earth-led roots decay for winter
Below my feet, below the fir seedlings
Planted in your place (one out of ten alive
In the summer drought),
Below the small green struggle of the weeds
For their own ends, below grasshoppers,
The only singers now.

The chains and cables and steel teeth have left
Nothing of what you were:
I hold my hands over a stump and remember
A hundred and fifty feet above me branches
No longer holding sway. In the pitched battle
You fell and fell again and went on falling
And falling and always falling.

Out in the open where nothing was left standing
(The immoral equivalent of a forest fire),
I sit with my anger. The creek will move again,
Come rain and snow, gnawing at raw defiles,
Clear-cutting its own gullies.
As selective as reapers stalking through wheatfields,
Selective loggers go where the roots go.

CONTEMPORARY
EXTREMES
1971–1993

"THE MAGICIAN'S UNDERWEAR had just been found in a cardboard suitcase floating in a stagnant pond on the outskirts of Miami." With that sentence Tom Robbins opened his 1971 novel *Another Roadside Attraction* and ushered in a new era in Northwest writing, one that contained visions of the region as disparate as the Olympic rain forest and the parched hills of the Palouse. At one extreme was Robbins, whose wildly hyperbolic stories were peopled with love children, Zen mystics, and terrorist bombers. At the other was Raymond Carver, whose spare, gritty, realistic style perfectly matched the broken-down, desperate lives of his characters. In between were fabulists like Katherine Dunn and Ursula K. Le Guin, contemplative essayists such as Annie Dillard and Timothy Egan, and spiritual environmentalists like Brenda Peterson.

With his lunatic prose, Robbins created a Northwest that might have been dreamed up by the surrealists. "The sky is as gruff as a Chinese waiter," he wrote. "The sloughs look like spilled tea." His characters, who bore goofy names like Plucky Purcell and Marx Marvelous, were counterculture misfits who rejected the strictures of an uptight society, preferring to explore the limits of personal freedom, sexual openness, and inner consciousness.

Over the next two decades, other writers added to the Northwest's menagerie of misfits. There was Sylvie Fisher, the wonderful nonconformist in Marilynne Robinson's 1981 novel *Housekeeping,* who settles in an isolated Idaho town to raise her late sister's two daughters. Sylvie spends hours meditating in a freezing lakeside forest, hops freight cars for fun, and stacks tin cans up to the parlor ceiling. Gus Orviston, the fly-fishing hermit in David James Duncan's 1983 novel, *The River Why,* finds spiritual completion in the rain that soothes an Oregon forest. In 1989, Portland writer Katherine Dunn created the ultimate band of outsiders, a family of circus freaks, in her dark novel *Geek Love*.

The Northwest wasn't only for the odd. In the late 1980s the region, and Seattle in particular, became the destination of choice for Americans looking for a better life. The Pacific Northwest's high "livability" level attracted young families who fled the nation's older, deteriorating cities. Chucking it all and moving to Seattle became such a popular sentiment that by the mid 1990s it had become a cliché. A thriving alternative culture of rock bands, fringe theaters, underground comics, upstart art galleries, poetry readings, and coffeehouses in Seattle and Portland made these cities the 1990s equivalent of San Francisco in the 1960s, drawing thousands of young artists, actors, writers, and musicians to the region.

Environmental writers flourished in the Northwest, continuing the tradition that began with John Muir a century before. Oregonian Barry Lopez became one of the leading American essayists with his ruminations on humanity, geography, and the natural world. Brenda Peterson, who grew up among trees in the Sierra Nevada, blended her strong environmentalist voice with an interest in multicultural spiritual practices and beliefs to craft essays exploring the effect of the Pacific Northwest wilderness on the soul.

Like Theodore Roethke, Raymond Carver did not write regional stories but used the region—he grew up in small-town Oregon and Washington and spent his final years in Port Angeles, Washington—to write some of the best short stories of the twentieth century. Carver's fiction was populated by people trapped in bad times, liquid habits, and shameful acts. He depicted their dour lives in sentences so spare as to define early-1980s literary minimalism. Carver's friend Tobias Wolff, who also spent part of his childhood in backwoods Northwest towns, also captured the cinderblock-tavern reality of the territory in his 1989 memoir, *This Boy's Life*.

Both writers explored the underside of the Northwest, the seldom-seen place where big Western dreams end in the despair of alcoholism, bankruptcy, and abuse. Carver's description of his own early adult life applies equally to many of his characters: "We had a lot of hope and idealism and strength," he once said, "and we thought that if we worked hard and did the right things, the right things would happen, things would work out. Well, as it turned out we did the best we could, and we worked as hard as we possibly could, and things did not turn out. There was never enough money to go around. Finally that kind of effort began to wear us down." Some of Carver's stories are set in the Northwest; many are not. But in all of them he fashioned quiet moments of humor and dignity out of the day-to-day struggle to get by. In his own way he continued the theme of economic and psychological survival—recall Vardis Fisher's Dock and Opal Hunter, and Ken Kesey's Stamper family—in the cold, gloomy country of the Pacific Northwest.

TOM ROBBINS

In 1970, Tom Robbins, a son of the South who had recently fled to the Northwest, sent the manuscript of his first novel to Doubleday & Company. Another Roadside Attraction, *written in Robbins's peculiarly joyous, anarchic prose, concerned the body of Christ, which had been stolen from a Vatican crypt and spirited to an abandoned hot dog stand in Washington's Skagit Valley. "To my mind," wrote a Doubleday editor, "it's a work of considerable genius . . . I'll go so far as to say that it has the potential to be for the youth of today what* Catcher in the Rye *or* Catch-22 *were for their times." The book became a counterculture classic, and Robbins went on to write a number of popular novels, including* Even Cowgirls Get the Blues, Still Life with Woodpecker, Jitterbug Perfume, *and* Skinny Legs and All.

from ANOTHER ROADSIDE ATTRACTION

THE JAPS ARE TO BLAME. Off the Pacific shore of Washington State the Japanese Current—a mammoth river of tropical water—zooms close by the coast on a southernly turn. Its warmth is released in the form of billows of tepid vapor, which the prevailing winds drive inland. When, a few miles in, the warm vapor bangs head-on into the Olympic Mountain Range, it is abruptly pushed upward and outward, cooling as it rises and condensing into rain. In the emerald area that lies between the Olympics (the coastal range) and the Cascade Range some ninety miles to the east, temperatures are mild and even. But during the autumn and winter months it is not unusual for precipitation to fall on five of every seven days. And when it is not raining, still the gray is pervasive; the sun a little boiled potato in a stew of dirty dumplings; the fire and light and energy of the cosmos trapped somewhere far behind that impenetrable slugbelly sky.

Puget Sound may be the most rained-on body of water on earth. Cold, deep, steep-shored, home to salmon and lipstick-orange starfish, the sound lies between the Cascades and the Olympics. The Skagit Valley lies between the Cascades and the Sound—sixty miles north of Seattle, an equal distance south of Canada. The Skagit River, which formed the valley, begins up in British Columbia, leaps and splashes southwestward through the high Cascade wilderness, absorbing glaciers and sipping alpine lakes, running two hundred miles in total before all fish-green, driftwood-cluttered and silty, it spreads its double mouth like suckers against the upper body of Puget Sound. Toward the Sound end of the valley, the fields are rich with river silt, the soil ranging from black velvet to a blond sandy loam. Although the area receives little unfiltered sunlight, peas and strawberries grow lustily in Skagit fields, and more than half the world's supply of beet seed and cabbage seed is harvested here. Like Holland, which it in some ways resembles, it supports a thriving bulb industry: in spring its lowland acres vibrate with tulips, iris and daffodils; no bashful hues. At any season, it is a dry duck's dream. The forks of the river are connected by a network of sloughs, bedded with ancient mud and lined with cattail, tules, eelgrass and sedge. The fields, though diked, are often flooded; there are puddles by the hundreds and the roadside ditches could be successfully navigated by midget submarines.

It is a landscape in a minor key. A sketchy panorama where objects, both organic and inorganic, lack well-defined edges and tend to melt together in a silver-green blur. Great islands of craggy rock arch abruptly up out of the flats, and at sunrise and moonrise these outcroppings are frequently tangled in mist. Eagles nest on the island crowns and blue herons flap through the veils from slough to slough. It is a poetic setting, one which suggests inner meanings and invisible connections. The effect is distinctly Chinese. A visitor experiences the feeling that he has been pulled into a Sung dynasty painting, perhaps before the intense wisps of mineral pigment have dried upon the silk. From almost any vantage point, there are expanses of monochrome worthy of the brushes of Mi Fei or Kuo Hsi.

The Skagit Valley, in fact, inspired a school of neo-Chinese painters. In the Forties, Mark Tobey, Morris Graves and their gray-on-gray disciples turned their backs on cubist composition and European color and using the shapes and shades of this misty terrain as a springboard, began to paint the visions of the inner eye. A school of sodden, contemplative poets emerged here, too. Even the original inhabitants were an introspective breed. Unlike the Plains Indians, who enjoyed mobility and open spaces and sunny skies, the Northwest coastal tribes were caught between the dark waters to the west, the heavily forested foothills and towering Cascade peaks to the east; forced by the lavish rains to spend weeks on end confined to their longhouses. Consequently, they turned inward, evolving religious and mythological patterns that are startling in their complexity and intensity, developing an artistic idiom that for aesthetic weight and psychological depth was unequaled among all primitive races. Even today, after the intrusion of neon signs and supermarkets and aircraft industries and sports cars, a hushed but heavy force hangs in the Northwest air: it defies flamboyance, deflates extroversion and muffles the most exultant cry.

Yet one inhabitant of this nebulous and mystic land had had the audacity to establish a Dixie Bar-B-Cue. There is a colony of expatriated North Carolinians up in the timber country around Darrington: perhaps Mom was one of them. Her enterprise had not succeeded, obviously, and a disappointed and homesick Mom may have packed her curing salts and hot sauces and trucked on back to the red clay country where a good barbecue is paid the respect it deserves. At any rate, that aspect of the history of the cafe meant little to Amanda and John Paul Ziller for they were immune to the mystique of Southern pork barbecue. Neither had ever tasted the genuine article. Plucky Purcell had, of course, and he once remarked that "the only meat in the world sweeter, hotter and pinker than Amanda's twat is Carolina barbecue."

Prior to signing a lease for Mom's Little Dixie, Ziller had warned Amanda of the rigors of her new environment. He explained to his bride that there was seldom a thunderstorm in Skagit country—simply not enough heat—so no matter whether the influence storms had on her was good or ultimately evil, she could expect to be free of it as long as she resided in the Northwest. He told her that there would be butterflies in the summer, but not nearly in the numbers to which she was accustomed in California and Arizona. Amanda knew, naturally, that cacti could not endure in these latitudes. And even their motorcycle would be impractical during the rainy season that lingered from October to May. "However," John Paul comforted her, "in those ferny forests"—he pointed to the alder-thatched Cascade foothills—"the mushrooms are rising like loaves. Like hearts they are pulsing and swelling; fungi of many hues, some shaped like trumpets and some like bells and some like parasols and others like pricks; with thick meat white as turkey or yellow as eggs; all reeking of primeval protein; and some contain bitter juices that make men go crazy and talk to God."

"Very well," said Amanda. "Mushrooms it will be." And it was.

———

Autumn does not come to the Skagit Valley in sweet-apple chomps, in blasts of blue sky and painted leaves, with crisp football afternoons and squirrel chatter and bourbon and lap robes under a harvest moon. The East and Midwest have their autumns, and Skagit Valley has another.

October lies on the Skagit like a wet rag on a salad. Trapped beneath low clouds, the valley is damp and green and full of sad memories. The people of the valley have far less to be unhappy about than many who live elsewhere in America, but, still, an aboriginal sadness clings like the dew to their region; their land has a blurry beauty (as if the Creator started to erase it but had second thoughts), it has dignity, fertility and hints of inner meaning—but nothing can seem to make it laugh.

The short summer is finished, it is October again, and Sung dynasty mists swirl across the fields where seed cabbages, like gangrened jack-o'-lanterns, have been left to rot. The ghost-light of old photographs floods the tide flats, the island outcroppings, the salt marshes, the dikes and the sloughs. The frozen-food plants have closed for the season. A trombone of geese slides southward between the overcast and the barns. Upriver, there is a chill in the weeds. Old trucks and tractors rusting among the stumps seem in autumn especially forlorn.

October scenes:

At the dog-bitten Swinomish Indian Center near La Conner, there is a forty-foot totem pole the top figure of which is Franklin Delano Roosevelt. One of the queerer projects of the WPA. Roosevelt's Harvard grin is faded and wooden in the reservation mist.

Outside of Concrete, boys have thrown crab apples through the colored glass windows of an abandoned church. Crows carry the bright fragments away to their nests.

On the Freeway south of Mount Vernon, watched over by a hovering sausage, surrounded by a ring of prophecy, an audacious roadside zoo rages against the multiplying green damp chill as if it were a spell cast upon the valley by gypsy friends of the sun. Events transpire within that zoo which must be recorded immediately and correctly if they are to pass into history undeformed. Things rot with a terrible swiftness in the Northwest rains. A century from now, the ruins of the Capt. Kendrick Memorial Hot Dog Wildlife Preserve will offer precious little to reimburse archaeologists for their time. No Dead Sea Scrolls will ever be found in the Skagit Valley. It's now or never for *this* bible.

Rain fell on Skagit Valley.

It fell in sweeps and it fell in drones. It fell in unending cascades of cheap Zen jewelry. It fell on the dikes. It fell on the firs. It fell on the downcast necks of the mallards.

And it rained a fever. And it rained a silence. And it rained a sacrifice. And it rained a miracle. And it rained sorceries and saturnine eyes of the totem.

Rain drenched the chilly green tidelands. The river swelled. The sloughs fermented. Vapors rose from black stumps on the hillsides. Spirit canoes paddled in the mists of the islands. Legends were washed from desecrated burial grounds. (The Skagit Indians, too, have a tradition of a Great Flood. The flood, they say, caused a big change in the world. Another big change is yet to occur. The world will change again. The Skagit don't know when. "When we can converse with the animals, we will know the change is halfway here. When we can converse with the forest, we will know the change has come.") Water spilled off the roofs and the rain hats. It took on the colors of neon and head lamps. It glistened on the claws of nighttime animals.

And it rained a screaming. And it rained a rawness. And it rained a plasma. And it rained a disorder.

The rain erased the prints of the sasquatch. It beat the last withered fruit from the orchard trees. It soaked the knotted fans who gathered to watch high-school boys play football in the mud. It hammered the steamed-up windshields of lover's lane Chevvies, hammered the larger windshields of hunters' pickups, hammered, upriver, the still larger windshields of logging trucks. And it hammered the windowpane through which I gazed at the Freeway reflection of Ziller's huge innocent weenie, finding in its gentle repose precious few parallels with my own condition.

"You know," I said to Amanda, "this whole awful business might be easier to endure if we were on a sunny Mexican beach instead of drowning under a Northwest waterfall." I gestured in the direction of the weather.

"The last time I was on a Mexican beach, some guy stole my transistor radio," sighed Amanda.

"Why, that's a dirty shame," I sympathized.

"Oh, it was all right," she said. "He took the radio but he left the music."

MARILYNNE ROBINSON

In 1981, Farrar, Straus & Giroux published Housekeeping, *a remarkable first novel by Marilynne Robinson. In the warm, intimate language of a friend recalling stories from her childhood during a long winter evening, Robinson captured the history of two sisters growing up in a small isolated northern Idaho town. Robinson was born in Sandpoint, Idaho, where her father worked in the lumber industry. She followed* Housekeeping *with* Mother Country *(1988), a nonfiction account of atomic poisoning in England.*

from HOUSEKEEPING

THE WEEK AFTER SYLVIE arrived, Fingerbone had three days of brilliant sunshine and four of balmy rain. On the first day the icicles dripped so rapidly that the gravel under the eaves rattled and jumped. The snow was granular in the shade, and in the sun it turned soft and clung damply to whatever it covered. The second day the icicles fell and broke on the ground and snow drooped low over the eaves in a heavy mass. Lucille and I poked it down with sticks. The third day the snow was so dense and malleable that we made a sort of statue. We put one big ball of snow on top of another, and carved them down with kitchen spoons till we had made a figure of a woman in a long dress, her arms folded. It was Lucille's idea that she should look to the side, and while I knelt and whittled folds into her skirt, Lucille stood on the kitchen stool and molded her chin and her nose and her hair. It happened that I swept her skirt a little back from her hip, and that her arms were folded high on her breasts. It was mere accident—the snow was firmer here and softer there, and in some places we had to pat clean snow over old black leaves that had been rolled up into the snowballs we made her from—but her shape became a posture. And while in any particular she seemed crude and lopsided, altogether her figure suggested a woman standing in a cold wind. It seemed that we had conjured a presence. We took off our coats and hats and worked about her in silence. That was the third day of sunshine. The sky was dark blue, there was no wind at all, but everywhere an audible seep and trickle of melting. We hoped the lady would stand long enough to freeze, but in fact while we were stamping the gray snow all smooth around her, her head pitched over and smashed on the ground. This accident cost her a forearm and a breast. We made a new snowball for a head, but it crushed her eaten neck, and under the weight of it a shoulder dropped away. We went inside for lunch, and when we came out again, she was a dog-yellowed stump in which neither of us would admit any interest.

Days of rain at just that time were a disaster. They hastened the melting of the snow but not the thawing of the ground. So at the end of three days the houses and hutches and barns and sheds of Fingerbone were like so many spilled and foundered arks. There were chickens roosting in the telephone poles and dogs swimming by in the streets. My grandmother always boasted that the floods never reached our house, but that spring, water poured over the thresholds and covered the floor to the depth of four inches, obliging us to wear boots while we did the cooking and washing up. We lived on the second floor for a number of days. Sylvie played solitaire on the vanity while Lucille and I played Monopoly on the bed. The firewood on the porch was piled high so that most of it stayed dry enough to burn, though rather smokily. The woodpile was full of spiders and mice, and the pantry curtain rod was deeply bowed by the weight of water climbing up the curtains. If we opened or closed a door, a wave swept through the house, and chairs tottered, and bottles and pots clinked and clunked in the bottoms of the kitchen cabinets.

After four days of rain the sun appeared in a white sky, febrile and dazzling, and the people who had left for higher ground came back in rowboats. From our bedroom window we could see them patting their roofs and peering in at their attic windows. "I have never seen such a thing," Sylvie said. The water shone more brilliantly than the sky, and while we watched, a tall elm tree fell slowly across the road. From crown to root, half of it vanished in the brilliant light.

Fingerbone was never an impressive town. It was chastened by an outsized landscape and extravagant weather, and chastened again by an awareness that the whole of human history had occurred elsewhere. That flood flattened scores of headstones. More disturbing, the graves sank when the water receded, so that they looked a little like hollow sides or empty bellies. And then the library was flooded to a depth of three shelves, creating vast gaps in the Dewey decimal system. The losses in hooked and braided rugs and needlepoint footstools will never be reckoned. Fungus and mold crept into wedding dresses and photograph albums, so that the leather crumbled in our hands when we lifted the covers, and the sharp smell that rose when we opened them was as insinuating as the smells one finds under a plank or a rock. Much of what Fingerbone had hoarded up was defaced or destroyed outright, but perhaps because the hoard was not much to begin with, the loss was not overwhelming.

The next day was very fine. The water was so calm that the sunken half of the fallen tree was replaced by the mirrored image of the half trunk and limbs that remained above the water. All day two cats prowled in the branches, pawing at little eddies and currents. The water was beginning to slide away. We could hear the lake groan under the weight of it, for the lake had not yet thawed. The ice would still be thick, but it would be the color of paraffin, with big white bubbles under it. In normal weather there would have been perhaps an inch of water on top of it in shallow places. Under all the weight of the flood water it sagged and, being fibrous rather than soft or brittle, wrenched apart, as resistant to breaching as green bones. The afternoon was loud with the giant miseries of the lake, and the sun shone on, and the flood was the almost flawless mirror of a cloudless sky, fat with brimming and very calm.

Lucille and I pulled on our boots and went downstairs. The parlor was full of light. Our walking from the stairs to the door had set off an intricate system of small currents which rolled against the floorboards. Glyphs of crimped and plaited light swung across the walls and the ceiling. The couch and the armchairs were oddly dark. The stuffing in their backs had slid, and the cushions had shallow craters in the middles of them. Water seeped out when we touched them. In the course of days the flood had made a sort of tea of hemp and horsehair and rag paper in that room, a smell which always afterward clung to it and which I remember precisely at this minute, though I have never encountered its like.

Sylvie came down the hall in a pair of my grandmother's boots and looked in at us from the door. "Should we start dinner?" she asked.

Lucille poked a sofa cushion with her finger. "Look," she said. When she took her hand away, the suppurated water vanished, but the dent remained.

"It's a shame," Sylvie said. From the lake came the increasingly terrific sound of wrenching and ramming and slamming and upending, as a south-flowing current heaped huge shards of ice against the north side of the bridge. Sylvie pushed at the water with the side of her foot. A ribbed circle spread to the four walls and the curves of its four sides rebounded, interpenetrating, and the orderly ranks of light swept and swung about the room. Lucille stomped with her feet until the water sloshed against the walls like water carried in a bucket. There were the sounds of dull concussion from the kitchen, and the lace curtains, drawn thin and taut by their own sodden weight, shifted and turned. Sylvie took me by the hands and pulled me after her through six grand waltz steps. The house flowed around us. Lucille pulled the front door open and the displacement she caused made one end of the woodpile in the porch collapse and tipped a chair, spilling a bag of clothespins. Lucille stood at the door, looking out.

"It sounds like the bridge is breaking up," she remarked.

"That's probably just the ice," Sylvie said.

Lucille said, "I don't think Simmons's house is where it used to be."

Sylvie went to the door and peered down the street at a blackened roof. "It's so hard to tell."

"Those bushes used to be on the other side."

"Maybe the bushes moved."

RAYMOND CARVER

Raymond Carver was born the son of a saw-filer in the mill town of Clatskanie, Oregon, in 1938. He grew up in Yakima, Washington, and spent most of his young adulthood in northern California, where he struggled to start a writing career and stay one step ahead of bankruptcy. He later taught creative writing in Syracuse, New York. With his four major short story collections, Will You Please Be Quiet, Please *(1976),* What We Talk About When We Talk About Love *(1981),* Cathedral *(1983), and* Where I'm Calling From *(1988), Carver changed the direction of American fiction, bringing stark realism back into vogue and starting a new short story renaissance. In the early 1980s he returned to the Northwest to live with poet Tess Gallagher in Port Angeles, and the region inspired an outpouring of poetry from the short story master. "I feel directly in touch with my surroundings now in a way I haven't felt in years," he said in 1984. Carver died four years later at the age of fifty. The following excerpt is from "Boxes," published in* Where I'm Calling From.

from BOXES

MY MOTHER IS PACKED and ready to move. But Sunday afternoon, at the last minute, she calls and says for us to come eat with her. "My icebox is defrosting," she tells me. "I have to fry up this chicken before it rots." She says we should bring our own plates and some knives and forks. She's packed most of her dishes and kitchen things. "Come on and eat with me one last time," she says. "You and Jill."

I hang up the phone and stand at the window for a minute longer, wishing I could figure this thing out. But I can't. So finally I turn to Jill and say, "Let's go to my mother's for a good-bye meal."

Jill is at the table with a Sears catalogue in front of her, trying to find us some curtains. But she's been listening. She makes a face. "Do we have to?" she says. She bends down the corner of a page and closes the catalogue. She sighs. "God, we been over there to eat two or three times in the last month alone. Is she ever actually going to leave?"

Jill always says what's on her mind. She's thirty-five years old, wears her hair short, and grooms dogs for a living. Before she became a groomer, something she likes, she used to be a housewife and mother. Then all hell broke loose. Her two children were kidnapped by her first husband and taken to live in Australia. Her second husband, who drank, left her with a broken eardrum before he drove their car through a bridge into the Elwha River. He didn't have life insurance, not to mention property-damage insurance. Jill had to borrow money to bury him, and then—can you beat it?—she was presented with a bill for the bridge repair. Plus, she had her own medical bills. She can tell this story now. She's bounced back. But she has run out of patience with my mother. I've run out of patience, too. But I don't see my options.

"She's leaving day after tomorrow," I say. "Hey, Jill, don't do any favors. Do you want to come with me or not?" I tell her it doesn't matter to me one way or the other. I'll say she has a migraine. It's not like I've never told a lie before.

"I'm coming," she says. And like that she gets up and goes into the bathroom, where she likes to pout.

We've been together since last August, about the time my mother picked to move up here to Longview from California. Jill tried to make the best of it. But my mother pulling into town just when we were trying to get our act together was nothing either of us had bargained for. Jill said it reminded her of the situation with her first husband's mother. "She was a clinger," Jill said. "You know what I mean? I thought I was going to suffocate."

It's fair to say that my mother sees Jill as an intruder. As far as she's concerned, Jill is just another girl in a series of girls who have appeared in my life since my wife left me. Someone, to her mind, likely to take away affection, attention, maybe even some money that might otherwise come to her. But someone deserving of respect? No way. I remember—how can I forget it?—she called my wife a whore before we were married, and then called her a whore fifteen years later, after she left me for someone else.

Jill and my mother act friendly enough when they find themselves together. They hug each other when they say hello or good-bye. They talk about shopping specials. But Jill dreads the time she has to spend in my mother's company. She claims my mother bums her out. She says my mother is negative about everything and everybody and ought to find an outlet, like other people in her age bracket. Crocheting, maybe, or card games at the Senior Citizens Center, or else going to church. Something, anyway, so that she'll leave us in peace. But my mother had her own way of solving things. She announced she was moving back to California. The hell with everything and everybody in this town. What a place to live! She wouldn't continue to live in this town if they gave her the place and six more like it.

Within a day or two of deciding to move, she'd packed her things into boxes. That was last January. Or maybe it was February. Anyway, last winter sometime. Now it's the end of June. Boxes have been sitting around inside her house for months. You have to walk around them or step over them to get from one room to another. This is no way for anyone's mother to live.

After a while, ten minutes or so, Jill comes out of the bathroom. I've found a roach and am trying to smoke that and drink a bottle of ginger ale while I watch one of the neighbors change the oil in his car. Jill doesn't look at me. Instead, she goes into the kitchen and puts some plates and utensils into a paper sack. But when she comes back through the living room I stand up, and we hug each other. Jill says, "It's okay." What's okay, I wonder. As far as I can see, nothing's okay. But she holds me and keeps patting my shoulder. I can smell the pet shampoo on her. She comes home from work wearing the stuff. It's everywhere. Even when we're in bed together. She gives me a final pat. Then we go out to the car and drive across town to my mother's.

I like where I live. I didn't when I first moved here. There was nothing to do at night, and I was lonely. Then I met Jill. Pretty soon, after a few weeks, she brought her things over and started living with me. We didn't set any long-term goals. We were happy and we had a life together. We told each other we'd finally got lucky. But my mother didn't have anything going in her life. So she wrote me and said she'd decided on moving here. I wrote her back and said I didn't think it was such a good idea. The weather's terrible in the winter, I said. They're building a prison a few miles from town, I told her. The place is bumper-to-bumper tourists all summer, I said. But she acted as if she never got my letters, and came anyway. Then, after she'd been in town a little less than a month, she told me she hated the place. She acted as if it were my fault she'd moved here and my fault she found everything so disagreeable. She started calling me up and telling me how crummy the place was. "Laying guilt trips," Jill called it. She told me the bus service was terrible and the drivers unfriendly. As for the people at the Senior Citizens—well, she didn't want to play casino. "They can go to hell," she said, "and take their card games with them." The clerks at the supermarket were surly, the guys in the service station didn't give a damn about her or her car. And she'd made up her mind about the man she rented from, Larry Hadlock. King Larry, she called him. "He thinks he's *superior* to everyone because he has some shacks for rent and a few dollars. I wish to God I'd never laid eyes on him."

It was too hot for her when she arrived, in August, and in September it started to rain. It rained almost every day for weeks. In October it turned cold. There was snow in November and December. But long before that she began to put the bad mouth on the place and the people to the extent that I didn't want to hear about it anymore, and I told her so finally. She cried, and I hugged her and thought that was the end of it. But a few days later she started in again, same stuff. Just before Christmas she called to see when I was coming by with her presents. She hadn't put up a tree and didn't intend to, she said. Then she said something else. She said if this weather didn't improve she was going to kill herself.

"Don't talk crazy," I said.

She said, "I mean it, honey. I don't want to see this place again except from my coffin. I hate this g.d. place. I don't know why I moved here. I wish I could just die and get it over with."

I remember hanging on to the phone and watching a man high up on a pole doing something to a power line. Snow whirled around his head. As I watched, he leaned out from the pole, supported only by his safety belt. Suppose he falls, I thought. I didn't have any idea what I was going to say next. I had to say something. But I was filled with unworthy feelings, thoughts no son should admit to. "You're my mother," I said finally. "What can I do to help?"

"Honey, you can't do anything," she said. "The time for doing anything has come and gone. It's too late to do anything. I wanted to like it here. I thought we'd go on picnics and take drives together. But none of that happened. You're always busy. You're off working, you and Jill. You're never at home. Or else if you are at home you have the phone off the hook all day. Anyway, I never see you," she said.

"That's not true," I said. And it wasn't. But she went on as if she hadn't heard me. Maybe she hadn't.

"Besides," she said, "this weather's killing me. It's too damned cold here. Why didn't you tell me this was the North Pole? If you had, I'd never have come. I want to go back to California, honey. I can get out and go places there. I don't know anywhere to go here. There are people back in California. I've got friends there who care what happens to me. Nobody gives a damn here. Well, I just pray I can get through to June. If I can make it that long, if I can last to June, I'm leaving this place forever. This is the worst place I've ever lived in."

What could I say? I didn't know what to say. I couldn't even say anything about the weather. Weather was a real sore point. We said good-bye and hung up.

Other people take vacations in the summer, but my mother moves. She started moving years ago, after my dad lost his job. When that happened, when he was laid off, they sold their home, as if this were what they should do, and went to where they thought things would be better. But things weren't any better there, either. They moved again. They kept on moving. They lived in rented houses, apartments, mobile homes, and motel units even. They kept moving, lightening their load with each move they made. A couple of times they landed in a town where I lived. They'd move in with my wife and me for a while and then they'd move on again. They were like migrating animals in this regard, except there was no pattern to their movement. They moved around for years, sometimes even leaving the state for what they thought would be greener pastures. But mostly they stayed in Northern California and did their moving there. Then my dad died, and I thought my mother would stop moving and stay in one place for a while. But she didn't. She kept moving. I suggested once that she go to a psychiatrist. I even said I'd pay for it. But she wouldn't hear of it. She packed and moved out of town instead. I was desperate about things or I wouldn't have said that about the psychiatrist.

She was always in the process of packing or else unpacking. Sometimes she'd move two or three times in the same year. She talked bitterly about the place she was leaving and optimistically about the place she was going to. Her mail got fouled up, her benefit checks went off somewhere else, and she spent hours writing letters, trying to get it all straightened out. Sometimes she'd move out of an apartment house, move to another one a few blocks away, and then, a month later, move back to the place she'd left, only to a different floor or a different side of the building. That's why when she moved here I rented a house for her and saw to it that it was furnished to her liking. "Moving around keeps her alive," Jill said. "It gives her something to do. She must get some kind of weird enjoyment out of it, I guess." But enjoyment or not, Jill thinks my mother must be losing her mind. I think so, too. But how do you tell your mother this? How do you deal with her if this is the case? Crazy doesn't stop her from planning and getting on with her next move.

TESS GALLAGHER

"Rain," Tess Gallagher once wrote, "is the climate of my psyche." The people of her Port Angeles, Washington, hometown "know the rain is a reason for not living where they live, but they live there anyway. They work hard in the logging camps, in the pulp mills and lumberyards. Everything has a wetness over it, glistening quietly as though it were still in the womb, waiting to be born." The daughter of a logger and longshoreman, Gallagher established her literary reputation with the 1976 poetry collection Instructions to the Double. *This is the title poem from* Amplitude, *published in 1987.*

AMPLITUDE

Twice this Christmas Day you tried
to get somebody to listen with
you to the new Ricky Skaggs tape somebody
gave you, and were
refused. You bummed cigarettes, ate
some hot pickles, ranged in and
out of the house, played a game of
"Fish" with your kids, dangling
a magnet from a string
over eight little magnet-mouthed
fish that snapped open their yaps, then
clamped shut before your mag-
net could suck onto them and lift
them out of the wind-up pond
on the coffee table. Your kids beat
you and laughed about

it. You laughed
too, a little. Then clearly
had to find something else
to do. Dinner settled in on our mother, her
mouth open to that other magnet, sleep,
drawing her god knows where
out of our warm, swirling pond of family and
the still excited clutter of gift-
giving. Then you remembered Ray's Mercedes

parked near the swing set and said to me, "Let's
go, Sis," handing me the Scaggs tape. Impossible, though, to get out of
the house without your wife, Jean, and the
kids who wanted not
to miss out. Errands thought of too, so
it wouldn't be *just*
a ride, presents could be dropped
off to friends so there'd be some place to go
to. All of this okay. And the company
of your kids and wife adding
to the solitude
because of how they travel like a beautiful wake
behind you even when you're alone and
silent at your work. So the car

gliding effortlessly through the nearly
vacant streets, under the sparse decorations of this mill town where we
were born, were kids together. Now, buckled in
to the dark, we adjust the volume and let
the cowboy sing his way down mainstreet, a
place he'll never see, with strangers he could care
less about. "Will you shut up so I can hear
the song, for Chrissake," you say into the back
seat, and, for a while we are all
with you, listening, because you said to, me

waiting until enough listening has gone by
to chance singing along, as you know
I have to, but not minding because it
beefs up the harmonies, a live track angling
in on studio vigor with the discrepancies
of the human. Real enjoyment leading then to

past hardship, so memory, that other fresh-
ness, cuts in to add value in a parallel key: "Did
you ever think, when we were kids and bare-
foot in the logging camps, we'd drive up Race
Street in a Mercedes listening to cowboy
music?" We blotted out a bar
or two of aggressive banjo just marvelling
at the unlikelihood. Vaguely, the
sense we shouldn't take such uncomplicated pleasure in
for long, or a magnet might
drop straight through the
roof and snatch one of us a-
way. Then, one by one,
the rest. But delight, pure and
simple, thanks to Ray's Mercedes, for having
pulled a fast one on this town and the invisible net over all, that said: You
won't amount to
a damn. And the triumph of it not even ours

as we passed the cemetery, lightly
dusted with snow, and our father there
with the others who came to this place and called
it good enough to hold a life and let it
go—some even, like him, who intended
to die here. The importance
of that choice unmade for me and humming along
with us. Then, looking over at you still
listening to the music, not
singing, but thinking about death or

whether or not you should be ashamed to be
seen motoring through the streets of our
hometown in the guise of those we'd learned to
hate as having more than their share. What

happened to those rocks we rushed from the house
to fling at bumper-to-bumper Californians, dragging
their mobile homes and over-
sized boats past the shack we were raised
in? In what far country did they
land, those heart-flung shards
of our untutored contempt? Here. They
landed here. And pelt down on me
because the violence of a kid's arm
is attached to more than stones and what
the world thinks of anyone's chances. Who's
to say if we could swing down Caroline Street and
pick up those two vigilantes they wouldn't
climb in—glad to have such mild
benefactors—ride along in wordless
awe, then the minute we put them out, set to
with a slingshot? Meanwhile I'm bartering
in the black markets of the mind for

the peace of a front yard nativity where
a kid's bike has tipped refreshingly onto the
baby Jesus so the spokes enhance his re-
solve toward bliss. Belief—the unspectacular
locomotion of childhood, gleams unremittingly
at me through the backlit curtains of
the house—that pyramid of wooly
lights anchored in the shadowy boughs. All
silent. All calm. House after
house. Until we hit
town and a little life stirs
outside the M & C tavern, two women
piloting a wobbly man into a back seat, then

genial shadows as they too climb in, reach
for the ignition and jerk away
from the curb. Suddenly over us a sign

above the used car lot: "Save Ethiopia! Send
money now." Our town shoots out into the starlit
map of the world where last night's TV news-
caster, in a voice dulled by the
ritualization of caring, hovers in-
visibly over a mother who has crawled forty miles
through desert with her child tied to
her back and will, he gives us
to understand, likely die
anyway. The bounce in the ad-break following
hurtles resourcefully on: "In a moment, how *you*
can pick up the tab on African hunger."
Ricky Skaggs careens into another verse
of relentless heartbreak, but it can't lift
an eyelid to this. Nor, inexplicably, that day

my high school chum, driving me down
Blue Mountain Road in his first car, hit
a child's puppy that had run in front of the
car, killing it outright. The kid weeping and
cuddling the mess and my friend, in a frenzy
of remorse, fumbling a dollar bill into
the kid's shirt pocket, then wordlessly sliding
into the seat beside me to drive us
away. That action waving now like a white flag
of surrender over a trench whose once embattled
defenders are safely imprisoned
elsewhere. Passing now the pulp mill and

my brother reminding me how our father
worked there three times, and quit
three times. The windows are fogged
with dirt and ingots of unhealthy,

fluorescent unlight. "Imagine
day after day working in there," I say, thankful
to dispose of a safely impossible fate
so near at hand. My brother looks hard at
the place, then like he could bash it
to bits, his voice low and even: "Jean's dad
spent thirty-nine years
in there." She makes a sharp
noise in the dark to let her father out
again and into his well-earned death. We drive

onto the spit of land that lets us look back
across the harbor at the lights of
the town. More red
in their glimmer tonight, I think, and then,
more gold. "It's
pretty," Jean says, "isn't
it?" The kids in their surplus of quiet, dreamily
then, "Yes, pretty. Really
pretty." We idle in the excellent rigor of
engine-pull de-
signed by Germans, until the same
child-voices, discarding beauty and
death as unequal to the moment, plead us
back "in time," as they put it, to give—unopened,
the gifts we are bearing.

DAVID JAMES DUNCAN

In 1983, Sierra Club Books ended its twenty-two-year policy against publishing fiction to bring out The River Why, *the debut novel of an unknown Oregonian named David James Duncan. The novel was a coming-of-age tale about Gus Orviston, a young man raised by fish-crazed parents in Oregon. Duncan's book celebrated and gently mocked the Northwest's cult of fly-fishing. Gus's blustery father, Henning Hale-Orviston (whom he calls H2O), in fact, bears a striking resemblance to Roderick Haig-Brown, a British-born North-westerner whose books* Return to the River *(1941) and* A River Never Sleeps *(1946) turned the region's rivers and salmon into the stuff of fly-casting legend.*

from THE RIVER WHY

SOUTH OF THE COLUMBIA and north of California, scores of wild green rivers come tumbling down out of the evergreen, ever-wet forests of the Coast Range. These rivers are short—twenty to sixty miles, most of them—but they carry a lot of water. They like to run fast through the woods, roaring and raising hell during rainstorms and run-offs, knocking down streamside cedars and alders now and again to show they know who it is dumping trashy leaves and branches in them all the time. But when they get within a few miles of the ocean, they aren't so brash. They get cautious down there, start sidling back and forth digging letters in their valleys—C's, S's, U's, L's, and others from their secret alphabet—and they quit roaring and start mumbling to themselves, making odd sounds like jittery orators clearing their throats before addressing a mighty audience. Or sometimes they say nothing at all but just slip along in sullen silence, as though they thought that if they snuck up on the Pacific softly enough it might not notice them, might not swallow them whole the way it usually does. But when they get to the estuaries they realize they've been kidding themselves: the Ocean is *always* hungry—and no Columbia, no Mississippi, no Orinoco or Ganges can curb its appetite . . . So they panic: when they taste the first salt tides rising up to greet them they turn back toward their kingdoms in the hills. They don't get far. When the overmastering tides return to the ocean, these once-brash rivers trail along behind like sad little dogs on leashes—past the marshes with their mallards, the mud flats with their clams, the shallow bays with their herons, over the sandbars with their screaming gulls and riptides, away into the oblivion of the sea.

The river I lived on is on the northern half of the Oregon Coast. I promised friends there not to divulge its real name or location, so I'll call it the "Tamanawis." The cabin was situated at the feet of the last forested hills—the final brash rapids just upstream, the first cautious, curving letters just below. There were a few fishing cottages near mine, empty most of the time, and upstream nothing but rain, brush, trees, elk, ravens and coyotes. A quarter mile downstream and across the river was a dairy farm, my nearest permanent neighbor. The farmer had 120 cows to take care of; he had it pretty easy. His wife had the farmer and their six kids to take care of; she had it tough. The farmer, wife, kids, and cows had an orange and purple and black house, two red and green and yellow barns, and a clearing of tree stumps where their yard should have been. (I used to thank Fathern Heaven for the trees that blocked that place from view. Something about those stumps and colors. Made me feel I'd been living on TV, Coca-Cola and doughnuts.) Below the dairy the Tamanawis Valley got more populated—a few farms, sportsmen's shanties, here and there one of those antennaed, yarn-floored boxes poor dumb suburbanites call "contemporary homes"; then a sawmill, a huge poultry farm, and a trailer court defacing the edge of a nice little town at river's mouth. (We'll call it "Fog.") Highway 101 runs through Fog, and the chuckholed asphalted Tamanawis River Road takes off from one of the five intersections in town, running up past my cabin, turning into gravel upstream, then into mud, and dead-ending in a maze of logging and fire roads. The only people who use the River Road are fishermen, loggers, hunters and an occasional mapless tourist trying to get back to the Willamette Valley by a "scenic route." The latter folk drive by my cabin all shiny-autoed and smiley, and two or three hours later come spluttering back with mud and disgruntlement on their cars and faces, hell-bent for 101 and screw the scenery. The Coast Range Maze does that to people.

Across the road from my cabin was a huge clear-cut—hundreds of acres of massive spruce stumps interspersed with tiny Douglas firs—products of what they call "Reforestation," which I guess makes the spindly firs en masse a "Reforest," which makes an individual spindly fir a "Refir," which means you could say that Weyerhaeuser, who owns the joint, has Refir Madness, since they think that sawing down 200-foot-tall spruces and replacing them with puling 2-foot Refirs is no different from farming beans or corn or alfalfa. They even call the towering spires they wipe from the earth's face forever a "crop"—as if they'd planted the virgin forest! But I'm just a fisherman and may be missing some deeper significance in their strange nomenclature and stranger treatment of primordial trees.

The river side of the road had never been logged. There were a few tremendous spruces, small stands of alder, clumps of hazelnut, tree-sized ferns, fern-sized wildflowers, head-high salal, impenetrable thickets of devil's club, and, surrounding my cabin, a dense grove of cedars—huge, solemn trees with long drooping branches and a sweet smell like solitude itself. The cabin was made of fir logs squared off Scandanavian-style and joined so tightly that I could light a cooking fire on a cold winter's morning, fish all day, and find it still cozy when I came home at dark. There was only one room, but it was big—twenty-two by twenty-eight feet—with the kind of high beamed-and-jointed ceiling that made you want to just sit back and study the way it all fit together. The bedroom was an open loft above the kitchen; the kitchen was the table and chairs, stove, waterheater and sink; the refrigerator was a stone-walled cellar reached through a trap-door in the kitchen floor; the bathroom was a partitioned-off corner so small you had to stand in the shower to take aim at the toilet, and if you bumped the shower walls they boomed like a kettledrum—so I took to voiding my bladder in the devil's club outside.

The cabin was dark, thanks to the grove, but some gloom-oppressed occupant had cut one four-by-four window in the south wall overlooking the river: I set up my fly-tying desk next to it, partly for light, partly so if something swirled as I worked I could be out there with a loaded flyrod in seconds. I didn't miss electricity at all—even preferred the absence of it—but H2O, convinced that I'd go blind tying flies by candlelight, left me three Coleman camp lanterns that blazed about as subtly as searchlights, and Ma, appalled by the lack of racket, bequeathed me a big battery-operated AM/FM radio: both earned an early retirement on a remote shelf . . .

The most outrageous housewarming gift was from H2O: a fifty-gallon aquarium. He keeps one of those monsters by his fly-tying vise and in his books recommends them to all serious fly-makers. The idea is to catch water bugs and larvae on fishing trips and stick them in your tank to use as living models; you can also test an imitation by tying it to a light leader, lowering it into the aquarium and jerking it around among its live prototypes: if it is attacked or raped you may conclude it a sufficiently deceptive fly. I've always thought this more than a little extreme. Trout are not entomologists; they don't care what your fly's Latin name is. I've suckered summer steelhead, brookies and bluebacks on a fly I call a "Bermuda Shorts"—an abstract imitation of a fat tourist on a golf course in a Caribbean travel brochure; my "Headless Hunchback" may one day be famous as a trout killer, and it imitates a thing that attacked me in a nightmare brought on by devouring half a box of Bill Bob's Sugar Pops just before bed. H2O and his pals rigidly adhere to the Imitation of Natural Food School of Fly Tying, but the truth is, trout are like coyotes, goats and people: they nibble, chew and bite for all sorts of reasons; eating is only the most common one. Sometimes Northwest lakes and streams are so rich in feed that their bloated denizens would sooner bite an Alka Seltzer than a natural imitation; sometimes a bored old whopper, like any decadent, affluent creature, prefers gaudy titillation to more of the mundane stone-fly-mayfly-caddisfly crap. (Remember Walton's "piece of cloth" and "dead mouse"?) Piscene ennui can arouse a taste for the bizarre that will skunk a Purist who insists on floating sacrosanct "name patterns" over his congregation all day. Bourgeois trout are like bourgeois people: after a week of three dull meals a day a man will empty his wallet and risk his life bombing belly and brain with rich restaurant food and eight or ten cocktails. The corresponding mood in trout is where the Bermuda Shorts comes in handy: of course it doesn't look like food; neither does a Double Margarita; and trout don't have to drive home afterward . . .

It took some time to get settled in the cabin: a day to stash gear, a day to build a fish-smoker, a day to set up and stock the aquarium, a day to clean, and salt in supplies, two days to cut three cords of wood. But on June ninth I hung the Ideal Schedule on the wall by my bed and began to live it: I proceeded to fish all day, every day, first light to last. All my life I'd longed for such a marathon—

and I haven't one happy memory of it. All I recall is stream after stream, fish after fish, cast after cast, and nothing in my head but the low cunning required to hoodwink my mindless quarry. Each night my Log entries read like tax tables or grocery receipts, describing not a dream come true, but a drudgery of double shifts on a creekside assembly line.

After two weeks of "ideal" six-hour nights and sixteen-hour days I got an incurable case of insomnia. It hardly mattered: sleeping I dreamt of fishing and waking I fished till there was one, undivided, sleeplike state. There was fishing. There was nothing else. A Kiluhiturmiut Eskimo song tells of a man like me—

> Glorious was life when standing at my fishing hole
> on the ice. But did standing at my fishing hole ever
> bring me joy? No!
> Ever was I so anxious for my little fishhook
> if it should not get a bite, Ayi, yai ya . . .

Like the Eskimo, my last thought before going fishing was "Won't it be glorious!" And like the Eskimo I then stood by the water, a needy, nervous wretch too anxious to wonder how "glory" could be so dismal. Ayi, yai ya!

CRAIG LESLEY

With the novels Winterkill *(1984) and* River Song *(1989) and his anthology,* Talking Leaves: Contemporary Native American Short Stories *(1991), Portland writer Craig Lesley brought the voices and lives of contemporary native Americans into mainstream literature. Danny Kachiah, the main character in* Winterkill *and* River Song, *is "Nez Percé, mostly," as he says, a failed bull rider trying to raise his teenage son, Jack, and scratch out a living on the Umatilla Reservation near Pendleton, Oregon.*

from WINTERKILL

DANNY LEANED AGAINST a telephone pole to watch the Westward Ho Parade. In the vacant lot to his left, some spectators were sitting on their pickups' tailgates, sharing beers and soft drinks from plastic coolers. To his right, several people put folding lawn chairs in the street, snugging the aluminum back legs against the curb. One man had a difficult time unfolding his chair because his arm was in a sling.

A railroad bull gang was pretending to work on a section of track just across the street, in front of four large grain elevators. Danny knew they had chosen that track section for the day so they could loaf and watch the parade. The railroad gang wore yellow overalls and orange hardhats. They were the only group of spectators not wearing cowboy hats.

"Look at those loafers," the man with the sling said to his wife. "It's no wonder it costs so much to ship grain."

"Everything's going up, all right," his wife said. She reached into the cooler at her feet and handed the man a beer. "Fred likes to have a drink when he's complaining about somebody else not working," she said to the man on her other side.

The man laughed at that and took a beer himself. He was wearing brown polyester pants and a dark green shirt with pens sticking out the pocket. A green feather in his hatband matched the shirt, and his silver-framed glasses were tinted dark enough to hide his eyes. His hands were soft and white, not the working hands of a rancher, so Danny thought maybe he sold real estate.

At a few minutes past eleven, six musicians shuffled down the street playing off key and stumbling into one another. Their wrinkled black ties matched their shabby suits, and a couple of them took flasks from their pockets and passed them around. One carried a drum that read "Happy Canyon Marching and Drinking Band." He had a plastic red nose and oversized spectacles. When they were pretty close to Danny they started playing for real, and everyone applauded because they were good. Danny figured they were from the college. The band finished the number and the drummer set off a buzz bomb and shouted, "Folks, there's a parade a-comin'!"

Danny settled back to watch. He had wanted Jack to see the parade too, but the boy had gone to the rodeo grounds early for a job tagging steers or cleaning pens, and Danny planned to meet him there afterward. From where he was standing, two blocks away, Danny could see the raised platform for the parade celebrities. The announcer had his back to Danny, and the loudspeakers were turned the other way, so Danny didn't have to listen to him gushing about the colorful Indian people in their ceremonial dress.

The parade had lots of good high school marching bands, but Danny liked the fife and drum corps from Athena best. They wore plaid kilts, even the men, and the leader had a small dagger on his belt. Queens and princesses from every festival around came by, mounted on horseback and waving slowly, as if they were washing windows. The queens from the Big Four rodeos—Ellensburg, Walla Walla, Lewiston, and Pendleton—had bouquets of roses adorning their horses. Danny tried to decide which women were the prettiest, but he couldn't make up his mind. It was hard to believe they were just a couple years older than Jack.

The man in the dark glasses kept yelling, "Throw me a kiss, sweetheart. I'll give it to my friend here to make him well." Danny became annoyed by his shouting.

The governor of Oregon rode by in a white Cadillac convertible with Brahma bull horns on the hood and pearly six-shooters for door handles. The dashboard was myrtlewood inlaid with silver dollars. The governor sat on the top of the back seat, smiling and waving both hands at the crowd.

He wore a light brown suit—Western cut—and a cream-colored rancher's Stetson. Danny thought he looked sharp.

Someone shouted, "Hey, Governor! Don't let that mount buck you off!" A lot of people laughed, and someone else yelled, "If the governor's in Pendleton, this must be an election year!"

More people laughed, and some started clapping and cheering. Then an Indian from across the way shouted, "Don't clap unless you have a job." After that, the clapping quieted a little.

Bands of little Indian children came walking up both sides of the street. They wore miniature headdresses, rabbit braids, beaded shirts, doeskin dresses, and colorful hand-sewn moccasins. Some of the people along the parade route started throwing handfuls of money at them, and the children scattered to retrieve the coins. After they had picked up the money, they put it in beaded fringed bags or hand-tooled coin purses.

"Getting these young ones ready for the dole," the man with the sling said. He was dipping pennies out of a half-gallon milk carton and flinging them backhanded with his good arm.

"Hey, Fred. You better pay them now or they'll get a sharpie lawyer and claim all of Pendleton is theirs," the man in dark glasses said.

Danny glared at the man, but he didn't seem to notice.

Caravans of covered wagons, prairie schooners, two-wheelers, and ox carts swept by Danny. Some of these had "Oregon or Bust" printed on the sides. There were Mormon carts, too, pulled by dark-suited men with the funny beards the early Mormons had worn. Two women in calico dresses followed the carts, carrying a sign that said FREEDOM OF WORSHIP. Next came marching missionaries holding Bibles and pretending to preach to the "Indians" who walked beside them. One man was dressed like Marcus Whitman, and he led a horse carrying a woman riding sidesaddle who pretended to be Narcissa. Their sign read GOD COMES TO OREGON. Danny shook his head as he thought of all the missionaries and settlers that had invaded the Oregon country.

He heard scattered applause and saw a lanky man accompanied by an immense woman in a tentlike prairie dress. The man was leading an ox and the woman carried an American flag in one hand and a basket full of Bibles in the other. Apparently the ox was trained, because it stopped and kneeled whenever the woman held out a Bible and shook it in the ox's face. Two dour children lagged behind carrying a homemade sign that said THE ANIMALS KNEEL BEFORE HIM.

"Isn't that just darling?" Fred's wife said. "Honey, we've got to get us a good camera."

A tractor pulling a mobile home came alongside advertising the Rancho Estate Trailer Park. Danny knew the owner, and some said he'd made a million selling "Mobile Homes on the Range."

The SUNCO float featured a giant rotating sun made from foil. Models in gold lame costumes posed under the sun, pointing to a large display banner that read: SUNCO PROGRESS BRIGHTENS YOUR ENERGY FUTURE. Danny shook his head because the float looked really professional and he knew it had cost a lot to decorate.

Behind this float came the Umatilla Sage Riders, a volunteer mounted posse riding palomino horses and wearing white suits, hats, and red silk scarves.

A small Indian boy trailed the Sage Riders. He wore a red shirt with bead trim and rabbit leggings. He looked as if he wanted to catch up with the other children but was hanging back because he was afraid of getting too close to the horses. As he walked his rabbit leggings slipped down, causing him to trip. Tears streaked his face.

"There's a cute one," the woman said. "Throw him some pennies, Fred. He's been crying."

Fred tossed out some pennies with his awkward backhand motion, but they rolled under the horses.

"Give that here," said the man in the dark glasses. After taking the carton from Fred, he reached into it and tossed out a few more. "There's your first handout, little buck," he said.

The boy picked up some of the pennies from the street and dug out those that had fallen in a crack between the pavement and the railroad ties. When the horses moved, some coins glittered where they had been standing, but the boy held back, not wanting to drag his rabbit leggings through the green horse turds.

"Throw him some more," Danny said, suddenly moving toward the man in dark glasses.

"What?"

"I said throw him some more." For a moment Danny wanted to grab the milk carton and dump the pennies into the street.

"We have to save some for the others." Fred's wife was talking. "They all expect something for getting dressed up and marching in the parade."

Danny saw her mouth working like a fish's. He walked into the street and knelt on one knee beside the boy. "Look, big fellow," he said. "You don't want to get those fine leggings dirty. Let's see if we can catch up to your friends." He lifted the boy onto his shoulders and started walking along the street, hurrying to pass the horses and the pioneer wagons. Behind him he heard the man with the glasses say, "That crazy Cayuse must be hitting the firewater."

"I like your rabbit leggings," Danny said. "Did you make those? Hey, quit crying now. It's okay." He walked a little faster.

"My sister made them."

"Which one's your sister?" He could see the children up ahead.

"There in the blue dress."

"Well, tell your sister she does fine work. What's your name?"

"Jimmy Sam."

"Where do you live, Jimmy?"

"Yakima."

"I'll bet you have a big pony."

He could feel the kid nod. "Her name is Betsy."

"Take good care of her, then."

When he had caught up with the group of children, Danny swung the boy from his shoulders and retied the leggings so the boy wouldn't trip. He took four quarters out of his pocket and handed them to the boy. "So long, little rabbit leggings," he said. "Buy some ice cream for your sister."

The walk had taken Danny close to the platform, and he stepped through the crowd behind it because he didn't want to see Taylor, especially if Tenley was with him. As he made his way through the crowd, he heard the announcer:

"Ladies and gentlemen, the *governor* of Oregon and his lovely wife. I hear you're up for reelection, Governor. Best of luck from all your friends in Pendleton. And behind him are some fine youngsters from the Indian encampment wearing their traditional native garb. They do look festive, don't they? And I am here to tell you that these fine Indian people are the most colorful and hospitable folks you'd ever want to meet. Every day, after the rodeo performance, you're invited to take a look at the traditional tepees and authentic craft displays they have set up behind the rodeo ground. Believe me, these wonderful people from the Umatilla

Reservation and their colorful cousins from throughout the Northwest are delighted with the opportunity to show you their ways and testify to how a little of the Old West still lives on today."

Danny couldn't imagine how the announcer could say so many words without getting confused, and he wondered if the man practiced for long hours in front of a mirror, all slickered up in his announcing outfit. "He probably shits just as smoothly," Danny mumbled.

KATHERINE DUNN

"The metaphor of the subterranean," Katherine Dunn once said, "is at work in a lot of Northwest writers and artists." Few Northwest writers have explored that metaphor as deeply as Dunn, however, whose life and work gravitate toward the weird and bizarre. Born in the Kansas town where the Clutter family (of Truman Capote's In Cold Blood*) was murdered, Dunn migrated with her family to the Northwest, where they lived like American gypsies, working as day laborers in Walla Walla bean fields and cutting salal in Puget Sound forests. Dunn eventually settled in Portland, where she made her name as a columnist for* Willamette Week *and as a nationally published boxing writer. Her novel* Geek Love, *about a family of circus freaks—proud outsiders, like Dunn—was nominated for the 1989 National Book Award.*

from GEEK LOVE

MY FATHER'S NAME was Aloysius Binewski. He was raised in a traveling carnival owned by his father and called "Binewski's Fabulon." Papa was twenty-four years old when Grandpa died and the carnival fell into his hands. Al carefully bolted the silver urn containing his father's ashes to the hood of the generator truck that powered the midway. The old man had wandered with the show for so long that his dust would have been miserable left behind in some stationary vault.

Times were hard and, through no fault of young Al's, business began to decline. Five years after Grandpa died, the once flourishing carnival was fading.

The show was burdened with an aging lion that repeatedly broke expensive dentures by gnawing the bars of his cage; demands for cost-of-living increases from the fat lady, whose food supply was written into her contract; and the midnight defection of an entire family of animal eroticists, taking their donkey, goat, and Great Dane with them.

The fat lady eventually jumped ship to become a model for a magazine called *Chubby Chaser*. My father was left with a cut-rate, diesel-fueled fire-eater and the prospect of a very long stretch in a trailer park outside of Fort Lauderdale.

Al was a standard-issue Yankee, set on self-determination and independence, but in that crisis his core of genius revealed itself. He decided to breed his own freak show.

My mother, Lillian Hinchcliff, was a water-cool aristocrat from the fastidious side of Boston's Beacon Hill, who had abandoned her heritage and joined the carnival to become an aerialist. Nineteen is late to learn to fly and Lillian fell, smashing her elegant nose and her collarbones. She lost her nerve but not her lust for sawdust and honky-tonk lights. It was this passion that made her an eager partner in Al's scheme. She was willing to chip in on any effort to renew public interest in the show. Then, too, the idea of inherited security was ingrained from her childhood. As she often said, "What greater gift could you offer your children than an inherent ability to earn a living just by being themselves?"

The resourceful pair began experimenting with illicit and prescription drugs, insecticides, and eventually radioisotopes. My mother developed a complex dependency on various drugs during this process, but she didn't mind. Relying on Papa's ingenuity to keep her supplied, Lily seemed to view her addiction as a minor by-product of their creative collaboration.

Their firstborn was my brother Arturo, usually known as Aqua Boy. His hands and feet were in the form of flippers that sprouted directly from his torso without intervening arms or legs. He was taught to swim in infancy and was displayed nude in a big clear-sided tank like an aquarium. His favorite trick at the ages of three and four was to put his face close to the glass, bulging his eyes out at the audience, opening and closing his mouth like a river bass, and then to turn his back and paddle off, revealing the turd trailing from his muscular little buttocks. Al and Lil laughed about it later, but at the time it caused them great consternation as well as the nuisance of sterilizing the tank more often than usual. As the years passed, Arty donned trunks and became more sophisticated, but it's been said, with some truth, that his attitude never really changed.

My sisters, Electra and Iphigenia, were born when Arturo was two years old and starting to haul in crowds. The girls were Siamese twins with perfect upper bodies joined at the waist and sharing one set of hips and legs. They usually sat and walked and slept with their long arms around each other. They were, however, able to face directly forward by allowing the shoulder of one to overlap the other. They were always beautiful, slim, and huge-eyed. They studied the piano and began performing piano duets at an early age. Their compositions for four hands were thought by some to have revolutionized the twelve-tone scale.

I was born three years after my sisters. My father spared no expense in these experiments. My mother had been liberally dosed with cocaine, amphetamines, and arsenic during her ovulation and throughout her pregnancy with me. It was a disappointment when I emerged with such commonplace deformities. My albinism is the regular pink-eyed variety and my hump, though pronounced, is not remarkable in size or shape as humps go. My situation was far too humdrum to be marketable on the same scale as my brother's and sisters'. Still, my parents noted that I had a strong voice and decided I might be an appropriate shill and talker for the business. A bald albino hunchback seemed the right enticement toward the esoteric talents of the rest of the family. The dwarfism, which was very apparent by my third birthday, came as a pleasant surprise to the patient pair and increased my value. From the beginning I slept in the built-in cupboard beneath the sink in the family living van, and had a collection of exotic sunglasses to shield my sensitive eyes.

Despite the expensive radium treatments incorporated in his design, my younger brother, Fortunato, had a close call in being born to apparent normalcy. That drab state so depressed my enterprising parents that they immediately prepared to abandon him on the doorstep of a closed service station as we passed through Green River, Wyoming, late one night. My father had actually parked the van for a quick getaway and had stepped down to help my mother deposit the baby in the cardboard box on some safe part of the pavement. At that precise moment the two-week-old baby stared vaguely at my mother and in a matter of seconds revealed himself as not a failure at all, but in fact my parents' masterwork. It was lucky, so they named him Fortunato. For one reason and another we always called him Chick.

"Papa," said Iphy. "Yes," said Elly. They were behind his big chair, four arms sliding to tangle his neck, two faces framed in smooth black hair peering at him from either side.

"What are you up to, girlies?" He would laugh and put his magazine down.

"Tell us how you thought of us," they demanded.

I leaned on his knee and looked into his good heavy face. "Please, Papa," I begged, "tell us the Rose Garden."

He would puff and tease and refuse and we would coax. Finally Arty would be sitting in his lap with Papa's arms around him and Chick would be in Lily's lap, and I would lean against Lily's shoulder while Elly and Iphy sat cross-legged on the floor with their four arms behind them like Gothic struts supporting their hunched shoulders, and Al would laugh and tell the story.

"It was in Oregon, up in Portland, which they call the Rose City, though I never got in gear to do anything about it until a year or so later when we were stuck in Fort Lauderdale."

He had been restless one day, troubled by business boondoggles. He drove up into a park on a hillside and got out for a walk. "You could see for miles from up there. And there was a big rose garden with arbors and trellises and fountains. The paths were brick and wound in and out." He sat on a step leading from one terrace to another and stared listlessly at the experimental roses. "It was a test garden, and the colors were . . . designed. Striped and layered. One color inside the petal and another color outside.

"I was mad at Maribelle. She was a pinhead who'd been with your mother and me for a long while. She was trying to hold me up for a raise I couldn't afford."

The roses started him thinking, how the oddity of them was beautiful and how that oddity was contrived to give them value. "It just struck me— clear and complete all at once—no long figuring about it." He realized that children could be designed. "And I thought to myself, now *that* would be a rose garden worthy of a man's interest!"

We children would smile and hug him and he would grin around at us and send the twins for a pot of cocoa from the drink wagon and me for a bag of popcorn because the red-haired girls would just throw it out when they finished closing the concession anyway. And we would all be cozy in the warm booth of the van, eating popcorn and drinking cocoa and feeling like Papa's roses.

ANNIE DILLARD

A few months before she was awarded the Pulitzer Prize for her 1974 essay collection, Pilgrim at Tinker Creek, *Annie Dillard accepted a position as writer-in-residence at Western Washington University in Bellingham. The Pittsburgh native lived and wrote there for five years, and the place continues to live in her writing long after her departure. Her experiences on Bellingham Bay and in the San Juan Islands provided material for her books* Holy the Firm *(1977),* Teaching a Stone to Talk *(1982), and* The Writing Life *(1989). In 1992, Dillard published* The Living, *an ambitious novel about a group of late-nineteenth-century white, Chinese, and native American settlers on the shores of Bellingham Bay.*

from THE WRITING LIFE

THAT ISLAND ON HARO STRAIT haunts me. The few people there, unconnected to the mainland—lacking ferryboat, electrical cables, and telephone cables—lived lonesome and half mad out in the wind and current like petrels. They had stuck their necks out. In summer they slept in open sleep shacks on the beach. The island lay on the northern edge of the forty-eight states, and was fantastically difficult of access. Once you had gone so far, you might as well test the limits, like an artist playing the edges, and all but sleep in the waves. With my husband, I moved there every summer; we spent a winter there, too. Our cabin on the beach faced west, toward some distant Canadian islands, and Japan.

The waters there were cold and deep; fierce tides ripped in and out twice a day. The San Juan Islands aggravated tidal currents—they made narrow channels through which enormous volumes of water streamed fast. If an ordinary tide flowed up the beach and caught an oar or a life vest, it swept it northward on the island faster than you could chase it walking alongside; you had to run. The incoming tide ran north; the outgoing tide drained south.

———————

Paul Glenn was a painter, a strong-armed, soft-faced, big blond man in his fifties; every summer he lived down the beach. He was a friend of the family. One summer morning I visited him, and asked about his painting. We sat at his kitchen table.

His recent easel painting, and his study of abstract expressionist Mark Tobey's canvases, and his new interest in certain Asian subjects, his understanding of texture in two dimensions, and possibly the mistiness of the Pacific Northwest and its fabulous, busy skies—something, I do not know what, had gotten him experimenting with dipping papers into vats of water on which pools of colored oil floated. He had such papers drying on the kitchen counters. Some of them looked like a book's marbled endpapers, or fine wallpaper—merely decorative. Some others were complex and subtle surfaces, suggestive and powerful. Paul Glenn was learning which techniques of dripping the colors on the water, and which techniques of drawing the paper up through the colors, yielded the interesting results. He had been working at it for six months. How he was going to use the papers was another matter, and the crucial one: he could cut them into collage material, he could fold them into sculpture, he could paint over them and into them. He was following the work wherever it led.

———————

The next summer, we returned to the island. Paul Glenn had spent the winter there. I visited him in his house on the beach in late June. He was tan of face already, and perfectly sane—witty and forceful, if a bit soft of voice.

I asked Paul how his work was going.

"You couldn't have known Ferrar Burn," he said. We were sitting at the round table by the kitchen window. There were white shells on the windowsill, and black beach stones. "He died twenty years ago. He was a joyful man, and a calm and determined one. He brought his family out here—June Burn, who wrote books and newspaper columns, and two little boys, you know North and Bob—out here to this island, where there's nothing but what you can find on the beach or grow."

Evidently Paul did not want to talk about how his work was going. Fair enough.

"Ferrar was striking: he had that same pale, thin skin his sons have, and their black eyes and hair. He and June built that cedar shack up on Fishery

Point. It was her study. Their house was near the woods—nice timbers."

Paul knew I knew all this, except what Ferrar looked like. Paul's hair had grown long; he kept moving pale strands of it behind his ears. I was fresh from the mainland, a little too bright and quick. He laughed openly at what he could easily see was my impatience; we had been tolerant friends for a few years.

"One evening," he went on, "Ferrar saw a log floating out in the channel. It looked yellow, like Alaska cedar; he hoped it was Alaska cedar. He rowed out to get it."

Everyone on the island scavenged the valuable logs, for building. If the logs did not wash up on the beach, it took a motorboat to get them in; they were heavy in the water.

"It was high tide, slack. Ferrar saw the log, launched his little skiff at Fishery Point, and rowed out in the channel. Sure enough, it was that beautiful Alaska cedar, that pale yellow wood—just a short log, about eight feet, or he never would have tried it without a motor. I guess he thought he could row it in while the tide was still slack.

"He tied onto the log"—such logs often have a big iron staple hammered into one end—"and started rowing back home with it. He had about twenty feet of line on it. He started rowing home, and the tide caught him."

From Paul's window, I could look north up the beach and see Fishery Point. One of Ferrar's sons still used that old rowboat—a little eight-foot pram, now painted yellow and blue. Paul's blue eyes caught mine again.

"The tide started going out, and it caught that log and dragged it south. Ferrar kept rowing back north toward his house. The tide pulled him south down the strait here"—Paul indicated the long sweep of salt water in front of his house—"from one end to the other. Ferrar kept rowing toward Fishery Point. He might as well have tied onto a whale. He was rowing to the north and moving fast to the south. He traveled stern first. He wanted to be going home, so toward home he kept pulling. When the sun set, at about nine o'clock, he'd swept south the length of this beach, rowing north all the way. When the moon rose a few hours later—he told us—he saw he'd swept south past the island altogether and out into the channel between here and Stuart Island. He had been rowing through those dark hours. He continued to row away from Stuart Island and continued to see it get closer.

"Then he felt the tide go slack, and then he felt it coming in again. The current had reversed.

"Ferrar kept rowing in the half moonlight. The tide poured in from the south. He kept rowing north for home—only now the log was with him. He and his log were both floating on the current, and the current was bearing them up and carrying them like platters. It started getting light at about three o'clock, and he rowed back past this island's southern tip. The sun came up, and he rowed all the length of this beach. The tide brought him back on home. His wife, June, saw him coming; she'd been curious about him all night."

Paul had a wide, loose smile. He shifted in his chair. He raised his coffee cup, as if to say, Cheers.

"He pulled up on his own beach. They got the log rolled beyond the tideline. I saw him a few days later. Everybody knew he'd been carried out almost to Stuart Island, trying to bring in a log. Everybody knew he just kept rowing in the same direction. I asked him about it. He said he had a little backache. I didn't see the palms of his hands."

Paul looked into his empty coffee cup, pleased, and then looked through the window, still smiling. I started to carry my coffee cup to the sink, but he motioned me down. He wasn't finished.

"So that's how my work is going," he said.

What?

"You asked how my work is going," he said. "That's how it's going. The current's got me. Feels like I'm about in the middle of the channel now. I just keep at it. I just keep hoping the tide will turn and bring me in."

Anthropologist Godfrey Lienhardt describes the animistic understanding of the Dinka tribe in the Sudan. A Dinka believes his own memories and daydreams to be external to himself, as external as the hills, and quick with substance. A man who had been imprisoned in Khartoum named his infant daughter Khartoum in order to placate Khartoum, which seized him from time to time vividly. He believed that as he walked about his village, Khartoum itself, the city with its prison, overwhelmed him with the force of its presence.

So that island haunts me. I was not in prison there, but instead loosed on the shore of vastness. As I walk about this enclosed bay on Cape Cod, or as I scroll down a computer file to a blank screen, then from time to time the skies part ahead of my path, or the luminous photons on the screen revert to infinite randomness, and I balk again on the brink. The irrational haunts the metaphysical. The opposites meet in the looping sky above appearances, or in the dark alley behind appearances, where danger and power duel in a blur.

There was no continental shelf; the island beach dropped to the deep and sandless ocean floor. The water was so cold throughout the year that a man overboard died in ten minutes. Once I saw two twenty-four-man war canoes race across a passage. Forty-eight bare-chested Lummi Indians paddled them, singing. Once I saw phosphorescent seas in a winter storm in front of the cabin; in the black night black seas broke in wild lines to the horizon and spilled green foam that glowed when the wind's pitch rose, so I wept on the shore in fear.

I lived on the beach with one foot in fatal salt water and one foot on a billion grains of sand. The brink of the infinite there was too like writing's solitude. Each sentence hung over an abyssal ocean or sky which held all possibilities, as well as the possibility of nothing. In June and July, the twilight lingered till dawn. Our latitude was north of Nova Scotia; the sun never dropped low enough below the horizon to achieve what is called astronomical night. The wide days split life open like an ax. When I sketched or painted the island shore, even with the most literal intentions, the work twined into the infinite again and dissolved, or the infinite assaulted the page again and required me to represent it. My pen piled the page with changing clouds, multiple suns, circles, spirals, and rays. I used the pages at night to light fires.

"I have been doing some skying," Constable wrote a friend. I have been doing some scrolling, here and elsewhere, scrolling up and down beaches and blank monitor screens scrying for signs: dipping pens into ink, dipping papers into vats of color, dipping paddles into seas, and bearing God knows where. The green line of photons forms words at the shore of darkness. Darkness empties behind the screen in an illimitable cone. Shall we go rowing again, we who believe we may indeed row off the edge and fall? Shall we launch again into the deep and row up the skies?

JONATHAN RABAN

*In each of his masterful travel narratives (*Old Glory, Coasting, *and* Arabia*),
Jonathan Raban created an authorial persona that is like, and yet is not,
Jonathan Raban, London writer and critic. For his 1990 book,* Hunting
Mister Heartbreak, *Raban assumed the role of a modern-day English immigrant to America. "He is, on the whole, younger in spirit, more enterprising,
more open to experience than Jonathan Raban," the author explained. As it
turned out, there was more of Raban in the character than he or his readers
imagined: soon after the book's publication Raban returned to Seattle, and he has
made his home there ever since.*

from HUNTING MISTER HEARTBREAK

ON THAT PARTICULAR MORNING, in hotels and motels, in furnished rooms and cousins' houses, 106 other people were waking to their
first day as immigrants to Seattle. These were flush times, with jobs to be
had for the asking, and the city was growing at the rate of nearly forty
thousand new residents a year. The immigrants were piling in from every
quarter. Many were out-of-state Americans: New Yorkers on the run from
the furies of Manhattan; refugees from the Rustbelt; Los Angelenos
escaping their infamous crime statistics, their huge house prices and
jammed and smoggy freeways; redundant farm workers from Kansas and
Iowa. Then there were the Asians—Samoans, Laotians, Cambodians,
Thais, Vietnamese, Chinese and Koreans, for whom Seattle was the nearest city in the continental United States. A local artist had proposed a
monumental sculpture, to be put up at the entrance to Elliott Bay, repre-
senting Liberty holding aloft a bowl of rice.

The falling dollar, which had so badly hurt the farming towns of the
Midwest, had come as a blessing to Seattle. It lowered the price abroad of
the Boeing airplanes, wood pulp, paper, computer software and all the
other things that Seattle manufactured. The port of Seattle was a day
closer by sea to Tokyo and Hong Kong than was Los Angeles, its main
rival for the shipping trade with Asia.

By the end of the 1980s, Seattle had taken on the dangerous luster of a
promised city. The rumor had gone out that if you had failed in Detroit

you might yet succeed in Seattle—and that if you'd succeeded in Seoul, you could succeed even better in Seattle. In New York and Guntersville I'd heard the rumor. Seattle was the coming place.

So I joined the line of hopefuls. We were everywhere, and we kept on bumping into each other and comparing notes. At breakfast in the hotel dining room I noticed that the woman at the next table was doing exactly what I was doing myself: circling ads on the Real Estate page of the *Post-Intelligencer* with a ballpoint pen. I was on *Downtown;* she was roaming round the city, going from *University* to *Queen Anne* to *Fremont, Magnolia* and *Capitol Hill.* She had the old-money equestrienne look—the boots, the khaki slacks, the hacking jacket, white silk blouse and gold chain that I'd once coveted for myself. Her expression, as she plowed through the small print, was avid: she was rolling the telegraphese of *3-bed, 2-ba* round in her head as if it were lines from Wallace Stevens.

"I got to find somewhere fast," she said. "Flew in last night. My furniture's all in store in Denver, Colorado, and that *costs.*"

For a minute or two, her eyes went back to the paper. She sucked on the end of her pen. Then she looked up from the advertisements in order to deliver a non-stop ten-minute advertisement for herself.

Yesterday was her birthday, her thirty-first birthday—she'd always said she was going to change her life when she was thirty-one—and it was on her chart; an astrologer had told her—she was a Scorpio—Scorpios were great decision makers—she'd had her own business back in Denver—real estate—and a big house—and a car, a silver BMW 520I—she'd sold the business—and the house—and the car—and just *come to Seattle.*

She was the heroine of an adventure story, and she was telling it like the Ancient Mariner.

"I was up here five days last year—I got friends over in West Seattle. I took one look at this city and I knew. Right then I said, 'Susan, here's where you're going to spend your thirties.' I had this gut feeling. Well—here I am."

It was hard to slide a word in edgeways, but there had to be some as yet unconfessed reason for this audacious and arbitrary move. Love, maybe? If so, why was she spending her first day here alone in a hotel?

"Susan . . . tell me. I still haven't got it. Why here? Why Seattle?"

I was violating her right to tell her own tale. She blinked at the question and shook her head in an impatient swirl of lacquered chestnut hair.

"Oh—the quality of the lifestyle, the good environment, the real-estate values; *you* know."

I had misjudged her. She was just a typical domestic flier with a low specific gravity.

Half an hour later, I was lodging a jacket and a pair of trousers with a dry cleaner's a block away from the hotel. The face of the man who took charge of them was a worried knot. He gave the clothes an empty, shell-shocked smile and said, "No problem." Then again, holding up the trousers by one leg, "No problem."

"Don't you want to make out a slip for them?" I said.

His gaze was distraught. "Thank you. Thank you. Yes, thank you."

A woman came out from behind the carousel of hanging garments and said something to the man in what I took to be Chinese. He scarpered.

"Oh, I am sorry," she said. "He is only in America two weeks. He not understanding English good. He learning very slow."

"Where is he from?" I asked.

"Inchon, in Korea. He start work yesterday. We train him as presser. But do not worry! We not let him loose on your pants yet, not this week." She laughed and touched her temple. "Jet lag. No 'on the ball.'"

"You're from Korea, too?"

"Yes, Seoul. But I am in America thirteen years. August 28, 1976."

The greenhorn was listening, peering out at us through a fringe of skirts and dresses. He was close to my own age, but his infancy in English gave him the facial expression of a fractious toddler. When I caught his eye, he ducked out of sight.

"And you like it here?"

"In America? Oh, yeah! It's good. It is so big! So green! So wide—wide—wide!"

Looking for somewhere to live, I quartered the city at the wheel of a new rental—a cherry-colored Spectrum with California plates and a painfully weak stomach. The steep little hills of Seattle made the car break wind with a sickly rumbling in its bowels. When I floored the gas pedal, the engine gave a shuddering sob and stalled.

The realtors turned up their nose at me. *No way*, they said, with lordly smiles, when I described what I had in mind. This was a sellers' market; house prices were up thirty percent on last year; the realtors didn't have time to talk even to *buyers* with less than a quarter million, cash in hand, and they certainly had no time to waste on me.

"Do you know where you're at here? This is Boomtown, U.S.A."

I drove on, through a cloud of pink dust. One could tell that Seattle was on a winning streak by the number of men in cranes who were trying to smash the place to bits with wrecking balls. The pink dust rose in explosive flurries over the rooftops and colored the low sky.

Pitched on a line of bluffs along Puget Sound, with Lake Washington at its back, Seattle had ships at the ends of its streets and gulls in its traffic. Its light was restless and watery, making the buildings shiver like reflections. It felt like an island and smelled of the sea.

It was a pity about the wrecking balls, for the city they were knocking down was an American classic; a survivor of the Theodore Roosevelt age of boosterish magniloquence. Where the high-toned buildings of Alabama had been cotton planters' daydreams of Ancient Greece, Seattle looked like a freehand sketch, from memory, of a sawmill owner's whirlwind vacation in Rome and Florence. Its antique skyscrapers were rude boxes, a dozen to fifteen stories high, fantastically candied over with patterned brick and terracotta moldings. Their facades dripped with friezes, gargoyles, pilasters, turrets, cornices, cartouches, balustrades and arabesques. Every bank and office block was an exuberant *palazzo*.

The whole thing was an exercise in conscious theater. All the most important buildings faced west, over the Sound, and Seattle was designed to be seen from the front. You were meant to arrive by ship, from Yokohama or Shanghai, and be overwhelmed by the financial muscle, the class (with a short *a*), the world-traveled air of this Manhattan of the Far West. If you had the bad taste to look at Seattle from the back, all you'd see would be plain brick cladding and a zig-zag tangle of fire escapes.

Until very recently, it seemed, Seattle had gotten along well enough with its turn-of-the-century Italian Renaissance architecture; but now the terracotta city was beginning to look dingy and stunted beside the sixty- and seventy-story towers that were sprouting over its head. Some were still just steel skeletons, with construction workers in hard hats swarming in their rigging like foretopmen. Some were newly unsheathed, with racing clouds mirrored in their black and silver glass. More were in the chrysalid stage, obtected in rough shells of scaffolding and tarpaulins. Then there were the holes in the ground, the wrecking-ball jobs, the molded garland going into smithereens.

I was having little luck. A "furnished executive suite" turned out to be a low-ceilinged room, as small as Alice's, on a new block, at a rent of $1,400 a month. *No way.* A promising one-bedroom apartment on First Hill at $550 was for nonsmokers only.

"Even if I do it out the window?"

"Even if you do it out the window."

I asked around the bars. It was possible, apparently, to rent a room in a rooming house in the International District for $60 a month.

"But they're kind of funny. They're Vietnamese. I don't think they take Caucasians."

I was told about the Josephinum Residence at a bar, where it was variously reported to be an apartment block, a Catholic shelter for low-income families, an old people's home and a hotel. But it was generally agreed that, whatever it was, the place was so big that it must have empty rooms.

The building was a richly encrusted pile on Second Avenue, three blocks back from the waterfront. Inside, it looked like the Medici Tomb. Its vaulted ceiling, forty feet up, was tricked out in flaky gold; huge veined marble pillars supported a balustraded cloister on the mezzanine floor. A fifteenth-century merchant prince might have found it homely, but it was hard to fit this heroic essay in the architecture of power and money to the people who now occupied the Josephinum's lobby. Shrunken, bald, leaning on sticks and planting walking frames ahead of them, they limped and clicked across the marble hall. Crayoned notices, in big round letters, advertised Bingo, flu shots, the arrival of the Bookmobile and Mass at 3 P.M. in the chapel. It had the institutional smell of Lysol and overboiled cabbage.

At the desk I apologized for making a mistake; but no, said the manager, there was indeed a vacant room, and she'd be happy to show it to me. No, you didn't have to be old—it was just that at this time of day most of the other tenants were at work. Nor did you have to be a Catholic, nor a nonsmoker; she was neither herself.

We stepped into the elevator with a spry centenarian whose black wig was a little askew on her head.

"She's as old as the state of Washington, aren't you, dear?" the manager said. "And you got a special telegram on your birthday from the President, didn't you?"

"Sure did," said the woman. "From the President."

"Mr. Bush."

"Lot of wind out there today." She tugged at her wig, bringing it down over her eyes.

"Oh, she could tell you a few things about Seattle; she's seen it all in her time, haven't you, dear?"

"Huh? Maybe," the woman growled. Being one hundred looked like a job that she had long grown bored with. As the elevator climbed the shaft, I watched her going through her flight-check routine: *wig*—okay; *afternoon paper*—okay; *specs*—roger; *room key*—where's that tarnation key? Yup, you got it. It's in your other hand.

On every floor we stopped at, a robed figure was waiting at the elevator doors. The first time this happened, I mistook him for a resident, then saw that he was St. Francis, with bluebirds, cast in plaster in the school of Dante Gabriel Rossetti. The centenarian got out at Joseph the Carpenter; we went on up to thirteen, Christ of the Sacred Heart. His beard was chipped, His blood had oxidized to chocolate; He was blessing the brass-bound rococo Cutler mail chute.

A long dark corridor led to an enormous room, empty of furniture but full of light. The air tasted as if it had been left to cook for many months, and there were some curious stains on the yellow shag carpet, but the view from the uncurtained windows was serene. The room looked out over turreted flat roofs to Puget Sound: beyond the cowled air vents, plants in tubs, fire escapes and satellite dishes, ships were on the move in Elliott Bay, whose wind-damaged water looked like knapped flint. A car ferry was coming in to dock from a suburban island; a big container vessel, flying a Japanese flag, was being taken in hand by a pair of shovel-front tugs.

"You want to see the bathroom?"

I was busy with the fishing boats over by the West Seattle shore, the shipyards, the line of buoys pointing the way in to the Duwamish Waterway. At this window, one could spend all day far out at sea, with the city laid out under one's feet. It was a cormorant's perch.

"If you want a phone, the point's right here."

The light was changing, the water turning from gray to a pellucid iceberg green. The ferry sounded its diaphone. The note, way down at the bottom of the tuba range, reverberated in the glass of the windowpane.

"It's a hell of a view."

"You'd better enjoy it while it lasts. It probably won't last long. We're lucky here. We're saved. They were going to pull us down, but we just got our official designation. We're a historic landmark as of last month."

The building had been put up in 1906, at the height of the craze for Italianate magnificence. It had been the New Washington Hotel, Seattle's grandest. Theodore Roosevelt himself was one of its first guests—and the gilded swank of the New Washington, its triumphant Americanism, was a perfect embodiment of the Roosevelt presidency. It had stayed in business as a hotel until 1962, the year of the Seattle World's Fair, when Elvis Presley had lodged in a suite on the penthouse floor. Then it had been taken over by the Little Sisters of Mercy, who'd run it as a home and hospital for the elderly.

Although the Josephinum was still owned by the archdiocese, it had caught the 1980s virus of free market economics. As the old died in their rooms or were packed off to nursing homes, younger and richer people were being recruited to fill their places. New tenants had to pass a means test to prove that they earned at least sixty percent of the "median income" of seventeen thousand dollars a year, and some well-heeled out-of-towners had begun taking rooms in the Josephinum as their Seattle *pieds-à-terre*. It was still a cheap place to live by middle-class standards—this big studio, with dressing room and bathroom, cost $425 a month—but the building was steadily hoisting itself out of the reach of the people it had housed for the last quarter-century.

When I went down to the lobby, all conversation stopped. Walking frames came to a squeaky halt; dog-eared magazines were lowered and eyes raised over the tops of halfmoon specs. I was shaken to see that on every face there was an expression of frank antipathy to the appearance of the latest cuckoo in the Josephinum nest.

I saw—and saw too clearly for comfort—the man who was reflected in the old people's eyes: a guy in a loud pink denim suit, with a foreign accent and money to burn. He was a sign of the times. When the papers talked about the great Seattle boom, about clogged freeways and massive rent hikes, this was the man they had in mind: a paunchy stranger waving a checkbook and driving a car with California plates . . .

The whole temper of the city was mild. The weather was mild. The driving was mild. There wasn't a horn to be heard and everyone made room on the road for everybody else. Even on empty streets, pedestrians waited in polite knots for the sign to flash WALK before they crossed. Life here, in daylight hours at least, seemed to be conducted according to the unwritten rules of an old-fashioned gentlemen's club. Even the street people had the air of members in good standing. A shaggy derelict, looking like the prophet Isaiah, was panhandling on Third and Pike. "Any chance you might have some loose change on you?" "Sure," I said, and dug out fifty cents. "Thanks, pardner. Have a good one." He was a world away from the desperate supplicants of Manhattan Island.

From a stool in Oliver's Bar, I watched the shoppers on Fourth Avenue. They were tacking, in ones and twos, between Bon Marché (Seattle's Macy's) and Frederick & Nelson (Seattle's Bloomingdale's). Ralph Lauren would have been appalled to see them. He had barely gotten a toehold on this city of crumpled dark suits, baggy corduroys, home-knit sweaters, plaid lumber jackets, thick golfing socks, dirndl skirts and sensible shoes. The men went in for beards and rubber-banded pigtails, the women for long, fair, frizzy tangles, as if they'd just come back from swimming. Nobody seemed to be dressing for show, or snobbery, or sexual conquest. The fashion in Seattle was to make yourself comfortable in quantities of wool and flannel.

Nowhere in the United States had I met such an air of gentility and reserve. Seattle, on first sight, was punctiliously dull. It was as if the city had come to believe in the legend of its own architecture; it seemed to think that it really was centuries old, a wise and ancient survivor in a flighty world.

Even the rain was subtle. It had been falling for hours, as light and finely sifted as talcum powder. It didn't splash or drip; you couldn't— quite—feel it on your skin. It was a spontaneous liquefaction of the air, and it imported an authentic antique gleam to the gargoyles, sculpted nymphs and cornucopias of summer fruits. It muffled, even further, the sound of the boom.

In an art shop above Pike Place Market, I was riffling through a stack of prints, searching for pictures to civilize the bare high walls of the room in the Josephinum. The woman who ran the store was an immigrant from the Midwest. "We like it here. It's so quiet after Chicago. Nothing ever happens. That's why we like it."

I chose a Georgia O'Keeffe poster, of blue and purple pansies enlarged to the size of giant sunflowers, and a big Hockney, half map, half picture, of Sunset Boulevard. The woman rolled them up and fed them into a cardboard cylinder for me.

"Well—" she said. "How long do you think it'll be? Before you die of boredom in Seattle?"

TIMOTHY EGAN

After spending five years as a reporter for the Seattle Post-Intelligencer, *Timothy Egan left the paper to write a novel. He spent two years on an ultimately unpublished manuscript, then sent his agent a proposal for a different kind of book: a nonfiction account of the Pacific Northwest. This one the publisher bought; in 1990, Alfred A. Knopf brought out* The Good Rain: Across Time and Terrain in the Pacific Northwest. *Egan's book captures the Northwest in a remarkable series of essays that combine history, reportage, travelogue, and personal insight, and touch on issues ranging from timber to salmon to volcanoes to relations between whites and native Americans. Egan has been the Pacific Northwest correspondent for* The New York Times *since 1988.*

from THE GOOD RAIN

A FEW HUNDRED YARDS from the Canadian border, I look for the home of Gerald Thompson, who grows apples on ninety acres of hillside above the valley floor. Even with the wind tossing dust and leaves and tumbleweeds throughout the bowl of the Okanogan, this country is astonishingly beautiful. Open sky. Clean water. Ice-covered mountains rising to the west, rusted mesas to the east, each level covered with bigger pines. And down the center of the valley, grafted to either side of the river, are nothing but miles and miles of fruit orchards. Thompson's house has no address; he had said I could find it by looking for green shake siding and a white roof. He greets me at the porch, frowning.

"I don't think you're gonna like me," he says.

"Why not?"

"I changed my mind. Not sure I want to talk to you."

Outsiders find either suspicion or open arms in this community, same as elsewhere. In the tradition of the American West, new arrivals have no past; tolerance is a high virtue, just as nosiness is a low crime. Usually, that holds for the Okanogan Country. For a hundred years, highbrows and hicks have lived side by side. The town of Winthrop, one valley to the east, was founded by a Boston-bred Harvard graduate, Guy Waring, and named for Theodore Winthrop's ancestor, the first governor of the Massachusetts Bay Colony. Another Harvard graduate, Waring's college classmate Owen Wister, spent his honeymoon here in 1898, a visit which he drew upon to write the first popular western novel, *The Virginian.*

Thompson is missing a few teeth up front, his gut hangs over his waistband and his face is blasted red from the wind and sun. I say I'm interested in getting a few things straight about the Goldmark trial of 1963. Thompson was one of twelve jurors who sat in a courtroom of linoleum floors and rough plywood doors while the idea of the international Communist conspiracy was put on trial. In passing judgment on themselves, they pondered the thesis that Communists could take over a farm community just as sure as a virus could invade a healthy cow. It was the only time that the postwar Red Scare was put up against the legal test of truth. Historians view the case as the turning point against the loose libels and conspiracy theories which coursed through much of American thought from 1945 to the early 1960s.

Beyond the historical implications, a man's reputation was at stake, a man who had embraced the Okanogan Country only to have it turn on him. John Goldmark, a war hero who'd given up the promise of his Harvard Law School credentials to become a cattle rancher and citizen politician here, had been driven out of state office by a campaign that labeled him a tool of the Communist conspiracy. If anything, Goldmark was a product of the New West—that which would blossom under irrigation and prosper with cheap public power. Tall, athletic, a voracious reader and superb outdoorsman, he became a sort of Northwest archetype of the American dream: a man who thought the land could enrich the spirit and harden the body. Delivering on Roosevelt's promise, he helped to put water to work producing electricity that freed farmers from burdens dating back to the Stone Age. Like timber and fish, public power was soon looked upon as a regional right. But those who had controlled electricity in the Okanogan Country did everything they could to hold on to it. In the dying days of a losing fight, they targeted John Goldmark, calling him a Communist and a traitor. His life in ruins following the 1962 smear campaign, he sued for libel. Witnesses flew in from all over the country to help the twelve Okanogan Valley jurors decide.

"Well, by God, I was a witness, all right," says Thompson, slowly warming to the topic. "As a juror, I spent the winter in that courtroom when I coulda been pruning my trees."

He has no trouble remembering the trial. The question is whether he *wants* to remember. The Big Lie of 1962 has yet to die; he is scared of what could still happen.

"You saw what they did in Seattle," he says, shaking his head.

On Christmas Eve 1985, Annie Goldmark was baking a ham for a holiday dinner of close friends and family. The dining table inside her Seattle home, a two-story Tudor overlooking Lake Washington, was set for ten. A thick fog which had covered the city for most of the week obscured any view of the lake or the Christmas ships which cruised near the shore. It was a few minutes before 7 P.M., and the guests were due to arrive in half an hour. Her dinner on schedule, Annie went upstairs to take a shower. A minute later there came a knock on the door. Her son Colin, a ten-year-old who spoke fluent French just like his Paris-born mother and fluent English like his Okanogan County father, answered the door and was greeted by a man with a dark beard and stocking cap over his greasy hair. He held a white box in one hand and a tiny black gun in the other. It was a toy gun, but looked authentic enough. When David Lewis Rice knocked on the door covered by a Christmas wreath, he had not expected a child to greet him. Inside, stockings hung over the fireplace and presents were piled high around a tree. Rice had planned this visit for six months; it was to be the act of a soldier against the imagined villain behind all that had gone wrong during his twenty-seven years. Rice blamed Communists for trying to subvert the country from within; he was part of the flotsam of urban castoffs who bounced from city to city, light-years removed from a fantasy such as Morning in America.

"Charles Goldmark, please," said Rice as the boy answered the door.

Born a month before his father went to fight the Japanese in the South Pacific, Charles Goldmark grew up on the Okanogan ranch. At first, the family had no electricity, and only a rough, deep-rutted twenty-five-mile road connected the Goldmark home to the handful of stores in the valley below. Chuck Goldmark eventually went to Yale Law School, served as an

Army intelligence officer and started a legal practice in Seattle. He used to say that the days of growing up on the remote ranch east of the Cascades provided the best education a boy could ever get: the eerie stillness before a thunderstorm, bunchgrass poking up through old snow in early spring, helping an infant calf get through the first days of life. No book could teach such things. It was an exalted life in a new land.

When Chuck Goldmark greeted the stranger at the door of his Seattle house, both sons now at his side, David Rice was momentarily confused. Chuck was handsome, with sandy hair and a build befitting his hobby of mountaineering. He seemed no older than thirty-five or thirty-six. Rice was looking for another man, somebody much older, the Okanogan Valley Communist he'd read about. Rice flashed the small black pistol and ordered them inside. One boy ran into another room. Rice told Goldmark to call for him. He directed them all upstairs. Hearing the shower, Rice told Goldmark to ask for his wife.

"Honey, can you come out here?" Annie put on a robe and walked into the bedroom. Rice ordered them to get down on the floor, face down. The two children, scared as they dropped to their knees at the foot of the bed, rattled him. Kids—this wasn't part of the plan. He pulled the sweaters of the two boys up over their heads so their arms would be bound. Then he handcuffed Chuck and Annie.

"Do you need money?" Chuck asked.

"Yes, I can use all you got."

Rice had pawned the cheap television set belonging to a woman he was in love with and used the proceeds to pay for the tools of his Christmas Eve plan—the toy gun, chloroform and handcuffs. Searching Goldmark's wallet, he found an automated bank card and asked for the identification number. Chuck gave the number of his law firm's bank card. Rice had intended to interrogate Goldmark about Communists in Seattle, but he didn't have time. Dinner guests were on the way over, he was told. He opened the white box and proceeded to apply chloroform to each of the family members. One by one, they lost consciousness. Annie struggled at the smell, but quickly went out like the others. Hurrying now, Rice went downstairs looking for a weapon. He found a small filleting knife and a heavy steam iron, then went back to the upstairs bedroom. Starting with Chuck, he bashed in the heads of each of the four people on the floor, using the sharp end of the iron. After hitting Annie several times, he saw her start to move, so he hit her again. The two children were bludgeoned in the same way. Checking the pulse of Chuck and Annie, he found they were still alive. "So I decided to complete the job with the knife," he said later, in describing how he plunged the weapon into their brains. Wiping his feet of blood, he walked downstairs and left the house.

The first dinner guests arrived a few minutes later. The lights were on, the table was set, but nobody was there.

They called out. "Chuck? Annie?" No answer. One neighbor went next door to call the house. No answer. Then they called the police, who arrived within a few minutes. Upstairs, officer Bane Bean found blood all over the walls, and the moaning, labored breathing of four people: Charles Goldmark, age forty-one; his wife, Annie, forty-three; and their two sons, Derek, twelve, and Colin, ten. Annie died that night; over the next thirty-seven days, the three remaining Goldmarks died one after the other.

On Christmas Day, David Rice showed up at the porch of one of his political mentors, a Boeing Company electrician named Homer Brand who had founded the Seattle chapter of an odd little right-wing group called the Duck Club. At their meetings at a smorgasbord diner in Seattle's Scandinavian community of Ballard, they talked about Jewish banking conspiracies and how paper money wasn't worth anything because it was no longer backed by gold. Somebody had to do something about the goddamn lawyers, one of the members would say, and everybody would roar in approval. And what about the federal income tax—it's unconstitutional. Goddamn right. Rice, a drifter, newly unemployed, took it all in. "Shut your mouth and open your eyes—that's what I always say," was a favorite phrase of his. At one of these meetings, Rice heard about the Goldmarks—not the family that he later slaughtered, but the first generation, the post–World War II pioneers of the Okanogan high country. What did he hear? An old story, a lie. Brand said something about Goldmark—living right here in Seattle—being the "regional director" of the Communist Party. As the target took shape in Rice's mind, he read some yellowed news clips about John and Sally Goldmark, who had been labeled tools of the kind of conspiracy in which Rice had come to believe. The voices inside his head told him to take direct action.

"Hey, Homer," Rice said excitedly to Brand on Christmas morning. "I've just dumped the top Communist!"

"Oh, yeah," Brand replied, skeptical. "So what else is new?"

Rice was caught the next day, after police were tipped off by another acquaintance. In the spring of 1986 he was found guilty of four counts of aggravated first-degree murder, the only crime in Washington State punishable by death. He had confessed to the killings. In a failed effort to save his life, defense attorney Tony Savage said Rice was mentally ill and easily influenced by talk that most people would consider irrational. "The extreme right wing did not cause his illness," said Savage. "But his illness provided fertile ground for their philosophy." After a short deliberation, the jury sentenced Rice to be executed. The jury foreman, Joel Babcock, said whoever planted the original thought that Goldmark was a Communist was as much to blame for the death of the family as was Rice. A grocery store clerk, age twenty-five, Babcock said the trial made him think hard about things he'd never thought about before. "This whole thing started with something that wasn't true," he said after the trial. "Whoever started such slander should feel a little embarrassed right now—a little guilt."

The seed that landed in the head of David Lewis Rice blew over the Cascade Mountains twenty-three years after it was shaken from the weeds of Okanogan County. When Gerald Thompson heard about the Christmas Eve carnage at the Goldmark house, he knew right away what was behind it.

Now, his face angry, his eyes watching the wind rip dead leaves from his apple trees, Thompson snaps his fingers.

"Just like that I made the connection," he says. "It came from these guys who first made up all these lies about John Goldmark. That was what killed Chuck's family."

John Goldmark first came to the Okanogan Country in 1946, looking for a fresh life in a land unencumbered by the rust of his native East Coast. As one of the most remote areas in America, the Okanogan fit the bill. While still at war in the Philippines, the young Navy ensign wrote his wife, Sally, about his urge to move west, "where people are less twisted up in traditions, class and inhibitions." After scouting the apple valleys of central Washington, he bought the ranch on the high plateau of the Colville Indian Reservation. From the house, a homestead structure in a grove of aspens, you could look across the plateau to wheat fields and pine in one direction and away to the blue curtain of the Cascades in the other. John, Sally and their infant son Chuck moved onto the ranch in early spring, when the ground was still covered with snow. He put his Navy officer's sword over the fireplace and set out to become a man of the land. Harvard Law School and a stint as a New Deal administrator in Washington had not prepared him for the life of frontier cattle rancher. But he listened. He applied pure logic and science to the sometimes illogical trade of farming. In time, he established a healthy herd, grew wheat and grain, and built an airstrip on his property so he could land a small plane. The boys, Chuck and Peter, learned about ranch life at home and the rest of the world at a one-room schoolhouse on the Indian reservation, a million-acre trust for nine tribes from the central Columbia River region. They both learned to fly the family plane, herd cattle, build fences and climb mountains.

At first, John Goldmark was not trusted by many ranchers in the valley, who were suspicious of his Ivy League credentials and his move from New York to the Okanogan. "People always wondered what a guy like him was doing in a place like this," says R. E. Mansfield, the oldest practicing attorney in the Okanogan Valley. The flip side of small-town security is a type of gossip that can be as lethal as big-city crime. John and Sally Goldmark were assaulted with the worst of this rural specialty. Rumors circulated that John was running a secret operation with his primitive airstrip up there on the plateau. And his wife, Sally—what sort of past had she dragged out from Brooklyn to the Okanogan?

John could be hardnosed—he did not suffer fools easily—and was always trying to do things differently. Initially, most of the other ranchers laughed at him. But over the years, they paid him the ultimate form of respect: imitating some of his ingenuities. Ten years of ranch life changed his look to that of a typical cowboy—lean, with a weathered face and crew-cut hair, always dressed in jeans and boots and plaid shirts. Yet, he could move just as easily inside a courtroom or a legislative hall as he could on the range. "John Goldmark was the only person I ever knew who made me think: 'There goes a great man,'" says Stimson Bullitt, a prominent Seattle attorney from the family that founded the KING Broadcasting empire. Others said he was too stubborn to like. In later years, he reminded some friends of Hank Stamper, the tough-nutted timberman in Ken Kesey's novel *Sometimes a Great Notion*.

In the mid-1950s, John served on the Rural Electrification Board, where he was an early proponent of public power, in part to help bring the twentieth century to his ranch and in part to help his neighbors. At the time, even though the Grand Coulee Dam had been operating for more than a decade, electricity in this part of the state was controlled by a private utility, the Washington Water Power Company, based in Spokane, 150 miles to the east. Most of the farmers couldn't afford its rates. Even those with money had difficulty convincing the company to connect power lines to their remote locations. With construction of the Grand Coulee Dam, then the biggest public-works project in American history, Roosevelt had said, "We are going to see with our own eyes electricity and power made so cheap that they will become a standard article of use." Such a thought seemed far-fetched. During the Depression, less than half the farmers of Washington had electricity, and only a third in Idaho and Oregon had it. Irrigation water was carried by horse, or hand, or primitive pump. Kitchen tables were lit by kerosene lamps. Homes were heated by wood-burning stove. Roosevelt looked at large sections of the dried-out American Midwest, where the earth was stripped of fertility by savage windstorms, and directed the blank-faced and bankrupt farmers to the area drained by the Columbia, new land holding the promise of accessible water and cheap power, with every farmer a shareholder.

Washington Water Power, through the faithfully supportive Spokane *Spokesman-Review*, fought public power and the Grand Coulee Dam as if they were a plague that would wipe out every community in the inland Northwest. The campaign was so relentless that for many years public power was kept out of the hands of the people whose rivers were being dammed for such purposes. Eric Nalder, growing up in the small desert town of Ephrata in the early 1950s, was ashamed to mention that his father was an engineer on the Coulee Dam for fear of being taunted by his neighbors. Advocates of the dam were called "Coulee Communists."

John Goldmark maintained that the ranchers and poor farmers of the Columbia had a God-given right to affordable electricity from hydropower, a campaign theme that helped him get elected to the state legislature in 1956, as a Democrat in a heavily Republican district. He was twice reelected. By his third term, he was chairman of the key House Ways and Means Committee, and used his position to push for increased public power, more park space, libraries, better roads. By the time 1962 rolled around, John's reelection seemed like a sure thing. But right from the start, things were different in this campaign. In announcing John's intention to run for a fourth term in the legislature, the local Tonasket *Tribune* carried a story in which it said that "Goldmark is a member of the American Civil Liberties Union, an organization closely affiliated with the Communist movement in the United States." The story mentioned that Goldmark's oldest son, Chuck, was a freshman at Reed College in Portland, "the only school in the Northwest where Gus Hall, secretary of the Communist Party, was invited to speak." John knew some people in the valley didn't like him; but this was poison.

The Tonasket paper was owned and edited by Ashley Holden, who for many years had been political editor of the *Spokesman-Review*, where he helped direct the long, losing fight against public power. "His hatred of anybody who advoated publicly owned electricity was so strong, it was almost like a mental illness with him," said Bob Dellwo, a lifelong Democratic Party activist from Spokane and an ex-FBI agent who spent decades fighting Holden and the *Spokesman-Review.* "If you were in favor of public power, the *Review* and the Washington Water Power Company considered you the closest thing to a Communist." However, one by one, the rural counties of eastern Washington shook off the Washington Water Power Company and set up public utility districts, which they used to provide their neighbors with some of the cheapest electrical rates in the world. In his sixties, Ashley Holden left Spokane for the small-town bully pulpit of the Okanogan Valley paper, which he endowed with the masthead slogan, THIS IS A REPUBLIC, NOT A DEMOCRACY—LET'S KEEP IT THAT WAY!

The second shot against Goldmark came from Albert Canwell, an embittered former legislator who operated as a self-described expert on international Communism from his home on the Little Spokane River. Some men play golf for a hobby, Cantwell once said, "I collect information on the Communists." With Holden's help, Canwell circulated a tape in the valley, a question-and-answer session in which the expert, Canwell, answered his own questions. In the tape, Canwell mentioned John Goldmark's affiliation with the ACLU, "one of the most effective Communist fronts in America." Next, he and Holden published part of that tape in a private newsletter, where they questioned why Goldmark, "a brilliant young lawyer, a graduate of Harvard Law School, a nephew of Justice Brandeis of the Supreme Court," had chosen to become a rancher in the distant Okanogan.

In late summer, Canwell and Holden took their campaign to a packed meeting at the American Legion post in Okanogan. Goldmark and his friend, local state senator Wilbur Hallauer, asked to speak, and were told they could not. The ACLU was the stated topic of the night, but Goldmark was the evening's true target. As several hundred people filed into the overheated Legion post on a summer night, Canwell handed out an open letter addressed to Sally Goldmark, in which he asked her if the Communist Party, "knowing your secret," had pressured her into drafting left-wing legislation for the state of Washington.

The Depression had been very hard on the family of Sally Ringe. The daughter of German immigrants, she was forced to give up her studies at medical school after her father went into bankruptcy. She worked in a New York soup kitchen for a while, seeing the faces of the broken men and women of the 1930s, day in and day out. Idealistic and outspoken, she joined the Communist Party in 1935. She paid her dues and attended meetings for six years. Shortly after she met John Goldmark, she lost interest in the party—Hitler's alliance with Stalin had changed the minds of millions in America and Europe—and then she quit. She later cooperated with the FBI when two men came to the ranch in 1949 to ask about her background. She was found to be so harmless that her husband, who had remained active in the Navy Reserve as a commander, was twice given top officer security clearances. In the Okanogan Country, she was active in the Grange, the PTA, the 4-H Club and the county-fair board. But Sally's years as a Communist would haunt her for the rest of her life.

At the Legion meeting on that summer night in 1962, Canwell preached against the Communist in their midst with the vigor of a televangelist reaching for a ratings point. He handed out a Washington ACLU chapter newsletter with Goldmark's name on the masthead, and then told the farmers and ranchers that the ACLU was "the major Communist front operating in the state of Washington." In those days, calling somebody a Communist was the same as branding him a traitor; it was a word effortlessly hurled at many prominent citizens. For nearly an hour Canwell spun tales about hidden agents and threats from within. You couldn't trust anyone. Communists were gaining force on both borders, and operated "both within and without," he said, "like an octopus." He sat down to thundering applause. Then John Goldmark tried to speak for five minutes, saying the ACLU reflected the principles of the Declaration of Independence. He was hooted down. When his friend Wilbur Hallauer tried to speak, the mob turned mad. "Get him out of here!" they yelled at their longtime state senator, and he was pushed off the stage.

Goldmark later said that looking into the enraged eyes of the people who had been his friends and neighbors for sixteen years sent a chill down his spine. He felt as though he were surrounded by a lynch mob. Who were these people? What had happened to the tolerant Westerners, free-thinking and independent, who would help you fix your fence if you bucked bales in return, who judged you by what you did instead of what was said about you, who never asked where you went to school or what your father did for a living? In the Okanogan Country, there was no hint of the restrictive class system of some circles of the East, where school ties and family connections could bind or exclude for life. But there was this, the noose of the rural West.

The Canwell speech was summarized that week in Ashley Holden's newspaper, under the headline COMMIE FRONT EXPOSED BY AL CANWELL IN LEGION TALK. In the same issue, he wrote an editorial in which he said John Goldmark "is a tool of a monstrous conspiracy to remake America into a totalitarian state which would throttle freedom and crush individual initiative . . ." Two weeks later, John Goldmark was defeated for a fourth term in the state legislature by a three-to-one margin. In a newsletter published after the election, Canwell described his Legion Hall talk as "the bullet that got Goldmark."

Shunned by neighbors, thrown out of his office, his family tortured by further gossip, John called on his friend Bill Dwyer, who at thirty-three was just coming into his own as one of the best young lawyers in the Northwest. Goldmark wanted to sue for libel. Dwyer said it would be tough. Goldmark had never directly been called a Communist—just a stooge, dupe and tool of their invisible conspiracy. Goldmark decided to press forward. On November 4, 1963, more than a year after the smear campaign, the trial opened. Twelve jurors—three sawmill workers, two apple farmers, an unemployed construction worker, a beekeeper, an Indian, two wives of cattlemen, a state employee and a cook at the local chow house—were impaneled to pass judgment on the claims of their neighbor, who had since become a stranger. They filed into court dressed in overalls and stained shirts and worn workshoes. The same type of folks who were ready to hang John Goldmark in the Legion meeting one year earlier were now asked to examine the truth behind their community's hysteria.

For two months, they heard from a range of national experts—United States Senators and prominent ex-Communists among them. A witness for Goldmark was Sterling Hayden, the actor, who said, "I was perhaps the only person who ever bought a yacht and joined the Communist Party in the same week."

Three weeks into the trial came some startling news—the young President, John F. Kennedy, had been shot.

"Who shot him?" Canwell asked Richard Larsen, a reporter for the Wenatchee *World*.

"Whoever it was, I hope he was a good shot," Ashley Holden replied.

Kennedy's accused killer had been to Moscow and Cuba, and was a professed Marxist. What would this do to Dwyer's careful dismantling of the conspiracy theory? Goldmark feared the worst. But jurors were already with him, Thompson said later. "We knew he'd been screwed," he told me. "You can't do that to a guy, no matter what you think of him, and get away with it." For all the experts brought from distant cities to the small town covered by ice-fog in midwinter, nobody was ever able to connect the ACLU or John Goldmark to a conspiracy to remake America into a totalitarian state. Testimony from twenty years of government Red hunts failed to provide a single nugget to back the claims made against him.

In closing arguments, Joseph Wicks, a defense attorney, again raised the question of why an educated man would choose to live in such wild country. Said Wicks: "He, the brilliant student of government, of political science and of law, of human nature, settles for a cow ranch in Okanogan County where he didn't know whether apples grew on trees or on a vine, where he didn't know which end of the cow gave milk or which end of the cow ate hay."

The vitriol pouring forth was so strong that Sally Goldmark started trembling. Wicks acknowledged that the smear had riled up the community. "Sure, it creates hatred. And isn't it about time that we had a little hatred for those people that declare 'We will bury you'?" Wicks quoted Scripture, then pounded his fist down. "What is God to an atheistic Communist?" At that, Sally burst into tears and ran from the courtroom.

In rebuttal, Goldmark's attorneys played on the jurors' sense of decency. Just as a terrible lie could spring from this wide-open country to ruin a man, so could a judgment of simple wisdom and fairness. "Life is only good in a community where freedom and justice are preserved for every-body, not just for a few," said Dwyer. His colleague, R. E. Mansfield, responded to the venom of Wicks with a Biblical quote of his own. He chose his words from the Book of Proverbs: "A man that beareth false witness against his neighbor is a war club and a sword and a sharp arrow." Twenty-two years later, the verse would prove to be prophetic.

The Goldmarks won; the first part of this story is an American fable, where truth, justice and tolerance win out over evil. After five days of deliberation, the jury returned with a verdict against Ashley Holden and Albert Canwell—the largest libel verdict in state history at the time. Gerald Thompson remembers sitting up in the attic of the old concrete-covered Okanogan County courthouse, watching the snow bury his car down below. The jurors were angry at what their community had done to the Goldmarks, he said, and they wanted to make it right. With the verdict, Thompson went back to his orchard near the Canadian border, convinced that never again would anyone call a decent man a traitor in the Okanogan Valley and get away with it.

More than a quarter-century after the trial, R. E. Mansfield is still practicing law in the Okanogan Valley, as he has done since 1937. In his law office hangs a poster-size picture of his hero, Franklin Roosevelt. The valley, slowing down for the winter, looks much the same as it did during the Goldmark trial. But some things have changed. The biggest employer, the timber mill in Omak, has just been purchased by its employees, making it one of the largest businesses in the West owned by its workers. A worker-owned timber mill—in the old days of the Okanogan Valley such a move would surely be labeled a Communist takeover; today, the local newspaper hails the employee buyout as a bold stroke for community ownership and self-destiny. Mansfield, who faced some lean times after he represented Goldmark, is a beloved figure in the valley; he now plays cribbage with one of his worst enemies, "a guy who hated my guts and believed I was a dyed-in-the-wool Commie." The John Birch Society, whose members saw Communists behind every apple-storage bin, has all but vanished.

What happened to the Goldmarks—both generations—brings tears to the eyes of a man who is usually never without a joke. Mansfield has never stopped thinking about that family. After the 1963 trial, the Gold-marks recovered their reputation, but never put their lives completely back together. Four years after the verdict, on a cold winter day, John was bucked from a horse in a distant part of the ranch. When Mansfield and others finally found him, he was seriously injured and near death from the onset of hypothermia. Several hip operations failed to restore adequate movement. He moved to Seattle, where he practiced law for several years. After a long fight with cancer, he died in 1979. Six years later, Sally Goldmark died of emphysema just before her oldest son and his family were butchered.

Still, the libel trial had done to the Red Scare what the Scopes monkey trial had (at least temporarily) done to Creationism. Bill Dwyer wrote a thoughtful and moving account of it titled *The Goldmark Case: An American Libel Trial*. In 1988, after one of the longest delays for any judicial appointee in modern times, Dwyer was approved by Congress as a United States District Court judge in Seattle. During the nearly two years that elapsed after he was first nominated, critics said Dwyer was unqualified to be a federal judge because he had done volunteer work for the ACLU.

Mansfield believes that the Goldmark trial changed life in the Okanogan Valley forever. It had always been the type of open country, in appearance, that could stir poets from Winthrop to Wister. What has changed following the Goldmark trial is that the people opened up a bit, too.

"I don't think the home folks will rise up in ignorance quite like that ever again," he says.

But John Goldmark was smeared not so much because he was different, says Mansfield; his crime was that he helped to pry the Okanogan away from the grip of private power. The tragedy that befell him did not fulfill any prophecy of Winthrop's, though Goldmark was certainly drawn to this country for the very reason cited by the Yankee prophet as a magnet for future generations; rather, the case brought out a truth penned by Richard Neuberger in his 1938 book about the Northwest, *Our Promised Land*.

"Class warfare of a sort has rocked the northwest corner over the principal ways proposed for using America's greatest block of hydroelectric power," Neuberger wrote. There were sure to be casualties from the fight over who controls the most elemental resource of the Promised Land, he said, but even with that struggle, the Northwest represented the best hope of America during one of its darkest periods.

Mansfield has seen the promise fulfilled, but he will always be troubled by the price. "They hated John Goldmark, these guys from the Washington

Water Power Company and all their shills," says Mansfield. "He fought them every step of the way. Then public power came in, the rates came down, and the farmers could afford to pump plenty of water to their orchards. They'd never go back to the way it was. The monopoly days were gone for good. Just too bad a good family had to die for it."

BRENDA PETERSON

Brenda Peterson spent the first five years of her life in an isolated ranger station in the Sierra Nevada near the Oregon-California border. She left the Northwest when her father, who would later become head of the U.S. Forest Service, was offered a scholarship to Harvard. The rest of her childhood was spent, she recalls, "following the trees" as the family moved from forest station to station. As an adult she moved back to the Northwest and wrote novels and a book of essays, Living by Water *(1990), which she describes as "a kind of mystical love letter to this region."*

from LIVING BY WATER

WATER CARRIED ME HERE; water keeps me here. I have most always lived by water—from Georgia's Yellow River to New York City's Hudson, whose winter ice floes crash with the sound of worlds colliding, to a wide irrigation ditch in arid Colorado, and now to this long embrace of Seattle's Puget Sound. Watching the water from my own window is so much second nature to me that in 1981, when I found myself staring at an Arizona sun boiling up over the horizon, heat glazing the low, red rocks like a mirage, I realized I had to do more than a rain dance for relief.

In a decision that capped my father's conviction that his eldest daughter was financially feebleminded, I sold my birthright to escape Arizona and move to Seattle. To do so, I traded in my precious and only inheritance: two water shares from my great-uncle's farm irrigation ditch company. My father didn't see the symbolism, that water was my medium of moving from desert to Northwest oasis. Now Father does note rather grudgingly that after nine years, my mutiny might have brought me more security than money because water seems to have at last settled me here.

"Water has more life in it than any part of the earth's surface," wrote

Thoreau. With 80 percent of our bodies liquid, water is literally life to us. Water is also the first element we experience. We spend our formative nine months afloat in an amniotic sea so rich it re-creates the primal ocean as we move again through all stages of evolution: from reptilian fetal tail to amphibious gills and at last to lungs. We have the memory of nurturance flowing into our bellies through that fluid umbilical—a liquid lifeline.

However could we forget this first watery bond, even beached as we become in bodies that struggle against gravity, breathe high, harsh, and fast air, and at last lie down in solid ground? I suspect those of us who still feel the deep draw of water—whether we're Northwest fishermen, Seattle houseboat floaters, islanders, weekend sailing skippers, river rats; whether we live by Lake Washington or Union, Puget Sound, the Duwamish or eagle-haunted Skagit rivers, or the fertile Strait of Juan de Fuca—are people who feel our true roots not in soil, but sea. In fact, our psychic roots might look more like the delicate float of jellyfish than grounded tree ganglia.

What is it about the element of water that shapes and characterizes our Northwest life? First, water is supportive. We've not yet worn it out as we have so much of our Earth. Water is also mutable; we cannot divide and determine it as we do our property. And by its very nature, water cannot be possessed—it flows right on through our hands.

To be supported daily by so yielding and yet strong a force as water perhaps lends the Northwest some natural grace that we would do well to consciously imitate. Compare a ferry full of commuters with a subway train tunneling through Manhattan stone. The first sails and rocks along with its lulled riders, while the latter jolts, thrusts, and speeds its passengers full tilt toward home. When I lived in New York City, I would never seek solace in a subway. But it is often to ferries I take my weary, sad, or forsaken self, as if the simple act of being on water will solve or erase. One of my friends stood on the slick deck of the Bainbridge ferry during a rainstorm and threw her wedding ring into the Sound. Only then did Deborah feel her divorce was final. Another friend got married on a ferryboat in the fog, those eerie foghorns sounding like the mournful celebration of whale songs . . .

Water is a world-changer. That's why in almost every mythology, it was water that once destroyed the world in a great flood. According to the Skagits, this great flood covered all except Kobah (Mount Baker) and

Takobah (Mount Rainier). One of my favorite Northwest Coast Indian deluge stories is the Vancouver Island *Daughters of Copper Woman,* by Anne Cameron, in which a solitary, sobbing Copper Woman cries all her tribe into creation.

If water is the original stuff of life, it's also a way of living. the ancient Chinese philosophy of Taoism, often called "the watercourse way," saw water as the most revered teacher. In the writings of Lao-tzu, the sixth-century B.C. master whose *Tao te ching* is still a classic:

> The highest good is like water,
> for the good of water is that it nourishes everything
> without striving.
> The most gentle thing in the world overrides the most
> hard.
> How do coves and oceans become kings of a hundred
> rivers?
> Because they are good at keeping low —
> That is how they are kings of the hundred rivers.
> Nothing in the world is weaker than water,
> But it has no better in overcoming the hard.

To the Taoists, water's intuitive, harmonious flow was wiser than the rathional attitudes of a linear, man-over-nature mind. Thus, according to the ancient Taoist Kuan-tzu, "the solution for the Sage who would transform the world lies in water." Our present-day willfulness has taught us much about our own separate selves and little about how to live wisely and at one with the world. Only now are we recalling that there is a Tao at play in the world; and understanding its way may well help us find reunion with our own, and the Earth's, body.

Here in the Northwest, where so much of our life is linked with water, where the Asian influence is keenly felt, we have a chance to follow this Tao or water's way. Perhaps that's why in the Northwest the most recent Stephen Miller translation of the *Tao te ching* is a best seller—especially during the long, gray rains of winter. What more ideal landscape (except China itself) to learn that, as Mitchell explains of Lao-tzu's sage, "the Master has mastered Nature; not in the sense of conquering it, but of becoming it."

I'm convinced that at some point those of us who stay in the Northwest do *become* one with our inward, watery winters. We may rant about the rain, but if there are too many days of straight sun, an odd thing happens to true Northwesterners: we feel exposed and quite disoriented. We have more automobile accidents, we get exhausted from bearing up under a brilliant sun's mandate to be outdoors and too outwardly active. At last, in those stunning summer stretches, we get overstimulated by sunshine and seek the shade. With too much light, we seem to lose our life, seeking, in Lao-tzu's words, a more meditative way that is "radiant, but easy on the eyes."

My first awareness of this underlying way, or Tao of things, was while learning to drive a stick shift in the Virginia countryside. My father taught me to master the clutch and to shift gears, "with authority." My mother advised me to coax the recalcitrant shift through its lugubrious gears. But one day, grinding my way into second, an old backwoods relative who had never driven a day in her life leaned forward from the backseat and suggested rather shyly, "Seems to me that stick *wants* to go into its next gear, don't it? Natural-like. Because ain't that where it belongs now?" Only then did I understand: I was not master of the machine, nor slave to its whims. I was an integral part of its workings—its way.

A decade later I stood on the other side of the country, knee-deep in Colorado mud, working a farm my family inherited. I stood amazed to see the strong gush of irrigation ditch water so mildly disciplined into narrow ditches flowing through my cornfield. The water moved humbly along my elaborate system of wooden gates and hoed rows. I worked with my shovel, turning the water easily this way and that. By midnight, when the moon made the rivulets into quicksilver veins pulsing through my garden, I saw the luminous arteries of the Earth revealed. And though I was supposedly directing the flow, I felt no power. I felt peaceful. And there was something else—awe at the subtlety of this water whose strength was in surrendering to another element, earth.

These are two times in my life I've felt the harmony of letting go and allowing another force to move through me. Most recently, I've had this sense while staring at Puget Sound. Beach life here is elemental. My first day on the beach, I was shocked to find a great blue heron dying in the gentle surf that lapped my bare legs. Blood pooled in its beak, its eye already plucked out by a predator, as the bird sank into the sand, its old neck broken. I carried the heron up from the water and buried its body deep in the forest soil. Overhead gulls cried and I placed sand dollars as gravestone markers. Even then, in death, I felt a naturalness, the rightful end of a cycle.

Since that day years ago, I've apprenticed myself to Puget Sound because I believe it will teach me more about living than what I've learned so far. Maybe I hope its watery wisdom will seep into me every night as I lie, listening to the whoosh of waves against my seawall. Maybe I'd like to hook up again consciously to the umbilical that first nurtured me when I breathed water.

Whatever the reason, I've found solace in living by water. Solace and a sense of humor restored. It amuses me to think that waterfront property rights ebb and flow with the tides. Today my property might extend well beyond my neighbor's buoy with a minus 2 low tide; tomorrow my property shrinks back to a plus 3 tide. It is water that shapes and defines my boundaries, not the other way round.

In learning to yield to water's having its way with us, we change our character. The Northwest Indians were not as warlike as the prairie or desert tribes. They were fishermen and whalers following the waters, not warriors claiming the land. Water, contrary to even our West's labyrinthian water laws, cannot be truly claimed. It's too malleable. Water may reflect us, mirror our deepest selves, but it won't bear our imprint, our scars. We can in a sense wound it through pollution and our contempt, but more often than not it will wash away those wounds over time . . .

Alan Watts, in his commentary on the Tao te ching, says, "The art of life is more like navigation than warfare, for what is important is to understand the winds, the tides,the currents, the seasons, and the principles of growth and decay, so that one's actions may use them and not fight them."

That first day on Puget Sound, I made a mistake in burying that blue heron. These years living by water have reminded me of what the Indians call the great giveaway of death. In the sea, all that dies sinks and rejoins the food chain. If one of the signs of our humanness was our Neanderthal Man burying his dead for the beyond, then perhaps one of our first signs of returning at last to the wisdom of the sea is to not always return dust to dust, but sometimes water to water.

So here where I have made my home, I am also making my own way, my Tao. Here in the Northwest, I at last claim my home, my resting place. And if it is my choice when I die, then let me go back to the sea. Slip my body into the waters of this chosen land and let me feed the birds as I do now from shore. Let my body live and let me die, by water.

SALLIE TISDALE

"The Pacific Northwest is my place, and consequently it is a kind of bound. I live here sometimes as though it fenced me in, and I can't leave even when I long for leaving," wrote Sallie Tisdale in her 1991 book, Stepping Westward: The Long Search for Home in the Pacific Northwest. *In that work Tisdale, a Portland-based writer and the great-great-great-granddaughter of Northwestern pioneers, explored the unremitting westward pull that the region has exerted upon generations of immigrants and residents.*

from STEPPING WESTWARD

PEOPLE SAY MEAN THINGS about Boise, and Idaho. (The poet Linda McAndrew calls it Idahohum.) One of my favorite postcards shows two men driving in a car with two shaggy dogs in the back seat. The caption is "Idaho Double-Date." People have always said mean things about Idaho, crawling over the hot, dusty southern basin and leaning ever forward, to the farther West. "In the raw new land of South Idaho it was shove and scrape, and if you had bad luck or lost your strength you were done for." So wrote Nancy Stringfellow, who is now eighty, of her childhood in Twin Falls, Idaho, "where the wind blows down like the hounds of hell."

Idaho was late settled, late to be a territory, a state, still an orphan of the West. In 1858, a travel writer, apparently serious, wrote, "Idaho is no chimera of the brain—*no terra incognita, no ignuus fatuus*—but an established fact." (Much later, after an extended visit to Idaho Territory, that same writer added: "Should we ever encounter an enemy, and his punishment be left to our decision, the sentence will be: 'Go, ride a fat, lazy, hard-trotting horse to Boise, and be forgiven.'")

Teddy Roosevelt liked to hunt in the varied wilderness of Idaho. He was that kind of man who is eminently logical to himself, and almost incomprehensible to me: the hunter who loves the virgin wilderness and the kill at once, who in fact connects the two. If Mr. Roosevelt had been

my passenger one night near Fossil, Oregon, when I drove past two perfect fawns standing like statues in the road, he would have wanted me to
stop and collect them. Roosevelt once had a piece of great good luck on a
hunting trip in the northern mountains in 1888. He was able to catch a
water-shrew, "a rare little beast," he wrote in his memoir of the trip. "I
instantly pounced and slew it; for I knew a friend in the Smithsonian at
Washington who would have coveted it greatly." He skinned the animal
and laid the treasure aside, while the night darkened and his Indian
guide—"He was a good Indian, as Indians go," wrote Roosevelt—prepared
the meal. In the process, the guide accidentally threw the skin on the fire
and that was the end of the rare little shrew.

Because it is stuck between the open land of Washington and Oregon
and the Continental Divide of the Rockies, Idaho gets left out. Is it Rocky
Mountain country? Perhaps. Is it the Northwest? Perhaps. Is it anything,
but Idaho?

   The Northwest would be another kingdom—isolated, anarchic, raising
itself up like a wolf child in the wilderness. The West's anarchy is another
terra incognita; unfound, unexplored. It has a dual nature, murky, a vague
combination of conservative and radical, pride and backwoods shame that
would be more interesting if it were more examined. The Pacific Northwest is provincial and progressive in the same breath, conformist, regres-
sive, excessively tolerant and intolerant by turns. It walks the conservative
line and then elects a Democrat. We have a history of escape.

   Not long ago, petitions for a new state circulated from Sandpoint,
Idaho, through Spokane in eastern Washington and Coeur d'Alene in
northern Idaho. The call was for a movement to form Columbia, the
fifty-first state—the Wilderness State—out of eastern Washington, western Montana, and part of Idaho. Columbia's state animal would be, of
course, the grizzly bear . . .

In places like Boise you can stop for a cup of coffee almost anywhere,
even in a gun shop. I crossed the wide, empty Boise streets, the short
buildings so far apart that whole chunks of sun seemed to fall between
them, to a gun shop for breakfast, remembering the sporting-goods store
on the main street of my hometown. The four high walls are covered with
taxidermy, examples of size and prowess cut off at the neck: a moose, a

buck with rack as wide as a park bench, a snarling, frozen bear. The center of the store is a U-shaped soda fountain, and around it, any time of the day, sit men—young and old, wearing cowboy hats and baseball caps, eating pastrami and tuna fish. If I can't find my father at the Elks Club, or the fire hall, or standing behind the counter at the hardware store, I know he'll be at Dan's Sporting Goods.

My companion at Moon's Cafe in Boise was a handsome, diffident man named Rick Ardinger, a Pittsburgh boy who dreamed of coming west. Rick found Pocatello, in eastern Idaho, then tried Albuquerque, and in 1977 moved back to Idaho City, a small town outside Boise where he feels permanently, and happily, settled. He has red hair, a bushy red beard, wire-rim glasses. Rick is a letterpress printer and, with his wife Rosemary, owner of Limberlost Press, one of the breed of small presses in the Northwest turning out handcrafted editions of poetry, journals, pioneer diaries. The evening before, Rick and Rosemary had hosted the poet Robert Creeley for a reading. It is Rick who gave me a copy of Nancy Stringfellow's memoir, a small, paperbound book he had set by hand, each copy bound singly, by hand. Nancy brought the love of serious reading to Boise in the form of a store called The Book Shop. She and her husband built a house that, her daughter Rosalie Sorrels writes, "looks like a bower and everywhere you put your foot a cloud of fragrance envelops you. The whole place seems to have grown from the ground."

We sat at a tiny table in the back, eating good, cheap food, and watched a succession of taciturn men examine shotguns and pistols. Hunting season was soon to start, and I could see boxes of ammunition pushed across the counter; a heavy-bellied man in a baseball cap sighted along a rifle toward the picture window at the far end of the narrow shop. We talked about the West's confusion, its adolescent ruminations on itself. "What is true for the West, is all most true in Idaho," Rick said, dipping into scrambled eggs. I could hear the murmur of men nearby, sipping good hot coffee, taking time. Idaho is isolated, Rick continued, running north and south the long way, split like a shingle by the Bitterroot Mountains. It is unclaimed, not quite set apart, but apart: Idaho is an orphan.

SHERMAN ALEXIE

In 1992 a small publishing house in Brooklyn, New York, Hanging Loose Press, issued a modest edition of stories and poems by a twenty-five-year-old Spokane/Coeur D'Alene Indian named Sherman Alexie. On the strength of positive, persistent word of mouth and glowing reviews, The Business of Fancydancing *became one of the year's surprising literary successes. Alexie's powerful mix of native spiritual mythology and sharply observed descriptions of reservation life marked him, in the opinion of a critic writing for* The New York Times Book Review, *as "one of the major lyric voices of our time." By the end of 1993, Alexie had published three more books of poetry and a story collection,* The Lone Ranger and Tonto Fistfight in Heaven. *The following selection first appeared in* The Business of Fancydancing.

THE BUSINESS OF FANCYDANCING

After driving all night, trying to reach
Arlee in time for the fancydance
finals, a case of empty
beer bottles shaking our foundations, we
stop at a liquor store, count out money,
and would believe in the promise

of any man with a twenty, a promise
thin and wrinkled in his hand, reaching into the window of our car. Money
is an Indian Boy who can fancydance
from powwow to powwow. We
got our boy, Vernon WildShoe, to fill our empty

wallets and stomachs, to fill our empty
cooler. Vernon is like some promise
to pay the light bill, a credit card we
Indians get to use. When he reach-
es his hands up, feathers held high, in a dance
that makes old women speak English, the money

for first place belongs to us, all in cash, money
we tuck in our shoes, leaving our wallets empty
in case we pass out. At the modern dance,
where Indians dance white, a twenty is a promise
that can last all night long, a promise reaching into back pockets of unfamiliar Levis. We

get Vernon there in time for the finals and we
watch him like he was dancing on money,

which he is, watch the young girls reaching for him like he was Elvis in braids and an empty
tipi, like Vernon could make a promise
with every step he took, like a fancydance

could change their lives. We watch him dance
and he never talks. It's all a business we
understand. Every drum beat is a promise
note written in the dust, measured exactly. Money
is a tool, putty to fill all the empty
spaces, a ladder so we can reach

for more. A promise is just like money.
Something we can hold, in twenties, a dream we reach.
It's business, a fancydance to fill where it's empty.

ROBERT HEILMAN

Robert Heilman's essays about working life in the Pacific Northwest, published in the Portland quarterly Left Bank, *have helped make that journal the region's best contemporary literary publication. Born and raised in southern California, Heilman has lived in the southern Oregon town of Myrtle Creek since 1975. He has worked as a carpenter, housepainter, mill worker, welder's apprentice, logger, tree planter, census taker, tillerman, and lately as a professional storyteller and writer. This essay was published in 1993.*

from OVERSTORY: ZERO

THE MAIN THING is to have a big breakfast. It's not an easy thing to do at 4 A.M., but it is essential because lunch won't come for another seven or eight hours and there's four or more hours of grueling work to do before you can sit down and open up your lunch box.

The kids on the crew, eighteen-year-olds fresh out of school, sleep in the extra half-hour and don't eat until the morning store stop on the way out to the unit. They wolf down a Perky Pie, a candy bar, and a can of soda in the crummy. They go through the brush like a gut-shot cat for awhile and then drag ass for the rest of the morning. But if you're an old-timer, in your mid-twenties, you know how to pace yourself for the long haul.

You're exhausted, of course, and your calves, hips, arms, and lower back are stiff and sore. But you're used to that. You're always tired and hurting. The only time you feel normal is when you're on the slopes, when the stiffness and fatigue are melted off by the work. It gets worse every morning until by Saturday it takes hours to feel comfortable on a day off. Sunday morning you wake up at four o'clock, wide awake and ready to stomp through downtown Tokyo breathing fire and scattering tanks with your tail.

Your stomach is queasy but you force the good food into it anyway, a big stack of pancakes with peanut butter and syrup, four eggs, bacon, and coffee. There is a point when your belly refuses to take any more. Saliva floods your mouth and you force back the retching, put the forkful of food down on the plate and light another cigarette.

It's dark outside and it's raining, of course. They aren't called the Cascades for nothing. It's December and the solstice sun won't rise until eight, three hours and a hundred miles from home, somewhere along a logging road upriver.

Raincoat and stiff pants, hard hat, rubber work gloves, cotton liner gloves, and a stiff pair of caulk boots stuffed with newspaper crowd around the woodburner. All the gear is streaked with mud except the boots, which are caked with an inch-thick mud sole covering the steel spikes. The liner gloves hang stiff and brown, the curving fingers frozen, like a dismembered manikin's hand making an elegant but meaningless gesture.

Tree planting is done by winos and wetbacks, hillbillies and hippies for the most part. It is brutal, mind-numbing, underpaid stoop labor. Down there in Hades, Sisyphus sees the tree planters and thanks his lucky star because he's got such a soft gig.

Being at the bottom of the Northwest social order and the top of the local ass-busting order gives you an exaggerated pride in what you do. You invade a small grocery store like a biker gang. It's easy to mistake fear for higher forms of respect, and as a planter you might as well.

In a once-rugged society gone docile, you have inherited a vanishing tradition of ornery individualism. The ghosts of drunken bullwhackers, miners, rowdy cowpunchers, and bomb-tossing Wobblies count on you to keep alive the 120-proof spirit of irreverence towards civilization that built the West.

A good foreman, one who rises from the crew by virtue of outworking everybody else, understands this and uses it to build his crew and drive them to gladly work harder than necessary. A foreman who is uncomfortable with the underlying violence of his crew becomes its target. It is rare for a crew to actually beat up a foreman, but it happens.

It's best not to look at the clear-cut itself. You stay busy with whatever is immediately in front of you because, like all industrial processes, there is beauty in the details and ugliness in the larger view. Oil film on a rain puddle has an iridescent sheen that is lovely in a way that the junkyard it's part of is not.

Forests are beautiful on every level, whether seen from a distance or standing beneath the trees or studying a small patch of ground. Clear-cuts contain many wonderful things—jasper, petrified wood, sun-bleached bits of wood, bone and antler, wildflowers. But the sum of these finely wrought details adds up to a grim landscape, charred, eroded, and sterile.

Although tree planting is part of something called "reforestation," clear-cutting is never called "deforestation," at least not by its practitioners. The semantics of forestry doesn't allow that. The mountain slope is a "unit," the forest a "timber stand," logging is "harvest" and repeated logging "rotation."

On the work sheets foresters use is a pair of numbers that tracks the layers of canopy, the covering of branches and leaves that the trees have spread out above the soil. The top layer is called the overstory, beneath which is a second layer, the understory. A forest, for example, may have an overstory averaging a height of 180 feet and an understory of 75 feet.

Clear-cuts are designated "Overstory: Zero."

In the language (and therefore the thinking) of industrial silviculture a clear-cut is a forest. The system does not recognize any depletion at all. The company is fond of talking about trees as a renewable resource, and the official line is that clear-cutting, followed by reforestation, results in a net gain.

"Old-growth forests are dying, unproductive forests—biological deserts full of diseased and decaying trees. By harvesting and replanting we turn them into vigorous, productive stands," the company forester will tell you. But ask if he's willing to trade company-owned old-growth forest for a clear-cut of the same acreage and the answer is always "No, of course not."

You listen and tell yourself that it's the company that treats the land shabbily. You see your work as a frenzied life-giving dance in the ashes of a plundered world. You think of the future and the green legacy you leave behind you. But you know that your work also makes the plunder seem rational and is, at its core, just another part of the destruction.

More than the physical exhaustion, this effort not to see the world tires you. It takes a lot of effort not to notice, not to care. When the world around you is painful and ugly, that pain and ugliness seeps into you, no matter how hard you try to keep it out. It builds up like a slowly accumulating poison. Sometimes the poison turns to venom and you strike out, as quick as any rattlesnake, but without the honest rattler's humane fair warning.

So you bitch and bicker with the guys on the crew, argue with the foreman, and snap at your wife and kids. You do violent work in a world where the evidence of violence is all around you. You see it in the scorched earth and the muddy streams. You feel it when you step out from the living forest into the barren clear-cut. It rings in your ears with the clink of steel on rock. It jars your arm with every stab of your hoedag.

DENISE LEVERTOV

The renowned English-born poet Denise Levertov became the latest addition to the Northwest's young poetic tradition by settling into a home near Seattle's Seward Park in the late 1980s. Her work since then has borne the subtle imprint of her surroundings. The Northwest is a place, she once wrote, whose people dwell "in a landscape that, with its mists and snowy mountains, often seems to resemble one of those great scroll paintings of Asian art." In this poem, which begins her 1992 collection, Evening Train, *Levertov captures the shifting spiritual and climatic atmosphere of her new home.*

SETTLING

I was welcomed here—clear gold
of late summer, of opening autumn,
the dawn eagle sunning himself on the highest tree,
the mountain revealing herself unclouded, her snow
tinted apricot as she looked west,
tolerant, in her steadfastness, of the restless sun
forever rising and setting.
                              Now I am given
a taste of the grey foretold by all and sundry,
a grey both heavy and chill. I've boasted I would not care,
I'm London-born. And I won't. I'll dig in,
into my days, having come here to live, not to visit.
Grey is the price
of neighboring with eagles, of knowing
a mountain's vast presence, seen or unseen.

ACKNOWLEDGMENTS

Sherman Alexie, "The Business of Fancydancing," from *The Business of Fancydancing*. Copyright 1992 by Sherman Alexie. Reprinted by permission of Hanging Loose Press.

Olive Barber, from *The Lady and the Lumberjack*. Copyright 1952 by Olive Barber. Reprinted by permission of HarperCollins Publishers, Inc.

Franz Boas, Kwakwaka'wakw songs, from *Songs of Kwakiutl Indians*, by Franz Boas. International Archive of Ethnography, 1896.

Robert Cantwell, from *The Land of Plenty*. Copyright 1934 by Robert Cantwell.

Raymond Carver, from "Boxes," from *Where I'm Calling From: New & Selected Stories*. Copyright © 1986, 1987, 1988 by Raymond Carver. Reprinted by permission of Grove/Atlantic Inc.

Horace Cayton, from *Long Old Road*. Copyright 1965 by Horace R. Cayton. Used by permission of Susan Cayton Woodson.

James Cook, from the second volume of *A Voyage to the Pacific Ocean: Undertaken by Command of his Majesty, for making Discoveries in the Northern Hemisphere To Determine the Position and Extent of the West Side of North America; its Distance from Asia; and the Practicability of a Northern Passage to Europe. Performed under the Direction of Captains Cook, Clerke, and Gore, In his Majesty's Ships the Resolution and Discovery in the Years 1776, 1777, 1778, 1779, and 1780*. London: G. Nicol & T. Cadell, 1784.

Ross Cox, from *Adventures on the Columbia River*. New York: J. & J. Harper, 1832.

H. L. Davis, from *Honey in the Horn*. Copyright 1935 by Harper & Brothers.

Annie Dillard, from *The Writing Life*. Copyright © 1989 by Annie Dillard. Reprinted by permission of HarperCollins Publishers, Inc.

David Douglas, from his journals as published in *The Companion to the Botanical Magazine*. London, 1836.

William O. Douglas, from *Of Men and Mountains*. Copyright 1950 by Sidney Davis, Trustee, William O. Douglas Trust. Copyright © renewed 1978 by Sidney Davis, Trustee, William O. Douglas Trust. Reprinted by permission of HarperCollins Publishers, Inc.

David James Duncan, from *The River Why*. Copyright 1983 by David James Duncan. Reprinted by permission of Sierra Club Books.

Katherine Dunn, from *Geek Love*. Copyright © 1989 by Katherine Dunn. Reprinted by permission of Alfred A. Knopf, Inc.

Timothy Egan, from *The Good Rain.* Copyright © 1990 by Timothy Egan. Reprinted by permission of Alfred A. Knopf, Inc.

Vardis Fisher, from *Toilers of the Hills.* Copyright 1928 by Vardis Fisher.

Francis Fletcher, from *The World Encompassed by Sir Francis Drake.* London: Nicholas Bourne, 1628.

Mary Hallock Foote, from *Coeur d'Alene.* Copyright 1894 by Mary Hallock Foote.

Tess Gallagher, "Amplitude," from *Amplitude: New and Selected Poems.* Copyright 1987 by Tess Gallagher. Reprinted by permission of Graywolf Press.

Zane Grey, from *The Desert of Wheat.* Copyright 1919 by Harper & Brothers.

Robert Heilman, "Overstory: Zero," from *Left Bank #4,* 1993. Copyright 1993 by Robert Heilman. Reprinted by permission of the author.

Bruno de Hezeta, from *For Honor and Country: The Diary of Bruno de Hezeta.* Translated by Herbert K. Beals. Copyright 1985 by Oregon Historical Society Press, Portland. Reprinted by permission of the publisher.

Ella Higginson, "The Blow-Out at Jenkins's Grocery," from *From the Land of the Snow-Pearls.* New York: Macmillan, 1897.

Stewart Holbrook, from *Holy Old Mackinaw: A Natural History of the American Lumberjack.* New, enlarged edition by Stewart H. Holbrook. Copyright 1956 by Macmillan Publishing Company, renewed 1984 by Sibyl Holbrook Strahl. Reprinted by permission of Macmillan Publishing Company.

Richard Hugo, from *The Real West Marginal Way: A Poet's Autobiography,* by Richard Hugo, edited by Ripley S. Hugo, Lois M. Welch, and James Welch. Copyright 1986 by Ripley S. Hugo. Reprinted by permission of W. W. Norton & Company, Inc. Poems from *Making Certain It Goes On, the Collected Poems of Richard Hugo,* by permission of W. W. Norton & Company, Inc. Copyright © 1984 by The Estate of Richard Hugo.

Chief Jo Hutchins, from his 1869 speech to A. B. Meacham, from Meacham's *Wigwam and Warpath, or the Royal Chief in Chains.* Boston: John P. Dale & Co., 1875.

Washington Irving, from *Astoria, or Anecdotes of an Enterprise Beyond the Rocky Mountains.* Philadelphia: Carey, Lea, and Blanchard, 1836.

Hathaway Jones, "The Year of the Big Freeze," from *Tall Tales from Rogue River: The Yarns of Hathaway Jones,* edited by Stephen Dow Beckham. Copyright 1979 by Stephen Dow Beckham. Reprinted by permission of the author.

Nard Jones, from *The Island.* Copyright 1948 by Nard Jones.

Chief Joseph, from "An Indian's View of Indian Affairs," *North American Review,* April 1879.

Jack Kerouac, from *The Dharma Bums*. Copyright © 1958 by Jack Kerouac, renewed 1986 by Stella Kerouac and Jan Kerouac. Used by permission of Viking Penguin, a division of Penguin Books USA Inc.

Ken Kesey, from *Sometimes a Great Notion*. Copyright © 1964, renewed 1992 by Ken Kesey. Used by permission of Viking Penguin, a division of Penguin Books USA Inc.

Rudyard Kipling, from *American Notes*. Copyright Rudyard Kipling, 1899, 1907. New York: Doubleday, Page & Co., 1916.

Amelia Stewart Knight, from her Oregon Trail diary, "Journal kept on the road from Iowa to Oregon," 1852. Original is housed in the archives of the University of Washington.

Louis Labonte, "Coyote Builds Willamette Falls and the Magic Fish Trap" and "Coyote and the Cedar Tree," from "Reminiscences of Louis Labonte," by H. S. Lyman, *Oregon Historical Quarterly* (v. 1), 1901.

Craig Lesley, from *Winterkill*. Copyright © 1984 by Craig Lesley. Reprinted by permission of Houghton Mifflin Co. All rights reserved.

Denise Levertov, "Settling," from *Evening Train*. Copyright © 1992 by Denise Levertov. Reprinted by permission of New Directions Publishing Corp.

Meriwether Lewis and William Clark, from *The Original Journals of the Lewis and Clark Expedition*, edited by Reuben Gold Thwaites, 1905.

Michael Lok, from *Hakluytus Posthumus, or Purchas His Pilgrimes, Contayning a History of the World in Sea Voyages and Lande Travells by Englishmen and others*, by Samuel Purchas, 1625.

Fitz Hugh Ludlow, "On the Columbia River," published in *The Atlantic Monthly*, December 1854.

Betty MacDonald, from *The Egg and I*. Copyright 1945 by Betty MacDonald. Copyright renewed 1973 by Donald C. MacDonald, Anne Elizabeth Evans, and Joan Keil. Reprinted by permission of HarperCollins Publishers, Inc.

Bernard Malamud, from *A New Life*. Copyright © 1961 by Bernard Malamud, renewed © 1980 by Ann Malamud. Reprinted by permission of Farrar, Straus & Giroux, Inc.

Anne Shannon Monroe, from *Happy Valley*. Chicago: A. C. McClurg, 1916.

Murray Morgan, from *The Last Wilderness*. Copyright 1955 by Murray Morgan. Reprinted by permission of the author.

Sidney Walter Moss, from *The Prairie Flower; or, Adventures in the Far West*. Published by Stratton & Barnard (Cincinnati), 1849, under Emerson Bennett's name.

John Muir, from *Picturesque California*. New York: J. Dewing, 1888.

Richard Neuberger, "The Biggest Thing on Earth," from *Our Promised Land*. Copyright 1938, renewed 1966 by Richard L. Neuberger. Reprinted by permission of Macmillan Publishing Company.

John Okada, from *No-No Boy*. Copyright Dorothy Okada, 1976. Copyright 1979 by the University of Washington Press. Reprinted by permission of the publisher.

Brenda Peterson, from *Living by Water*. Copyright 1990 by Brenda Peterson. Reprinted by permission of the author.

Archie Phinney, "Coyote and Monster," from *Nez Percé Texts*. Copyright 1934 by Columbia University Press, New York. Reprinted by permission of the publisher.

Peter Puget, from his journal aboard the *Discovery*. Original journals are housed at the Public Record Office, London.

Jonathan Raban, from *Hunting Mister Heartbreak*. Copyright © 1991 by Jonathan Raban. Reprinted by permission of HarperCollins Publishers, Inc.

Tom Robbins, from *Another Roadside Attraction*. Copyright © 1971 by Thomas E. Robbins. Used by permission of Doubleday, a division of Bantam Doubleday Dell Publishing Group, Inc.

Marilynne Robinson, from *Housekeeping*. Copyright © 1980 by Marilynne Robinson. Reprinted by permission of Farrar, Straus & Giroux, Inc.

Theodore Roethke, "The Rose," copyright © 1963 by Beatrice Roethke, Administratrix of the Estate of Theodore Roethke. From *The Collected Poems of Theodore Roethke* by Theodore Roethke. Used by permission of Doubleday, a division of Bantam Doubleday Dell Publishing Group, Inc.

Chief Seattle, from his 1854 speech, as recorded by Henry A. Smith. Published in the *Seattle Sunday Star,* October 1887.

Walker C. Smith, from *The Everett Massacre* (I.W.W. Publishing Bureau, Chicago).

Gary Snyder, from "Night Highway Ninety-Nine," from *Six Sections from Mountains and Rivers Without End, Plus One*. Copyright 1970 by Gary Snyder. Reprinted by permission of the author.

Monica Sone, from *Nisei Daughter*. Copyright 1953 by Monica Sone; © renewed 1981 by Monica Sone. Reprinted by permission of Little, Brown and Company.

Wallace Stegner, from *The Big Rock Candy Mountain*. Copyright 1938, 1940, 1942, 1943 by Wallace Stegner. Used by permission of Doubleday, a division of Bantam Doubleday Dell Publishing Group, Inc.

John Steinbeck, from *Travels with Charley*. Copyright © 1961, 1962 by The Curtis Publishing Co., copyright © 1962 by John Steinbeck, renewed copyright © 1990 by Elaine Steinbeck, Thom Steinbeck, and John Steinbeck IV. Used by permission of Viking Penguin, a division of Penguin Books USA Inc.

Hazard Stevens, "The Ascent of Takhoma," published in *The Atlantic Monthly,* November 1876.

James Stevens, from *Paul Bunyan.* Copyright 1925, 1947 by Alfred A. Knopf, Inc., and renewed 1953 by James Stevens. Reprinted by permission of the publisher.

Anna Louise Strong, "Britt Smith," from *Rebel Voices: An I.W.W. Anthology,* edited by Joyce L. Kornbluh. Copyright 1964 by Joyce L. Kornbluh. Used by permission of the University of Michigan Press.

James G. Swan, from *The Northwest Coast.* New York: Harper & Brothers, 1857.

Jonathan Swift, from *Travels Into Several Remote Nations of the World, by Lemuel Gulliver (Gulliver's Travels),* 1726.

James A. Teit, "Origin of the Columbia River," as told by Red-Arm. First published in *Folk-Tales of Salishan and Sahaptin Tribes,* edited by Franz Boas, 1917.

Sallie Tisdale, from *Stepping Westward: The Long Search for Home in the Pacific Northwest.* Copyright © 1991 by Sallie Tisdale. Reprinted by permission of Henry Holt and Company.

George Vancouver, from *A Voyage of Discovery to the North Pacific Ocean and round the World, 1791–1795.* London: C. J. and J. Robinson; J. Edwards, 1798.

Frances Fuller Victor, from *Atlantis Arisen, or Talks of a Tourist about Oregon and Washington.* Philadelphia: J. B. Lippincott, 1891.

David Wagoner, "Elegy for a Forest Clear-Cut by the Weyerhaeuser Company," from *David Wagoner: Collected Poems, 1956-1976.* Copyright 1976 by David Wagoner. Reprinted by permission of the author.

Narcissa Whitman, from *The Letters of Narcissa Whitman.* Fairfield, Washington: Ye Galleon Press, 1986.

Theodore Winthrop, from *The Canoe and the Saddle.* New York: J. W. Lovell, 1862.

Owen Wister, "The Second Missouri Compromise," from *Red Men and White.* New York: Harper & Brothers, 1896.

Walter Woehlke, "The I.W.W. and the Golden Rule," published in *Sunset,* February 1917.